THE PHOENIX GENERATION

HENRY WILLIAMSON

THE PHOENIX GENERATION

'Thou knowst how drie a Cinder this worlde is
That 'tis in vaine to dew or mollifie
It with thy tears, or sweat, or blood'

John Donne

faber and faber

This edition first published in 2011
by Faber and Faber Ltd
Bloomsbury House, 74–77 Great Russell Street
London WC1B 3DA

A CIP record for this book is available from the British Library

ISBN 978-0-571-27808-4

CONTENTS

PART ONE
FELICITY

PART TWO
MELISSA

PART THREE
WAIFS & STRAYS

Part One

FELICITY

Chapter 1

'FARM BOY'

The guests were still arriving, to judge by the crowd waiting on the pavement outside the Oxford Street shop. The two young men, sitting in a black sport's car with fabric body, drawn up by the kerb across the street, watched for a while. The upper part of the building was illuminated. "Bogus," said Piers. "Look at that 'ornate Ionic' pillar. I wonder they didn't put Mickey Mouse on them as well."

But Phillip was thinking of the safety of his new possession, his Silver Eagle, a six-cylinder, three-carburettor sports car. "Perhaps it would be safer to park down a side-street, in case someone pinches it."

Piers thought that his friend had paid far too much for that second-hand car. It was less than a year old, but the exhaust smoked blue, the engine used a gallon of oil every hundred miles. Obviously the previous owner had caned it. Phillip had employed the Motor Association to vet it before buying. The engineer's report had been equivocal: *Provided the excessive smoking can be abated it is in good order.*

"Have you insured it against theft?"

"Oh yes!"

Piers thought that the sooner it was stolen the better. He said, "It should be fairly safe here, don't you think?"

Having removed black-leather flying coats and helmets, the two friends walked bare-headed towards the American-style department store, said to be the only one of its kind in London. Not quite the place, Phillip had understood from Piers, where one would buy one's shirts, ties, and socks. Piers had taken him to his shirtmaker in Burlington Arcade.

It was a fine night in May, 1929. Stars shone above the roofs of London. The sky had a tawny glow. As they re-entered Oxford Street a large yellow limousine drew up outside the flood-lit building. The commissionaire, a tall ex-Guardsman wearing the Victoria Cross on his uniform greatcoat, walked down to the kerb to open the door. The principal guest was to be the Earl of Lonsdale. The yellow Rolls-Royce of the famous sporting peer was known everywhere. But instead of the expected figure with large red side-whiskered face from which jutted what gossip-columnists called the inevitable cigar, a small dark man wearing opera hat and cloak alighted and, after giving the commissionaire a tip, walked alone to the entrance. Some laughter greeted this odd figure.

"Dikran Michaelis, Piers. He bought one of Lord Lonsdale's old buses. I had a lift in it once. I rather like his books."

Piers thought it strange that one who could write so well himself should be taken in by such bogus stuff. Phillip was very nearly two distinct people in one body: a strange mixture. In his talk he was penetrating and amusing about some of his past encounters with women; but when Piers read what he had written about essentially the same episodes, the wit and penetration was absent. The trouble with Phillip was that he still idealised girls, who were either sexual bitches or sentimental leeches. That girl Felicity was no good for Phillip. She made him irritable and moody, but he would stick to her. It was the same with the Silver Eagle: it gave continuous trouble, but he wouldn't get rid of it.

They were taken up in the lift, shown the way to a large room leading through to an entire floor, and announced.

"Sir Piers Tofield! Captain Phillip Maddison!" as they went forward to Mr. Gordon Selfridge and their hostess.

Stringed music from one of five bands present was audible through the massed chatter. It was nearing midnight. "Let's find the champagne bucket," said Piers. "Ah, that's better. Prosit!" Glass in hand, Phillip looked around. Many of the younger men wore red carnations in button-holes. He recognised Sylvester Card, once an almost unknown member of the Parnassus Club of young writers who had met, just after the war, once a week in a small room in Long Acre to discuss Literature and Life. Card was now famous as a writer of witty comedies and revues. Phillip felt they had nothing in common. Sylvester Card collected all the urban moods of the moment.

He saw, with a mild shock, the bearded face of Tenby Jones, 'the lion of Chelsea', who had been painting in the ruins of Albert when he had been wheeled past on a stretcher on July the First. That moment belonged to the past which must not be thought of until the time came when it could be written. He glowed within; then suffered with the thought that time was passing; and nothing done.

A woman with a smooth face recognised Piers. She wore a pink frock frothy with chiffon. Her neck lanced sapphire and richer-than-rose-red rays.

"Julia, may I present Phillip Maddison. Lady Abeline."

Another mild shock. Would Lady Abeline recognise him as the patient in the Royal Tennis ward at Husborne Abbey whom she had taken for walks in the park in May 1918, when he had been temporarily blinded by mustard gas? . . . he lived again in scenes of the Western Front, stricken, accompanied by that sudden piercing awareness of mortality whence come images of paradise clearness, realm of all beauty, poetry, art.

"Lady Abeline, w-we met at Husborne——"

She smiled with total confidence, showing splendid teeth. "Yes, you discovered a hawk-cuckoo, didn't you? Uncle Bohun has never let me forget it," she said gaily. Then to Piers, "How is Virginia? You must bring her to the Yacht Club. Of *course* it doesn't matter about the divorce. My dear, one *never* heeds the old women, who have nothing better to do than talk. 'Yes, my dear, have you heard, my dear?' Of *course* you must bring Virginia to see us."

They made their way to the buffet. "Champagne, no thank you. Never touch it." She lit a cigarette. Then winsomely, "A pink gin, thank you so much," throwing a swift smile with Sirius flashings below the tall neck. Phillip, swallowing more champagne, began to feel that the whole scene was one of grace and light.

The string orchestra sank to silence. People were turning to a screen being crossed by letters and figures. From loudspeakers came the voice of the Controller of the B.B.C.

"Labour gain."

"Oh lor'," said Lady Abeline. "I did the horoscope of Ramsay Mac. and knew this would happen. And *what* a doleful voice."

"The wreathing voice," said Piers. "Why doesn't he leave it to John Snagge."

A tall man with a grey moustache and an assumed easy manner sauntered up. Standing upright, he bobbed his head before Lady Abeline. After greetings Piers said, "May I introduce Phillip Maddison. He's a neighbour of mine and has just given up farming."

"Ah," said the elderly man. "Never forget what O. Henry said, 'Once a farmer, always a sucker'."

The affable and bewhiskered figure of Lord Lonsdale approached with a debonair, lightly-stepping man whose nose was slightly flattened. The four standing there appeared not to notice these celebrities, but all had observed them with the slightest of eye-movements. Phillip felt elation. He was among the great ones. Georges Carpentier, boxing champion of Europe . . . 1914, friends on the Hillies, warblings in the summer twilight, such happiness of life going on for ever and ever . . . until that strange and exciting suspension of life at the beginning of August.

The night glass-bubbled away and became early morning with a slight air of dishevelment. The screen continued to throw on election results. The monotonous voice of Sir John Reith—*Labour gain.* There was gentle booing in the vast crowded space: counter-cheers of the intelligentsia led by Sylvester Card, the actor-playwright with a red carnation in his button-hole. Phillip felt like cheering too: everywhere the Tory landslide. Thank God. No more hard-faced war-profiteers becoming knights, baronets, and peers giving millions of pounds for Lloyd George's 'honours fund', while denying the workless ex-soldiers who had broken the Hindenburg Line and now were breaking their hearts on the dole.

He moved about in the crowd, happy with thoughts of one day writing this very scene. There was a kangaroo in a boxing ring with a young man. Most amusing. The animal gave a sudden kick at the bottom of the young man in boxing gloves as he tried to get away over the ropes. He fell. The kangaroo hopped over him, and stopped, appearing to stare at Dikran Michaelis standing alone with his back against a pillar: dark wavy hair, sharp Armenian-Jewish face cast in reflective melancholy. He said to Phillip, "It must be a French kangaroo, ignorant of the Marquess of Queensberry rules."

Phillip laughed. "My name is Maddison."

"I remember your face of Christ crucified. You are now famous, God help you."

"Not so famous as you are."

"A brief candle which guttered. From gutter to gutter, one might say."

"I'm awfully glad to see you, Michaelis."

The Armenian novelist looked even more depressed after a man and a woman had come up to say, "Dikky darling, how *wonderful* to see you again", and passed on.

"They don't really mean it."

More people came up. Obviously Michaelis was popular. Why could he not believe it? Every affectionate greeting appeared to leave him more melancholy.

"These English ladies and gentlemen carry good manners beyond the point of insincerity, Maddison."

Phillip thought Michaelis must be unhappy because he, too, was cursed by a misplaced sense of time: occluded by shadow from childhood. He remembered that Armenians had been massacred by Turks. Dikran was rootless. A blank feeling overcame him. What if his own work ceased to be the mainspring of living? The work that he was not doing; feeling the presence of Lucy too much to struggle against in the dull valley life, the daily walk beside the brook to the Longpond. He must start his book on the trout.

A string band was playing *Tales from the Vienna Woods*. The music sank to a murmur as of leaves.

"Here is another result that has just come in——" the slow deep voice growled once more. "Labour gain——"

Phillip saw Piers beside a tall girl watching the screen. He went to them. Piers said, "You remember Gillian?"

"Yes indeed. We met at Colham market just about three years ago, when I bought my first cow."

"'Rosebud'! And those too, too sweet calves you bought because they were starving, poor mites, and Rosebud had so much milk. Have you still got them?"

"I had to give up farming." The tone of his voice, with its hint of resignation, prevented her asking further questions as he sat beside her, to receive the full look of her big brown eyes. She was drinking brandy and soda.

"How is Felicity? I haven't seen her for ages. Didn't she become your secretary?"

"Yes. Do you ever go to the 'Game Pie' now?"

"Not since it was taken over by 'Ma' Merrill. It's become too, too bogus."

"Ugh!" said Piers. "Sweet champagne at three guineas a bottle. Well, I'm going to take Gillian home. If I don't see you here, I'll see you at the flat. Here's a latch-key."

About two o'clock there was a movement towards the screen about to relay further election results. Applause announced another

Labour gain: Lady Georgiana Birkin had won a Staffordshire constituency from a Conservative candidate, with a majority of nearly 8,000. This was followed by a second announcement that Mr. Hereward Birkin, her husband, had not only held the seat in Birmingham he had taken from the Conservatives during the previous election, but had increased his majority by over 3,000 votes. A roar went up from the crowd in the street outside to add to the cheering within. Phillip was standing beside Lady Abeline and heard her say to the grey moustached man beside her, "Pouff! Birkin goes round in an old motor, 'Boy', pretending to be the friend of the working man."

"A damned buffoon," replied the other as though genially. "I know his father. The young pup was born with a golden spoon in his mouth, but if he had his way there would not be one country house remaining in England. What?"

"It's quite a problem, sir," replied Phillip, thinking that he had been addressed.

"You're the friend of Piers Tofield, aren't you? You're the farmer——"

Lady Abeline took this chance to get away. Left with the grey-haired man, Phillip said, "Well, I *was* a sort of farmer, sir."

"Won't you join me at the bar, and drink to the damnation of all politics? Allow me to introduce myself. Owing to the general decay of manners among the so-called post-war generation, you were not permitted to hear my name, which is Runnymeade."

"I remember Piers speaking of you, sir. He's putting me up for the Yacht Club."

"You must get 'im to bring you over to my place. The racin' starts this month, so we shall meet again soon. And don't call me 'sir'."

There was an euphoric glitter in the unfocus'd grey eyes that warned Phillip to keep his distance: was it pederasty? To his alarm he heard Captain Runnymeade asking for two large whiskies and soda. Whisky on top of champagne—fatal. But he finished the drink out of an uneasy politeness, and was wondering how he could get away when a woman's screams followed by laughter amidst a scattering of figures revealed that the kangaroo had again hopped over the ropes of the boxing ring, and was loose among the gold lamé'd, chiffon'd, tulle'd, and boiled-shirted crowd. It stopped against no resistance as men and women stood still. Its keeper arrived with a small bunch of carrots and dangled them against its nose. The kangaroo held the carrots between paws clobbered by boxing gloves and munched away as the room began to swirl around Phillip, who made for the door and hurried away down some stairs. He must get to the darkness of the side-street where his sports-car was parked. He was going to shoot his bundle.

After an hour he recovered sufficiently to open the top of the tonneau cover and drive slowly west until he found the Uxbridge road to Acton Vale and so to Ealing Common. Felicity was spending the night alone in the house during her mother's absence. She helped him into the bedroom and took off his shoes, while he sat shuddering on a chair.

"You're icy cold. Oh, Phillip, I should have been with you, to look after you. Come into bed, darling, and I'll warm you."

She moulded herself against his body. Gradually he ceased to tremble, and turned to enter her. She lay still, suffering because he did not make love to her first; he never wanted to kiss her, or do more than fondle her breasts. She understood this from what he had told her about his childhood: a mother forbidden to 'make him a nambypamby' by comforting him when he cried: a father who had insisted that he sleep in a cot, and at one year old had taken away the part of an old silk petticoat his mother had given him as a comforter. Had this warped him, driven him into himself? Had he made love, ever, to his dead wife, Barley, whom she pictured in her mind as perfection? Oh, would Phillip never be entirely hers? He had turned away, he lay still. She remained quiescent beside him. After awhile he rolled over and, putting an arm around his own neck, settled to sleep.

For some time she lay without movement, hardly breathing. The muscles of her stomach became hard with frustration. When he was asleep she got out of bed and swallowed four aspirins.

Phillip arrived home by train the next day with Felicity, after sending a telegram to announce their arrival. Both had made new resolutions to make a success of this second attempt to work together: not to see one another before noon, when he would have finished the morning's writing: not to ask nervous-foolish questions about office details while he was by the river, observing and taking notes. He must be clear to write at regular hours every day, and finish at certain times. The afternoon was free. After tea, until supper, he would write his war novel. Every morning he would write his book on the life of a trout. That was the programme.

On arrival at Skirr Farm, Lucy told him that Piers had telephoned and left a message.

"He asked if we'd care to go with him to the Yacht Club on Saturday, and dine afterwards with Captain Runnymeade."

"Well, Saturday is to be a whole holiday—relaxation—no writing. Can you leave the children with Felicity?"

"I didn't know you were coming, so I told Piers that I'd have to look after them, as Mrs. Rigg has Saturday at home." She hesitated. "Yes, I suppose I could leave them with Felicity."

"No," he said. "Not after last Christmas."

Felicity had been left alone with the children on Christmas night, when he and Lucy had gone to a party. She had only recently arrived to work for him, and had told them she would be quite happy alone; but overcome by melancholy and finally despair, she had written a letter to her mother describing her loneliness, and in an unhappy attempt to prove her feelings for Phillip, had brought her mother's reply to his writing room. He had glanced at it, but read no further after *My Darling Girlie, How dreadful for you to be left all alone on Christmas night of all nights! I was most distressed to read your letter——*

"But she was new then, wasn't she? Anyway, I'll be quite happy to remain here. Why not take Felicity? Piers said he wanted two more to crew him."

"She's never sailed, and I don't know much about that sort of racing yacht. I'll go alone."

"I wrote down the telephone number. Piers is not staying at his home, apparently, but at an hotel in the New Forest."

"I'll telephone now."

He thought that Piers was with Virginia, his wife, and he kept back his surprise when another voice, which he recognized as Gillian's, cut in and said, "Do bring Felicity. She's such a pet. I haven't seen her for simply ages."

He imagined Gillian with an arm over Piers' shoulder until his friend's voice said, "Get off the line, you bitch. Are you there, Phillip? That girl's listening from the bedroom."

"How's that adorable Rosebud?" the voice continued. "And those too, too sweet calves?"

"Oh, they're quite happy together."

"Do come," continued the voice, liquid-sloppy with drink. "I do so want to see Felicity. She's a pet."

"Yes, come," Piers cut in.

"I haven't got a car, I'm afraid."

"What's happened to your Silver Eagle?"

"It's in London with the firm that sold it to me. As you know, I had it vetted, before buying, by the Motor Association Engineer. He said the engine would be all right if the excessive oil consumption was put right. The salesman said it probably needed the oil-flow adjusting. I bought it on the understanding that it would be.

"I'm pretty sure one of the cylinder bores is badly worn, by a loose gudgeon pin on the piston."

Piers, bored by these mechanical details, said:

"We'll pick you up."

He never touched a spanner. His Ulster 1½-litre Aston-Martin was serviced by a mechanic who had a converted Mews stable near Piers' South Kensington flat.

"How long will it take us to get to the yacht club?"

"Forty minutes. I can take you and Felicity if you don't mind rather a tight fit. We must be there not later than four. The race starts about an hour before high water. Right, three o'clock tomorrow."

"Hold on, Piers. Lucy wants to say something to you. Oh, she says, will you come to lunch here?"

"Love to. One o'clock tomorrow, then."

"I like Piers," said Lucy.

Phillip warned Lucy not to mention Virginia when Piers arrived with Gillian. "One never knows about wives or girl-friends these days."

After luncheon they sat in the sunshine by the Longpond, and Phillip told them that he would have to look for another house to live in. The War Department was taking over the land, which his Uncle Hilary had sold, at midsummer.

"It will be hell with all the Tank Corps hutments going up. I'd like to be somewhere nearer the sea."

"Are you giving up Fawley?"

"Oh no. I've invited my parents to live there, in one of the flats. I shall perhaps let the other two."

"Officers' families," suggested Piers.

Trout were rising to the surface of the Longpond. A hatch of duns was drifting.

"The trouble is, to write my book about a trout I must be near water. And when the army comes, this brook will be poached to death."

It was time to leave for the coast. Piers' car had two bucket seats only.

"Would you care to drive? Gillian and I can sit on the hood."

Phillip, feeling this to be a courtesy offer only, replied that he was looking forward to seeing the view from the back. So Felicity sat in front beside Piers, and Gillian got up behind the driver, fitting her right foot with difficulty in the narrow space beside Piers' seat. Her left leg was bent back to be sat upon, while she supported her body with spread fingers. It was a precarious position, and higher than the top of the windscreen. When Phillip tried to adjust himself beside her there was no room for his legs, so Felicity took off his shoes and tucked a foot under each of her arms. She felt her warmth flowing into them as she hugged them to her body. Darling Phillip.

Lighting a cigarette, Gillian said, "Piers, you won't blind, will you? I'm hanging on literally by my fingernails."

With a crackle of exhaust they were off, watched by the entire village, it seemed, at cottage thresholds. Piers drove slowly at first, until the two perching behind said that they were all right; but he never exceeded 35 m.p.h. He slowed up and changed down well before corners, so that brakes were not needed. The wind blew Gillian's hair about her eyes, she laughed at Phillip and shook it out, while he supported her with an arm behind her woolly coat, feeling the warmth of her thigh pressed against his own.

"Very matey, isn't it?" she said to Felicity. "Are you most frightfully tired, holding us down, darling?"

"Oh no."

"It's too, too heavenly up here, Piers. One can see over the hedges."

The car swerved to avoid a bicyclist. She clutched Phillip, and laughed. "Do you mind if I put my arm round you?" holding her face close to his, while her air tickled his forehead. "Aow, now I want to scratch."

He tried to work the loose strand under her Norwegian ski-ing cap, conscious of what Felicity was feeling as she sat with the hug of his legs relaxed. They drove beside a river.

"Piers, may we stop a moment?"

The car drew in under an avenue of lime trees. Phillip climbed the tarred railings, and was in a park. He strode to the bank. Water flowed glass-clear. Bines of crowsfoot lifted and swayed in the current, their white flowers sometimes drowning but to re-appear. Beyond, among trees, was the long thatched roof of a house. He went on to look at it, leaving the others leaning over the railings.

In the garden of the thatched house an elderly man and a woman were playing croquet. Both wore faded panama hats. He determined to return, when he had his Silver Eagle, and explore this country.

Before they went on, he asked a villager who lived in the house: to be told 'twas the Colonel and Mrs. Gott, and they was leavin' come Michaelmas.

"Do they own it, d'you know?"

"'Tes the Lord's. 'Twas once the steward's house, but 'a ban't livin' there no more."

"I suppose you don't know if it's to be let?"

"Us ban't heard nothin', sir. But then us doan't hear nought about the gentry's goins-on."

"Who's the owner?"

"'Tes the Lord's, zur."

Phillip went back to the others with this information. Piers said, "It belongs to George Abeline."

Before they went on Gillian insisted on changing places with Felicity. "The view is too, too wonderful darling."

So Felicity sat beside Phillip, who put an arm round her waist.

"Are you happy, Felicity?" he whispered.

"Oh yes! I love the wind on my face."

From their perch they saw masts and rigging as they drew nearer the port. Hulls of yachts, tarred schooners, and small coastal steamers were moored at the quay. Beyond was a row of white Georgian houses, one with pillars which was the Customs House.

They stopped farther down the quay. There was a view of sea and distant trees across a broad bay. Nearer, a low green-painted house was set back behind a stone wall. A flagpole was visible. They entered by an iron gate into a garden, where elderly men and women in blue jackets and yachting caps were sitting at tables having tea.

"There's 'Boy' Runnymeade," said Piers.

Captain Runnymeade sat at a table by himself. He held a large tumbler of whisky and soda in one hand. Two trays stood on the table. One covered by a white cloth held teapot and cup, a plate of rolled bread-and-butter and another of cakes. Beside it was a silver tray with decanter and syphon of soda. The handsome face held a slightly mocking look as it regarded the newcomers. Then the pepper-and-salt suited figure, wearing brown-and-white golfing shoes, half-rose to say to Piers, "How are you, m'dear fellow? Glad you could get here in time for the race."

Captain Runnymeade, seated once more, with a half-careless wave of a hand indicated the empty chairs around his table. Then beckoning a young waiter in a white jacket he said, "Jerry, take this stuff away and bring some tea for my guests," after which he drained his tumbler and put it on the silver tray. "And give me a whisky-and-soda. Piers, have a drink?"

"Not for the moment, thanks. I must see about my boat, if you'll forgive me." Gillian went with him.

"Will you have a drink, Maddison?"

"Not at the moment, thanks."

The young waiter filled the tumbler, placed it within reach of his master, and took away the tea-tray.

"We met at the Election party the other night, Captain Runnymeade."

"So we did. You are a farmer," replied the other man, with an air of amused scorn as he looked about him. "Are you sailing?" he said to Felicity.

"Oh no, Captain Runnymeade."

"Then perhaps you'll be so good as to pour out tea for me when it comes."

Piers returned to ask Phillip if he would crew him, as someone had telephoned to say that his car had broken down on the way.

The breeze was stiffening with the tide; it might mean sickness; at the same time, to be left with Runnymeade, who looked to be the sort of man who drank to escape the depression of a false nature, might be worse. While he hesitated an unexpected report shattered the air. From behind a tamarisk bush the lanyard of a small cannon standing with two others on the sea-wall, had been pulled by the steward.

Seeing the hesitation on Phillip's face Piers said, "That's the fifteen-minute gun. Come with me to my locker. I'll see if I can fit you out," and in the dressing room he said, "If you don't want to go, I'll take Gillian, she has crewed before. Only I thought you might be stuck with Runnymeade."

Phillip remained away from the table while Piers and Gillian went to change. Two boatloads of men and women were being rowed to the yachts at their moorings. The 10-minute gun had gone when the two returned, dressed alike in blue jerseys, serge trousers, peaked caps, and carrying oilskins and kapok life-belts. Phillip saw them into a praam below the slip, and watched them while they boarded their yacht, to set about hauling up main and foresail. Last to be run up was a little triangular flag at the top of the mast.

Returning to the garden, he saw the steward, in a white jacket, hoisting a duplicate of Piers' flag.

"Isn't it good to think that flags are still used for signalling, as in Nelson's day, Felicity?"

"Yes."

"Piers' has just been run up."

Captain Runnymeade said heavily, "We call it a burgee."

A broad man in white flannel trousers and double-breasted blue jacket with brass buttons, wearing a large cap with a white cover, appeared. He had a gold watch in his hand. The last of the yachts were running up burgees. Sunlight flickered off the waves.

"According to Piers," went on Runnymeade, "You are a farmer——"

"I *was* learning to be one, Captain Runnymeade."

"I was about to say that, before you come to the inevitable end of a farmer, like Stephen Leacock—who, no doubt you will remember, in a good year, managed to get his seed back—and resume the pen—may I offer you a drink? Jerry, give Mr. Maddison a whisky and soda." He nodded to himself several times, and turned to Felicity, who was pouring out tea. "You have read O. Henry, of course. It was O. Henry who said, 'Once a farmer, always a sucker.' Oh, I beg your pardon. What will you drink?"

Phillip gave her a look as much as to say, Beware—this man is an alcoholic. Felicity replied, "I'd love some whisky, if I may, Captain Runnymeade."

"Good girl."

The Commodore was staring at the gold hunter watch open on the palm of his left hand. His right arm was raised. The steward, lanyard wrapped round fingers, was watching him. Down went the arm; steward's tug on lanyard, *bang!* the echo rolled.

"I think I'll watch the start," said Phillip, getting up to go to the quay.

A strong tide was flooding the harbour. The waves had little white tops. Yachts were sailing to and fro, each with its burgee fluttering taut in the wind. Some boats were heeling over as they tacked across the tide. Others were beating up against wind and water, close-hauled. It appeared to be a matter of getting as near as practicable to the starling line, marked by two buoys, before the starter gun. He had observed the synchronising of the captains' watches with that of the Commodore's before the crews had gone out to the boats.

A man watching told him that any boat that crossed the line before the starting gun would be notified by the running up of its burgee on the flagpole, to recall it.

Feeling mean that he had left Felicity alone to cope with Runnymeade he returned to her saying, "Would you like to see the start? We'll be back, Captain Runnymeade."

The other man waved a hand. They went to the wall and stood near a telescope on a tripod pointing to the starting line.

"Why did you have that whisky? He's only trying to make you tight."

"I rather like him," she replied gaily.

"What were you talking about?"

"Oh, he has heard that the Swannery is likely to become an R.A.F. bombing range, so he is not going to renew the lease of his country house, but move to a cottage he's bought somewhere on the East Coast, where he wants to paint in water-colour. He said I must go and stay with him when he's had the place done up."

"He's a ram in wolf's clothing, as Dikran Michaelis would say."

"He's a dear."

"A father-figure."

The steward, now in blue jacket with Naval ribbons and small peaked cap under white cover, held the lanyard of the red cannon. His eyes were on the Commodore, who was crouching with an eye against the telescope fixed to the flagpole. Most of the boats were now criss-crossing near the starting line. Some were lagging, sheets at right angles to let slip the wind, while bows pointed on course.

The Commodore began to count.

"Five seconds—four—three—" he raised a hand—"two—one—"

BANG!

One of the boats had crossed the line prematurely. Another gun spoke: up went a burgee to the top of the flagpost. The yacht turned stern to breeze, its boom lifting over with the flapping sail which the helmsman hauled in to lessen the weight of wind as the boom was hurled over. The boat appeared to stagger before it recovered and went fast with the tide until put about; to hang in the wind before plunging after the other boats.

There followed, for Phillip, a tedious time with Captain

Runnymeade. He had to accept a drink since he felt it was expected of him. Then someone mentioned that there was table tennis in the next room. Here he passed an hour with Felicity, playing with his left hand since she was a beginner. While they were sitting down, resting, looking at yachting magazines, the steward came in and said that Captain Runnymeade had left a message that he would be most grateful if they would go over to the Castle that night to help him entertain some old ladies to dinner. Sir Piers Tofield and Miss Templecombe had accepted. The Captain would send his motor to fetch them at eight o'clock, but they were not to hurry, as dinner was at half-past nine.

"I wonder if he thinks we're married?"

"Darling, of course he knows I am your girl friend."

"Then he'll expect us to sleep together."

She said happily, "Good. I must telephone Lucy that we won't be back to supper."

"I wonder why he invited you to stay with him at his cottage? I bet he's a sensual old devil."

"Most of 'Boy's' friends are painters, dancers, and writers."

"You seem on familiar terms with him already."

"He asked me to call him 'Boy'."

"He doesn't look the artistic type."

"Perhaps he enjoys their company. Everyone isn't sexy, you know."

"So I'm 'sexy', am I? I thought I didn't come up to expectations."

"Darling, I love you."

"I thought it a bit *outré* when he repeated that bit about O. Henry. He said the same thing to me at the party on Election night."

After the race, the crews crowded the bar before changing. There was loud talk about points in the race. Phillip began to feel that this was the life. Piers had already put him up for membership. His fear of a social life, in the belief that a writer to be any good must keep apart and live in his own world, was temporarily abated. All was experience! He took his fifth whisky and soda from Piers.

"I rather fancy there will be quite a crowd later on tonight, coining down from London with Stefania Rozwitz, his girl friend."

"Isn't she one of the Russian ballet?"

"Yes. Runnymeade has the whole company down sometimes,

by special train to Bournemouth, which gets in about half-past twelve."

"Is that where he lives?"

"His place is west of where we are now, about twenty miles. The Aston usually does it in under the half-hour from here."

"What time d'you think the party will end?"

"Oh, sometime tomorrow."

It was getting on for nine o'clock.

"Have you telephoned Lucy yet, Felicity?"

"Oh dear, I'd quite forgotten——"

He pushed past her to the box. Lucy said it was kind of him to have rung up. Billy and Peter were happily asleep in the same bed, everything was all right, and she would expect them when she saw them. When he came back to the bar he saw that Felicity was biting her nails. They were bitten down to the quick. It annoyed him to see them.

They arrived at the Castle soon after ten o'clock. Runnymeade saw them briefly, apologised for having to leave them to write letters, and asked Piers to do the honours. After dinner the four went to the billiard room and played slosh. At one corner of the room was an oak door beyond which were stone steps leading down to the cellars—cave after cave lined with bottles. There was no dampness down there, the floors and walls having been rendered with a special kind of waterproof cement, Piers explained.

"He took the Castle on lease after the war. I've no idea where he comes from. I don't think anyone knows, except that he had an American mother who left him a fortune. He told me once that he was with the sixteenth cavalry at Mons, and then went on the staff. What else he did in the war, if anything, I don't know."

"I tried to talk to him about it at the club, Piers, but all he said was, 'Who wants to talk about that goddam war?'"

It was midnight. Champagne suspended time. They sat with backs against the wall, glasses in hand. When Runnymeade reappeared he was wearing a claret-coloured smoking jacket. "Let us await our guests in the hall," he said.

A light flashed at the top of the flagpost on the lawn beyond the entrance drive, announcing the convoy passing under the arch of the eastern lodge. At once lights went on in all the rooms and the great oak door, iron-bound and studded, was opened. Two footmen stood by this door, while a red light glowed below the light on the pole. The chamberlain, wearing some sort of brocaded eighteenth-century coat with black silk knee-breeches and silver-buckled shoes, went forward as the tyres of the first motor stopped on the gravel. It was like a film set, Philip thought: the chamberlain bowed, in came the guests, led by Stefania Rozwitz dressed in a pale fur toque and coat, gliding towards Runnymeade with arms held out, a dozen young women behind her moving with level movements as though the bodies floated on air. Curtsies were dropped while the ballerina received clasps from a beaming host. The men stood behind them with less assurance, automatically feeling themselves to be in a supporting role.

Last of all, velour hat in hand, came a figure with a moon-face and the eyes of a children's-book owl in spectacles.

"I say, Piers, do introduce me to our host, won't you? I heard you were going to be here. Hullo, Phil. What a pleasure to see you again. And Gillian, my dear, I *am* delighted."

"And what might be your connexion with the ballet, Mr. Plugge?" asked Runnymeade, when Piers had introduced him.

"Oh, I hire out the chairs to the gallery boys and gels, sir."

Archie Plugge was soon at home. He praised the 'simply marvellous' dancing of the ballet as he held a large whisky and soda beside Runnymeade.

They moved into the banqueting hall. There were two enormous flaming hearths at each end. The loftiness below the roof was interrupted by a gallery running around three sides of the hall, up among dark beams and kingposts. On the floor of heavy oak planking stood a refectory table long enough to seat a hundred guests but now looking bare with a mere score or so of places laid amidst a profusion of flowers, candelabra, crystal glass, and gold plate.

"Seat yourselves anywhere," cried Runnymeade. "We don't stand on ceremony here."

Even so, the footmen served, the under-butler carved and sliced, the wine went round with dignity. At last the servants left, with the exception of Jerry the valet, who had looked after his master at the Club-house.

"This is a party," cried Runnymeade, his eyes between glaze and glitter. He had eaten only oysters with whisky and soda. Along the table corks popped. Laughter was continuous.

Phillip sat with Archie Plugge, who explained that he was in partnership with a chap who hired out the collapsible chairs at sixpence a time to people in the queues for the ballet and opera.

"I'm still on *The Wireless Times,* old boy, the chairs are a sideline—literally so, ha-ha. It's a gold mine—fifty per cent pure profit on our outlay." He went on to say that he had telephoned Piers' home to propose himself for the week-end, but when he found he was not there he rang up Lucy, and since some of the ballet company were going to a party not far from Piers' place, made enquiries and found they were on his doorstep, so to speak.

"Have you seen 'Le Spectre de la Rose,' Phil? I saw it for the first time tonight. It somehow reminded me of you. Rozwitz was marvellous."

"Tell me about it, Archie."

"It's rather the same theme as 'The Flying Dutchman'. A girl dreams of a lover in the rose she has been given, and her feeling calls up the vision in a material form."

"Poor girl," said Phillip, thinking of Felicity.

"I say," whispered Plugge, confidentially, "What is our host, d'you know?"

"Retired cavalry. Rich American mother."

Plugge raised his glass towards the head of the table, and then went for the lobster, with a side-glance at the chicken on his neighbour's plate, mentally approving it for the second course.

Felicity sat on one side of Runnymeade, Stefania on the other. 'Boy' appeared to live in a private world, served by Jerry and an almost colourless Scotch whisky. It was not so much a party, as an assembly of parties. Phillip tossed a roll which fell at the other end of the table, where sat the male dancers in a separate gathering, some talking with feminine voices and gestures. The roll was gracefully tossed back. The host then picked up another roll and hurled it at Phillip.

"Now then, 'Farm Boy'," he called out. "Come on, pay a dividend! You're a writer. Amuse us. Remember what O. Henry said, 'Once a farmer, always a sucker.' You haven't said a goddam word all the evening, Maddison. Tell us somethin' amusin'."

"What sort of thing amuses you, Captain Runnymeade?"

"What does that mean exactly?"

"I haven't quite got your wave-length, but I gather that you're not a sucker."

"What d'you mean by that?" asked Runnymeade, in a voice suddenly quiet.

"Hush, 'Boy,' hush," said Stefania putting a hand on the sleeve of his jacket.

"I meant merely that you're apparently not a farmer yourself. Nor am I—it gave me up."

Runnymeade sat back, nodding his head to himself. "At any rate, my other friends don't call me a sucker to my face, although they probably think it."

"Oh no, 'Boy'," said Stefania. "Don't pretend that you're hurt. You were playing with Farm Boy, now Farm Boy is playing with you."

"Very well. I can see I am in the way, so I'll say goodnight all, and leave you to enjoy yourselves." He pushed back his chair and toppled over.

"I can tell you one thing," said Piers, when 'Boy' was back in his chair. "I saw this farm boy once doing a very fine stroke of business in the market. Made a good profit, too, over Rosebud. She was beautiful. What did she cost you, Phil? A tenner, wasn't it? Quick work, I must say, and worth every penny of it. Don't you agree, Gillian?"

"She was a pet. A love. She was simply too, too sweet," sang Gillian, and, draining her glass, she gave a loving glance at Runnymeade across the table.

"You're a dark horse, Maddison," said Runnymeade, smiling to himself. "Why didn't you bring Rosebud?"

"She was looking after two other suckers at the time."

"I don't get you. Who or what is this Rosebud?"

"An Ayrshire heifer I bought at market."

When the laughter had ended, Runnymeade said, "Pay a dividend, and tell us more about this Rosebud."

"I bought two calves at market. They were starving. For all animals to be sent to market is tragedy. Market Hill at Colham is a place haunted by lost love, anguish, and fear. So I bought a cow from a milkman, so bagged up, as they say, that——"

"A milkman bagged up, did you say? Or was he baggered up, possibly a euphemism for the familiar state of all farmers today?"

"In a way, yes. But it was the cow who was in pain. She hadn't been milked that morning, in order to show off the size of her bag."

He told them about the honest milkman, how Piers and Gillian waiting apart gave him a calmness to know that the cow was good, as was the milkman's word. It was all a true play of social instinct, he said, feeling foolish.

"God bless my soul," said Runnymeade. "I don't know what you're talking about."

"I suppose a ballet could be written around the incident—'The Honest Milkman'?" said Piers.

"Good God," said Runnymeade, "And that's how you spend your time. You're a do-gooder, Maddison."

"You're a do-gooder, too. Look at your wonderful party."

Cheers and handclapping seemed to depress the host. Phillip knew what he was feeling: the loneliness of the would-be artist, the dream of happiness that was built on the broken inner self. The mockery, the touchiness, the semi-scoffing attitude toward others were but signs of inner despair. He felt affection for Runnymeade.

"Are there any more animals on your goddam farm, Maddison?"

"I'm afraid not. I lost my land through my own stupidity. Ideas pass, the land remains."

This simple statement caused silence. He was conscious of sympathy from the feminine young men at the end of the table. They had been listening to the talk with absorbed interest. Then one of their number took a mouth-organ out of his pocket and began to play a melancholy tune, improvising as he went on, bringing in bass notes to represent the noises of market. Suddenly the tune lifted into life, and another of the feminine young men got up and began to dance with hardly a sound of feet on the oak floor. Another joined him, throwing off his jacket, and another, until they were passing to and fro in the candlelit hall with a suggestion of the grace of swallows meeting and turning and circling over a lawn when the glass is falling and the gnats are flying low because of damp membraneous wings. Phillip felt tears coming to his eyes as he sat, hands folded as though meekly on his diaphragm, with a feeling of being borne above life, aware of Stefania moving her feet out of her low-heeled shoes and floating down the other side of the table, giving him the passing glance of a dove among swallows. The other girls joined in. He felt the part-communicable truth of the moment: of Rosebud and her gentleness, her grief for her own lost calf, her love given to the two calves he had bought: of Runnymeade, also aching under his bravura for lost love.

They were miming the story: Rosebud was being danced by Stefania, the Honest Milkman by a male dancer, the calves by two girls. The others made the market-day crowd, all in silence, through motion: the flow of feeling transformed to movement.

Then everybody was clapping and laughing—except Runnymeade, who sat at the head of the table, leaning back a little in his chair, his manner of faint mockery that of a man wilfully apart, watching in a surrealistic world of cubes and angles, Phillip dancing with Stefania.

As for Phillip, he felt himself to be moving on air while holding and being upheld by air.

The morning star had risen in the east when, feeling his way down a dark passage with feet and hands, a swirling vehicle of acidity remaining after two bottles of champagne, he was aware of Runnymeade's voice, now petulant, now pleading, now angry, repeating the same words again and again—behind the closed door—*Beat me—beat me—Goddamit, why don't you beat me!*—ending the pleas with a crash. What was Runnymeade doing?—his conscience demanding punishment?—and for what? God, how easy it was to lose one's true self . . . and with a pulling movement of hands along the wall he counted to twenty-three before stopping, to proceed again with caution, until he found and overcame the obstacle, sought and found the glass handle of the 'throne'—a large glass knob cut with a score of facets. He had observed this potential bolt-hole, making a mental map-reference to it as it were, on the way down to dinner.

He turned the cut-glass knob; and after a timeless period of surgent repentance on his knees lifted the plug and left the hide, his bearings beyond tight-closed eyes fixed upon the length of the passage, particularly the step—*up* this time—now twenty paces on—slowly——

He tripped and fell over. The jolt upset everything—he must go back to the cut-glass handle—he was conscious of someone helping him up, leading him into candle-light. A voice was saying *Drink this*. Fizzy stuff. His legs were lifted and he was floating on a bed; but not, thank God, with saliva coming into his mouth for the dreaded return.

Later, he knew that his forehead was being sponged with cold water. The candlelight revealed an oval face enclosed in a white bathing turban. He felt better.

"Stefania, how very kind of you."

"How do you feel, 'Farm Boy?'"

"Better, thank you."

She sat on the side of the bed and looked at him.

"Why do you men drink? I know what 'Boy' is looking for—his mother. But what are *you* looking for?"

"I don't drink much, as a rule."

"But you are looking for something. Isn't Felicity enough, and your writing? You are sad about your farm. Why? Tell me. Do you know what it is? If so, tell me. Don't be afraid of me. I have known many men—I have known Nijinsky, yes, I still know Nijinsky. There was a contradiction in his life that overwhelmed him, just as there is in 'Boy', only a different contradiction. I try to help him. I try to help you. Tell me, 'Farm Boy'."

"All life is a search for 'le spectre de la rose'."

She looked at him again and said, "You are a poet, as well as a Farm Boy."

"'As a necromancer raises from the rose-ash, the ghost of the rose'—I must raise *my* 'spectre de la rose'—or die."

"You will die in any case, 'Farm Boy'. Who was she?"

"My first wife, who died at nineteen, having a child. The wrong way round. Feet first."

"Did the child live?"

"Yes."

"Where is the child now?"

"Lucy—my second wife—looks after him. She loves him more than I do. With a true, human love, which I lack."

"Go back to Lucy, and love your son, 'Farm Boy'."

She kissed him on the forehead, and he returned to Felicity's room, got in beside her, and fell asleep.

Felicity lay in her bed, unmoving. She was thinking, or rather feeling, that she had lost Phillip. She had seen him returning along the passage, and entering the bedroom of the beautiful, the graceful Stefania Rozwitz, whom she adored. If only her mother had allowed her to train as a dancer, as she had wanted to when a child.

Chapter 2

FLUMEN MONAGHORUM

Phillip went to London to make a complaint about the engine of his car. The Portland Street salesman was suavely repetitive.

"The Motor Association engineer's report made it clear, surely, sir, that the oil-flow needed only a little adjustment. The regulating screw on the oil-pipe to the overhead valve tappets needed a turn or two, I thought I heard him say."

"I fancy that is what *you* suggested."

"Really, sir? But I'd not seen the car before, it only came in that morning. Have you tried adjusting the oil screw, sir?"

"Oh yes. There's no compression in one of the cylinders. You can hear the air hissing past the piston when you turn the handle."

"A broken ring, perhaps, sir. If you'd like us to take off the cylinder head for you, and can spare a couple of hours, I'll get a mechanic to draw the piston."

Phillip went back that afternoon. The front cylinder was badly scored. "The gudgeon pin apparently came adrift, sir. It looks like a rebore."

"How much will a rebore cost?"

"We might do it for ten pounds. She'll require new pistons, of course. Shall we say fifteen pounds for the job?"

"I suppose it wouldn't be fair to ask you to pay for the entire job, since I bought the 'bus as it was. Caveat emptor, you know."

"That's very sporting of you, sir. I'll tell you what, we'll throw in the pistons. How about a tenner for the job, sir? By the look of the toe-mark on the floorboard by the accelerator pedal, the last owner caned your engine somewhat."

When the work was done he drove home at thirty miles an hour. The dipstick showed clean oil, and none used. He must take Lucy for a drive, at once.

"You look after the house while we're gone, Felicity. I'm going to take Lucy to look over that house at Flumen Monachorum we saw on the way to the Yacht Club last Saturday."

Felicity felt unhappy because Phillip did not invite her to come, too. Had he forgotten what he had said to her? 'We'll go over together, and if the place is all right, I'll take it, then well bring Lucy and let it be a surprise for her.'

Now she watched them driving away, and felt forlorn. He did not really love her. Was he in love with Stefania Rozwitz? Had he slept with her that night of the party?

"Lucy, d' you think Mother will mind if we move some miles south of Fawley, now that they're going to live there when Father retires?"

"Well, all Mother's letters have been about how wonderful it will be for her to be so near the children."

"But Skirr farmhouse is sold, as you know, with the rest of the estate, and we've got to give vacant possession by Michaelmas. And frankly, I don't fancy living in one of the flats at Fawley, right on top of my parents."

Lucy thought that this was perhaps not the time to tell Phillip that Mother had written to her, asking her if it were possible that she, Lucy, might take Doris' two little boys, so that Doris could go back to her old job of teaching in London, and spend her holidays in the country with them. Mother had said in her letter that, when she and Father came to live there, it might result in a reconciliation between Father and Doris, now that the marriage between Doris and Bob Willoughby had failed.

Lucy would love to have Doris' two little boys, it would be so good for Billy and Peter to have some cousins to play with. After all, Fawley was big enough, and there was plenty of garden, and the downs behind. But Phillip did not get on with either of his sisters, Elizabeth or Doris. So Lucy said nothing about the letter from his mother.

"I don't want to live at Fawley. The downs will be out of bounds, tanks churning up the turf. Instead of rooks cawing there'll be the crack of tank cannon, and splintered trees." He thought of Bourlon Wood in the battle for Cambrai in November 1917, and drove on slower than before.

"Didn't they say at the enquiry that there wouldn't be any firing this side of the downs, Pip?"

"Well, to be honest, it isn't altogether a question of tanks or a firing range. It's the fact that I've failed in what I undertook to do. As you know, Uncle Hilary bought back the family land my grandfather threw away, so that I could succeed him, and I—well—I threw it away, too. And I want to be near a trout stream, to watch fish, for my book. And I'd like to move nearer the sea, and I think I've found a house. It was to be a surprise, but I've told you before we get there. We're on the way now."

"How lovely!"

"It's got plenty of room," he went on with a stir of optimism, "and it's all by itself in a hamlet called Flumen Monachorum. There used to be monks in the Abbey, but Henry the Eighth dissolved them. Lord Abeline lives at the Abbey, he's the landlord."

Lucy blushed. Should she tell Phillip that George Abeline was her cousin, by marriage? No, it was not important.

The elderly tenants were only too pleased that someone had come to look at the house. Over tea Colonel Gott said that he and his wife wanted to move nearer a town, the place was rather isolated for them, they had been thinking of going back to Cheltenham to be among friends. It was a jolly little place, he declared, not too difficult to run, and plenty of help was available in the hamlet. The bath-water was fed to a tank in the roof from a ram beside the river, and drinking water came from a well, as was usual in the district. They were shown round the bedrooms, five in all, and three living rooms in addition to kitchen and scullery. There were the usual outhouses, and drainage by septic tank.

"There's a couple of miles of fishin', the rent is moderate, forty pounds a year, tenant paying rates, another twenty. The very place to study trout, if you want to write about them. I've read your book on the otter's wanderings with interest, knowing the Devon moorland country more or less. We took this place and the fishin' on a seven-year lease, two of which are yet to run. I'll speak to the Steward, if you like, and may I tell him that you're prepared to consider taking over the unexpired portion of the lease?"

"Thank you, Colonel Gott."

Lucy and Phillip went away happy at the prospect of living in such a secluded place. They drove into the town, and visited the Steward, a solicitor to whom Phillip made a formal application to take over the remainder of Colonel Gott's lease at Midsummer. For references he gave the name of Lucy's father, his uncle Sir Hilary Maddison, and his bank.

"I'll put your application before his Lordship, who will want to see you, Mr. Maddison."

The following week, wanting to run-in the rebored engine, he set off for London to break the news to his parents. He took Felicity with him, she was going to stay at home for awhile. He said he was determined to begin the trout book, for which he had had the advance royalties more than a year ago. She had heard that before.

"I don't see why I can't do the book on the trout at the same time as the war book, once I get into a routine. I'll send a chapter of each to you every day, and not re-write one sentence. Then when I'm in full flow, you can come down. I mean, if you can live at home for awhile, you can also begin the novel you want to write, can't you?"

She remained silent: she felt depression growing upon her: this was his way of telling her it was over. She tried not to cry. A little farther on he stopped beside a wood near Andover and said, "Come on." She trembled: she prayed she would not fail him by remaining tense, so that he would turn away from her. They lay on dry leaves. She was thrilled, by his sudden fierceness, and hearing from him the 'three little words' of the current revue song, felt herself becoming tumescent with a feeling of love beyond desire; holding him in her arms she felt that the earth was rocking, while involuntary cries came from her. And afterwards as she lay beside him staring at the sky beyond the canopies of the trees she was lapped in happiness that now her dream of having a child before she was twenty-one might be fulfilled. If she became pregnant she would go away without telling him, so that he would never feel burdened by her ugly presence, and have her baby alone in a remote cottage somewhere.

They drove on to London in silence, and Phillip put her down by the underground station at Hammersmith Broadway.

"Take care of yourself, dearest," she said, hoping he would want to kiss her goodbye. But all he said was, "I'll telephone you as soon as I know what I'm doing. I'm going to see my parents, who are coming to live at Fawley, then I'll be at the Barbarian Club. Would you care to meet me there tonight?"

"Oh yes!"

Phillip felt guilty when he saw how much his mother was looking forward to a new life, as she called it, among her children's little ones. Had Lucy spoken to him about having Doris' two boys when she went back to teaching?

"Well, as you know, Mother, I don't get on very well with

either Doris or Elizabeth. Also—now please don't be upset—Lucy and I may not be living at Rookhurst. You see," he went on, speaking quietly to control a feeling of exasperation, "all the estate is sold, including Skirr Farm, so we've got to give up the farmhouse. Then the brook, and the Longpond, all belong to the Army authorities, and there'll be officers fishing for trout there. So I must move, to be beside a stream, to observe fish, before I can write about them. But we'll be quite near."

"Oh, I am so relieved, my dear son."

How like a child she was, she had never really grown up——

"You see, Phillip, your father is a very lonely man, and looks forward to going for walks with you, where he walked with his father when he was a boy. He talks about the walled garden, too, and how he will be able to grow fruit again, against the walls. Now tell me all about Lucy, and Billy, and little Peter and Rosamund——Oh, I cannot tell you how I am looking forward to seeing them all together, and in that lovely country, Phillip. I am counting the days to next spring, when Father retires from the office! Oh, must you go so soon? Won't you wait to see your father? He will be so disappointed. Yes, I'll give him your love, my dear son. You are a good son to us, we can never thank you enough for inviting us both to live at Fawley."

"Oh, Mother! You're doing me a favour, by occupying part of it."

An old soldier wearing the riband of the 1914 Star arrived on a bicycle one morning when Phillip was looking over the new house with Billy. He had a most woeful expression, as though he had found himself homeless after some years of fancied security. This indeed was the case.

"Sir, permission to speak to you. Rippingall, sir, at your service!"

Phillip knew the soldierly address. He liked it. He took the old fellow into the house. After a cup of tea, he decided that he was that rare thing, a gentle soul. Also he was of a literary turn of mind, having read Shakespeare, Tolstoi, and other classical writers.

Rippingall explained that he had been the gardener and house-parlourman to the old vicar of Flumen Monachorum, who had allowed for his occasional bouts of malaria; but the new vicar—"His Reverence bears the name of Scrimgeour, sir, I expect you know the gentleman, he comes from Liverpool, I believe"—had shown him no sympathy after one of his bouts, and had told him to go.

Rippingall had a pinched, bluish look about him, and was so earnest in offering himself for work of any kind that Phillip took him on, especially when he told him that he had been a mess-waiter in a regular regiment of foot, and had also worked as a house-parlourman since the war. He could cook, wash clothes, keep accounts, paint, do a bit of masoning, carpentry, "and what not".

"Well, you've told me what you can do, so I won't bother with what you can't do."

"I am a trained soldier, sir, a trained valet, house-parlourman, cook, gardener, and what not, sir."

"Have you been in service other than the Rectory?"

"Sir, I was valet to Captain Runnymeade for nine years," replied Rippingall, giving him a salute, while the smart raising of the right arm revealed a half-bottle of gin in the pocket of his threadbare tweed jacket.

"How often do you go on a blind, old soldier?"

"Only when those who are, in a manner of speaking, my betters, become more or less critical of me, sir," and he gave Phillip another salute.

"How often is that?"

"About twice a year," replied Rippingall, trying to click heels which were worn down.

Rippingall was such a success, the garden beginning to look so orderly, and Lucy so pleased, that Phillip wrote to Felicity, and asked her to come back. He was now, he said, sure that things would be different.

Billy had a passion for the tar-engine which was then working on the London road. It was a beautiful thing in his eyes, which shone whenever it was praised by his father when they passed it in the sports-car. But sometimes Phillip teased Billy about it, pointing out that it gave off an unpleasant smell, that it was sticky and never washed itself, that in fact it was a detestable if useful mass of congealed tar. This would enrage Billy, and his tea-things were liable to be pushed away, and a word shouted at his father that always displeased Lucy—"Bug off, Daddy, bug off." Lucy would attempt to explain that Billy felt strongly about the tar-engine and that Phillip was upsetting him and also encouraging him to use silly words.

"He is being inoculated against such words," Phillip said to Felicity.

At the tone of his father's voice the child would show a confusion of feeling, as he glanced first at Lucy's face, then not at his father's but on the ground. He would pout, frown, go away by himself; and Lucy would return to her sewing, or her cleaning, or another of the duties which kept her working from early morning to late at night. Phillip would feel in himself something of the confusion of what the little boy was suffering, and return to his writing room, to potter about, doing anything but write, waiting to bring himself clear and as it were into focus again. Was it not good that the boy should swear and shout, if he felt like it, he demanded of Felicity, who had come into the room almost on tiptoe lest she interrupt his thoughts.

"I did *not* teach Billy to swear. He picked up 'words' as Lucy calls them, from the other little village bipeds playing in the village street. One of the first things I heard him calling Lucy, with a happy smile, was 'dirty old cow'."

Felicity laughed with delight. She looked so young, so fresh, so tender that he pushed her gently backwards into his leather arm chair and, kneeling before her, wound arms about her with that sudden impulse that always made her yield with beating heart and desire to bring him fully to herself—her wayward, her distraught, her innocent child.

"Parson Scrimgeour was a prison chaplain at Strangeways Gaol in Manchester, Lucy. He is obviously used to executions, for he said to me, 'Why did you, of all people, write that horrible book, *The Phoenix?*' So I turned the other cheek and gave as my own, Bernard Shaw's reply on the first night of *Arms and the Man*, when the audience applauded wildly, and called for a speech. G.B.S. held up a hand. In the silence a voice from the gallery cried 'Rotten!' G.B.S. held up his hand again for the laughter to stop, and said, with the friendly, open manner of a man who has been trained and self-built in pain, 'Yes, I agree with you, sir, it is rotten, but what are we two against so many?'"

Lucy had heard that story many times, but all she said was, "I hope it made the vicar laugh."

"No, he didn't get the joke. 'So many?' he said. 'I don't understand.' 'Oh, only my bad joke,' I replied. 'Oh,' he said. Then he asked me if I had seen the notice in *The Ecclesiastical Times* when it appeared a year ago. I said, 'Oh, yes, my wife's father saw the review before he read the book, and remarked, after he had read the book, "H'm, my son-in-law's an ass".' Scrimgeour then gave me a toothy smile and said, 'Well, do better next time,' and asked me to play badminton in the winter at a little club he had got up, by permission of Lord Abeline in the old coach-house of the Abbey."

Out of friendship for the new vicar, who was not popular, Phillip went to church after they moved to the new house. Whether by chance or design, on his first Sunday the sermon was on the theme that Truth had been discovered among men already, and there was no need for further search in the world among individual writers and philosophers. Afterwards, while the vicar stood by the porch, to bow to and pass a word to the more established of his parishioners going out, he said to Phillip, who had remained in his seat hoping not to be noticed, "I haven't the gift of words that you have, Mr. Maddison, but I did my best to make the Christian point of view clear."

"I listened with great interest, Vicar."

"It is up to men like you, who have gifts, to help influence others for good. I think your hero is wrong-headed, but I wouldn't go so far as your respected father-in-law as to say he is altogether an ass."

"Oh, that was applied to me as a person, Vicar. At the same time, it is only fair to add that, as my father-in-law considers that the novels of Dostoievsky are unreadable and the music of Wagner a horrible noise, in a way perhaps he was paying me a compliment."

"Oh."

"Well, I must not keep you, Vicar."

"No hurry, I assure you. How is Rippingall behaving himself? Well, I hope?"

"Yes, he is in good heart, I think. He and I have already worked happily together for several weeks, drinking only tea."

"Oh yes, Rippingall goes 'dry' as the Americans say, but you'll have to watch him all the same."

Monachorum House stood among trees, a couple of hundred yards outside the deer park of the Abbey, home of the landlord, built of chalk and limestone blocks and thatched. Pear, peach, and greengage trees grew against the south wall, with hollyhocks and sunflowers. It had paths of limestone chips, and two small lawns. Lucy loved it. Soon a cheerful cottage woman, glad to have extra money, since her husband earned little more than twenty shillings a week, took the place of Mrs. Rigg, who had promised to work for 'Mr. Phillip's mother' when the old people moved down from London.

The first guests at Monachorum were Piers, and his wife Virginia who had been living in Austria with her mother. Phillip did not ask questions, but he had the idea that there had been some trouble, but the two were now reconciled. The three went sailing together, Phillip now a member of the Yacht Club, from the quay of which they set out to distant parts of the bay, spending long sunny hours lying on the sand, talking and idling. Felicity joined them, bringing her pencils and pad, in case Phillip wanted to dictate; but Phillip told Piers that he would start writing seriously in the early autumn. Piers agreed that he would be better for a long rest, lying in the sunshine.

"After all, you've had a pretty hard time since leaving the army, one way and another, and your batteries need recharging."

The valley lay in a dream of sunshine, it was St. Martin's Little Summer. Rosamund, lying in her perambulator, struggled against late morning sleep and the straps which confined her. She was weary of the shade of an apple tree. She wanted to be with Dad and the boys playing in the river water. She understood nearly all that was said, taking in expressions and sounds with her ears and translating life away from her pram as all-smiling, no shushing and no babydarlinggotosleeptheresagoodgirl. The sixteen-month-old girl screamed at times because she was strapped in when she wanted to climb over the side and walk away.

When the apples began to drop the pram was moved to the lawn, beside an overgrown box hedge. The lawn was humpy, she could rock the pram. It was uneven because often the drainpipe from the kitchen was choked, and every time this happened Phillip had to dig up the lawn. Not only were the pipes choked at the open joins by the movement of earth worms, he told Lucy, but far too much muck went down the 4-inch-diameter pipes. Would she ask Miss Kirkman, the lady-cook (as she described herself) to try not to let any solid matter go down the kitchen sink?

Baby Rosamund—'Roz' to her brothers—slept every day, well wrapped, in the shade of the bushy box-tree, while Phillip tried to work up above in his writing room. He felt a dark eye half-concealed in hair topping the fat little naked body regarding him. While Dad was up there, Roz was content. And hearing the gurgling of the kitchen drain, and seeing a grey fluid spreading over the path below, she knew Dad would come downstairs and play with her. Before digging up nice wet grey mud.

Rippingall now worked outside, in the garden. His headquarters were in a thatched summerhouse with open walls of rustic work.

There, being of a literary turn of mind, he planned his cultivations and croppings for the year, writing many notes and reminders of what should be done. These details were interspersed with ideas for 'Monograph on Trutta trutta, or the common brown trout', which he planned to write in order to present it as a birthday present to help 'Phillip my gentleman'.

In the kitchen a local girl helped the lady-cook, who had been a governess in Brussels with a Belgian baron and his family. Miss Kirkman had advertised in *The Lady,* a periodical taken by the vicar's wife, who had brought round, on her bicycle, a marked copy for Lucy to see. Miss Kirkman was overweight, reddish in colour, and overwhelmed by the primitive cooking stove—a paraffin-burning Valor Perfection—which filled the kitchen with fumes. Phillip thought that the genteel Miss Kirkman was best avoided. A rancid odour seemed to accompany her presence. This did not altogether originate, he thought, in the condition of the drainage pipes which lay, irregularly, under the lawn. They were field drains, of the kind laid in the nineteenth century under heavy land, without collars and unglazed.

"Lucy, *do* ask Miss Kirkman to let only liquid go down the sink."

"I have asked her. She is careful, you know. However, I'll speak to her again."

He said to Miss Kirkman, "I know it's the fault of those field-drain-pipes. I'll replace them when I've finished my book."

There was no St. Martin's Little Summer that November, it was washed away in rain, rain, rain. The springs broke early, soon the river was swollen, but never turgid, swilling bank-high and drowning, below the park, the water-meadows which gleamed grey and cold with the reflections of low clouds dragging past in the sky.

Billy, the elder boy, was now rising five years. He and Peter and tiny tottering Rosamund had their nursery in one of the damp downstairs rooms, all of which burned coal in early Victorian grates. Phillip missed the open hearth of Skirr farmhouse, and went to the Steward's office behind the Abbey to ask permission to uncover the wood-burning fire-place in the large square sitting room. This grate, like the others, threw out almost no heat since it was virtually a hole through which flames roared into the cavernous chimney enclosed behind a square of thin cast-iron.

"Cold air is sucked under the doors the more fiercely the flames roar up the chimney. And just as James Watt watching a kettle boiling got the idea of harnessing steam, so our sitting-room fireplace gives the idea of a refrigerator combined with an oven, for while the flames draw the cold air to freeze the back of the body, one tends to be roasted in front."

The Steward laughed and said he would send round the Clerk of Works.

This individual, upon arrival, told Phillip that the house had once been three cottages in a row, but a century before had been made into one for the then-Steward's occupation. Phillip thought that in those days the iron hearth must have appeared to be a most genteel thing, burning gentlemen's coal instead of the common oak or beech sticks which still smouldered under the iron crocks and hanging kettles of the cottages upon the estate.

"I suppose all social aspirations are in a sense anti-social," he said to Felicity, when the Clerk of Works had gone. "Look at this great black shell, entirely anti-social. The more coal we shove into it, the more scoured of warm air becomes the room."

At night while tawny flames edged by smoke roared up the chimney to join with the remote thunder of the gale above the square exit of the blackened tun, he and Lucy and Felicity drew up their chairs and thereby were in the more concentrated bore of cold air feeding the flames. Lucy usually went to bed early. She felt sad, while concealing the feelings that her dream of herself and Phillip being like her father and mother—inseparable and hardly wanting any visitors—was not to be.

And every day the valley views were dissolved in rain. Every walk by the river, now swirling past the stick-matted trunks of the willows, was ended for Phillip with sopping trousers and squelching shoes. Trying to dry his legs before that early Victorian grate, while he waited for the mason to come, was a nightly act of frustration, for he winced from the idea of making a complaint as the weeks went by and no one came to open up the hearth. At last he wrote to the Steward, apologising for not having said during the interview that of course he would pay for the work to be done.

The elderly Clerk of Works reappeared one morning and gave Phillip more local history, mixed with scandal of the previous century, and at last took his leave, saying that he would see what he could do. Phillip gave him his idea of what the back of the open hearth should be, not straight up, another warmth stealer, but with a back built to slope forward until four-fifths of the frontal area of the fire-, or rather flame-place, was reached; then it should go back sharply in order to allow the flow of flame to take itself up the chimney, passing the smoke-box where the slope joined the ascent of the chimney proper.

"I've been reading about this in the *Country Gentleman's Magazine*," he explained. "It's the same with water. There's always an eddy at a bend of a river, I've noticed, where the water tends to travel backwards. And so with air. In a straight-up old-type open hearth, the hot air revolves just under the lintel, and in turning round causes the smoke to bounce off the hot-air ball, and into the room."

To this the Clerk of Works made no reply. He hadn't understood a word of it.

A week before Christmas a mason arrived and Phillip repeated his idea of what an open hearth should be: it must have a back sloping forward, then sharply back. No gate-crashing cold air must be allowed up the chimney.

"Aye, zur. I'll 'ave 'e out in no time," and bringing a pick the mason took a swing at the cast-iron shell and then lugged it out in a cascade of soot and mortar dust. Sheets were brought down from off the children's beds to cover chairs, table, and bookcase.

There was a worn blue Delabole slate before the hearth, and Phillip knew that this would conduct the heat from the fireplace and make it pleasant to stand on in his socks, after writing, which usually made his feet cold—November, 1914: the flooded Diehard T-trench under Wytschaete ridge——

"So leave the slate. Delabole slates are wonderful things. They warm the farmer's feet in life, and stand guard above his skull when he's dead. I've got to go to London now, to give my first broadcast. I'm scared stiff, like the poor old farmer under the stone, because I've got to do it without a script—you know, all written out and read from a script, I mean—but this is to be without a script. Have you got a wireless set?"

"No, zur. Us poor men can't afford it, like the gentry do do."

"Good. Then you won't be able to hear what a fool I make of myself."

This made the mason laugh, and he forgot the idea, which was to leave the splendid slate, worn by centuries of feet on winter nights, in position.

Phillip left before dawn the next morning, to be able to rest in the Barbarian Club before the talk, which was one of a weekly series on Tuesday nights after the nine o'clock news. Richard and Hetty listened, and found it embarrassing; for Phillip had stopped on the way at a friend's house, and had drunk claret most of the day, with various cheeses; to arrive only a short time before he was due on the air. He had rehearsed his talk on the way up so many times, each with a variation, and when the green light changed to red in the studio he felt hopelessly mixed up. The producer, a Scotsman, stared at him almost with anguish; then after a gulp of water Phillip began.

"It was G. K. Chesterton who wrote, I seem to remember, that Noah said, while in the Ark, 'I don't care where the water goes, so long as it doesn't get into the wine.' I live by a river—er—a trout stream—usually I walk—or—er—rather splodge by the river, looking for signs of life—I am almost duck-footed, and quack before meals——"

Richard told Phillip afterwards, when he called at Hillside Road, that he had to switch off because there were so many er-er-ers, and he could not bear the feeling that his son was so nervous.

When Phillip returned to Flumen Monachorum the slate was gone. In its place was a concrete slab, two days set.

"But I told you I wanted the slate left, Felicity. Damn it, wasn't that enough? Why didn't you remind the mason? Where is the slate?"

"He broke it up with his pick before I could stop him."

Her face was made-up. She had been eating little or nothing for days, and drinking only a glass of lemon juice and water every morning, in the hope of losing some of the fat she had put on, almost to her horror: for she had been vain of her figure, and was now fearful of losing it.

"But it takes a lot to break up a slab like that. It could only be broken up by scores of blows. So what do your words mean, 'before you could stop him'?"

"I was in my room, typing your notes about the river, and I didn't hear anything."

The new hearth had been much in Phillip's thoughts during the cold wet drive from London. It had rained at Chiswick, he had not stopped to put up the hood, longing to get home, to relax before the new hearth, flaming with beech logs. She stood there, feeling numb that he was cross with her.

"Where's Rippingall?"

"I'm afraid he's not very well."

Phillip went to the boiler room. There lay Rippingall, blotto. When he returned to the sitting-room Felicity said timidly, "Shall I get you some tea?"

"Billy at least might have helped. He knew."

Billy and Peter, who had hurried out of the kitchen when the headlights had flashed across the window, sat beside his feet as he stood, still in soaked leather flying coat and fur collar, before the cold dull hearth. He felt a sense of shame at his outburst now, for his arrival had had the effect of making their faces so animated. He saw Billy hang his head, before the boy turned away pouting. Then Peter came and stood at his knee, looking up innocently into his face. Billy caught his father's eye and frowned, before going out of the room.

"Dad," said Peter. "It wasn't Billy's fault. Billy was up to school, Dad."

The nursery door was ajar; it moved; he saw a face under tousled black hair looking earnestly at him out of very dark eyes. Rosamund was inspecting him, finger in mouth. The head disappeared, the door moved back, then round the corner came a crawling object which pulled itself up to his knees and stood there, continuing its stare. This object made a noise like *hur-hur* when he picked it up and, opening his coat, sat down with Roz on his knee and hugged her. She turned round and almost threw herself on his chest, burying her head in its warmth.

The concrete hearth was not entirely set. With a piece of stick he gouged the outline of a trout in the cold grey gritty stuff. There were stones in the concrete and some made the engraving unsmooth, and when he dug them out with Rosamund's help, left the grooves rough. He worked on his knees, the child silent beside him, while Peter watched earnestly. When he had finished, observed all the time by the little girl, he looked round, uncramping his back, and saw that Billy had returned.

"Billy, I'm so sorry. I beg your pardon. Of course you were at school."

"It don't matter."

And giving his father a mournful look Billy hung his head and again went out of the door. Phillip wondered how much of Billy's attitude came from the fact that he had been told, some time before, by a woman who came to look after Lucy when she was ill, that Lucy was not his real mother.

But this was not the cause; it lay in his own inability to give the child the warmth of his body, in love. Oh God, was he passing on the *mort cordum* to his son, as Lucy's father had passed on the *mort main* to *his* children? The dead-hand of laziness, of selfishness, of lack of imagination, which had been the cause of the once-great

Copleston family estates coming down to the derelict Works in the garden at Down Close? But who was he to criticise, he who had thrown away all but the house, that shell of a family, at Rookhurst?

"Billy, Billy, come and help me make a fire. Billy, Billy, come back, you are my best boy."

"Billy is, y'know, too," said Peter, staring up with his mild gaze.

It turned out to be a good hearth for burning wood, throwing out heat and giving contentment to legs stretched to the mass of beech ember and flame, while the kettle of cast-iron gently steamed as it hung from the serrated lapping-crook. Occasionally he grilled steaks and bloaters over the glowing embers, eating them beside Lucy and Felicity. Alas, that the mason's hammer had cracked up that old slate slab. It had been a lovely thing, blue and gentle, hollow with so many stocking'd feet resting on it, and mellowed by fat-spreckles jumping out of a score of heavy frying pans and roasting spits of the past. The new concrete slab was without feeling: even the fish did not give it baptismal life: to Phillip, it was a symbol of post-war soullessness.

On New Year's Eve he invited Rippingall to sit with them and share a couple of bottles of champagne. Except for the one lapse the house-parlourman had behaved impeccably; he had dug the garden, polished the silver plate (left to Lucy by an ancient spinster aunt—delicate Caroline spoons and forks, coffee-pot and teapot, salt cellars, pepper pots, candelabra, asparagus tongs, cheese-scoop, etc.) and 'made himself generally useful in the house', as Lucy told Pa.

When not on duty Rippingall was to be found in the boiler house, which he had fitted up with shelves for books, and pictures torn from old illustrated magazines of actresses, generals, battleships, and photographic scenes of the Great War. Sometimes the reedy strains of an accordion, muffled by the warped oak door, floated into the kitchen. Rippingall was singing to himself in a nasal voice as he boiled water over a methylated spirit lamp for his nightly mug of cocoa. He had a pair of steel-rimmed spectacles, and was a great reader. Phillip's novels about Donkin, he declared, were the real stuff.

Rippingall, with the points of his moustache held in a fixed position by *pomade hongroise*, was a man of gentleness, deep feeling, and understanding. After awakening from that drunken stupor he had wept, saying that he had betrayed the whitest man he had ever known. He would devote his life to Phillip, if only given another chance; he would renounce liquor for ever. Poor Rippingall, said Phillip to Lucy, he must find life with an author even duller than living in the dark background of a vicarage, the incumbent of which was low church almost to Calvinist simplicity, believing literally in the constant war between Heaven and Hell; and with the temptations of Hell there could never be compromise.

Now it was the start of another year.

"Ring out the old, ring in the new, ring out the false, ring in the true . . . *'for God reveals Himself in many ways, lest one good custom should corrupt the world'*. Rippingall, you old sweat, a man must break his principles now and again, to show that he is master of them. Who said that?"

"It sounds like Thomas Carlyle, sir."

"I've never read Carlyle."

"I must confess that I myself have but the slightest acquaintanceship with the Sage of Chelsea, sir."

After that first lapse, Phillip made Rippingall sign an agreement that provided for his wages to be paid into a fund which Rippingall could use only at the age of sixty. Even so, he felt that he had let down Rippingall, allowing him only five shillings a week for pocket money. On odd occasions, chosen by himself, Rippingall got into his dress suit in the evening, and rewaxed the ends of his moustaches to points which, to the low church vicar, must have resembled the horns of the Devil himself. Never a glass of beer had he taken, true to his promise, since that one lapse.

"On this New Year's Eve let us drink to Liberty, Fraternity, and Equality, Rippingall. What a wonderful suit you are wearing. I wish I had one like that."

"One of the Captain's" said Rippingall. "He gave me, as was my perquisite, all his wardrobe when I relinquished my post at the Castle."

Phillip understood that Rippingall had worked as valet and, at times, companion to 'Boy' Runnymeade. He had been his opponent at billiards, snooker, cards, chess and picquet, with the ultimate job of the day of hauling his master upstairs and undressing him on the bed—a confidential job, for Captain Runnymeade had a fixed dread of appearing drunk before the other servants. On leaving his service at the Castle, Rippingall had taken with him a score or so of suits, shirts, shoes, etc. which had been replaced that year, as annually, by new patterns.

The next morning, in bowler hat, yellow goatskin gloves, whangee cane, and brown shoes patterned all over with holes and shining like glass, Rippingall, having brushed himself free of boiler-room dust and withered potato fragments, lit the remains of his cigar of the night before and set off to wish the Reverend Mr. Scrimgeour the compliments of the New Year. Rippingall wore the 1914 Star, with bar, on the lapel of his pepper-and-salt jacket.

"How do you do, everything all reet?" he greeted the parish priest, who was about to leave on his bicycle to go the rounds to some of his aged parishioners.

The vicar, moving his new Raleigh bicycle—a present from his congregation—between them across the front door to prevent entry, caused Rippingall to lurch to the other side, but he recovered his stance with the aid of the cane bent like a bow.

"Go away, you're drunk again. Why have you come, you silly fellow? Been dismissed, as you deserve, no doubt. And do not smoke when you address me."

"This——" replied Rippingall, removing the cigar from between yellow teeth and inspecting it "—is a weed, known first to Sir Walter Raleigh, whose name is spelt, but not pronounced, like your bicycle. Our West Country still shelters Rawleys, your reverence, not Rallys."

"Go away, you impertinent fellow. And don't puff smoke in my face. I told you never to come here again."

"All reet, all reet," retorted Rippingall with spirituous amiability. "I came to wish your reverence the compliments of the season, together with——" puff, puff—"a Happy New Year." He added, "In my father's house are many—bicycles——"

"Leave these premises at once!"

Rippingall spun round, recovered, and pointing the whangee cane upwards with one hand, removed the brown bowler with the other and said, "I will go——" puff, puff—"to my father——" puff, puff—"who is in heaven."

As January's dull windows and leafless trees repeated themselves, so the form of Rippingall was in decline. Like most people of irregular sensibility, caused by an early malformation of the will and usually known as artistic temperament, Rippingall became untidy. He could be very smart indeed when in full starch, wax, and tail; but his bedroom was a mess, his kitchen—for Miss Kirkman had left her situation before Christmas—in disorder. He was ail-anyhow. Phillip felt that he had let-down Rippingall, given him a formless example—almost nothing to live for. Lacking someone to keep him in order, by example, Rippingall was reverting to the bottle. His sink was a greasy mess of old tea-leaves and potato-peelings. Glasses came on the table with the water-stains of porridge and bacon-fat residue.

Phillip became more and more critical of Felicity and one day she departed, while he was in Colham, leaving behind a letter saying that she felt her presence was only a hindrance to him, and an obstruction to his writing.

Staring at the choked drainpipes under the lawn, the untidy cupboards, the chaotic woodshed and boiler-house, the scatter of toys everywhere in the day nursery—a room which Lucy said she liked to look "lived in"—Phillip told himself weakly that he needed order and competence about him so that he could do his writing, and keep on doing it, without strain. That work was for the future, the tidying up of human minds by 'enacting a full look at the worst', in the past; or rather the growing of young minds in a way entirely different from the past. What was needed, he told Lucy, was a revolution—but without bloodshed. Yet he knew that it must first begin with himself; while it seemed there was nothing to begin it with.

The newspapers told of struggle everywhere. Unemployed men, many without work since returning a dozen years ago from the Armies in France, Flanders, Mesopotamia, the Balkans, were sent from the Distressed Areas of the North to dig ditches in the South. Married men on the dole were paid 26*s.* a week, out of which rent at 7*s.* must be paid. Coal was 1*s.* 6*d.* a bag of 112 lbs, while the poor family's main meal of the week was based on what was known as a butcher's shilling bag—a bit of mutton, portion of black pudding, and scraps of stewing steak: a meal for two days. The butcher threw in 'a bone for the dog', out of which broth was made, with vegetables.

Winter dullness held the valley. Frosts whitened the lawns. For three months sunshine ceased to enter the lower rooms of Mona chorum House, which had dry rot under all floors. Then the top of the sun was seen again over the wooded crest of the Chase.

Chapter 3

HARD VOICES

And every day at breakfast-time the sun's curve rose a little higher over the hill. Missel-thrushes were in bold song, rooks speculating about their old nests. And with the primroses Felicity came back.

The exterior alterations to Fawley House had been completed. The bill exceeded £1,200. One roof still required new rafters and purlins and slates.

Every day a working party left Monachorum for Fawley, eighteen miles north on the Shakesbury-Colham road, and every night it returned. While Lucy and Felicity worked in the rooms of the old house, Phillip and Rippingall worked in the walled garden. During the back-end of the year it had been cleared, ploughed, harrowed, rolled and threeparts sown down to alsike, a pink-flowered plant of the clover family. This alsike, when dug in, would enrich the soil.

The remaining half-acre was for tillage. Here, thought Phillip, Father will want to spend his time. He must remove the ruinous green-houses and cold frames, and so give the old boy a decent start. A small potting-shed had already been erected near the two circular lily ponds. The cast-iron garden seats were scaled and repainted dark green.

All was now ready for Phillip's parents to come down and occupy the ground-floor flat.

Hetty was living in a flow of excitement that soon she would be in the beautiful country near her son and his wife and the little ones; and with this feeling was an undercurrent of sadness, even of fear, that she would be leaving the house where her children had grown up—it was almost all of her life. More than thirty-five years in Wakenham: first in the little house in Comfort Road near the railway cutting, which once had been part of the Sydenham-Deptford Canal, where old Pooley, who was nearly a hundred years old when she had gone to live there with Dickie, had once seen a salmon taken on rod and line, at the time of the Napoleonic wars. Thirty years of her life had passed in the house in Hillside Road: now she was about to say goodbye to all the landmarks of her marriage—the Hill, the trees, the church across the grass, the view of the Crystal Palace from the crest of the Hill. O, those far-off summer days, and Phillip flying his kite on what he called the Hillies!

And now everything appeared to have a life of its own, to be appealing to her to be allowed to remain as it had been when Papa and Mamma were alive, and living next door—and brother Hughie—sister Dorrie—her boys killed in the war. At such re-visitations in memory Hetty prayed silently, as she stood in her bed-room with its wide brass bed, seeing the faces of the dead with instant emotion before the expunging of all personality under another vision of the white marble forests of the cemetery. Then she would laugh as she thought of the joke of Hughie, about the engraving of the church on the cover of the *Parish Magazine*, newly built of red brick when they had moved into their own house. The church garden was still a wilderness of grasses tangled above the yellow clay soil. *Note*, the words declared below the engraving of the church on the blue cover of the Parish Magazine, *the tower is not yet built.* And all the years had passed, and the church had never had its tower.

Once the church had been full every Sunday. Now it was more than half-empty. People had given up going to church since the end of the Great War.

She peered through the nearer of the two bow-fronted windows, watching her husband wheeling his barrow up Charlotte Road. Dickie still kept on his war-time allotment beyond the farther side of the cemetery. He was tidying up his rod of ground for his suc-cessor, whoever he might be, and thereby keeping himself in trim for the work ahead in the walled garden at Fawley. He had spent the past two days picking up flints and making a neat heap of them in one corner, and cleaning and digging the ground as a matter of routine; while all the time happy thoughts of returning to Rookhurst, the village where he had been born and bred, had given him secret satisfaction. He was aloofly proud, too, of his son's success as a writer, and looked forward to ending his years happily in the dwelling place of his forefathers.

Richard had an idea of repaying his son's generosity by inviting him to use the house in Hillside Road as his own whenever he came to London. This was a happy solution to a problem which had been worrying him: what to do with the house. He did not want to sell it, nor yet to let it. The district was not what it was, a new class of people had been moving in during the past few years. Not that he felt that Wakenham was, or ever had been, in any sense a superior place to live in; but the newcomers generally did not care for gardening, and many were, moreover, distinctly untidy in other ways. Motor-bicycles stood on the uncut grass of lawns, paper was left to lie about, paint was not renewed. Dinginess was the word for it. No, he would not want his well-kept house and garden occupied by one of those fellows who went about with cigarettes in their mouths and hands in pockets and thought so much of themselves that they never raised their hats to a woman when they spoke to her: the sort who invariably sat about in their rooms, and at table, in their shirt-sleeves.

He would ask the police to keep an eye on the house, and have the plate chest put in the bank. Master Phillip living there would keep the house alive. He and Lucy might want a holiday; it was handy for London, and theatres and restaurants; and since they would need a comfortable bed, he had ordered, in plenty of time, a modern one, with spiral springs and low centre of gravity, and walnut panels, from the Stores. That was to be his surprise; and when Hetty came to London to visit—whosoever she wanted to visit—she would find it the very thing for sound sleep, nervous little thing that she had always been.

Fawley having been put in order, Lucy and Felicity set about spring-cleaning at Monachorum. The swallows were back. Stimulated by the sight of these migrants, and by the habit of physical work, Felicity was confident that now she would be able to help Phillip much more than in the past. She must organise his writing room for him, as a start. Having watched him often enough pawing over the contents of a drawer, pulling out old envelopes, worn-out typewriter ribands, stumps of pencils along with shells, nails, odd stamps, German 1914–18 cartridges and bullets, and other relics supposed to be of use later on, she determined to free him of worry by tidying up his room, together with the cupboards, boxes, and contents of his kneehole desk.

Phillip sat in the shade of the cankered apple trees in the orchard, wearing dark glasses, writing pad on knee. A goldfinch had a nest in the fork of a branch. Voices floated from the house, and the noise of water gurgling down the drain; the gurgling stopped, and he knew that once more the wretchedly inadequate field-drain pipes were choked. When the paper-boy brought the morning papers he got up to meet him, and returning to the deck-chair glanced through the London paper. By this act he broke his rule never to look at the papers until after the morning stint, of a minimum thousand words, was done.

On the front page was the news of a junior minister's resignation from the Labour government. The name of Birkin was prominent. Where had he heard it before? Ah, at the Selfridge Election party. GREAT SPEECH TO THE HOUSE, ran the headline.

> 'If this loan of one hundred million pounds cannot be raised,' continued the Minister, 'then unemployment, as an urgent and immediate problem, cannot be dealt with. We are told by the City of London that we cannot have the money to help the workless back to work—in reclaiming land, in afforestation, in building great new roads to replace the narrow, wandering tracks that so frequently link town with town, creating obstacles for traffic and danger to life; in electrification projects; and in everything needed to bring this great country up to date in the public utility services—all these things are needed for our survival. More important still, for our true wealth lies in our people, not only should children be kept out of industry, but an *ad hoc* pension scheme must be instituted whereby old people shall be encouraged to retire from industry at sixty by payment of pensions of twenty-five shillings a week. Thus more jobs will go to those who urgently need them—those on the threshold of adult life who are now growing up in idleness and subject to demoralisation of every kind——

Phillip had read so far when Lucy appeared. "Are you busy?"

"I'm trying to formulate my thoughts, although it may appear I'm only reading the paper. No, that's untrue, I'm not busy."

"I'm awfully sorry to worry you just now, but Uncle Hilary has just telephoned to say that he and Irene are on their way here, and I've asked them to luncheon. Of course, the kitchen drain would choke now."

"Where's Rippingall?"

"I haven't seen him, otherwise I'd get him to do it. The washing water is all over the path."

It was eleven o'clock. There was an hour before they were due to arrive. He dug up the pipes and continued a trench through the turf of the lawn, then covered the trench, through which grey liquid was seeping, with nine-inch boards, bought recently to extend the garage. Having washed and changed his shirt, for he had worked neurotically fast, he went back to his seat.

> 'The Chancellor of the Exchequer has told us that the unemployed figures have risen, that they are bad and getting worse. He has told the House that if the unemployed problem is regarded from a purely Party point of view a tremendous case can, in the light of the published figures be made out against the Government.
>
> 'The solution lies in the system of an import control board. Applied to agriculture, and particularly to wheat, an import control board can increase the price to farmers by ten shillings a quarter above the present world prices without any increase in the price of bread. Many thousands of men can thereby be found employment on our derelict arable farms, and the policy of controlled imports can be applied no less to other trades. For if we are to build up a home market, it must be agreed that this nation be, to some extent, insulated from the electric shocks of present world conditions. You cannot build a higher civilisation and a standard of life which can absorb the great force of modern production if you are subject to price fluctuations from the rest of the world which dislocate your industry at every turn, and to the sport of competition from the virtually slave conditions in other countries.'

Footfalls were coming along the garden path. He dropped the paper and took up his writing pad, ready as an excuse should this be an unwelcome caller. It was. With distaste he saw the grinning face of A. B. Cabton, a writer originally sent to him by Edward Cornelian, the critic and publisher's reader, during Phillip's time as an improver on his Uncle Hilary's farm. Cabton had shot birds in June with a walking-stick gun, also trout in the Longpond. After that visitation neither Phillip nor Lucy had heard a word from him.

"Hullo. How's everybody? Don't get up. Just be your natural self. How's Lucy? Felicity still with you?"

"I thought you lived in Cornwall, Cabton."

"So I do. But I thought I'd like a break. My novel is held up. You don't mind if I fish in your river, do you?"

"Well, I don't really want the fish disturbed, Cabton. You see—well—I'm studying them. I haven't fished myself yet."

"Studying them by reading the paper, eh? I saw you put it down and take up that pad. Why pretend?"

He took out a packet of Bonville's cigarettes and tossed them at Phillip. "Thought you might like them."

"It's good of you, but I have given up smoking."

"Keep them, anyway. I get them for nothing, my sister works in Bonville's. What about this fishing?"

"Well—I'll show you a place later, at the end of my beat—I'm not watching that water particularly, just yet, anyway."

Cabton sat down and picked up the cigarettes.

"Have you see Birkin's speech in the paper, Cabton? It looks as though something will be started at last. May I read you a bit?" Without waiting for a reply, he read, "'If then, this loan'—that is, a hundred million pounds to make new motor roads, using the unemployed, nearly three million, Cabton—'if this loan cannot be raised in the City of London, let us confess defeat honourably and honestly; let us run up the white flag of surrender. Why is it right and desirable that British capital should go overseas to equip factories to compete against us, and by means of sweated labour to undercut our prices, to build roads in the Argentine or in Timbuk too, while it is supposed to shake the whole basis of our financial strength if anyone dares to suggest the raising of money by the government of this country to provide work for the people of this country? In conclusion, let me say that the situation which faces us is, of course, very serious. Everybody knows that; and perhaps those who have been in office know it even better. It is not, I confidently believe, irreparable, but I feel this strongly, that the days of muddling through are over, and this time we cannot muddle through."

"Hear, hear," said a voice from over the fuchsia hedge behind the summer house. Phillip saw with exasperation the weak and vacuous face of Rippingall above the shoulders of Runnymeade's old pepper-and-salt suit.

"Everything all reet, old dear?" Rippingall drew himself to attention and went on, with an attempt at clear articulation, "I have—just—seen—the ghost—of—the Rascal Monk—of—Mona-Mona-Monaquorum Abbey—sir."

Deciding to treat Rippingall as though he was his normal self, Phillip said, "Come here and meet Mr. Cabton, old soldier. I want you to show him Fossett's pool, where I've given him a day's fishing, fly only, of course. Come and listen to Birkin's speech of resignation."

Rippingall walked on down the lane to the gate and came into the garden. Gravely he took off his brown bowler and bowed to Cabton, saying quietly, "Sir, Fossett's pool—is haunted—by the Rascal Monk." Then turning to Phillip he said, "Sir Olive Lodge—Physical Society. Sir, with respect, there are ghosts—in—the—old Abbey, sir." He added as an afterthought, "It is said to be haunted."

Cabton took out his pocket knife and began to clean his nails as Phillip said to Rippingall, "This is the peroration of Birkin's speech. He was pleading in the Commons yesterday for a hundred million pounds to make new motor roads for the future, and also to give work——"

"—to three million unemployed," said Cabton, inspecting the long nails with their raised half-moons.

"Per-or-ration," said Rippingall, solemnly. "The climax, as the Greeks would say."

"Do listen to this. Birkin has just said that this time we cannot muddle through, or there'll be a smash."

"All politicians are crooks," remarked Cabton.

That comes well from you, thought Phillip. "Listen to this, Rippingall.

"'I feel this, indeed, from the depths of my being: I believe with all the hopes of all the soldiers of our nation who lived for a better world and died on the battlefields of the Great War—on the rolling downlands of the Aisne and the Somme—upon the vast and featureless crater-zones of Flanders—in the March retreat across the waste lands of nineteen-sixteen—in the last summer-time advances to the Hindenburg Line, which they finally breached and led the way to victory, leaving nearly a million dead on these and other battlefields—dying in the hope, in the belief of a better life for their children—and the years drift by, and those children are on the dole, and who can rally their comrades who survived, who can mobilise and rally for a tremendous effort, and who can do that except the Government of the day?'"

At this point Rippingall said, "I've seen the ghost of the murdered priest."

Ignoring this drunken fantasy, Phillip read on, "'If that effort is not made, we may soon come to a crisis, to a real crisis. I do not fear that so much, for this reason: that in a crisis this nation is at its best. This people knows how to handle a crisis; it cools their heads and steels their nerves. What I fear much more than a sudden crisis is a long, slow crumbling through the years until we sink to the level of a Spain, a gradual paralysis beneath which all the vigour and energy of this country will succumb. That is a far more dangerous thing, and far more likely to happen unless some effort is made. If the effort is made, how relatively easily can disaster be averted. You have in this country resources, skilled craftsmen among the workers, design and technique among the technicians, unknown and unequalled in any other country in the world.

"'What a fantastic assumption it is that a nation which within the lifetime of everyone has put forth the efforts of energy and vigour unequalled in the history of the world, should succumb before an economic situation such as the present. If this situation is to be overcome, if the great powers of this country are to be mobilised and rallied for a great national effort, then the Government and Parliament must give a lead. I beg the Government tonight to give the vital forces of this country the chance that they await. I beg Parliament to give that lead'."

Rippingall stood to attention. As a serving soldier, he had been up for more 'crimes' than any other man in his regiment. As an old soldier, he made a parade of the military virtues, so-called. Rippingall now said, "Up the rebels!" and took uncertain steps into the summerhouse which he called his G.H.Q.

"Here's what the first leader of *The Crusader* says, Cabton. 'Here was evidence of hard work, concrete thinking, and of a real political conscience, and the House, after the soft abstractions of Mr. Ramsay Macdonald, the Prime Minister, rejoiced to feel solid ground beneath its feet. After today's speech no one can think of Sir Hereward Birkin as a rich dilettante in politics. This industrious and able young man, if he keeps his health and his industry, must be regarded as a candidate, some day, for the highest honours'."

Cabton shut his knife and said, "Where can I find that pool, what d'you call it, 'Fossetts'?"

"Rippingall will show you."

Rippingall returned, and said to Phillip, "The monk asked me if I knew where Miss Felicity was living."

Phillip was trying to write when an open car drew up in the lane with Hilary and Irene. He went to meet them.

Irene's smile made him exclaim, "How good it is to see you," as she held her face to be kissed on the cheek. "Hullo, Uncle Hilary, this is an unexpected pleasure. Lucy will be glad to see you. You both look awfully well. She and her helper, you know Felicity, don't you, are in the midst of a spring-clean." He added, "I hope it won't disturb you."

The two girls came out to meet the guests, who were on their way to the south coast of Devon, to stay at Turnstone and play golf, said Hilary.

Phillip noticed how much fitter his uncle looked, he had shed some of his fat. He heard him telling Lucy that he had been dieting under the eyes of Irene, after a visit to Finland where both had regularly had sauna baths, in steam from water poured on hot stones, followed by beatings with birch twigs and a plunge into ice-cold water.

"There's nothing like it, Phillip, for clearing away the cobwebs."

"Talking of cobwebs, have you read Birkin's speech following his resignation from the government, Uncle Hilary?"

"Yes, I have, and in my opinion it's a lot of unrealistic idealism. Birkin was born with a silver spoon in his mouth, and yet he pretends to be the friend of the working man."

"He is the friend of the working man, Uncle Hilary, surely? His generation led them in battle, after all."

"That's not enough to run a country in these difficult times, with a world slump threatening to become worse. Noble sentiments I agree, but they come from a hot head. Birkin wants to ignore world conditions, which rule our overseas markets. He knows nothing about finance, which is ruled by the world situation, as I said," replied the older man, his voice between the persuasive and conciliatory. "I hold no brief for Churchill, but he was right when he urged the raising of the Bank Rate, which stopped Labour's wild-cat schemes. Now Birkin, in resigning, has turned his coat again, as once before he turned it when he was a Conservative. The fellow lacks stability."

"Birkin said that Churchill, who raised the Bank Rate, is like a man who sets fire to his house, then throws stones at the fire brigade."

"If these wild-fire socialists came to power, the first thing they would do would be to block Sterling. Then where would our export markets be?"

"We could export to the Empire, surely, and invest all Sterling there, chiefly in raw materials."

This did not please Hilary, who wanted to be free to invest his capital where he could get the biggest yield.

"Now look here, Phillip, we've had all this out before. Such ideas as yours will get you nowhere in your writing. Look at this——" He held out a copy of *The Morning Post*. "Read it out. That bit there."

Phillip read, "'The sounds of cheering in which the explanation of the resignation terminated were—ominous sign—common to all three parties'. I should say hopeful sign, instead of ominous sign, Uncle Hilary."

"We're a democracy, Phillip, and not a dictatorship. You should have been with us in Finland, and heard what they said there about their neighbour, Russia. And Germany is on the verge of civil war. Although," he added, "Hitler is at least anti-red."

Seeing the bleak look coming on Phillip's face, Irene said, "How is your trout book going?"

"I'm still trying to find a theme for it, Irene."

"That's your line, you know," declared Hilary. "Now, my boy, show me where I can wash my hands. I had to change a sparking plug just outside Salisbury."

When Phillip returned, Irene was waiting. "Come and show me the river, P.M."

On the way through the garden she peered at Rosamund lying naked in her pram. "Isn't she a darling? I can't wait to see Billy when he comes home. It's over a year since I saw my grandson. How are you, my dearest P.M.?"

"Oh, getting along, more or less."

"Isn't the scent of the meadow-sweet wonderful. And those ragged robins. Don't you love it here?"

"I'm really offset from it, thinking how to do my book all the time."

"I suppose you get more freedom now that you have help with your correspondence?"

"Oh, yes, but there's not much to be done, really."

"Felicity seems to be a nice girl."

Phillip led the way upstream, away from the figure of Cabton, who, despite the request that fly only be used, was casting with a spinner. As the two walked on, a heron flew up before them. "That bird does a lot of damage. I thought of asking the keeper to shoot it."

"Oh, it's such an addition to the landscape."

"Yes, I suppose you're right."

They stopped to watch the heron now at the top of a tree a hundred yards away.

"Phillip, you don't sound very happy."

When he did not reply, she said, "I'm probably leaving myself wide open to a snub, but what does Lucy think about that girl being here?"

"Oh, she doesn't mind. We have only the children in common. Nothing else, really."

"And what do you have in common with Felicity?"

"Oh, I don't know."

"That girl adores you."

"I wish she didn't."

They walked on, watched by the nervous heron until the bird could bear its anxiety no more, and with a curse flew away.

"Irene," he said, stopping to face her, "I can't ever forget Barley."

"Of course neither of us can ever forget that darling child. I am still her mother, and seldom is she out of my thoughts, Phillip. But we must let her spirit sweeten our lives, not embitter them."

"I try not to let my thoughts sap me, Irene. My father kept his dream, or illusion, shut up inside him, and so became chronically irritable with my mother. He loved Jenny, Uncle John's wife, you know, who died when Willie was born. Are *you* happy, Irene?"

"Oh yes, as much as one can expect to be happy, I suppose. Hilary is a pathetic little boy at heart—and it means something to a woman to be wanted, you know. But, P.M. darling—there's always Billy, remember. Barley lives in him, you know."

After a light luncheon of herb omelette with watercress, Hilary suggested that he and Irene take Lucy and the children, together with their little nurse-maid, to see her father and brother at Down Close. Felicity continued her re-arrangement of the writing-room—her surprise for Phillip, as she called it. Meanwhile Phillip had gone back to the river to look for Cabton. To his relief the fellow was gone. As he walked beside the familiar runs and weed-beds, he stopped and peered for signs of trout having been gripped by a heron's beak—dark lines across their shoulders like a scissor-cut—in the shallows of the gravel beds. He had come to regard the heron as his particular enemy, thus venting his own frustrated feelings upon the thin, grey, cautious bird.

Alone in the house Felicity worked happily, and with animation at the thought of the writing-room being more orderly for Phillip by the time he returned. She was also quickened by an idea to go to London to have a sauna bath to get rid of what she thought she was now too old to regard as puppy fat. Her growing plumpness had continued despite exercises in her bedroom, and running with the boys on the lawn every morning before breakfast—a device to get them promptly out of bed. Felicity wanted to be slim and admirable in Phillip's eyes always, as Barley, from her photographs, had been.

When Phillip came back from the park, where the heron had, as though lazily, oared itself by its wings from the gravelly shallows long before he could get anywhere near it, he was in a constricted mood. He had waded in to get a fish lying on its back by a weed-bed, with a cut on its head from the bird's beak. Going upstairs he smelled furniture polish, and saw to his surprise that the door of his wall-cupboard was open, with the key left in. Here, some time before, he had placed relics of his dead wife, including the pair of shoes she had been wearing at Malandine just before she had gone to the maternity home. The shoes were missing; also the lace which she had broken when she had been tying it.

At once feelings of anguish and resentment arose in him. He ran downstairs to where Felicity was sitting at the sewing machine in the day nursery, and said, "*Who* has opened my private cupboard? *Where* are the shoes that were in it?"

Rippingall heard the distraught voice as he was sitting in the summerhouse reading, with every approval, Birkin's speech of resignation from the Labour Party. He listened for a few moments, then getting up, took the almost empty wine-bottle which that morning had been filled with methylated spirits, dyed blue, and drank the remainder. He was putting the bottle down when through the thin hedge he saw the priest, seen up the river, standing there.

"Christ Almighty," said Rippingall, just as Phillip's voice was heard shouting through his open upstairs window, "*Why don't you answer me? Answer my question, damn you!*"

Rippingall crept under the eaves and stood still. He heard Felicity's soft voice saying, "Oh, I'm terribly sorry. I thought they had been left there by someone before we came."

"They were left there by someone before *you* came! What did you do with them?"

"Oh, I think I put them in—in the summerhouse—for Rippingall to burn—with the other rubbish."

"But *why* in the summerhouse?"

"I—I—don't know. I get nervous sometimes and hardly know what I am saying."

Rippingall floated to the kitchen door as the voice cried out, "If those shoes are burned I'll never see or speak to you again!"

Phillip jumped downstairs, slid on the lime-ash floor, recovered, and ran into the garden. He saw Rippingall taking off the lid of the dust-bin outside the kitchen door. There the shoes were, placed side by side on top of a Quaker Oats carton. The lace that Barley had broken when trying to tie her shoes on the morning of her labour pains, before the night of her death, was inside one shoe.

"Did you put them there, Rippingall?"

"I can't remember, sir."

He turned to Felicity. "Did *you*?"

"I think I must have done."

Without a word he carried the shoes back to his room and locking them in the cupboard put the key in his pocket. Then ignoring the tearful apparition at the bottom of the stairs he returned to find Rippingall sitting in the summerhouse with a foolish smile on his face. The empty bottle lay on the seat beside him. Rippingall struggled to stand up and salute but fell back, murmuring, while his eyes glassed over, "All pres'nt an' c'rect."

Still unspeaking, Phillip left the garden and, getting into his motorcar, went to his bank in Colham, drew out ten pounds, had the tank filled with petrol, and set out for London.

When Lucy returned with the children in her brother Ernest's motorcar, the house was empty. She saw Cabton sitting in Phillip's chair in the garden. Had he seen the others?

"No."

"Oh well, they'll come back sometime, I suppose."

Cabton stayed to supper, and when about ten o'clock Lucy said "What are your plans for the night?" he said, "I never make plans." So Lucy made up a bed for him, and he stayed three days, fishing all day up and down Phillip's beat, while Lucy said not a word. She thought Phillip might have given him leave to fish there; but knowing Cabton, she very much doubted it.

Phillip went through Randiswell hoping that no-one would recognise him, and feeling that he never wanted to see the place again. Most of the shops had been modernised and the place looked like any other conglomerated suburb. It was no longer a village with its own distinctive character. Driving up Charlotte Road he turned the corner and saw a furniture van, and a shallow looking as though it belonged to a scrap merchant, parked outside No. 11. At the door his father met him with the well-known exasperation on his face. He heard voices above.

"What's happening, Father?"

"You may well ask. Better to go upstairs and see for yourself, old chap. Your mother's ways are beyond me."

Upstairs Phillip found three men, bare-headed, standing outside his mother's bedroom door. Two wore green baize aprons. The third looked particularly humble to find himself in what he seemed to believe to be such posh surroundings.

"Ver lady's upset, just a little, sir."

"I'll speak to her. Hullo, Mother, may I come in?"

He found her wiping her eyes, and trying to smile. A hammer of the kind for breaking coal lay on the floor. The brass bed was dipped forward thirty degrees to the normal, its back detached and leaning against the wall. The mattress and bedclothes were piled against another wall. Hetty said nearly inaudibly, "All you children were born in this bed, Phillip." More tears fell.

"Whose bed is it, legally speaking?"

"It's—it's—your father's. He has sold it to the barrow man."

"I know exactly how you feel, Mother dear. I've inherited some of your genetic traits, don't forget. I know the power of past association."

"Of course you do, Phillip. I am being silly, I know."

"That's not altogether complimentary to me, Mother. Do you want this bed? I can get it stored for you quite easily."

"What will your father say, Phillip?"

"Nothing. Leave it to me." He went to the open door. "Did you buy this bed?" he asked the humble barrow man.

"That's right, guv. Paid the gent a dollar fer it."

"Will you take a profit?"

"Oo me, guv?"

"Yes, you, mate. I'm a farmer, I buy and sell. Will you take a profit of half a dollar?"

"Phillip, may I have a word with you, please?"

Hetty was hovering by the door. He went to her, saying audibly to the men, "The chaps will need a wet after all this. Now what is it, you poor dove mourning for its nest?"

"Perhaps after all it would be best for the bed to go. I know I'm being very silly——"

"No, you're not being silly. But my presence has fortified you, and three pints of Bass in the Barbarian Club have fortified me. In addition to your presence, of course. You know what you told me once about Barley, not to let thoughts of her spoil my life with Lucy?"

She smiled and took his hand. "Father has bought such a comfortable new bed, for you and Lucy when you come and stay here. There now, I've given away his secret. Promise you won't let him know? He wants it to be his surprise, you see."

The barrow man went down Hillside Road whistling with his bargain. The bed was an affair of many thin steel lathes which supported a mattress transversely. Brass knobs and rods comprised the upper frame. He had been given an extra half-crown by the young gent.

The new walnut-veneer'd bed from the Stores' van had replaced it, together with a thick and sumpy mattress of dark blue ticking with pompoms, patented with the name of Driftasleep. Thanking the guv'nor (Phillip) the two green-apron'd removers departed, each, like the humbler scrap-man, with the price of five pints of best. Everyone was pleased; but while Phillip was driving on the Dover road he could not rid himself of the feeling that he had let down both Father and Mother, for he had told them that he and Lucy would definitely not be living at Fawley.

At Maidstone he stopped and sent a telegram to Piers, saying that he would be staying at Skindles Hotel, Ypres, for three days.

"Well," said Mrs. Ancroft, sitting upright in her chair and switching on the shaded reading lamp beside her, "Now you can tell us all about it, my girl."

Felicity's guardian sat in the armchair across the unlit fireplace. He felt pleasure in the sight of the young woman in distress before him. Felicity was sitting, as though half-collapsed on the sofa. She had arrived in a hysterical condition, in tears and almost incoherent. After an omelette and tea she had recovered a semblance of composure. Now, behind the timid mask of her face in the presence of both inquisitors, she had decided to say nothing about the real reason of her sudden return.

"Philip asked me to go up and see his publisher about his trout book."

"But by your general appearance of being upset, I might almost say in a state of shock when you arrived here, I imagine that something must have occurred to upset you. Besides, my darling," Mrs. Ancroft went on, "your letters have not been altogether happy letters. I have thought I could read between the lines, and so concluded that all was not well with you." Her voice took on a winning note. "After all, Girlie, I am your mother, and I have not known you since you were my dearest little baby, without coming to understand your inmost thoughts."

"Oh mother—please——"

"Very well, dear, I won't play the heavy parent. But I am naturally concerned for your welfare. You may speak frankly before Fitz who has your interest at heart almost as much as your mother has."

When Felicity said nothing, her mother went on, "How do you

get on with Mrs. Maddison—or rather, Lucy, whom I feel I know so well from your letters?"

"She is a very sweet person, Mother.'

"You are good friends?"

"Oh yes."

"What are the children like, Girlie?"

"Oh, Rosamund is a darling. So are the two boys. Billy is rather a problem child, in a sort of way——"

"Billy is the son of Phillip Maddison's first wife, I take it?" remarked the guardian.

"Yes, Fitz."

"Tell me more about Billy, Girlie. I very nearly popped down the other morning to see how you were getting on. The excursion trains are running again, and cost only eight-and-six return. That would have been a surprise for you, wouldn't it?" She spoke pleasantly, while waiting nervously for her daughter's reply.

"Oh, Mother, never do that. People who live in the country always call by appointment."

"I suppose the Maddisons have many visitors?"

"Only the local people call, about a dozen in all, to leave cards. It's a good thing really, for Phillip is always very busy writing."

"Does he dictate to you, or write in longhand?" asked the man in the armchair.

"He did try once, but I think my presence got in the way."

"Oh really?"

"In what way, may I ask?" said Mrs Ancroft.

She felt a nervous flutter about her heart, and prayed that she was not going to have one of her attacks. She saw with some relief that her box of tablets was in place on the marble shelf beside the clock.

"He says that he can feel what other people are thinking."

"I see," said Mrs. Ancroft, who wondered what exactly her daughter meant by that. Could it be—but no, the child had had a Christian upbringing. Such a thing was unthinkable. Her daughter knew the difference between right and wrong. Besides, she had had her own example of duty always before her.

"You're looking tired, Girlie. I'm going to give you a bath and then put you to bed with a cup of hot Maltine. Then tomorrow, after a good sleep, you can tell your mother all your troubles."

When Felicity was in bed Mrs. Ancroft returned to the sitting-room where her old friend (with reservations) was doing the cross-word puzzle of *The Daily Telegram.* Dare she tell Fitz her forebodings? Or was it better to wait until she had spoken to Girlie in the morning?

"I'll make some tea, Fitz. China tonight, or Indian, which is it to be?"

"Oh, China, if you've got any lemon."

"Of course there is lemon. I should not have asked you otherwise."

"I fancy I've caught a bit of a cold."

"Girlie is putting on weight, Fitz."

"Too much clotted cream," he replied, wondering what it was that began with LA, had eight letters ending with IS, and would be greeted by hysterical screams if seen crossing the carpet of a lady's bedroom in Golders Green.

"She told me she was trying to 'bant'—what an expression—and thought of having a sauna bath tomorrow."

"Puppy fat. What would make you scream if you saw it crossing your bedroom floor with eight letters beginning LA and ending with IS, although you don't live in Golders Green?"

"I should not scream in any event, but can the answer to your problem be one of the Three Fates of Greek mythology, 'Lachesis'?"

Mr. Fitzwarren calculated. "Well, it fits in. I'll look in the dictionary."

When she returned with the tray he said, "How clever of you to guess first go off. 'Lachesis' is also a species of venomous rattlesnake found in Suninam."

"I remember my brother George telling me about the Three Fates, Fitz. Poor George. He worked so hard that he damaged his eyes, working at night by a single candle. He got a first in Greats, only to die four days after joining his regiment at Zillebeke."

She poured the tea, and added two thin slices of lemon to the cup before putting it beside him.

"Did she say what had upset her?"

"I didn't dare to ask."

Their eyes met.

"Better take her to a doctor, Nora, and forget about the sauna bath."

Desperately she said, "Do you think he could have turned her away?"

"I wouldn't put it past him. He came here, you know, one night two years ago, and hung about to see me off. I thought then that there might be something in the wind, and so awaited an opportunity to take him with me. It was when you were away seeing your mother."

"You never told me that, Fitz."

"I didn't want to alarm you unduly, old girl. If you remember, you asked me to keep an eye on her while you were away, and so I came round about ten o'clock, as usual, to see if she was all right."

"But why ever didn't you tell me about him being there when he offered her a post of secretary? My mother knew that I should never have let her go so far away from home, at her tender age. I distinctly recall her words—'Mark what I say, you'll regret letting her go.'"

"Well, don't meet trouble half way. Take her to the doctor tomorrow."

Phillip and Piers had walked from Ypres to Poperinghe, and were making their way to the rue d'Hôpital to find Talbot House.

"I came here with 'Westy' in nineteen seventeen, before Third Ypres, and again just before the last battle for Passchendaele."

Toc H was found to be next to the chemist's shop, a three-storey building behind iron gates. Phillip called at the chemist's to ask if it would be possible to see the chapel in the hop-loft, where many thousands of men had received the Sacrament before going up to the battles beginning at the end of July and ending with the occupation of the Passchendaele crest in early November, 1917.

"The chemist won't know me, of course, but I remember him. He has a face like that of Hindenburg, and I told him so once."

They went into the shop. The chemist said that the owner of the house would welcome them.

"Thank you, m'sieu'. Do you remember my telling you, thirteen years ago, that you were like a famous German general?"

"To whom do you refer, m'sieu'?"

"To the President of the German Republic—Marshal von Hindenburg, m'sieu'."

The face went hard. Phillip left the shop hastily. Piers remained to talk.

"I see that his ideas have not changed," said Phillip, when his friend came out of the shop.

"Nor would yours, perhaps, if your country had been invaded."

Phillip rang the bell of the tall grey house. Almost at once the inner door opened and a young girl appeared. She unlocked the gates, and drew back with a movement quiet and charming, bidding them enter. "To see the chapel, messieurs?"

She led the way up bare white enamelled stairs to a room austerely furnished, up another flight, and so to a door, which she held open for them before leaving with a slight movement of her head, neither bow nor nod, but a gesture of sensibility and understanding.

Phillip remembered the last flight up, very steep, poplar wood unpainted and thin—worn by thousands of nailed boots clumping up and clumping down. He sat on the bench at the far end, where the altar, a carpenter's bench, used to stand.

The sun came out of a cloud, and light shone whiter through the five semi-circular windows. Sparrows were chirping on the roof. Slow rattle of wheels on the *pavé* of the road below. Phillip was standing with eyes closed, trying to recall 'Spectre' West in the loft, when there came, as from far away, a dull report. Ah, the terror and dreadfulness of Third Ypres, during those four months, a horizon without hope, every tomorrow as today. How could it ever be written?

"The chemist told me they're blowing up German pillboxes in the cornfields near Brandhoek," said Piers, who was thinking that he would like to get hold of the girl who had shown them the way up. "How about some lunch, or do you want to go on?"

"What would you like to do?"

"Anything you like."

"You're not bored?"

"Not at all, my dear Phil. But I think a drink might do us both some good."

"I'll take you to La Poupée, where all the chaps used to go. It's down one of these streets off the Square."

Where was it? The sun was hot, the streets narrow. They went up and down several streets, then finding themselves back in the rue d'Hôpital, Phillip said that he remembered: *La Poupée* was a name given by the soldiers—The Doll—its real name was something else.

"I think this is the place, Piers."

They entered, and out of a dark kitchen came a plump and pleasant woman with a reserved smile on her face. They asked for an omelette. Chairs were piled on a long table covered by a soiled and worn American cloth.

"I lunched here with a chap called Teddy Pinnegar, when I

was a transport officer in the Machine Gun Corps. I think it might be the same girl." But not the same spirit. The room was dreary and lifeless. Should they cancel the order and find somewhere else, he asked Piers, who said that the cooking was the thing. They finished their glasses of wine, and were about to ask for more when a smell of burning drifted into the room.

"It could be the eggshells, of course," remarked Piers. "Did you read Birkin's speech?"

"Yes, it got through to reality. Tell me about him."

"I've met him at the Minotaur Club. He's first-rate with the foils. Represented us at the Olympic games."

"He was in the war, wasn't he?"

"Yes. He went straight from school to Sandhurst in August on an abbreviated three-month course, and was in the first battle of Ypres, flying as an observer in the Royal Flying Corps. He crashed, and nearly lost a leg, but hearing that his Lancer regiment was in the trenches at the battle of Loos, nine months later he left hospital and joined them, in mud up to his thighs. His wound opened and became septic. But he wouldn't have his leg off, and now rather resembles Byron, with a club boot to take up a couple of inches. He talks about 'the hard-faced Parliament of profiteers and money'. You must meet him. He thought your novel *The Phoenix* was an authentic voice of his generation."

"Now he's up against the hard-faced men of the money-power."

The woman with the Mona Lisa smile moved towards them bearing a black and yellow omelette. She put it before them with slices of bread.

"I suppose it was like this in the war, Phil."

"Oh, no, the cooking was first-rate."

They scraped away the burnt parts, and washed down the rest of the omelette with two bottles of white wine.

They returned to Ypres, with feet blistered from walking on cobbles. It was late afternoon. They drank glass after glass of beer while sitting under an awning, and watched the passers-by.

Ypres to Phillip was unrecognisable. Wipers existed in the memory only. The new city was clean and hybrid-English. Its Grand' Place held enough air and sunlight to give a feeling of freedom in space. The rectangular ruined fragment of the Cloth Hall was contained in a scaffold box. Grasses and wildflowers on the tops of the walls made the ruin beautiful. American tourists noticing the four-way trumpets of the local Fire Brigade's siren on the top of the ruin repeatedly asked their guides if it was "the old original gas-horns of the British."

Phillip rested on his pavement seat in front of an hotel, and sipped pale yellow beer, and looked at some printed papers which had been thrust into his hand by touts.

> Carefull drivers. Highly recommended and very populair with visitors' tours to Belgium, the prices quoted as for first-class car including experienced guide explaining all places of interest and are inclusive absolutely nothing extra.
>
> You may go to Schrapneel Corner or Tyne Cote cemetery, absolutely largest in district, about 12,000 graves. Highly recommended and most interesting point of view Trip No. 7 which includes St. Julien, Poelcapelle, and the famous Houthhulst forrest, Deat trench kept the same state up as it was in the war and can be visited for small fee of one franc.
>
> Trip No. 9 . . . after lunch a most extensive visit to Bruges (often referred to as the Venice of the North) including amongst others the Blood-chappel with the casket containing a drop of the blood of Christ brought back from Palestine by one of the Crusaders, with its famous painting, recommended highly to all desiring a real pleasant and interesting day . . . £2 10s.

They ordered more beer, and stretched their legs, for the pavé had been hard going. Then Piers drank brandy, and Phillip followed him. After four glasses Piers said to Phillip, "This place is haunted by the spirit of love."

"Yes," said Phillip. He wanted to think of 'Spectre' West, whose lecture he had attended before the opening of Third Ypres, in July 1917. He remembered 'Spectre', then a G.S.O.3 attached to G.H.Q. D(a) telling them that the massive walls in red brick had been built by Vaubain to withstand seige by the Spaniards. The sun was going down below the rooftops as he reached the broken curve of grass-grown rubble by the new Menin Gate. Below lay the moat; but no longer foetid and shallow cloacal scum. Water-lilies lay on the surface, a grey wagtail skipped from one palette leaf to another. The brickwork rising sheer from the moat had somehow withstood the German bombardments of the years, but he had to go carefully. Where were the dugouts within the ramparts, once lit by electric light from a power station by the Menin Gate? The building of the power station was said during the war to be the only one remaining of 1914 Ypres.

He remembered the dugouts behind the ramparts. The roofs had been shored by steel girders and sandbags. At night rats used to squeal whenever a light was shone, because it was usually followed by a revolver shot. The rats used to eat everything, even to climbing down the string of a suspended sandbag to eat the candles inside.

He walked on the ramparts with the wraith of his old, or was it his very young, self? That wraith fluttered with fear and disquiet and homesickness; it thought of the sorrows of a mother's face equally with the smiling obliteration that was Lily Cornford vanished in the great livid light of a Zeppelin torpedo fallen on Nightingale Grove above the railway cutting on that September night of 1916, after he had come back wounded from the battle of the Somme. How the love of the dead remained, to be passed on to another. Lily whom he had kissed only once, in a love that had sustained the spirit through all things.

Below lay the calm new waters of the moat. The lilies were withdrawing their flowers with the going down of the sun. Fish were rising, swallows taking last sips as they flew. Children were running out of the Shannon cinema built on the bank across the water.

Motorcars were now bumping down the Menin road, carrying people to a jolly Saturday night in the Ypres cafés with their friends and relations. The cars bumped and swung over the uneven pavé surface, their horns filling the lighted hollow under the new white pantheon of the Menin Gate.

He could not face the idea of the new Gate; the wraith with him was with the long night columns of men moving east out of the city, stumbling in sweat and fear amidst clatter of limber and waggon wheels—horses, mules, men not knowing why they were there in the roar and flash and appalling terror of bursting shells. Everything was silvered within the semi-circle, the salient, of the swamp east of Ypres. Here was the dreaded Menin road with its spiky tree-stumps; here the quaking track of swilling beechwood slabs; his horse, Black Prince, had been left behind near the prison with the groom, before entering with his men each leading a pack-mule into the nihilism of water-glitter, curses, whooping shells and cries for help from wounded lost under the lilies of the dead, in a land beyond all imagination, all longing, almost all hope.

Here rose the new houses, all without chip or loose tile; but they did not obscure the passing of the men. No, it was not men; it was a force that was passing, like an invisible wind that hurled down brick and stone soundlessly, that filled the Grand' Place and the streets with cries and shouts and the screams of the dying, yet all was without sound. He left the ramparts and sought the hotel where they were staying. Piers was not to be seen. He drank several brandies. There was too much noise, the lights were too bright. Men were playing billiards, others talked with animation at the tables. Waiters hurried with trays of filled glasses. It was Saturday night, this was the happy chatter of men who knew they need not work on the morrow. Smoke straying from pipe and cigar. Many neat blue British serge suits, British voices, faces of old soldiers who had learned, in Conrad's phrase, to submit. Their wisdom was immemorially wiser than that of the old or the young—but not to be communicated. O Christ, when could he begin his war novels?

He sat there, the wraith of himself merging with remembered darkness rushing by, yet stagnant amid soundless cries, viewless flashes of field guns lighting broken wall and scattered rubble, the subdued fears of men moving in broken step, laden and sweating, through the gap called the Menin Gate. He drank more brandy. Now he was with the reliefs going up: slouching shapeless men coming out, holding to one idea—sleep, sleep, sleep: troglo-ditic shapes against the great shimmering horsehoe of the Salient, slouching on desperately, puttees over boots, some bare-footed, feet swollen and unfelt, stumbling on and thinking only of sleep, sleep, sleep as they passed files of men moving up, rifle slings cutting into shoulders, thighs and ribs and arms overhot with sweat as they approached Hellfire Corner. Christ, Jerry's five-nines were crumping, and sending the timber track before them into the air.

Alas, prayers do not deflect the hissing flights of bullets that rip, or dissolve the shell that scatters trunk and limbs into charred fragments among the upheaved tree-stumps of Polygon Wood.

Feeling unable to face the *café*, he went back to the Ramparts. The last of sunset, the purple-red bars and flecks of the damp Flanders sun, lay over the oakwoods to the north-west; but there was hope, the evening star was a rayless serene globe in the west. The edges of the moat below were dimly whitened by cement rocks tipped from the bank. Perhaps these were from the blown-up German pillboxes, made of Rhine gravel and cement. The lime in the cement would gradually dissolve in the water, and be used by shrimps and snails to make their shells, and so become food for fish. There were still some concrete machine-gun shelters on the farther bank—now the homes of nettles. How feeble they looked in comparison with the massive German shelters in the

Salient, the *mebus* called pill-boxes by the tommies. But the British had never, until 1918 anyway, thought of the B.E.F. as a defensive force, but as one eventually to cross the Rhine. And they had done it.

He saw a flat-bottomed boat pushed into the reeds below. An old man was fishing. Was everything normal for him? The war but an interruption in a life of trade, a profession? Did he think only of money as the true basis of life?

He sat still, longing for love. The fisherman was using bread-pills for the roach which roamed in shoals from the Menin to the Lille gates. The border of ground, under the ramparts where the boat was moored, was tilled with dwarf beans and potatoes. It looked to be his allotment; he had finished hoeing weeds, and was now enjoying a pipe and the watching of his quill float. Did he see only reed, water, lilies, his quill and the peaceful evening sky above the cultivated fiélds of dark brown soil east of the city; hear only the impatient horns of motorcars passing under the Menin Gate ... the confident song-chatter of the warblers in the reeds?

The old man looked up.

"Soldat, M'sieu'? Anglais? Revenu?"

"Oui, Monsieur."

"Sale boche fini, hey?"

"Bon soir, Monsieur."

That night he could not sleep.

Through the open door of her room Mrs. Ancroft heard her daughter turning and turning in bed, and sometimes it sounded as though she was crying. Once she went in, and stood by the bed, summoning up resolution to whisper, "Are you all right, Girlie?" When there was no answer she went back to her room and, lying in bed, prayed that no harm had befallen her innocent child.

Her daughter had been born during the year of King George the Fifth's succession. When the child was barely out of her third year the marriage had come to an end. Shouting with anger at his wife, calling her every hateful name that came from the years of his frustration, and, towards the end, hatred, her young husband had picked up the terrified child and shaken her, threatening to hurl her out of the window unless her mother altered immediately what he had often called her obstructive mentality. *I never want to see you again!* and putting down the child, who was too shocked to speak, or utter any sound, he had left the matrimonial home for ever.

The war came the following year. Mrs. Ancroft's three elder brothers at once were commissioned in the militia, or reserve battalion of the county regiment. The eldest was killed at Zillebeke in 1914; the second at Festubert early in the following year; the third was reported missing after the flame-attack at Hooge Château in the Salient in 1916. Meanwhile she had learned that her husband had joined up, and after service at home, had transferred to the Royal Flying Corps. He had survived the war. Mrs. Ancroft meanwhile had thought it best to tell her little girl nothing about her father. He was, in his deserted wife's eyes, 'a mixture of half-saint, half-devil.' How else could he—who had obviously loved his little girl from the time that she had first smiled at him, to be taken upon his lap and fondled—how otherwise *could* he have behaved with such fiendish cruelty as to pick her up and shake her violently in order to spite her, the mother? He had been indulged as a small boy, certainly, by two of his aunts, who had made themselves responsible for his upbringing after his parents had died of typhus in India, while he was at a private school in England.

Mrs. Ancroft had refused to divorce him. He had made over all his wordly goods to her; and when she had last heard of him, he was working in the Congo as a lay-brother among an order of friars which called themselves Laurentians.

Mrs. Ancroft, in a weak moment, had told her daughter that her father had died in the war.

She had had a proposal from Mr. Fitzwarren, a widower, but had held firmly to her principles regarding divorce, despite a clear case of desertion. It must be stated that, to some extent, she had been helped to maintain this attitude by the knowledge that the name by which 'Fitz' was known was an assumed one; and that he had not fought in the war.

Altogether her life had continued in a vacuum: a wasting sense of loss was never far away from a consciousness fortified by her faith, by her loving care for Felicity, and the belief that in the end she would be with her brothers.

Phillip was writing to Felicity,

Near St. Julien, opposite Triangle Farm, at a place called Vancouver, stands the Canadian Memorial, but for me it is the memorial for all the soldiers in the War. It faces towards Ypres, not towards a vanquished enemy as do so many of the memorials to be seen in France today, such as the Gallic cock crowing triumphantly on a broken cannon at Roclincourt, or the caribou roaring eastwards from Beaumont Hamel, or the defiant artisan-soldier standing firm and fierce at Lens.

Do the dead feel cock-crowing triumph over the dead? No; the colossal head and shoulders of the soldier with reversed arms emerging from the tall stone column has the gravity and strength of grief coming from the full knowledge of old wrongs done to men by men. It mourns; but it mourns for all mankind. We are silent before it, as we are before the marble figures of the ancient Greeks. The thoughtless one-sided babble about national righteousness or wrongness, the *clichés* of jingo patriotism, the abstract virtues so often parasitic on the human spirit fade before the colossal figure of the common soldier by the wayside.

The genius of Man rises out of the stone, and our tears fall before it.

Chapter 4

SCYLLA

When Felicity's mother returned from seeing the family doctor she telephoned Mr. Fitzwarren, asking him to drop in on his way home from the office.

"I cannot talk over the telephone, for reasons which will be obvious when I see you. Yes, you were right, I am afraid. I can still hardly believe it."

When the two were together she said that Girlie was in her fourth month of pregnancy, and that the father was an American she had met in London. He had come to Europe on a travelling scholarship and was now back in the United States.

"The awful part about it, Fitz, is that she says she did not love him. How *can* it be true? A chance meeting at a Chelsea party, she says."

"It looks to me as though she's covering up for someone else, Nora."

"Phillip Maddison, you mean? Oh, why did I let her go down to work for him? I knew she should have stayed in London until she had had a chance to mature."

"We must make sure who the father is, old girl. Let me talk to her. Where is she?"

"Upstairs in her room."

"D'you mind if I go up?"

"My dear Fitz, you are one of the family, you are my trustee and executor when I'm gone——"

When Mr. Fitzwarren knocked on Felicity's bedroom door she was sitting on her bed writing a letter, and at once hid pad and pencil under her pillow.

"Come in."

"I'll not beat about the bush," he began, while the phrase aroused erotic thoughts. "Who was it? Maddison?"

"No, it was an American, I think."

"You *think*? Were there others then? How many?"

"I don't remember. I'd had too much to drink at a party in Chelsea."

"When?"

"In the summer. I forget the exact date."

"My poor darling."

Mr. Fitzwarren sat himself beside her and put his arms protectively around her shoulders. The propinquity of young flesh aroused him; soon he was fondling her breasts while kissing her neck. She put up with this for a space before removing the arms gently.

"Haven't you still got some feeling left for me, eh?"

"I'm fond of you."

"You used to love me."

"I suppose I did. But love isn't just sex, you know."

"It often begins like that. After all, it's the natural way. Romantic love is an illusion. I suppose you imagined yourself in love with Phillip, after reading his book? I read it—the tinge of self-pity here and there probably aroused protective feelings in you. But that isn't love, my pet. You did let him have you, didn't you?"

"I'll tell you if you promise not to tell Mummie."

"All right, I'll promise. No—don't tell me. I knew already who it was. The point is, you've got to get rid of it as soon as possible."

"I'm not afraid of having a child. I'd love it. But I don't want to hurt Phillip in any way at all."

Mr. Fitzwarren told himself that his promise was not valid, since she had not told him that it was Maddison. He pretended to be sympathetic, while erotic desire arose to possess her again.

"Of course you don't. I shouldn't have loved you as I did, if you'd been a hard little creature," he said, unbuttoning her blouse. "Would you really like to have the baby? I'm not the jealous type, honestly. If you marry me, that will give the child a father, and I love you so much that I swear I'll care for it as though it were mine."

He put his hand over her heart, but did not knead her breast again. "God, you are lovely. How I've missed you, darling. Don't go back to that chap. I can get you a job in London, and we can be married at a register office as soon as you're twenty-one. I suppose it will be a shock for Nora, but much better than having an abortion."

He took her hand and pressed it to his lips. He saw himself in a generous, almost noble light. At the same time he thought that the baby would hold her to him, and he would have someone always in his bed, years younger than himself, who would be middle-aged about the time that he started to become impotent. A splendid idea, to be looked after in his old age.

"Why are you crying, honey?"

"I don't know."

"Did you tell Phillip about me?"

"A little——" She added, "I had to. He found out."

"How could he find out without your telling him?"

"He guessed when he saw me home that night two years ago. If you remember you were waiting here when we returned. You both left together."

"Did he creep back afterwards? Did you let him sleep with you?"

"Of course not. He wouldn't have done such a thing. He's an honourable man."

"Oh, I see. The perfect, gentle knight, is he? Well then, I take it that it was Phillip who put it across you?"

"No he didn't, if you want to know. It was all my fault."

"You'll marry me then, darling?"

"I can't tell you yet, honestly."

"Don't be upset, Baby. I'm with you, remember. Not a word to anyone, mind."

He resisted running downstairs.

"Well, did you manage to influence her in any way, Fitz?"

"Oh, I think so. I pointed out that her present infatuation with a charming experienced man couldn't possibly last, and that she'd spoil her chances of marriage if she insisted on having the baby."

"She is a minor, we must not forget, Fitz."

"What we need, Nora, is another doctor beside our own to certify that she is either mentally or physically unfit to bear a child, and the way is clear. Then she can come home here and get a job in London and no one will be any the wiser."

"What I'd do without your moral support, I just don't know, dear Fitz. Ah, there's the front door. Well, I must answer it."

"Let Felice go, why not."

"Felice? I've never heard you call Girlie that before."

"Oh, I've always thought of her as Felice, since she was small. Such a happy child she was always—*felix, felicis*—'producing happiness'. It was in a cross-word puzzle some years ago, I recollect."

"I thought it derived from *felix,* a cat, fruitful."

"Oh, I don't think so. No. The *felidae* is a genus of fissified carnivora—lions, tigers, pumas, et cetera. My cross-word mind," he laughed.

"It's hardly a moment for levity, Fitz, surely?"

Phillip was walking down the garden path.

"Oh, hullo," said Lucy, blushing. "We wondered where you were."

"I went to the Ypres Salient."

"Didn't Felicity go with you?"

"No. Isn't she here?"

"We came back and found everyone gone and the house empty."

"What about Rippingall?"

"I haven't seen him either. Oh, before I forget, your post is on the table in your room."

He ran upstairs and searching through two score of letters tore open an envelope with Felicity's writing.

My Dearest,

I hope that my sudden departure has not put you out too much. I hoped you would return after my very foolish act and tell me I was forgiven. Of course you could only be but upset but I do promise you that I did truly feel that the shoes gave me a feeling of such tenderness when I held them in my hand, for I could see the shape of the feet which had worn them, and sense the balance, too, for sole and heel were evenly worn, not like my own clumsy feet which tread down the backs of all my shoes.

Now I have a confession to make. As I think you know, I have been imagining that the tightness of my frocks was due to laziness and perhaps eating too much, so I was going to have a sauna bath before writing to ask you if you would give me another chance. But Mother thought that I was not well, and in need of a tonic, so we went together to our doctor who told me that I was over three months gone in pregnancy. My periods have always been irregular, due to something that happened when I was very young, so I was not unduly worried, when I was more late than usual.

I have discussed it with mother, and told her that the father is an American who was a temporary member of the Yacht Club, and I had a brief affair with him before he returned to the United States. So while it is my dearest wish to have a child while I am young I have decided that with so many responsibilities weighing upon you, and considering that Lucy will have more to bear with now that she too is to have another little one, I must fall in with my mother's suggestion that I have an operation.

At the same time, I feel it is not right to do so without letting you know of my intentions. Will you send me a little note saying that you approve, so that my conscience may be clear?

Who knows, it may be my fate to follow her whose shoes I was about to cast away in so ungracious a manner; if this is to be, I pray that it will not be a cause of grief to you. But if a homeless ghost has any love left in its wanderings upon the battlefields where my father lies, mine will be watching over you, dearest of friends.

Felicity.

The next letter he opened seemed strangely to add to Felicity's letter. It was signed Bro. Laurence. At once Phillip thought of Rippingall's 'rascal monk' by the river, who had made enquiries about Felicity. The writer declared that he had read all of Phillip's books, and had been deeply moved by *The Phoenix*. He went on to say that he had come recently to call on Phillip, finding himself in the neighbourhood of Rookhurst, but had not realised he was so busy. Might he propose himself for a brief visit later on, when perhaps Mr. Maddison might be able to see him? With the letter was a page of what the writer called 'random impressions', which he hoped would not be taken other than in the spirit by which they were written: if, however, they did offend, he hoped Mr. Maddison would forgive him for his good intentions.

Your hero, Donkin, believes that by a change of thought the blind will see, the selfish will love, the cruel have pity, and the dead of the war will rise again. He is wrong, and fails; for although all he meets are stirred for a moment and see with his vision, he is cast out and dies; the living are unchanged, the dead remain dead. But he is also right, and succeeds, for the act of the artist-misfit-messiah, which in this world can only be symbolic, is reality in the kingdom which is not of this world.

I beg that you will not consider this letter from a stranger to be merely impertinent, but I was coming to see you in your house recently when I heard your cries, and realising that you were in some distress, I went away. May I therefore, with trepidation, make a confession about myself when I was a younger man, and thought that by a change of thought, like your Donkin, I could alter the attitudes of those about me. All I can say now, with respect, is that there are deep things in us, and you know what they are as well as I do. Something flows into us that enlarges our personalities and when that flows out of us our personalities shrink. At the moment you are void of this something, so your personality is rather shrivelled——

Phillip put the letter aside, feeling that it verged on the impertinent. He read it through again. No, it was pertinent. The writer had divined what he himself had seen in the character of Donkin. He was opening another letter, from his New York publisher, when Lucy came into the room.

"I think you had better read this," he said giving her Felicity's letter.

Lucy read it and said with a wavering smile, "Of course she must have her baby if she wants it, don't you think so."

"I must tell you that there wasn't any American, it was me."

"I thought it might be," she replied, now more sure of herself. "Oh well, it can't be helped now."

"Do you mind very much, Lucy?"

"Well, I suppose it will steady Felicity to have a child," and she laughed a little, blushing.

He showed her the letter signed *Bro. Laurence*. She said, "Isn't it good?"

"Yes, I wonder why he asked where Felicity was living."

At dawn next morning Phillip set off for London, driving into the sun rising over the Great Plain. At Staines he went into an eating house for breakfast of coffee with eggs and bacon. He had some time to wait. At half-past nine, telling himself that he must always keep calm, he arrived at the house on the edge of Ealing Common. Felicity came to the door.

"Oh, I am so glad you've come!"

"I've been with Piers in Flanders."

"Yes, I had your letter."

She kissed him, he kissed her. Taking his hand, she led him into the sitting-room. "Mother, this is Phillip."

"How do you do. I think you've met Mr. Fitzwarren, Mr. Maddison? Come, let us be seated" she said, as though brightly. "Have you just arrived from the West Country? The country must be at its best just now. Have you had breakfast?"

"Yes, thank you."

After more small talk, Mr. Fitzwarren said to Mrs. Ancroft that he must be going, but would telephone later. Mrs. Ancroft saw him to the door.

As soon as her mother was out of the room Felicity sprang up and said, "Oh, darling, I can hardly realise that you are here!"

He said quietly, "Lucy says you must have your baby. I think so too. By the way, am I still an American?"

"I haven't said anything more about it. Only Mother is shocked because she says I seem to be so casual about it." Her face glowed with happiness.

Mrs. Ancroft returned.

"Please sit down, Mr. Maddison. You must be tired after your journey. Would you like some coffee?"

"May I?"

"Certainly. Felicity, will you attend to it?"

"Yes, Mother," replied the girl, going out with an adoring glance at Phillip. There was a pause; then Mrs. Ancroft said, raising her eyes, "I wonder if you have anything to tell me about my daughter, Mr. Maddison?"

"Felicity tells me that you think it best that she does not have her child. In which case," he said, with a stammer of awkwardness, "I hope that you will regard me as your banker."

"Does that mean that you assume responsibility for my daughter's condition?"

"Oh yes, Mrs. Ancroft."

Part of Mrs. Ancroft's face seemed to glitter, as though with petrifaction: it was the eyes that gave this effect, in a red, rock-like face. She suffered from heart-trouble.

"How could you, a married man, behave in that way towards one so young, and so inexperienced?" she said. "It is a terrible thing to have happened to one so gently brought up. Mr. Fitz-warren, my daughter's guardian, is greatly shocked. I will say quite frankly that he was against her going so far away from her home to work, from the very first. I foolishly considered that country air would be good for her, since she was often pale and inclined to be depressed. But had I known then what the situation between you and Felicity already was, I should certainly never have given my approval, but on the contrary, taken her guardian's advice."

To this he was silent. The coffee arrived. "Girlie, will you bring some more hot milk? Thank you, darling."

When Felicity was out of the room, Mrs. Ancroft continued, "What will your wife say when she knows, Mr. Maddison?"

"She said she thought it would be the very thing to give Felicity some sort of balance, Mrs. Ancroft."

She looked at him curiously, as though unable to resolve the puzzle of this man who had written *The Water Wanderer,* such a delightful, revealing book; only to follow it with *The Phoenix*, a mixture of saintliness and blasphemy, of wonderful descriptions of natural beauty hand in glove with such appalling sentiments.

"*I* cannot understand why the hero of your novel, *The Phoenix,* who is presumably based on yourself, should hold such dreadful ideas about his own country! Oh yes, well do I know that war is a tragedy. But surely, Mr. Maddison, love of one's country counts for something? Three of Felicity's uncles, my brothers, died in that war. You survived. Is that all the war meant to you, what you put into the mouth of your hero, Donkin?"

"Mrs. Ancroft, my novel is not autobiographical. But I may tell you that Donkin was a real person. I hoped that it would be clear that he was his own tragedy, but I expressed it poorly, I'm afraid."

"At least I am glad to learn that from your own mouth." She looked at the ormolu clock. "Now I must leave for my appointment with an eminent surgeon, if you will excuse me. I expect you to be here when I return."

When her mother had left, Felicity took Phillip for a walk on the common.

"I'm sorry I was angry with you, Felicity."

"Ah, but it was my foolishness over the sandshoes that made you so upset. But you are here now, that is all that matters." She took his hand. "O, I am so glad to see you! I thought I would never see you again. I ran last night on the common, in my nightdress. I thought of my baby being taken away from me. I could see it with its unsunned eyes lying in a hospital bin, wrapped up in a parcel. I had wanted to drown myself, to save everyone trouble, but I knew this might cause more trouble to you, so I went home."

"You poor darling. Hold on, never give way. And when your baby comes, about the same time as Lucy's, I'll get both registered as twins. Then there will be no stigma. If I'm copped I'll probably do porridge, but people will be on the side of a man who thinks of the baby before himself. It might even sell my books!" he laughed.

When Mrs. Ancroft returned she said, "Oh, that specialist is such a fool. He had already agreed to do the operation for a hundred guineas, after *merely* glancing at the doctor's certificates, but when I said, 'Isn't it a pity that we are the only country which is so hypocritical about abortion?' he looked at me and said, 'Madam, if, as your words appear to infer, these certificates are not authentic, then I refuse to consider the matter further' and with that he pressed the bell for me to be shown out. Such a stupid man."

Phillip avoided the ravaged eyes in the haughty suffering face which looked for a moment almost forlorn; then the mouth recovered its former determination.

"Felicity shall come down in a few days' time to pack her things. I have told her that she must return the same day and you must not dissuade her. I need hardly remind you that she is a minor, Mr. Maddison."

"Very well, I'll go back now. Perhaps you'll let me know when you are coming down, Felicity?"

Mrs. Ancroft called out to Mr. Fitzwarren waiting in the next room, "Come in, Fitz, and be a witness to what Mr. Maddison has just said. He has promised never to see Felicity again."

Phillip said firmly, "That is not true, Mrs. Ancroft," at which the lady, hitherto masterful, murmured, "Oh, my heart, my heart," and supported by Mr. Fitzwarren on one arm and her daughter on the other, she sank back on the sofa.

Phillip left the room, lest his presence cause further upset. He was near the front door when he heard slipper'd footfalls behind him.

"Don't worry, darling, don't worry. I'll never leave you so long as you want me."

"And I'll stand by you always." They kissed hurriedly. "Make my apologies for leaving so abruptly. I'm with you, remember, and so is Lucy." And kissing the back of her neck, so slender under the fair soft hairs, he was about to go down the steps when she said, "I'll come with you to the car. Oh, I love the Silver Eagle."

Mr. Fitzwarren was saying, "Now don't forget what I said, Nora. I know of a cottage in the woods in Oxfordshire, which I'm prepared to buy now against my retirement in a couple of years' time. It will be the very place for you to take Felice until it is all over. Meanwhile I'll find out about the adoption and let you know." And putting on his black Homburg hat he went down the steps, thinking, as he saw Felice returning, that he would marry her.

Mrs. Ancroft had her own ideas for her daughter's future. "You and I will go away together, Girlie darling, just as we did when you were little, and be all in all to one another. We'll find our own little cottage in the country, far from anywhere, perhaps in the Lake District, and you shall have your baby there. And we three shall be all in all to one another, won't we?"

Felicity pretended to herself that the three were Philip, her baby, and herself, living somewhere in Scotland. He would study trout by some loch or burn, and catch their breakfast at the same time. Tears filled her eyes as she thought of this hopeless fantasy; yet it persisted; and she wondered if Phillip was thinking the same thing —perhaps all of them together—Lucy, Billy, Peter, and Roz—herself and her child. Then no one would be unhappy. Had he not offered to take the baby and have it registered as Lucy's, which would mean all of them together again? It was with a shock she heard her mother saying, "And Girlie darling, I shall adopt our baby when it is born, and then we shall always be together, shall we not?"

Two days later Fitz made his proposal to Mrs. Ancroft. "I'll marry Felice myself, old girl, to keep the good name of Ancroft."

"A noble gesture, Fitz," she replied, equably, "but I could not think of allowing you to make such a sacrifice," while she thought that *she* would adopt the baby when it came; then in due course, when Girlie met some nice young man, no one need be any the wiser.

When Phillip returned to Monachorum he read the letter from his New York publishers, MacCourage & Co., Inc. John MacCourage asked how the book on the trout was coming along, and when could he see a copy of the typescript. Phillip replied that he could not see the form the book should take: there was so much to be seen by the river; and to be frank, it was not easy to concentrate at the present time, with so much domestic detail filling the Imagination, as Keats wrote of his muse, with a capital 'I'.

When this letter reached New York his publisher replied at once with a long night cablegram asking Phillip to come over at his expense, tourist class, and stay with him at his apartment in Manhattan where he might be able to help him co-ordinate some of his ideas, since he himself was a keen fisherman. If Phillip brought his rods he would take him north to spend two weeks at his Fish and Game Club in Canada.

Phillip thought at once that he couldn't possibly go. How would the family get on without him? He went to see his father.

"Ah, old chap, now you are beginning to feel what it is to be a family man, I can see."

Richard laughed as he struck his spade, with its work-bright blade, into the plot of alsike, with its pink clover flowers, he was about to dig-in. "I thought of dibbing-in my first early potatoes under this wall next March. It will give shelter from the frost wind from the east. How's the trout book coming along? Have you started your garden yet?"

"More or less."

"Shall you go to America?"

"Well, Father, I dare not allow anything to come before my eyes until I can see how to do the trout book. I've got somehow to link the theme with the *Zeitgeist*—the spirit of the times. It isn't only knowledge of fish that I'm groping for. I've been reading back numbers of the *Salmon and Trout Magazine,* as well as the *Flyfisher's Journal.* Also many books. What I want to cohere—to bring to life—is something beyond local things. I mean—well—civilisation is threatening all wild life—rivers being polluted——"

Hetty came into the walled garden.

"I know you are so very busy, Phillip, but do tell me, how are Lucy, and the little ones? I am simply longing to see them."

"Lucy sends her love, and says she will come over shortly to see you both."

"Ah, then she can ask her father about the artichoke tubers. When the other day I saw Lucy she said she would get some from her old home. I thought of putting them in the corner over there."

"I'll tell Lucy to remind Ernest to bring them, Father."

"How do they manage, those two alone?" asked Hetty.

"Oh, Ernest and Pa muddle through somehow. I've tried again and again to persuade Ernest to sell the machinery, which was hardly used when his brothers Fiennes and Tim went to Australia years ago, but Ernest does nothing. He says, 'Oh, I shan't bother,' while nearly a thousand pounds worth of lathes and milling machines depreciate. Ernest is living on his capital, which isn't much. He potters about the semi-derelict Works and feeds spiders in their webs, trying to see which will grow the biggest. Still, I used to do that, as an impotent young boy, so who am I to criticise Ernest?"

"Who looks after Ernest and his father, Phillip?"

"No one except themselves. I suppose there isn't enough money left over to pay the so-called cook's wages. I don't know, I never go there," he said with a trace of irritability. "I can't bear to go over to Down Close. But who am I to talk. Look at the mess I've made of my life so far."

"But you've done ever so well, really, Phillip. It seems a shame to waste all these beautiful rooms. I suppose you aren't thinking of letting Lucy and the children come over here to stay, now and again."

"I'm sure she'll be much happier away from me, so it's not a bad idea, Mother. I'll suggest it to her."

"I thought that perhaps she should not be left alone in the house when you go to London."

"*Yes*, Mother," he replied, quietly. "Yes."

"I wish I could do something about your sisters, Phillip. There they are, both in London, Elizabeth all day in her office, and living in a rented room in North London, and Doris as a school-teacher. It seems such a pity that Father won't allow either of them to live in the house in Hillside Road. I don't suppose you are going to London soon, are you?"

"I wasn't, mother."

"I'm sure it's not good for either of the girls to live so far apart. Now do come in and let me give you some tea, you look rather tired. I've had a fire lit in the drawing room, it gets so damp, I find."

They sat in the drawing room, close to the fire around which two screens were drawn in a vain attempt to exclude the east wind.

"How do you like living here, Mother?"

"Well, as I was saying, Phillip, without Elizabeth and Doris it will be lonely, at times, for me, after all those years in Wakenham. Still, your father seems to like his garden—he spends all his time on it. But the house is so big, after what we've been used to. What a pity you decided to give up the land——"

"Oh, for God's sake, Mother! I did *not* give up the land! Uncle Hilary sold it—or made up his mind to sell it—before we had the promised conference—in order to marry Irene. I was quite prepared to set aside all my plans for writing, to which he'd never shown any sympathy—on the contrary, he was dead against it."

"Ah well, no one can put back the clock, my son. And as Father says, land has never been so cheap for more than a century, so perhaps it is all for the best that it was given up. Still, I can't help thinking it is a pity. I've been looking at some of the records

Father found in one of the oak chests—I wondered if they would interest you, as a writer, I mean. But perhaps you've already seen them? Father brought these in from the library."

She pointed to a heap of parchment deeds on the table.

"Your father says he remembers your grandfather telling him that there were boxes and boxes of them in the attics. Have you time to glance at them?"

"Well, at the moment my mind is rather pre-occupied, mother." To avoid letting her feel disappointed he added, "Yes, of course I'd like to look at them."

She got up, and taking one from the table said that she found the details very interesting.

"I made a summary of the will of William Beare Maddison in fifteen hundred and seven, just think of it, before Shakespeare was born. Here it is, so very interesting."

> In the will (*circa* 1507) £4 was left to the poor of Colham, and to his most beloved wife W. B. Maddison left part of the barton, namely the 'smalle parlour on the north side of the hall', the buttery and the cellars under it, the 'kitchin' and the 'bowlting house' (bakehouse), with wainscot chamber, the chamber of the 'kitchin,' the 'dornix chamber' with the hangings of coarse damask, and the two chambers and the garret on the south side of the house.
>
> His wife was 'not to meddle at all with the building or garret or cellar on the north side of the barton, but to suffer my son William Beare to have the same'. She was to have the 'smalle room at the stairfoot, and the lodging over it, the newe house for the capons, and one of the two hogstyes, and 'the newe stable and loft over all, with free ingress, egress, and regress to herself, her children, her servants, so long as she continued sole and unmarried.'
>
> This widow left to her daughter Elizabeth 'parcells of her apparel'. One gown of 'wrought velvet, one kirtle of the same, a gown of damask, two kirtles of velvet, a kirtle of wrought velvet and one of trifet taffeta, a petticoat of crimson Callymancho, and all linen appertaining to her proper wearing, a turkey grograyne gown with two yards of velvet, a mourning gown of cloth, a petticoat of cloth with fur of lysle grograne, another of silk grogane with six welts of velvet.'

"Well, Mother, it's not exactly in my line. You see, I have to shut my mind to some things, in order to think about the trout book."

"Yes, of course, naturally. But I thought this might interest you particularly, after our walk to the Coppice, all of us together, when we were here for the christening of Billy and Peter. Do you remember? Hilary, Irene, Dora, Uncle John, your friend Piers—Oh, I did so enjoy that visit. You told us about the prices of coppice wood—well, this is about another coppice, Father said, because the Hanger Copse was chestnut and hazel, this was for oak, grown for tanning leather as well as for firing. It was written in seventeen eighty-five, in the Steward's book."

Dead—dead—dead stuff—the blind trout slowly dying of—inanition——

> Upon a Statute Acre of Coppice Oak Wood of seventeen years Growth there should grow two tons of Bark and twenty two cords of Wood.
>
> Three Wood Acres make very near Five Statute acres. One Good Load of Wood in a kiln will burn Fifteen Yard of Lime.
>
> 16½ ft. to a Perch to a Statute Acre.
>
> 21 ft. to a Wood Acre.
>
> A Cord of Wood is 8 ft. 4 inches long, 4 ft. 6 inches high, 2 ft. 6 inches in length of Billet.
>
> Half a year's land tax and window money at 4/- comes to £8:04:11½ Tax in All thus—

Land Tax. . . .	£3:14:5½
Window Tax . . .	4:10:6
fervantf	1:00:7½
Horfes	0:15:0
	£10:08:1

"I make the total ten pounds and sevenpence."

"Here's a list of the names of the men employed, Phillip. There were forty in those days. Just think of it."

"I don't want to think about it, Mother. I want to think of the blind trout. Why don't *you* write a book about all this?"

"I would if I had your gift, my son."

"As I told you when you first came down here, Mother, my talent is buried, with most of my generation. No, that's sentimental. But as a fact it is not possible to give all my imagination to what I want to write just now. Perhaps I'll be able to write it in my field at Malandine."

It was an idea. That was the place. A writer should have a secret pied-à-terre—

As he was leaving she dared to ask about his secretary. "Has Miss Ancroft finished her secretarial duties, Phillip?"

"Yes, Mother. Felicity left because she wants to be on her own—to write. And meanwhile, keep herself by typing. She's going to advertise for work in *The Writer.*"

Dearest Phillip,

I'm awfully sorry, darling, but however hard I try, I *cannot* feel myself to be a ruined girl—no, I am not the ruin*able* sort—though perhaps ruin*ous*. And as no-one else feels that—three rousing cheers. All the same, I seem to sense that you are not altogether happy. I wish I could determine once and for all if you would be better away from your home—and act upon it. Why should you, as you write from your field in Malandine, be 'almost afraid' to go back to your lovely valley? Darling, you must not let your heart wither away. It must not be wasted by a sort of slow petrifaction, but allowed to flow out easily and without strain.

I have rented a room here from mother, and am typing a novel—as I told you—I have advertised in *The Writer.* And am also doing my own work. When I see you again I shall be a new girl for you, without any more silly mistakes.

Always yours,
Felicity.

If only he could settle to a clear prospect of what to write. If only life were simple, as in those years after the war, in the cottage at Malandine. Now to think. The first rough draft of water-scenes was done; now to determine the dramatic theme. It was fishing weather in the West Country with hatches of fly every noon, and trout on the move. He stood beside the river, watching the rises of trout, and the insect traffic upon the water; making notes of the times of flies hatching, and identifying them with a book with coloured plates by Halford. He made notes on the buoyancy and grace of cloud formations high in the dome of the sky which brought lightness of heart to man, bird, and fish—the nymphs swimming to the surface of the stream, to arise tremulously to the shelter of willow and alder, there to cast their pellicles, those diaphanous coverings of wing and body, to await the nuptial flight into the sky of late afternoon. He came to know the regular stances of the trout, day after day, when they were feeding just under the surface.

One morning he noticed a fish, over three pounds in weight, darker than the others, a lean fish the colour of which was almost black. As the days went on he saw that it was always in the same place, in relation to the rise, but never seemed to take any flies. He used a telescope to watch it; and seeing smaller trout, again and again, rising to flies just under the surface, observed that this fish never appeared to feed. It stayed in one place, using small slow movements of fin and tail and evenly opening its mouth to breath —but nothing more. Could it be blind?

How could a blind fish feed? Had it a sense of smell, like an eel? Was it hovering in its stance by day, at the times of hatching, only out of habit, having nothing else to do with its life? Did it feed on minnows in the shallows, by sensing the nearness of the little fish by the nerves along the lateral nerve-lines of its body?

Now for a theme, to relate observation to a story with its own life. Take several fish and relate their lives as individual fish, with the blind, black, and aged trout symbol of the obsolescence, leading to its death. A symbol, hidden and never revealed directly, of dying Europe? No politics. Keep to the blind trout. Relate its condition to the pollution of so many rivers due to the industrialisation and the squalor of the machine age. Be neither romantic nor sentimental: a fish is a fish is a fish, as Gertrude Stein said of a rose. It existed; no more than that. The problem to solve was, How did this blind trout exist? And was it black because the sense of protective colouration was put in action by the optic nerve? A blind trout living through eternal night? Pollution? The Flumen was one of the purest rivers in the West Country . . .

He hurried home, packed up his note-books, addressed and posted them to Felicity. Would she type them at once and give any ideas, or reactions from the notes, about how the story might go? He would pay her for this work at the rate of fifteen shillings a day.

Darling,

Of course I will give you priority for the trout and river notes and impressions which arrived just now, and tell you exactly how they strike me. I am sorry you have to chip every word from your breast-bone. What you tell me about the blind trout is exciting. You are wonderful in your scenes of darkness, cold starlight, and the first electric pallor of dawn arising before the 'rosy fingers' of the Greeks.

Now I don't want one speck of Ancroft pollen—mère ou fille—for I can hardly describe myself a *jeune fille*—to touch the opening flower, but the fact is, I am in a quandary. I must leave home at once, but it is difficult, almost impossible, for me to begin looking for a cottage because I have no money of my own. There is 'alternative accommodation', as they say, but it involves a tentative acceptance of an offer of marriage which I do not want to consider, even, feeling as I do. Also it would be rather a shock to my mother. I am sorry not to be more explicit, perhaps I should not have mentioned it, anyway it is 'out'.

Do you think you could let me have an advance of, say, £5 for the typing, so that I could look at some cottages offered in *The Lady*? They are usually very cheap ones advertised in that magazine. I would not ask this were I not desperate, for I know you must not stop writing when 'the honey flow is on'. Also you have so many mouths to feed.

Could you come up for a couple of days, and take me in your lovely Silver Eagle to look at various cottages? As I said, I am most loath to interrupt your work, but a cottage of my own would enable me to feel free and unencumbered in mind, so that I can give all of it to help you in your work. I myself am in my usual health and feel buoyant and optimistic.

Later. Perhaps it would save you a journey to London if, in the course of your wandering, you come across any cottage that is to be let, the humbler the better. Will you let me know?

He would go to London on the morrow. He must take her a basket of trout. He was tired: the idea of putting on waders, oversocks, and nailed canvas boots was too much. The sun was going down behind the hill. How lonely, bereft, was the earth without sunlight. Even under morning and afternoon light there was a vacancy in the valley: sameness of walks by the river: the same trout to be caught on barbless hooks and put back, to disappear for a day or two and then they were back at their stances, before and below the old blind trout slowly waving its life away.

It was no good fishing now that a mist was beginning to lie upon the meadows. He couldn't see to tie the fly properly. Was his eyesight failing? Could it be due to that temporary blindness by mustard gas in his youth? The knot was wrong anyway, he could not see to bend the gut round the eye of the shank. It became a grannie knot. He cast badly. The fly *struck* the water, he *snatched* it back—he was all jangle, disintegrated, no harmony between eye, arm, and heart. He tried again. The fly was caught in an alder branch. He snatched it back and the cast snapped. He was always meaning to cut back the branches, and here it was June, he hadn't really fished properly that season, no time to do anything. He waded across but could not see where the fly was caught. His legs felt chilled and heavy. He got out of the water and walked to the bridge, to look down into the pool from his usual place in the centre of the parapet.

The sinking sun was lengthening oak and alder shadows. Red spinners of the midday hatch of olive dun were now rising and falling regularly over the gliding copper-plated surface of the river.

He stood below the bend, with no desire to fish, his mind empty save for an impersonal feeling of sadness which he knew came from nervous exhaustion. For some time now the river had been *him*. He had known, sensed, and *lived* in every gravelly stone, bubble, grain of sand: yet that part of his life, because it had remained unwritten, was as ephemeral as the air-life of one of the spinners, those creatures, frail and delicate, their mouths sealed against the need of food or water, living only on air during their brief winged life between the rise and setting of their one day's sun.

Love is a full growing and constant light:
But his first minute after noon is night.

The water was low and clear. Cattle in the morning and afternoon heats had been cooling themselves under the shade of the alders, but the slight cloudiness of loam in the gravel had settled, so that, peering down into the water at noon, he had seen every stone and speck of gravel, every tiny spotted samlet of the late winter's hatching.

During the early part of the year the water had been high, the spring-heads in full gush, salmon coming in from the Channel had been able to run up higher than was usual at the beginning of the season.

As the level dropped in April, the salmon sought the deepest water they could find, in the pools and by the hovers of the banks.

And as the springs lessened their upwelling in May, the salmon were forced to spend most of the daylight under the muddy roots of the waterside alders, waiting for twilight and cooler water from the great reservoirs of the chalk downs and safety from the glare of day.

There was a solitary salmon lodged under a clump of roots a few yards below where Phillip was standing at the bend. The water there was about two feet deep, and the salmon was trapped.

He had been watching that fish for more than two months. Its life was one of solitary confinement. When it had first appeared, in April, it had been a bluish-silver, and very lively. Now its scales were a pinkish brown and the fish was dejected.

Its tail could usually be seen sticking out of the roots about eleven in the morning, before the shadow of a branch hid it.

Sometimes when he had gone to the bridge about noon he had

seen the fish sidle out of the roots, turn slowly into the wimpling current, to idle there like a great trout for a few moments, its back-fin out of water, and then to gather way while it prepared for a leap—a great splash, and it had fallen back, while the narrow river rocked and rippled with the impact. After remaining in midstream for a minute or so the fish would drift backwards to its hiding place, slowly, almost wearily, and push itself under the roots again.

Now, on this evening in late June, Phillip was standing beside the run, a small seven-foot rod of split cane weighing two ounces in his right hand. He was about to drop lightly an imitation of a red spinner—the olive dun which had shed the pale green pellicle or sheath of morning for its one dance of love-and-death—upon the wimpled surface when something made him pause and remain quite still.

The water in which he was standing was about ten inches deep. It blurred as it began to deepen towards the edge of the run. The sky-reflecting water had shown a gleam as he had raised his rod. The salmon was swimming slowly up the run, to pass within a few inches of his wet trouser-ends.

Very slowly he turned his head to watch the fish. After some moments of quietude it turned on its side and sinuated along the gravel as though trying to scrape away the itch in its gill-rakers, for freshwater maggots were clustering there. It actually pushed itself against Phillip's left foot. And there it idled before beginning a series of gentle rolling movements, porpoise-like . . . until it accelerated up the run, pushing waves from bank to bank, to make a slashing turn in water shallower than its own depth and to hurtle down the run again, making a thruddling noise as it passed.

Entering deeper water above the bridge it leapt, and smacked down on its side. It came up the run once more and idled there, maintaining place with the slightest of slow sinuating movements, scarcely perceptible now that the sun had gone down in the west.

He stood there, still as a heron, watching the lonely salmon playing by itself—a fish, three feet long, imprisoned in a few square yards of space, threatened by asphyxiation in warm water, by gaff of poacher, by beak of heron; by eels which would eat it alive when the fungus grew in yellow rosettes on its wilting scales; by otters; by many other hazards. He stood there while the sunset faded to dusk, and full darkness came to the earth. Moths whirred past, sometimes alighting on his hair, their wings brushing his brow. It was nearly midnight when he went back to the house. There were no lights in the bedrooms. Lucy, and the children were asleep. He wrote until the first light of day, and when he set out for the London road the downs were dark against the sky, and 'the rosy fingers of dawn' (a physical love-image, surely) were arising in the east.

11 Hillside Road,
London, S.E.

One moment I am in despair, dearest Lucy, with my guardian urging me to go to live in his Oxfordshire cottage, and my Mother wanting to let this house and take me to the Lake District with my grandmother, when a certain sports-car draws up round the corner and within ten minutes all my things are under the tonneau cover and we are crossing the Thames and safe upon the Surrey side! A wonderful day for a joy-ride through Richmond and on to Kingston and over the chalk downs to Cheam and Cross Aulton and the lovely country which Phillip told me was once all herb fields and dog-carts when he was a baby and his mother left her home to have him in her very own little house in Wakenham.

We drove past the Crystal Palace, where we stopped awhile to gaze up at the tall glass towers and the roof glittering like the wings of an immense dragonfly. And at last up Hillside Road, with the beautiful park-like Hill opposite. I can hardly believe it—that I am in Phillip's bedroom where he lived before going down to Malandine after the war.

I have already met one of Phillip's sisters, the younger one, whom I saw in Devon during that lovely holiday by the estuary. Of course, she is very unhappy, her husband having left her. Doris is very kind, and I like her very much, but poor woman, her irritability and pessimism and don't caredness are all against my nature. However, I look forward to helping her with the two small boys. It will be grand to have her company for the time being, but I don't think this house will be suitable when my babe gets lively later on and wants to start crawling and possessing. The front, or drawing room, is the most unlived-in room I have ever seen, I don't suppose Phillip's mother often, if ever, had any time to rest, let alone relax here.

So I'm still keeping my fingers crossed and hoping to find a 5*s.* a week place somewhere in Phillip's old haunts near Reynards' Common; and where I can grow my own vegetables. I know such cottages are to be had in plenty.

By the way, I am known here in Wakenham as Mrs. Rivers, wife of an absentee American husband. (I choose Rivers as a good luck symbol for Phillip's new book.)

During my first evening here we went for a walk in the High Street, and Phillip showed me 'Freddy's' which he used to haunt during the war with Desmond Neville his friend, whom he hasn't heard of for years, he said. We also went to Nightingale Grove, and saw where the Zeppelin torpedo fell, destroying eight cottages and killing Lily Cornford, who is to be a heroine of his Somme novel, which he feels he will never be able to write; but we shall see! The cottages there are all rebuilt and only here and there a gash in a brick wall remains. Phillip seems more than ever wanting to avoid the present; I suppose his mind is, like Shelley's, always dwelling in the past. He did not speak of Barley (whom I resemble but fail to live up to) but I felt that she was very much behind those sad and speculative eyes. Also he seems to feel that in some way he has let me down, but as I told him, he needn't worry on my account, because I am perfectly content here for the time being and there is the green Hill to go to, with its views and sunshine and many shady trees. At the same time, I am finding, as Phillip told me I might, that D. is obstinate as a mule. She is obviously worn out physically and mentally, but all my efforts to get her to talk, not by being inquisitive of course, are without effect.

She lives too much in the past. I already knew, of course, about her boy being killed on the Somme, and that she had married, after the war, his friend in the army. She did tell me, however, that he tried to strangle her before he left home. Apparently he argued with her all that night, before he lost control. She is extraordinarily obstinate. Phillip told me that she was set as a child against her father, because he used to make her mother cry. He explained it all to me. "Doris was the only brave one of us three children; she set herself against Father, and was thus petrified in part of her. When Percy Pickering was killed, she reverted to the rock." It all seems very tragic.

Doris told me that her mother had offered to pay the fees for her to see a doctor and get a tonic, which she needs, and which probably would make no end of difference to her health and spirits. But she says she can't be bothered to go. Well that seems to me to be utterly inexcusable. There *must* be something wrong: she goes to bed never later than 10 and sleeps very well, gets up at 7.30 feeling heavy and cross and half-awake. I feel desperately sorry for her and wish I could be allowed to nurse her. However, there you are. But I shall continue my gentle pressure and as I always feel very cheerful and full of energy in the morning it may react on her some day.

She is rather naïve. The other day she asked me if Phillip was going to the U.S.A. to find my absentee husband, Rivers!

Later. I'm afraid I've held this up for a couple of days. In the meantime I have met Phillip's mother. She stayed here last night and seemed very cheerful. She, also, asked after my American husband. Doris persists in calling me Mrs. Rivers, by the way: I wonder if this is transference, (if that is the Freudian term) because her father still refers to her as Mrs. Willoughby?

I have met Phillip's other sister, Elizabeth, who arrived here last evening with her mother in Phillip's car. She brought three large suit-cases. According to Doris, she spends all her money on clothes and must always have the latest fashion. Elizabeth would be very pretty were it not for her sharp, almost imperious manner of judging others and abruptly dismissing them. Thus much of what Phillip said to her she scoffed at—I could feel her underlying tenseness. Also she is unkind to her mother, indeed when she asked her for money she was so persistent in a neurotic way that I could not bear it, and left the room, following Phillip, who had a drawn look on his face. Later Doris told me that Elizabeth has fits at times and her mother always gives in to her because otherwise she gets very upset. What a desperately unhappy home it must have been for Phillip when he was a small boy. No wonder he says that the war was the happiest time of his life.

Phillip's mother is very sweet. I enjoy hearing her merry little laugh. I can see where Phillip gets his sensibility, and also his sense of fun.

Well, my dear, I do hope you and the children are very well and happy, and that the coming summer will be full of sunshine, physically and metaphorically.

My love to you,
Felicity.

P.S. Phillip told me that he is going to do some sailing this season, and wants to buy Piers' twelve-foot sailing dinghy. I am so glad he has Piers for a friend. Phillip is full of Hereward Birkin too, as a saviour of Britain and the Empire. He talked of a small field he used to lie in, rather high up above Malandine, and said he thought of buying it, if he can get it cheap, and making a cattle shippon there into a place where he can work. He says he cannot work here, now that Elizabeth has joined the household, he feels she is filled with broken glass.

Why does she want to write and tell me all this for? thought Lucy. As for Phillip's sisters, he and they are worlds apart, and should stay apart.

Then she thought, Would Phillip be happier if I went away with the children, and looked after Pa and Ernest? I know I am no good for him, nor is Felicity, I suppose. Yet how well she writes. Oh dear, what a muddle. Well, I must make my blackcurrant jam now.

The dinghy Phillip had bought from Piers was built for bass-fishing in the running seas of the Channel beyond the inland arm of the harbour. It was clinker-built with bluff bows and broad in the beam, with a high strake or combing above the gunwhale against lipping seas.

He had an idea of sailing down the coast, putting in at various places for the night, until he arrived at Esperance Cove, and so to the village of Malandine in South Devon which he had first known a decade previously. There, in a linhay on the hilltop field he had often visited, with Barley, he would be able to write. He had the money to buy the field, because—his literary agent had written to tell him—his New York publisher had agreed to pay 3,000 dollars advance for *The Blind Trout*, half on signature of contract, half on publication day.

As a safety measure against the hazards of the down-Channel voyage—particularly past the turbulent tides of Portland Bill—he had had two long cylindrical tanks of phosphor bronze—called yellow metal by the boat-builder—fitted under the thwarts. If *Scylla*, as he had already re-named the boat, were to capsize, she would float.

First, he must explore the mouth of the harbour. One late July morning he hauled up the brown lugsail and put the nose of the boat westward. The sail, filled with the offshore wind, drove the dinghy to ride and slither over the smooth waves of the ebb while leaving behind a satisfactory pattern of foam and bubbles. Running before the wind at six knots, he came to a large wooded island to leeward. It was marked Bere Island on the 1 inch Admiralty Chart. The channel beyond was marked by buoys.

There was a Club race that morning. A flight of white sails was down by the Bar Buoy, which they would round before returning on the next leg of a triangular course. Piers had told him of sudden swells on the bar at low water; but the tide had another two hours to lapse, so the sandbars on either side at the harbour mouth were well covered. He would be safe with an offshore wind.

So far, he had not sailed in any of the Club boat races, and knew nothing of the hazards of a spring-tide ebb—the moon was new—with an offshore wind.

The leading yachts, which had presented broad sails before the wind, were now putting about, close-hauled against wind and tide.

Lolling in the stern seat of his little boat, tiller under arm, sheet held in hand, Phillip passed west of Bere Island, and recognised one figure in the leading boat now creaming through the water past him. He was hailed. "Hullo, 'Farm Boy'. Come and dine with us tonight."

"It's very good of you, but I shall probably be too late returning." He didn't want to go to the Castle, to have drink forced upon him.

He noticed one of Runnymeade's crew: a young girl with fair curls to her shoulder. It was almost a shock to see her looking at him, so startling was the resemblance to Barley.

Runnymeade hailed him again. "Where are you bound for?"

"Oh, just to have a look at the form."

"You won't get back on this ebb tide, 'Farm Boy'."

Phillip waved and sailed on. His mind was held by the image of the field on the high ground above Malandine, where he had lain in the grass beside Barley, watching a pack of swifts—those strange thin, unearthly birds—flying with faintly shrill cries a thousand feet in the air above and barely visible to his eyes. *Do swifts beat first one wing, then the other?* he could hear her voice saying. His admiration had grown from that moment: for the poise, the observation, the penetration to essential truth of a mere child of fifteen, who on the way back to the village had taken his hand and led him to Irene, her mother, and their cottage during that wonderful summer of nineteen twenty-one, so that they should be friends again, after a slight misunderstanding over Julian Warbeck, that arrogant young poet, with whom he shared his cottage at that time. God, how time passed, leaving only ghosts. What remained of that bright image of Malandine—only the grave among the tombstones of drowned sailors, a solar wraith among ghosts of the sea: a fret and scatter of piteous bones under the headstone carved with reaping hook and severed rose-bud.

Selfishly transfixed by the past, by hopeless thoughts, he sailed into a choppy sea of waves raised by wind against tide, and, still steering south, passed a chequered buoy wallowing on its chain visible with green weeds clinging to its links. *Scylla* rolled past the great sea-top turning its head as though with weariness this way and that. She began to plunge and rise as her bows were smacked by waves which broke into spray and wetted sail and thwarts alike. The wind had changed, it was now coming up channel from the sou'-west. He dare not put her over, she would capsize and swamp with the brutal weights of water in conflict from all directions. So he steered to run before the wind, to edge the boat round to avoid losing way, while realising that he was being carried into the open sea.

The small brown sail was being watched by telescope from the roof of the clubhouse. The owner of the motorboat which took the crews to their yachts and brought them back to the slip after the race was hailed by the Commodore.

"I'd never get through the white water of the Race, sir."

The Commodore accepted the opinion, and telephoned to the Lifeboat station. He was told that the coastguard lookout on

Horsabury Head had already reported the sail, now approaching the five-fathom contour line a couple of miles offshore. The Commodore accepted responsibility for calling out the Lifeboat. A warning maroon was fired. The shell travelled up leaving a thin white thread, broke into a red ball, and slowly descended. The echoes of the explosion rebounded over the water. It was followed by a second maroon. The Lifeboat crew left their jobs and assembled at the slip.

An everlastingness of sliding, white-streaked slopes was passing in long roll and lip past the combing, each crest a yard or more above his eyes succeeded by a trough opening well below the combing of the gunwale. He was wet and cold. His mind forked; should he put about and make for the white water of the Race over the bar, or continue in this dreadful wallowing, with waves sometimes almost masthead-high above where he sat in the stern? Before he could decide he put the helm over and at once hung fearfully sideways on a crest, before slithering. The tiller swung idle as the sail flapped loose. Thank God he had tied the end of the sheet-rope to the ring beside him, so that the rope could be hauled in. The sail filled; bow responded to rudder, but he had shipped gallons of water. Thereafter *Scylla* was a toboggan, wallowing along a ridge, bumping into a crest, water showering past his eyes before the inevitable pitch downwards. He was going to be drowned. O God, why had he done it? He thought of Conrad's admiration for Stephen Crane's phrase in *The Open Boat*—'the waves were barbarous and abrupt.' These waves were monstrous and crashing. If only she would hold herself steady before the tip, stagger, and bump of the next wave.

Ahead of the bow lesser waves were hurtling down and spreading into a grinding bickering of white water. He pulled up the centre-board, remembering Piers' words about the shifting shingle bank during the heavy spring tides. Should he tie himself to the sheet-rope? No: if the boat rolled over he would be entangled. He must keep the sail filled, *drave* into the white water—*drove*——*Keep you a-goin'*, he heard the voice of Ned the bailiff of Skirr farm saying, *keep the ploo-point a-draving on so far as the meat soil*—the thin four-inch top-soil turning over with the share or shear. The ship ploughs the ocean. *Keep you a-goin'*! Poor Ned, was he on the dole now?

They were lurching and sliding. *Scrash!* She was hanging in a massive shower of water and pebbles. She staggered. Christ, pebbles were showing in the waves. We'll go down. Billy—Peter—Roz——

Scylla was riding, she was passing over the shingle tongue. Pebbles were rolling with the bilge over his feet. Bere Island was coming nearer. He was over the bar. The Lifeboat approached. A rope was flung. His hands were too cold and feeble to hold it. With detachment he saw the strake of *Scylla* held by a boathook. He was being pulled over the smooth side of the red and blue of the tubby white boat. Men in oilskins. Stiffness of wrapped tarpaulin. Brandy was gasp hard. Thank you. Feeble. Tears.

While he was being helped up the quay steps someone in the clubhouse poured away a quart bottle of Swan ink and filled the bottle with hot water, which was then wrapped in the cover of a cushion which had been ripped up. He felt ashamed and stammered an apology to the Commodore and thought with anguish that he had forgotten to thank the cox of the lifeboat.

He saw the girl who had crewed 'Boy' Runnymeade looking at him. When he had slept after being given hot milk and sugar and brandy, he got up and put on a tweed suit belonging to Captain Runnymeade, and went downstairs among the faces in the bar, feeling as foolish as the youth-masked old-man dancing in the Guy de Maupassant story.

In character, he insisted on driving himself home. Left the Silver Eagle with the front section of the tonneau cover unfastened against the rain. Walked with hands before him and stinging eyes half-closed—lids raw with salt—up the stairs and felt his way to his writing room.

When Lucy came in he was sitting on the couch.

"Hullo," she said.

"The sleeves are too short for me. This suit belongs to 'Boy' Runnymeade."

Her hand sought his. "You are a poor one, aren't you? Why did you do it?"

"You know, then?"

"Yes. Melissa told me on the telephone."

"Melissa?"

"Melissa Watt-Wilby. She said she recognised you from when you were in hospital at Husborne during the war."

"Lady Abeline's daughter! Good Lord!"

"I'll bring you a hot-water bottle, my man, then some hot milk."

The water-meadows were in flood, there was nothing to do. It was quieter than ever in the house by the river now that Billy had gone to the village school, wearing so proudly his father's cheap old leather satchel with its frayed and ink-stained leather.

Every morning he sat in his room, paper before him. Something was wrong with the trout story. He did not know enough about fish. He started a novel *The Irritable Man,* using his parents as characters, but the narrative was thin. He was not wholly in mind to portray his father as he had been; nor his mother; nor grandfather Thomas Turney and other faces of the past. What he had once thought of as satire, with the title of *Soot,* had become—tragic. His father had dreamed all his life of the downs and the hangers, the Longpond and the family home—and now the reality of being back was almost too much for him. The weather was partly to blame; it rained nearly every day; he could not work in the garden at Fawley. But the truth was that both he and Mother were lonely. Father missed the cinema. He was too nervous to ride in a motor-car. As for Mother, she was homesick for the old faces, she missed Doris and the two little boys, she missed Elizabeth, she even missed her occasional flutter on horses with Chamberlain the Randiswell butcher, who privately kept a book for a few of his customers.

His parents were not happy at Fawley. Hutments were being built near the spring-head which fed the Longpond. The enquiries from army officers about renting the upper and middle flats seemed to upset both his parents.

He sat at his desk, staring at the panes of glass in the casements before him. They were old and discoloured. Some were curved, flawed with bubbles and twists in the glass which distorted the trees outside. The view from the window was enclosed, for the house stood in a combe descending from a spur of the wooded Chase. Cancelled drafts of *The Irritable Man* followed scrapped pages of *The Blind Trout* into a drawer.

What could he do, where could he go? He knew every grain and crack and mark on the surface of the table; day after day and night after night he had heard the same lesser sounds about the house—the *crack-crack* of the hand-sawn oak floorboards when the hot water was turned on in the bathroom and the iron pipe along the joists expanded and tried to push up the boards; the rustling gallop of solitary rat down the interior of the wall just after half-past eight every night; the voices of small children crying 'appul' or 'bikky' or swear words which Lucy tried not to notice; the chirping of sparrows at the thatch; the dry flitter at the window of tortoiseshell butterfly regretting that it had missed some of the autumn sun; the varying notes of the van engines of newspaper man, baker, butcher, and fishmonger; the distant cawing of rooks at the October-sown corn; the voices of children coming home from school, Billy with them; the *tottle-tonk* of the African cattle-bell which called the members of the household to meals at the long oak table in the room below—the table which took five men to lift, and which Lucy kept polished by a 'secret receipt' given her by the vicar's wife.

How fortunate to be like Lucy: to accept all things as they came with an equal-mind. A mere writer saw the same walls and the same row of books every day, and the flawed grey window-panes with the dull and distorted trees on the combe-side. He saw these things as insubstantial surfaces. They were not of the real world, which for him was in his mind. He wrote, he saw, he lived in past scenes, which arose before and around him with an integrity to which he trusted. He must *trust* that other self, that scarcely-known visionary ghost which lived independently and often with torment within his being, if his work was to have any authentic life.

Billy knocked on the door. "Let me in, please, Father! Let me in!"

"Why, what's the matter, Billy?"

Billy stood before him, then pushing a grubby hand into his leather satchel he pulled out an envelope marked *Special Delivery*.

"Where did you get this?"

"Mrs. Chowles gived it me up to shop, Dad."

"Thank you, Billy. The telegraph boy usually has sixpence. Here you are."

"Thanks, Dad. Goodbye."

"You off?"

"Aye. There be some good conkers in the Lord's park. Isn't the sun lovely?"

"Yes, let's go for a walk, shall we? I must read this letter first. Wait for me downstairs, Billy."

"Yes, Father."

Ward 16
Queen Alexandra's Hospital
Marylebone Road, N.W.1 Tuesday

Dear Phillip,

I am very happy that I have a son, tho' I can't really believe it yet. He was born today, at 2 a.m. which was what I wanted, as it's a 'special' anniversary for me—three years ago I first read the Wanderer, so I fixed it, and here we are. It wasn't too bad, and very interesting and exciting. I'm sorry I couldn't write before, but my hands are still very silly and flabby, from clenching them I suppose. Will you please help me to choose a name for him—do you like any of these—

Wilfrid, Richard, Douglas, Anthony, Hubert, Gerard, Charles, Edward, Simon.

I am avoiding fancy names, but like any of these. But mind you I am still very flabby and can't think of much, so am open to any suggestions. But I shall register him while in this district—I believe a man comes round here. But I'll see.

It's hateful not to be out in this sweet sunlight of St. Martin's Little Summer. They are not very keen on fresh air here. Do you remember in the Game Pie nightclub where I imposed a piece of purple prose on you as though it was spontaneous, about the nightingales under the downs 'ringing the night with song'. I did it to impress, and now look at me. I'm a bad girl, but so happy, bless you.

It's now 8.15 a.m. and I've been up and tidy since 4.45 a.m. Not bad, after what the nurses called my little do.

Just before I came here I was in the middle of writing you a letter about a lovely walk I had the evening before. I was alone on the windy Hill with the rain coming down like aught out of a sieve, as countrymen say. All the usual crowds were in their brick boxes and only me on the grass. And I pretended that you and I had put on macs and rubber boots and were walking beside the Longpond in the moonlight and the mayflies were hatching and Major Bill Kidd was poaching trout 'of aldermanic proportions' as fast as he could pull them out, but we left him to it and returned wet with dew to Skirr farmhouse for supper by candlelight. But it was a lovely walk we had though there was no Longpond on the Hill, never mind.

For I'm very pleased with everything. Thank you for this nice present. It is a very sweet one. I must write to Lucy, I had such a sweet letter from her, full of rapture for David. (Don't be alarmed, it's her private name for him, when he deigns to come forth to greet the sun.)

Bless you, my sweetheart. I want to cry when I think of you too much, you are so very dear.

Love from
Felicity.

"I'll tell you a secret, Billy. You have another little brother."

"As well as the bastard, Father?"

He looked sharply at Billy. "Where did you get that word from?"

"From my friend Chugg Boy, Dad, you know, the one at my school you call 'Owl Eyes'." Seeing Phillip's face, Billy went on, "Have I said anything wrong, Father?"

"No, but never say that word again, will you? I'll take you in to see Mum and David now, with Peter and Roz."

On his return he sat at his table, and took the pile of unanswered letters. He must reply to them. Heavens, he hadn't even replied to the perceptive Brother Laurence. Now there was a possible friendship in the feeling of this letter. Why not send these fan letters to Felicity to reply to on his behalf? He made notes on each one, giving a suggestion of what line to take, as an editor of a newspaper proposes a particular idea for one of his leader-writers. "Phillip Maddison asks me to send his apologies for not replying personally, but he is at the moment deep in a new book——"

Then making a parcel of the letters, he put them in a drawer to post them to her when she was out and about again.

Part Two

MELISSA

Chapter 5

RENAISSANCE

In the New Year Lucy and Phillip were invited to join the Abbey dinner party for the Hunt Ball before going on to Captain Runnymeade, who had lent the Castle.

"Do you think I should accept, Lucy? I suppose they know about Felicity——"

"Why not? After all, it isn't as though you've behaved badly towards her."

'Boy' Runnymeade had written to Phillip asking him and his wife to stay the night, and saying that he would be happy to provide them both with mounts for the meet the following day. So Rippingall put Phillip's top boots, boned and polished in their trees, into the back of the car, with his ratcatcher coat and breeches, before they drove to what locally was known as the big house.

There they were the first guests to arrive. The Abelines were still dressing, so while the housekeeper took Lucy upstairs, Phillip was left in the smoking room. There Abeline joined him, appearing round the door suddenly in a grotesque mask. Phillip hardly knew his landlord. The usual cards had been left by Julia. Later, after a return call, they had been invited to luncheon. And once again with the two boys to tea, with other neighbours and their children, on Christmas afternoon.

Lord Abeline was the second baron. His father, an industrialist, had represented his Liberal constituency for a score of years under Gladstone before being raised to the peerage. His son had inherited the foundries and shops on forty acres in the Black Country, and kept away from them ever since, preferring to live as a country gentleman with his own pack of hounds. Since the war and increased taxation the Hunt had been taken over by a Committee which allowed him, as Master, two thousand pounds a year to hunt the country.

To Phillip, he did not look like a Master of Foxhounds, he lacked the healthy, lean brown face; the spare frame, the keen eye. He had a big, rather pale face, and was going bald; his body seemed soft.

"Help yourself to a drink, Maddison."

While Phillip poured a tot of whisky the host was opening a drawer in a desk, his back to him. When he turned round his face was covered by another leering mask, from which came sounds of self-scoffing, which made Phillip think that he was not altogether sure of himself.

"You quite startled me, sir. It was so realistic."

"What about this one?"

A fat jolly face peered at him. It was succeeded by others, all more or less macabre.

"Look out of the window, will you, until I tell you to turn round? Don't draw the curtains, just open them a bit." Phillip looked at the leaded casement. Nothing beyond the black diamond panes was visible. He heard rustling behind him, and when told he could look, saw a simpering face with protruding teeth and yellow curls above a black Victorian bombazine dress. The figure pirouetted around the room in the manner of a stage Charley's Aunt. A memory of a picture in an illustrated weekly, years before, made Phillip remark on the likeness to the actor Brandon-Thomas.

"You like it, what?"

"Very much."

"Will you take me into dinner, if I put on a bodice and skirt?"

Phillip pretended to laugh, embarrassed by the feeling behind the foolery.

His host got out of the costume, and having pulled his nose as if to narrow the nostrils, rubbed his hands together.

The butler entered to say guests were arriving. Among them were Piers and his wife. Julia was already there to greet them; and beside her, standing back a little, was a young girl whose face and carriage of head upon a long neck rising from a small white wrap, or shawl, upon the shoulders, was immediately arresting. She seemed more grown-up than the girl who had passed in 'Boy' Runnymeade's yacht when he went over the bar and had to be rescued. So this was the child who had sat beside him in the brougham during a drive in the park at Husborne Abbey, before he had removed the bandages around his eyes after the mustard gas at Byron Farm below Wytschaete ridge in 1918. Yes, it was the same honey-coloured hair, the same large, china-blue eyes, curve of mouth, strong chin. She was smiling, her eyes lowered as he went to Lady Abeline, who having given him a smile of what looked like candid pleasure, said, "You remember Melissa?"

Having shaken his hostess's hand, he turned to the young girl to feel the calm gaze of her eyes going into him and taking his secret self into the air about her smiling lips.

At dinner he sat beside her, refusing all but one glass of wine. He felt calm and poised beyond himself. Was she going to dance? he dared to ask. Oh yes, she replied, for a little while, until twelve o'clock.

Neglecting Lucy, he had the first dance with her. Afterwards she led him up the stairs. The moon in its second quarter seen through glass above the Castle battlements was serene. Clouds moved in from the Channel.

"May I have the next dance?"

Again she was within the oval of his arm, hardly touching, feather-light on her feet and head held high, dancing to the *Saxophone Rhapsody*. He thought of Felicity and her baby: that disaster would follow and an aching heart: but O glorious, glorious —dance on, dance on——

"Where shall we sit? Or would you like some fresh air? There's a good view from the battlements, but perhaps you might catch cold?"

"Oh, I never catch cold. In fact I don't feel the cold any more."

"I don't feel the cold either. I have a cold tub every morning at school and at home."

"Are you still at school?"

"It will be my last term."

They went on the roof, by the way of stone steps. The night lay in an unearthly silver stillness below them. She wanted to tell him that she had loved *The Water Wanderer,* and that sometimes when she was swimming she thought herself into the form of an otter, but it might sound pretentious.

They returned to the ballroom. The third dance had not begun. "Have you seen the orchid house? I thought I saw Daddy taking Lucy there."

How tactful she was. "I must dance with Lucy. But first with your mother."

"Mummy would love it, you are so light on your feet."

The band started. Lady Abeline was dancing with Captain Runnymeade. Lucy and Phillip fox-trotted together round the floor.

"Are you happy, Lulu?"

"Oh yes. But my legs are still inclined to ache a little, after David. It's my silly veins."

"Let's sit out, it's warm in the orchid house."

Lucy said what he thought was rather a strange thing.

"Don't you think Melissa is beautiful?"

"She reminds me of one of Rodin's white marble figures come alive. How long have you known her?"

"Oh, I saw her first at a children's party at Grannie's house years ago. We're sort of cousins once removed, something like that. Pa knows all about relations and connexions, it's a hobby of his." She could see that Phillip was still anxious when he said to her,

"Do you think the Abelines will have heard about Felicity?"

"Even if they had, I don't suppose they'd bother one way or the other."

Lucy had felt more about Felicity than she had admitted; but then, she told herself, the girl had not been at all happy when she came. Also, Phillip had had a lot of worry from Uncle Hilary. But in her heart she was sad, with a feeling of her own inadequacy; almost a sense of failure.

Supper at midnight, and Melissa must go to bed. She was not very strong, and went away to have a bowl of bread and milk with meat extract and glucose, in her room. Afterwards she lay in bed, on her back and breathing quietly, evenly, her eyes closed, hands folded over her bosom, ankles crossed in the posture of a figure carved in stone, but breathing slowly, calmly, feeling herself almost to be levitated by his image.

Phillip stood at the champagne buffet with Piers.

"You've made a hit with Melissa."

"Oh no, surely not."

"Watch out for George Abeline. He has a jealous eye."

"I wonder why he puts on those masks?"

"He was the only boy among too many sisters. He likes bathing young girls, and photographing them naked. All the signs of an artist *manqué*. How's Felicity?"

"I had a letter from her mother's solicitors telling me to keep away."

"That let's you out, anyway."

"I must go to Lucy."

"May I come too? I'm very fond of Lucy."

They found her sitting with their host in a room looking like a museum. There was a long buffet table displaying gold plate.

"Is this the museum, or the salon?" he asked.

"We're not frenchified here, we call this the saloon," Captain Runnymeade replied heavily. "Help yourself to some salmon-trout, 'Farm Boy'."

"That fish, 'Horse Boy'," retorted Phillip, "we call a sea-trout."

"*Touché,* 'Farm Boy'. Jerry, give Mr. Maddison some wine."

Towards one o'clock Lucy said she felt tired, and slipped away up the stairs, followed by Phillip, who wanted to remember where their room was, for when he should go up later. Seeing him going up, George Abeline called out in a semi-scoffing voice, "Don't you let him go into Melissa's bed by mistake, Lucy."

"I won't," cried Lucy, as she waited to take Phillip's arm. Along the landing she said, "George is like that to everyone, so don't take any notice. Well, my man," she said at the door, "I'll see you later. Don't let Runnymeade give you any more to drink, will you?"

Phillip went up as five o'clock was striking on the stable clock. He managed to find the throne, and after a long time upon his knees, crept back to Lucy's bed.

"Did you bring any salts, Lucy? Thank God."

He could eat no breakfast. The meet was at eleven. He hadn't ridden a hunter for nearly ten years, and was nervous. The sight of Melissa, cool and upright, in bowler, breeches, and short dark West of England jacket like himself, made him further regret that he and Piers and 'Boy' Runnymeade had stayed up to play snooker, and drink, good fun as it was.

Hounds moved off; Master and field followed. A fox was found in the first covert. The *Gone Away* seemed to panic brightly. Bits jingled as hunters threw up heads, eager to gallop but held back at a canter. Beyond the park and across ploughed work, clots of earth flung up from hooves. It was a bold fox, stole-bred, he heard someone say, and was away into the east towards the distant pines on the ridge, below which lay a sandy land of heath and scrub, scene of Hardy's *Return of the Native,* he had been told by Lord Abeline.

It was hard going; he sweated much; the gelding was used to a side-saddle, he thought, it had a screwy action, which shook him even when sitting down at the canter. Perhaps it was too much corned up? He galloped, and passed Melissa; bore back on the horse's mouth, and felt a stab in his back, as though the spine had been pierced by a splinter of glass. He was forced to ride half standing in the irons while holding his breath. He dropped behind, one of a long column of riders now extended across the heath. By the severity of the pain he thought he had torn a muscle.

He made his mount trot, then walk, as he watched Melissa disappear among the pines on the skyline. The horse was lathered; he cursed the image of Captain Runnymeade, who must have put him on this dud nag for one of his heavy-handed jokes. When the horse stopped he spurred it, but the rowels had been filed down, and the animal remained still. Then without warning it kicked its hindlegs into the air, and losing gas, broke into a lumbering trot, flinging out its forelegs as though it had been trained to draw a fast gig in a trotting race.

The fox had been killed when he arrived to see dismounted riders eating sandwiches and talking. Melissa was laughing with two young men, who looked as though they were more used to tanks than horses. He saw her looking his way out of the corner of an eye, and pretended to withdraw into himself.

He became suddenly happy, the crick in his back forgotten, when she walked to where he stood by his now patient mount.

"You look so cool," he said.

"Do you play badminton? Do come along, we've got a room fitted up over the old stables. How's your back?"

"How did you know I'd ricked it?"

"By the way you were holding your breath. I suppose I should add, 'Jolly sporting of you to carry on like that, old boy.' Did you sleep well?"

"Hardly at all."

"Oh, bad luck."

"I drank too much."

"You weren't the only one."

The huntsman and whips were mounting. A groom approached leading her hunter.

"Don't forget next Wednesday afternoon," she said. "Badminton in the old stables," and lifting a foot, allowed herself to be thrown into the saddle.

Lucy had already gone home, so after poached eggs on muffins he said goodbye and left, thinking to give up this pleasant social life, and really begin the trout book. Melissa's image filled his mind with grace. After a cold bath, despite the pain in his back, he sat before the sitting-room hearth in dressing gown and slippers, while Lucy with needle and thread went over a pile of baby long-clothes, neatly folding them away after examination and repair.

"We're asked to play badminton on Wednesday. I don't think I'll go."

"Oh, won't you? Melissa will be disappointed."

"What makes you think that?"

"She likes you, I could see that at once. She's your sort, I think."

"I've never played badminton."

"You'll soon pick it up. It's only a sort of tennis. Lots of local people go. They play in the old stables."

He bought a racquet and went along, to see a number of elderly parsons with their wives.

One man present who introduced himself as Becket Scrimgeour, the younger brother of the rector, was as open and friendly as the vicar was closed and withdrawn. He and Phillip got on well, and Becket asked if he might come and see him.

"Yes, do, any time."

They played as partners. Phillip soon got his eye in, after one game under the electric lights. On the side-board was a tea-urn, with plates of split scones daubed with cream and jam. He missed Melissa: but perhaps she would appear with her mother to preside over tea. But no; when the time came a parson's wife took charge of the urn, filling it with water from two kettles heated over oil stoves. They took turns every week, it was explained to him. Then Julia Abeline came up the stairs, and joined them as they sat round the table. She said brightly that Melissa had caught a chill after the meet, and was in bed. He wondered if this was an excuse, and perhaps a hint; and her absence on the following Wednesday seemed to confirm what Piers had told him of her father's jealous eye. But no; the daughter of the house had merely invited him as she would have asked anyone else who had mentioned the need for exercise. He wrote a letter to her, thanking her for the invitation to play badminton, and telling her about his perplexity over the trout book. How could it be cast? In what form?

It rained all the next day. The interior of the house was gloomy; always the fringe of thatch seemed to be dripping. Abruptly his outlook brightened and he felt himself to be young again, after a letter in a strange, firm handwriting.

Dear Cousin Phillip,

How I wish I could write something helpful and intelligent about trout and running water—alas, I am not gifted. I often think of that night when we all went to a dance at 'Horse Boy's' after dining at home, and I had to say goodbye to you at midnight, like Cinderella. I was brimming with love, completely undesigning, naïve, *unthinking*. It didn't impinge on my mind that I could be hurting Lucy. I *felt*; I was sensitive to all others, somehow you gave a focal point to what the French call *sensibilité*. At least that's how I see that evening.

I hope it's not the wrong thing to say to an author, but your Donkin novels, and *The Water Wanderer*, how fine they are. I cannot praise them too highly, they are beautiful. They are wonderful, all the scenes and characters so true, every page full of grace. Can you wonder that I fell at your feet, because it was you that opened my eyes to beauty.

Dearest Phillip, you were so very sweet and vulnerable at that dinner and dance. In an aerial way: no demands, no possessiveness, no words, you seemed completely mine. I expect you saw a schoolgirl's crush on my face, but how could you have known what was in my heart. Yet you have been here since I was a small child sitting beside you in the brougham in the park at Uncle Bohun's long ago in the war. When first I saw your eyes, after the bandages had been taken off, your look went right down inside me.

With love, Melissa.

P.S. Captain Runnymeade is quite bucked by being called 'Horse Boy'. He said to me, 'I believe Farm Boy likes me.' I told him of course you did, so did we all.

In February Phillip, who had revised the scenes of river, estuary, and sea-coast for his book, had the copies returned by Felicity.

Dearest,

Here are the landscape, riverscape, and seascape scenes, and wonderful they are, too. I am certain that the book, when you have woven in the story of the Blind Trout, will be a great success. The typing of them has been a great relief to my mind, perturbed otherwise by petty worries. I hope you will not allow them to distract you, but I think I should let you know that my mother is determined to adopt my baby, because I am still a minor, I suppose, and in her eyes in need of 'care and protection'. So I went up to Somerset House to ask about adoption, and got the enclosed printed reply.

I wrote asking if they could tell me if it meant much publicity, in a public court, etc., as I had been told by the Registrar at Marylebone that it was a simple matter, and they replied that they could not tell me about this, and I would be advised to ask the Clerk to the local court. Would you like to write to the Clerk (at Marylebone I suppose) or would you rather do it yourself when next you are in London, just to find out what the procedure is, as I imagine you would not care for a public business. I am sorry to bother you, but I thought that you and Lucy might want to adopt him after what you said about the registration of twins, but please just say yes or no. Of course I would make the enquiry quite impersonal, not mentioning any names or revealing that it concerns me personally.

Love to you both, Felicity.

P.S. My mother's idea in adopting Edward is, I think, to leave me legally free of him should I want to marry later on. What do you think about it? I am rather confused, and personally want to keep my baby, but perhaps my mother's way will be best for him in the end, if you do not like the idea (as you once expressed) of you and Lucy adopting him. Do say exactly what you feel about it, dearest.

Phillip went to see his solicitor in Colham. He asked what he, as father of the child, could do to stop its adoption against the wishes of both its parents. The solicitor said he would seek counsel's opinion, and then would write to Phillip. This opinion arrived three days later.

Re. An unmarried mother's dilemma to retain her infant while she is a minor.

Under the Administration of Justice Act, 1928, the guiding principle laid down is that of the welfare of the infant. Any proposals of the putative father must be considered to the extent that they contribute to that welfare. His position as putative father might enable him to urge recognition, in the child's interests, of the ties of blood and natural affection, but it does no more for him than that. So strong, but no stronger, is his position in equity, and he has no further rights, whether against the mother or third persons. So it comes down to this: the Court will consider if adoption is in the interests of the child, not because it is the putative father's proposal, but *per se.*

Deciding that it would be better to let his mother know about this natural child of his, Phillip wrote and told her. He asked her to respect the confidence, because 'there is no point in upsetting other people'. He meant his father. Hetty, in distress, replied in a scrawled note in pencil.

Dear Phillip,

I can hardly tell you what horror and grief your letter has caused me, I cannot believe a son of mine would let down his young wife and children in this fashion, also I cannot understand why you should have brought her to Wakenham. It is such a hole-and-corner business, and what about Lucy? I have always been so fond of her. What is she going to do? No wonder she has not written to me. And she has no Mother! I think of your last school report, do you remember the remark of the Magister, 'His standard of honour should be raised?' Well, Phillip, on consideration I have decided to keep your secret but I hope it won't be for long. Why doesn't 'she' go to some of her own people?

Your Mother.

Phillip drove Felicity, baby in arms, to the windmill on Reynard's Common. There was a cottage to be let in the hamlet, advertised in *The Lady*. It was built of red brick and had a small garden. Rambler roses grew over a decayed wooden porch. Felicity got the key from a neighbour. They lit a fire of sticks in the small brick hearth in the parlour. Smoke in skeins drifted out into the room. Obviously the chimney was blocked, perhaps by a jack-daw's nest. They made rolls of newspapers and thrusting them up the chimney set fire to the base. More smoke poured down. He opened the window, and a pane of glass fell out, the putty having cracked and loosened. Suddenly the chimney roared and going outside he enjoyed the sight of an accelerating column of smoke ending in a burst of flame and shower of sparks ending in a minor explosion which burst the chimney pot and sent pieces rattling down the tiles. Neighbours had come out to watch.

"Anyway the next tenant won't require a sweep."

The kitchen was dark and dirty. Wallpaper curled away from cracked plaster. Sooty cobwebs drooped. There was an outhouse with a copper for boiling clothes, an earth closet at the bottom of the garden almost hidden by docks, burdocks, thorn-apples, and deadly nightshade.

"A warlock must have lived here."

"I'll do it up, and soon have the garden cleared and dug over. That is, if you approve." She stopped herself adding "dearest".

"Well, it's your cottage, if you'll allow me to arrange the rent and reconditioning. Let's go and have some bread and cheese and beer in the Greyhound."

Ale and cheese with bread and pickled shallots put heart into them. Phillip paid £5, half a year's rent. Then upstairs again, and looking closer at the two small bedrooms. One had a cast-iron grate.

"The very place for my favourite author."

"I wonder how much the whole place will cost to have done up?"

"I shall earn it. And do some of the work myself."

"I hope you won't lose heart."

She wanted to say, Darling, let me be your heart, and then I shall never again lose mine, but she said bravely, "I'll never lose my heart again."

"I wish I could say the same thing."

"Oh darling, I wish I were the right one for you."

"You're a good friend to me, Felicity."

"Let's find out if there's a mason in the hamlet, shall we?"

"All right. The ground floor, at least, must be made waterproof before you can move in. Walls replastered where loose, after hacking off the old plaster. It's loam and cowdung, by the look of it." He wrenched off a cracked slab, it fell with a thud. "Now for that mason."

An out-of-work mason would start at once. He would keep the score, he said, by the hour. Could they provide the materials—cement, and hair-plaster? Sand was local, in the pits on the common, he would get that. "I've got me tradesman's tools." They motored into the town and returned with distemper in tins, a brush, a couple of sacks of cement, seven pounds of Medusa porcelain dust for water-proofing, a pail and shovel. That would do for a start.

Felicity enquired of the mason if he knew of a bedroom to let. The mason said his wife had such a room. After seeing and approving this, Felicity said, "I'll hire a bicycle, and go about looking for furniture at local auctions. It will be fun."

He unloaded cot, blankets, and other gear, and carried them into the downstairs room.

"I'll get the cot over to the mason's cottage" she said, hoping that he would want to stay with her.

When the unloading was done he said, "I nearly forgot. I've got some fan letters for you to reply to. You'll find directions inside the parcel."

"Before you go, may we have one more look upstairs, all three of us together?" She held her face near the baby. He saw that she was crying.

"It's dull weather now everywhere," he said.

"Oh, Phillip, I'm a silly girl, but I shan't be able to bear it if, you leave me."

He tried to comfort her, putting an arm around her, while supporting the baby with the other. "I'll always be your friend, Felicity."

"Then there *is* someone else?"

"Not in the sense of an affair. And anyway, I'm tied, whether I like it or not, to my work."

"I wish I could be of more help to you."

"You are closer to my work, which is the real me, than anyone else I know."

"Truly?"

"Yes."

"Cross your heart?"

"Of course you are."

She looked so young and bright-eyed that he kissed her. She put down the sleeping child and clung to him.

"Darling, you are so sweet. Please forgive my base suspicions. If I lost you, I think I should not want to live."

"What about Edward?"

"I'm being a selfish girl, darling. I'm all morbid and stupid today. Won't you stay the night? You look so tired."

He stayed. He was happy for twelve hours. Then restlessness. He returned to Monachorum.

The snowdrops had gone to seed, the primroses were withered. Throughout the lengthening days of high cirrus and falling blossom, the throbbing notes of turtle doves came from the downland thorns as though the very flints upon the uncultivated arable were crying for love, Phillip felt, as he walked over the fields of his lost land. Even the nightingales' songs coming from many points under the line of the downs were a reproach. Through his head ran again and again a line from Marlowe. *And what is beauty saith my sufferings then.*

At the moment Richard had no such feelings.

"I'm another man, Phillip."

Richard drew pleasure from meticulous sowings, from the straight rows of eschalots, lettuces, onions, carrots, and brassica seedlings. Morning after morning he spent within the walled acre. With loving care he avoided giving distress to the various small birds which had their nests about the secluded garden—goldfinch in fork of apple bush—whitethroat in the black-currants—nightingale among the nettles beyond one of his squared compost heaps—swallow on a purlin across the rafters of the potting shed—wren in the sleeve of an old jacket—blue titmouse in a hole in the wall against which an espalier pear had been planted a year before.

Billy knew them too, sharing the secret with 'Dickie'. Richard felt complimented, he told Hetty, on being accepted as an equal by the small boy, his grandson.

"A child of love. Look at his shining morning face." He went on, "And to think that we owe our presence here to 'the wild boy'."

This unexpected reference to Phillip delighted Hetty.

"Ah well, it all turned out for the best."

"When is he returning, do you know? I understand that he went to Wakenham recently, to write his book on a trout."

"Oh yes, Dickie, I had a letter this morning."

"Did you, b'jabers." Richard had revived, for Billy's benefit, some of the slang of his boyhood. "Still moving about, is he? What a restless creature he is; just the same when he was in the army. Well, what did he say, old girl? Or was it something private between you and your best boy?"

Hetty hesitated. She had ever been a dissembler, for the sake of peace; but now she was unable to say anything. As a fact, even the thought of Dickie seeing the letter was bringing on one of her bilious headaches. Phillip had written to say that he was going to live alone in his field above Malandine in South Devon.

"I put the letter down somewhere. How silly of me to mislay it."

"I expect it came from Hillside Road? I've half a mind, old girl, to go up and see how things are up there. The trouble is, I ought not to leave this blessed garden just now."

When Hetty had gone into the house the thought came to him, Who was there to eat all the vegetables he had grown in the shelter of garden walls? One of the flats, he understood, had been let to an engineer officer who was due to arrive any day now to supervise the building of new hutments on the old war-time site beside the Longpond. Lorries had already driven up, making ugly tracks in the grass, with bricks and other building materials. Only the previous afternoon, when he walked up the borstal to the Hanger, drawn by the sunshine of a still day, he came upon a gang of men with a tractor in the act of rooting up, with winch and wire rope, the hazel and ash stoles of the Coppice. Richard was told that there was to be a machine-gun firing range, and here the butts were to be built.

"Hetty, it is simply awful what they are going to do. The entire countryside will be ruined. Well, I suppose we've got to face it. I'll run up to town tomorrow and see how things are getting on at Number Eleven, Hillside Road."

Felicity was sitting at a three-legged cricket table she had bought at auction for half-a-crown. A candle was burning in a battered brass candlestick on the table. No curtain was drawn across the casement window. It was a warm night, owls were calling.

Felicity felt extraordinarily happy. In fact, she told herself, she had never really been happy in her life before.

Her novel was flowing. She lived in its scenes, which were more vivid to her than anything in 'real' life, except Edward her son, sleeping in his cot beside her; and the man in the room adjoining her own, whose gentle breathing was audible. She told herself that now her life had suddenly changed, and so completely that never again would she think about Phillip other than as a friend.

My heart has come back to me, she said to herself, as she sat at the cricket table, pen in hand, living in the images of words written in pencil upon the pages of a ledger souvenir'd from the B.B.C. when she had been one in the pool of typists at Savoy Hill. She felt slightly nervous every night when beginning to write, even anguished, for it was the story of a young woman who fell in love with a married man, whose personality the heroine was not able to share. Even when her heroine was in bed with her lover, she knew he was thinking of a younger, prettier and more enchanting girl than herself. The heroine's feelings were further complicated because she wondered if she ought to try to make him passionate by action taught to her by the elderly man who had seduced her at the age of fourteen; but she was unable to bring herself to act thus, there was something forbidding in her lover's attitude to sex.

The heroine's seducer had taught her to enter his bed at the foot, between the sheets, to move slowly up while kissing and caressing his body until she had drawn herself to his lips, to enter his mouth with her tongue. But the heroine was unable to act thus with her lover, although she believed still what she had been taught as a young girl 'with one petal out', in the words of her seducer, who had told her about the need of a man for stimulation which, he had declared, was the woman's natural function in courtship.

So the heroine was confused; as had been the authoress until recently, believing that Phillip was afraid of natural love: a fear originating from an act of his father's in thrashing the young boy at the age of seven years for wanting to examine his sister's body under the nursery table. And inevitably, later on, he had found emotional refuge, or desolation, in Wagner's *Tristan*.

And so, despairing that her true love would ever love her—never lose that part of him which had turned to stone—Felicity's heroine had yielded herself, in abandonment of her dream of true love, to her original seducer, while imagining him, in bed with her, to be the hero: one who was possessed by the essences of the war-dead. Those haunted eyes, when first her heroine had met him, had made her long to cherish him and bring back all the sunshine that he had missed in his youth upon the battlefields of the Western Front. And the Great War was the epitome of lovelessness in Western Civilisation. This was a sub-theme of her novel. Her heroine saw herself as Persephone leading one back to life from the gentian-blue halls of Dis, in D. H. Lawrence's last poem before he died at Vence in the south of France.

Often the heroine had cried voicelessly to herself, in the loneliness of the nights in her cottage in the village of Lavenham in Suffolk (which Felicity had known as a child, when her father had been with her mother). At times her lover seemed to be struggling spiritually against the love which she wanted to give him: a circumstance which had had the effect, at times, of giving her physical cramps which blighted her spirit. And having sighed through so many lonely periods, at last Felicity's heroine had given in to the pleas of the one she tried to make herself believe was a kind and fatherly man.

It's no good, Felicity said to herself, it's sentimentality. I would never have gone back to Fitz. I'll scrap it all, and recast it as a straight autobiography, and publish it under another name, while using made-up place-names. Besides, if ever Mother found out about Fitz, it would kill her. What shall I do?

She felt depressed, and lit a cigarette. She was about to go downstairs to make herself a cup of tea when she heard the noise of a motorcar coming up the lane. She blew out the candle-flame and listened by the open window. The motorcar had stopped by the gate.

Peering out, she saw the low outline of Phillip's sports-car. Her blood seemed to gush into her head, making her dizzy for a moment. She managed to whisper, "I'll come down and let you in."

At the door he said, "Are you alone?"

"I was writing upstairs."

"I saw you blow out the candle."

He held her and buried his face in her neck. She felt relief, but restrained herself. "You're cold, come in, and sit down. I'll light a fire. I've got some kindling drying beside the hearth."

This was soon blazing.

"Are you hungry?"

"I am rather."

"I'll do some eggs and bacon for you."

She filled a cast-iron kettle from a jug and with a fire-pic hung it on an iron crook. "I got this from an antique shop the other day."

While he was eating hungrily, she said, "Well, this is a pleasant surprise. What brings you here?"

"My father came up unexpectedly, and found Elizabeth and Doris at home. He left again without a word. I suppose he was bound to find out, sooner or later."

"He'll get over it. Would you like tea, or coffee?"

"Oh, tea, please." He ate in silence. At last he said, "Is there anything the matter?"

"Why should there be anything the matter?"

"You seem changed."

"I am changed, Phillip."

He sat still, looking at the fire. After a while he said, "In what way?"

"I suppose I've grown up."

"And grown out of me. Yes, I ought to have known it would happen. You had an illusion about me, which I couldn't live up to."

"Perhaps it was that," she said. "But I am still very fond of you, Phillip. And shall always be grateful for the way you have helped me."

"Or hindered you, and used you."

"I think I used you."

He finished the meal somehow. "Then you are going back to Fitz?"

"Are you making any progress with Melissa—your Isolde?"

"You're more real to me than Isolde. In Wagner's opera everything happens in the mind."

"Ah! You say that because you haven't slept with Melissa."

He wanted to leave. Had she gone back to Fitz? She was transferring her own feelings to him.

"I was going to write to you, Phillip——"

"All right, give it me straight. There's someone else?"

"Not in the way you mean," she replied, sitting beside him and taking his hand. "Do you remember sending me those fan letters to reply to?"

"Yes. I suppose one of them came to see you?" he said, not believing what he said. Even so, he was shocked when she replied, "Yes, someone did, Phillip."

"And you've fallen in love with him?"

"Not fallen in love, no. I love him. Do you remember Brother Laurence?" She took a deep breath. "He is my father."

"Do you know, I had an idea—vaguely—of something like that when I had that letter from him? He must have come to Monachorum to find you. And on that day I screamed at you—over those sandshoes."

"I was a very foolish girl in those days. Poor you, it was an awful shock——"

"Where is Brother Laurence now?"

"Sleeping in the spare bedroom. Oh, Phillip, he is so sweet! I can never forgive my mother for telling me he was killed in the war."

"Your mother must have been dreadfully unhappy."

"So was I. I used to cry myself to sleep."

"Perhaps she didn't want you to feel different from the other girls at school."

"She was thinking only of herself!"

He said reflectively, "Horatius holding the bridge alone until it became a habit—unable to be relieved—and an orthodox Christian, never again to be free from guilt because of her own falsehood."

"But he was *my* father, as well as her husband! All those years I felt incomplete—not like the other girls in the office—because they had fathers and I didn't. Don't you *see,* Phillip?"

He stood up. "Well, I'm so glad, Felicity," he said with a suggestion of formality. "Now I must be getting back."

"But you can't go at this time of night! All that long way to Monachorum. I simply won't allow it," she declared, with assumed gaiety. She put her arms round his chest, and laid her head against the rough tweed jacket, swaying gently, as though to soothe a child. "Come, darling, sit down by the fire, and rest that weary head."

She sat at his feet, her arms round his knees, resting her own head. This was not comfortable, so she got upon his lap and with arms round his neck kissed first one eyelid then the other, and descending with light kisses on each cheek-bone, she gave him a gentle kiss on his lips, saying, "Bless you. There now, lie in this chair, while I make up a bed on the couch."

When the bed was made up she lay beside him and stroked his hair. He turned to her and laid his cheek against her neck so that she felt the soft hair of his head against her cheek, gentle upon her flesh like a little boy's hair. She felt tenderness.

"How Barley must have loved you." She sighed. "So must Melissa. You belong to one another, my dear."

"I love you, too."

After tucking him up she went upstairs to her room, thinking joyfully, Now I can see how my novel should go. But this afflatus departed with her excitation. An inner dullness returned. This, too, went in the morning light when she saw how Phillip and her father took to one another. She felt a richness in her living, she was happy at last.

Chapter 6

RESURGENCE

Richard returned, after walking from the Halt with steady stride and tense face, in the late evening. He said nothing of what was on his mind, avoiding all his wife's hesitant questions, until it was his time to go to bed.

"I don't know what your wishes are in the matter of remaining here, Hetty, but I intend to leave in two weeks' time, at the quarter day, and return to live out my days at Wakenham."

"Oh dear, is anything the matter, Dickie?"

"You should know the answer to that question. I'll say good-night," and with that he went to his bedroom.

After trying in vain to read his newspaper, he went to her room, knocked on the door, and at the threshold said, "I should like one matter to be made clear. Did you—or did you not—help, or advise, or help to procure in any way—the presence of Elizabeth and Mrs. Willoughby at the house I particularly lent Phillip for his own use?"

This was the old Wakenham Dickie speaking, the side of him which she hoped had gone for ever. The tone of voice was higher.

"I am waiting for an answer."

"Oh no—well, you see—I really can't say, Dickie."

Richard had held to the illusion of all being changed in his life while he had been at Rookhurst, despite disappointment over what he had anticipated, with a feeling almost of the renewal of his youth, that his son would prove to be the friend and companion he had always lacked since, at the age of seventeen, he had gone to London: that together they would follow the old paths he had walked with John and Hilary—perhaps even so far as the Chase—that sunlit tract of down and woodland which had lived in his memory as a symbol of unclouded childhood.

As he lay in bed unmoving he said to himself, I am a broken man, I might as well be dead.

Some places, equally with some incidents, retain throughout life a power of illusion which determines the personality. In this, both father and son were alike. The continuity of both lives had been broken in early youth: Richard's by the extravagances of his father, by which the base of life, the land, was lost: Phillip's by the obliteration of the country adjoining London. In those woods, along those paths through field and heath which he had followed in boyhood, often alone, Phillip had experienced an ecstasy, a joy of living, which was now lost under bricks and mortar in row upon row of little houses, killing the land, mortifying the spirit of love.

Hetty met her son at the door, with a smile to hide her dread. "It's Phillip, Dickie."

"Good morning, Phillip. I'd like a word with you in private in the smoking room, if you please. Hetty, will you kindly allow us to be alone."

The door of dark oak closed. Hetty hovered in the passage, then went to her boudoir to sponge the leaves of her aspidistra—that faithful friend, as she thought of the fern, which had been with her ever since the early days of her marriage. Things will be all right, she thought to the lank dark leaves.

Richard began formally. "Well, Phillip, first I must thank you for coming to see me so promptly upon receipt of my letter."

"I've just arrived from London, and came over to see you at once, sir. May I say one thing now—please believe me when I say that your feelings are more important to me than my own." When his father did not reply he went on, "You lent your house to me, and I lent it to others. That is inexcusable. Father, I must offer you my sincere apology."

"What?"

There was another pause, then Richard said, "Oh well, old chap, let us say no more about it."

Made curious and apprehensive by the unexpected silence at the end of the passage, Hetty left the aspidistra and went on tiptoe to the smoking-room door. The silence continued. Then she heard Dickie's voice saying, "There now, Phillip—no harm has been done. Let me offer you a glass of sherry."

"Thank you, Father."

Hetty went back to her boudoir, in tears of thankfulness.

"Well, old chap, I have a confession to make to you. After all your consideration and kindness—well, I won't beat about the bush—but the fact is, Phillip, I find the garden too big for me. I have thoroughly enjoyed the work, but, all things considered, I fancy I ought to think of giving it up.

"You see," he went on, "I can't bear to think of what those fellows are doing beside the Longpond, putting up huts again, as though the war were still on."

"I feel the same, Father." Phillip finished his sherry. "I don't want to be argumentative, but in a way the war is still on."

"I agree with you, Phillip. It's those Prussians, thinking again in terms of world domination. I tell you, we should have gone on to Berlin in nineteen nineteen. I don't like the look of that fellow Hitler, with his ideas based on revenge. The old Prussian spirit that destroyed my mother's family, the von Föhres of Württemberg, is active again. 'Those junkers will deceive you yet,' I remember Castleton in *The Daily Trident* repeating that over again and again before the Treaty of Versailles."

"I remember it, Father." Phillip, to avoid an argument about the war—father torn between his English and German blood—went on hastily to say, "I suppose it's never any good going back. I went to Reynards' Common recently, and on the way passed the new housing estate between Cutler's Pond and Brumley, built on the Seven Fields of Shrofften. That's where I first awakened to the beauty of the country."

"I knew it when there were pheasants among the turnips, in the fields by Whitefoot Lane, Phillip. Your mother and I had our honeymoon in the keeper's cottage at the edge of one of the woods there, or shaws, as they were called."

"I know, those long strips between some of the fields. I used to take my Bloodhound patrol of Boy Scouts there, in the years just before the war."

"I used to bicycle there, on my 'Sunbeam', Phillip. You and I used to go to the Fishponds together, do you remember? They were jolly days."

"Yes, Father."

Hetty knocked at the door.

"Come in, come in," cried Richard, jovially. "Phillip and I are talking of old times. He has recently been on Reynard's Common, of our bicycling days before the war. Looking round for local colour, no doubt, Phillip? I suppose," he continued shyly, "you would not care for a walk together on the downs, so that we could, as it were, see out the last of the old order together?"

"I'd love it, Father. I really would."

"Are you sure you can spare the time?"

"Of course, Father."

"Phillip and I, Hetty, have a feeling in common that Fawley has outlived its usefulness. What do you think? I find the large garden becoming too much for me, and you, I fancy, will not be averse to returning to Wakenham, now that Lucy and Phillip have moved to Monachorum. I thought you would be relieved, old girl. Phillip, too, as I have said, feels the same way."

"I thought of selling the house, Mother."

"Oh, wouldn't that be a pity, Phillip?"

"If the war comes again, Mother, as cousin Willie prophesied, all this area will become a tank practising area, with live shell and England under martial law. As I'm still on the reserve I'll go back again to the army."

And be killed this time, he thought.

"How about tomorrow for our walk, Father? I'll bring sandwiches for us both, and some ale."

"Yes, tomorrow will suit me, Phillip. I don't know if you have any ideas, but my father, when we were boys, used to take us along what he always considered to be an extension, or possibly a switch, of the Roman road between Bath and the harbour where you have your yacht club. Shall you use your motor, for part of the way?"

"Anything you like, Father."

"If you don't mind going slowly, old man—I'm not used to them, remember. Well, as I was saying, my father used to tell us that the Romans liked to keep well above us, in order to see the surrounding country, and any hostile Saxon troops. We could, if you agree, start near the springhead feeding the Longpond, and walk due north—here is the route, marked in indelible pencil by my father, God bless my soul all those years ago—I can see him pointing out the route now, in this very room—it was a great treat to be invited into his smoking room, you know, old chap. Now we can either go north, as you wish, passing the Deverills here"—Richard's forefinger, with the long almond-shaped nail lightly touched the worn map—"or go south, to where we cross the main Roman road to Sarum. The legions brought lead here from the Mendip mines, I recollect my father saying. I can't tell you, old man, what a wonder it was to climb up the ox-drove of the Chase and see a distant gleam of the Channel, before going down again through the Tarrants and so to the south coast. Uncle John and I did the entire walk from here one summer, during the holidays, and back again after a rest, nearly fifty miles from one sunrise to another."

They decided to go north, and to start at nine o'clock on the morrow, if the weather remained fine.

On his way home to Monachorum, Phillip passed Melissa riding with a groom. He pulled up and spoke to her, and was enlightened by the glow of happiness in her eyes. She had four more days of holiday, and said, "Will you be at the Yacht Club on Wednesday for the Lantern race? Do come if you can," and with a smile at Phillip she touched her mount with her calves, and gave him a nod before he turned back to the car.

Thus enlivened, Phillip arrived at Fawley and greeted his parents with enthusiasm. Father and son set out on a walk which was to be remembered all their lives—the first and the last walk together since Phillip was a child. Richard, in later and inevitably sadder years, relived many times the same walk, linking it with the 'tramps' of his early years, he told Phillip as he stopped to remark upon the air the scent of wild thyme.

"Ah," said Phillip, daring to show emotion, "the sense of smell, in the words of one of the most homeless of poets, 'raises from the rose-ash the ghost of the rose'," words which had for Phillip a living exactitude with Marlowe's heavenly line, *What is beauty saith my sufferings then*, as they walked a little apart along this myth of a Roman road, sometimes a wide and cambered paleness, a ghostliness as of grass itself weary of time, pale with the sunshine of nearly two millennia of a dwarf-yellow star 'bursting through untrodden space', he said, "That's Jefferies' phrase, Father."

"Why," replied Richard, "when Uncle John and I walked here with our father we may indeed have passed by Jefferies himself. My father appreciated his writings, and once he visited him when Jefferies was living near Brighton."

"When he was young, I expect Jefferies would have gone by with eyes downheld, and unspeaking, Father."

All was passing, all would pass: the dwarf-yellow sun burn itself out, even as Jefferies, in the fury of creation and despair within his own short life.

"Ah, he too was a wild boy, Phillip."

The pale thinness of the grasses growing upon the buried road led to a church, where the ghost of the road was lost. Beyond the flint tower hung the feather of the moon, pale for very weariness.

From the wall of the churchyard, that acre of stone and silence, the road led up the hill, no longer visible as an interred way, but divined by the boy in Father, arisen out of the past. "Now this way, Phillip"—and so to a grassy lane, where honeysuckle hung in budding fingers and the wild rose was yet unborn. Whitethroats churred among the feathery wild carrots and taller purple-splashed hemlock. Now they had come to a field being harrowed for a catch-crop of white turnips the horseman said, glad to rest and talk a while. His toecaps were worn by kicking apart clods which had slewed past the tines of his harrow. Glad to see them, he was, as he pointed to a white-speckled riband just discernible in the loamy soil, a braid of broken flints curved with the camber as of a roadway once metalled.

They came to a spur of the downs, Phillip thinking of the long chalky slopes above the Somme, planning what dispositions he would make if he were commanding a company holding this spur above the lower ground and the road lying almost parallel a mile to the east. *Emulate the porcupine, never forget your flanks.*

Walking up a lessening combe or valley they reached a hill which led down again to the main road lying under tarmac; and climbing once more, passed by a barrow, burial place of some ancient warrior, and following the now familiar camber under the sward along the reverse slope of the hill descended to another valley where a spring-water stream wimpled under a bridge.

"Glassie, cool, translucent," said Richard, peering at the stream dreamily awave with water-crow's-foot and white blossoms along the green lengths of Sabrina's hair.

"I didn't know you'd read Milton, Father!"

"I recall that passage of *Comus* from my private schooldays, Phillip."

Richard was dreamed out, he was not used to long walks. They reached Colham, and waited for the local train to the Halt.

"A wonderful, wonderful day, Hetty," he said when Phillip had gone home. "I shall never forget it as long as I live."

When his parents had returned to London, Phillip missed them. If only he had been to see them more often. And when a month later the house was empty, for the sapper officer who had rented one of the flats had gone by then, he felt that there was no life left in Fawley. Better to put it up for auction; and clear off his overdraft. The house and grounds made £1,100.

On the day before the sale Phillip walked round the walled garden for the last time, and, driving away, left the car halfway up the borstal, going on foot to the beech-hanger where he rested, below the crest of the downs. There was no relief up by the sky. Below him lay the scene of defeat brought about by his own vacillating mind. Upon the gentle breeze came the familiar scent of wild thyme. He was sitting on an almost continuous mat of purple flowers. Large blue butterflies were fluttering about the flowers, and each other. He walked on, coming to the footpath above the white road where sometimes he had sat among the throb of turtle-doves. Now he walked sideways down the sheep-path to the brake of blackthorns and sat among the bushes to listen to their voices. One bird flew to her nest within a yard of him: had she remembered him from three previous summers, for without fear she poured the milk of her crop into the throats of her two squabs crouching side by side on the raft of twigs, while the cock bird poured his feelings into the sunshine—throb—throb—throb—love—love—love—Father, Mother, Lucy, little children—Melissa——

He went home to Monachorum, and was happy with Lucy and the children.

It was August, and the Royal Wessex Yacht Club, at the end of the crescent of Georgian houses along the western curve of the bay, was in full burgee. There were dances (to the gramophone or the wireless) in one or another of the seaside summer houses every night. The Navy was in harbour (a small cruiser). The pennant of the South Wessex cricket ground fluttered in the breeze. The club was swelled by temporary members—friends, relations and members of the three services and the only three possible professions. Gone were the days when there were only three possible schools. The war had brought its social compromises within the Royal Wessex Yacht Club.

Phillip was rowing Melissa from the shore in his dinghy. The lug sail was not yet up: a race was imminent: yachts with unreefed canvas were skimming up and down the fairway. He felt himself to be in a state of grace, with Melissa sitting at ease on the thwart before him. She wore serge trousers loosely almost baggily cut, with rope-soled shoes and a blue jersey. Her curly hair fell to just below her shoulders.

Phillip was now on intimate terms with the family. He wondered if George and Julia Abeline had parted company, for George never appeared at the family seaside house where Julia lived with her children—Melissa, and her brothers Giles and Nigel, when home for the holidays. Phillip privately thought this was a good thing, for once after the Abelines had come to dinner at Monachorum, George had taken him aside and whispered, apropos of something Julia had said, "She must have left her brains in her mother's womb."

At least Julia had poise and charming manners, he thought, which was more than George had. Julia more than once had offered to put him up, after a late evening at the club, but Phillip had always refused, since he did not feel altogether at home with her; but after he and Lucy had spent a couple of days there with the children, he lost the feeling of slight constriction, which, Julia had remarked once to him, in a frank talk after several drinks, was due to pretentiousness on his part.

Like Dikran Michaelis, he thought, of whom it was said, 'Not so much brilliant, as brilliantine'. Or, 'Every other inch a gentleman'.

"Yes, I suppose I do seem pretentious, Julia, but the fact is I've never lost the feeling of nervousness with you, after our talk in May, nineteen eighteen, about that rare cuckoo. I felt I was a bore."

"Not at all, Phillip, not in the very least. They still talk at Husborne about your marvellous sound-ranging by echo on the front of the house, before your bandages came off. It was simply marvellous. I was amazed I can tell you. Oh yes," she said, lighting another cigarette, "you were simply marvellous. Oh yes. Uncle Bohun still talks about it whenever I go there."

After that Phillip often stayed a night, sometimes two. One morning he saw through the open breakfast room door two strange men at the table. Julia took him aside before he entered the room and said in a whisper, "Don't let on this isn't the Ocean Hotel, you know, the house next door. They arrived here this morning just as I was taking in the milk at the top of the steps. They said they'd driven through the night from London."

"It must have been one of them that tried to turn the door handle while I was having my cold tub."

"I'm simply longing to see their faces when they find out this isn't their hotel."

Julia led the way in. The two strangers continued to eat eggs and bacon, until Julia said, "May I introduce Colonel Maddison?" One nodded, then went on cutting up a rasher, the other half got to his feet. Both looked slightly embarrassed.

"Phillip, may I cook you some porridge, or would you prefer cornflakes?"

"I'm afraid we arrived rather early," said the one who had half got to his feet. "When will our rooms be ready?"

"Oh—well—you see——" Julia's smile lit up her face. "May we talk about it after breakfast? I have two small rooms at the back, if you won't mind having them for a few days."

"But in your letter you said we could have the two rooms facing the harbour, surely?"

"My letter?"

"Isn't this the Ocean Hotel?"

"Oh, no," said Julia vaguely. She added briskly "The Ocean Hotel's next door. That way, Number Three. Oh yes, the Ocean Hotel's next door."

"I say, I'm most fearfully sorry. We'll go at once." Both men were on their feet now, alert and deferential as became sahibs.

"Ah ha, you came to the wrong door!" laughed Julia. "What fun! Anyway, stay and finish breakfast, won't you? I'm awf'ly sorry the bathroom was occupied when you came. Yes, the Ocean's next door," said Julia, with a laugh, and with her style of repetition that had maddened the neither-one-thing-nor-the-other George Abeline.

"It's most awf'ly good of you. May I be so bold as to ask the name of our charming hostess?"

"I'm Lady Abeline," said Julia promptly, like a busy person at the telephone saying "Wrong number". "Have you come to do some sailing? You have? Oh well, Colonel Maddison and I will take you round to the Club this morning, if you've no other arrangements, and you can meet the secretary, and arrange about temporary membership."

"That is most kind of you, Lady Abeline."

"And how is Kenya?"

"Sisal and coffee not so good, I'm afraid."

"You'll meet a number of fellows also back on leave, I expect."

When the two men had gone next door Phillip said, "Oh, by the way, Julia, when I was at Husborne in nineteen eighteen I was only an acting lieutenant-colonel——"

Julia appeared not to have heard this remark. She and Melissa were laughing at what they appeared to think of as a tremendous joke. "Oh Lor', you should have seen their faces when they found out this wasn't the Ocean! My dear, it was *killing*," to Phillip.

He felt happy, life was light, easy: Ariel had come again—the summer sun of boyhood, of the first visit to the West Country in May, 1914. "Well, I'll leave you two together," said Julia, taking her coffee and dry toast (rye bread) and honey upstairs. So Phillip hovered around the kitchen while Melissa cooked his breakfast. They sat at a bare wooden table, scrubbed until the grain in the wood stood out. Giles and Nigel, Melissa's brothers, who had returned from the Abbey very late the night before in an old Scripps-Booth runabout, were sleeping on.

"I suppose I should ask you if you slept well?" said Melissa.

"Very well, thanks." He added, "I suppose I ought to go back home this morning."

"There's no need to go unless you have to."

"Are you sure?"

She looked at him steadily. "Unless you want to go."

"I want to stay."

She sparkled, her tongue darted out and in again like a bumble-bee's first sip at honey. He heard himself saying, "Would you like to come sailing in *Scylla*? I expect you're much in demand to crew."

"I'd love to come. There's a race on, it'll be fun to watch from the water."

He got up and standing before her said, "You wrote me a beautiful letter after the dance at Runnymeade's. I've read it many times."

She was pale. He sat beside her, putting his arms around her, feeling her curls on his cheek with his nose, and as gently kissed first one cheek bone then the other.

"Your feelings are important to me," he said as he stood back, smoothing her hair from crown to ears. "You are beautiful in your own right."

"I must turn off the gas under the coffee." She returned to put her arms round his neck and hug him. "And your feelings are important to me, Phillip." She added, "They always were."

"Since you were five, at Husborne, in nineteen eighteen?"

"Yes, ever since then."

"I often wonder if, when I am thinking about you, the waves are coming from you to me."

"I think about you now and again."

"Only now and again?"

"Well, quite a lot." She was now self-possessed. "Sit down and get on with your breakfast. Quince jam or marmalade?"

"Whichever you like."

"It's what you like."

"Sorry. Quince, please."

"'Sorry'—'sorry'—don't say that word to me again. You are so much *stronger* than your Donkin."

"Donkin was my cousin Willie."

She put toast before him. "Yes, Lucy told me. How's the trout book getting on? I'll type it for you if you like."

The 6-metre class race began in a stiff breeze from the south-west. The first leg of the course was due south to the chequered channel buoy, Fisher's; west of Gull Island to round the Campion buoy for the long haul east to the first harbour buoy and home to cross the starting line.

After the first hour the sun was obscured by low overcast cloud, while the wind freshened. Cat's-paws on marbled waters became lion-rushes to the growl of gusts while reefs were rolled around booms and the recall signal was run up the Club mast. A 7-force wind was blowing.

He felt not the slightest anxiety. Melissa sat calmly amidships, adjusting her weight to the drive of the dinghy. They were a mile west of the starting line when the last 6-metre reached its mooring. Tide was lapsing, wind against water. *Scylla* on the homeward run banged and bumped into waves and shook off all sheared water.

Gale cones were hoisted. The wind was violent. They were watched from the upper windows of the Club house through binoculars. The motor-boat came to meet them, and returned alongside to starboard. All was well. *Scylla* had proved herself. So had Phillip. And Melissa. Cheeks glowed. When they landed on the slip the motorboat man said, "Well done, sir," as he helped off the lady's oilskin.

"May I have a cold tub?"

"Isn't that what otters require?"

He was making whistling and yipping noises when Melissa came through the unlocked door and walked to a cupboard to get him a hot towel.

"Do you always utter odd cries when you are in your bath?"

"Always at the full of the moon."

"But it's the new moon."

"I'm practising."

She hung the towel on a chair-back and with a satisfied glance over her shoulder walked out.

Julia said, when they were drinking pink gins before supper, "Thanks for bringing back Mel so promptly, Phillip. No, I wasn't alarmed in the very least, but Mel's not been well, and you know the danger of getting cold at her age. Do stay the night if you want to."

Melissa was drinking milk with glucose. After supper, with two hot-water bottles, she went to bed. And sat up while trying to put her feelings into verse.

How could you have known that I loved you so,
When, with a child's heart and eyes
I followed your moods and ways,
Your look, and the homeward road whence
A receding you journeyed to that troubled place
In Flanders?

Do I, in tidal flooding twilights, link
The shore-birds wet-sand prints
And starry pipings,
To you, remote across the hills, yet infinitely mine
As with a child's simplicity, I feel in me,
In man and nature, the divine
Love stirring?

After breakfast Phillip said, "I have so enjoyed myself, Julia."

"Do stay on if you want to."

"Thank you, but I'm afraid I've got to be in London to meet Piers. We're going to Birkin's party at Olympia."

"Oh lor', that fellow."

"I've never heard Birkin speak," said Melissa.

"Would you like to come?" he dared to say when alone with her.

It was arranged that she should stay with an aunt in London where Phillip and Piers would call for her.

For nearly two weeks the morning newspaper owned by the Trades Union Council and the Labour Party, together with the two Liberal papers and the Communist news-sheet, had been urging all men who believed in the principles of equality, democracy, and free speech to protest against the advertised massed rally of Birkin's Imperial Socialist Party. Birkin's face displayed on thousands of posters stuck to suburban walls and boards had been torn down and defaced; to be replaced at night by volunteer members of the I.S.P. The route was marked by arrows at key points. As the Silver Eagle passed one arrow, some men were in the act of reversing it.

"What a pity all political parties can't combine," said Melissa. "Only necessity unites dissident parties, in a war."

"But the other species don't fight amongst themselves," said Phillip.

"'Homo rapiens', as my father's old friend Henry Salt called us."

"He wrote a fine pamphlet about Richard Jefferies."

Kensington High Street was dark with figures. Phillip noticed a group of men in horn-rimmed spectacles leaning forward to peer at each car as it moved slowly past. Across the road another group was watching the first group.

"Birkin's boys," said Piers. He was wearing the party badge, a warrior with a sword confronting the minotaur. "We must find a garage. I don't want your Eagle overturned."

This was done, and they walked back along Exhibition Road. Two hundred yards short of the main entrance the crowd was solid. While they waited, a clip-clop of mounted police edged a way through the crowd, followed by others on foot. With linked arms these tried to maintain a passage for ticket holders. Cries of 'Fascists', 'Enemies of the Workers', 'Scabs', etc., were drowned when another group started to sing the *Internationale* to the waving of small red flags. Farther on towards the narrow street beside a railway line which led to the main entrance counter cries broke out, sharp and staccato, "Two-four-six-eight-who do-we-appreciate-B-I-R-K-I-N—BIRKIN!" At this, booing spread across the crowd which, to Phillip's eye, seemed about the size of a division of infantry—ten thousand men.

"Juden," said Piers. "At least they haven't got machine guns, as in Red Charlottenburg."

Piers had recently returned from Germany. He had been writing scripts for a film company which had studios in the woods north of Berlin appropriately called Neubabelsberg, since films were made simultaneously in German, French, and English. The same star was used in all three versions since she was tri-lingual, but the dialogue was rewritten and the minor parts acted by nationals of each of the three countries. Piers had been writing the English dialogue, together with the English director. He had watched some of the nightly fights in Berlin between the Communists and the Brown-shirts of the N.S.D.A.P., or Nationalsozialistische Deutsche Arbeiterpartei led by Hitler, of whom he partly approved, because the Brown-shirts were cleaning up the worst of the vice shops in the city; nearly all of them, he said, run by Polish profiteering Jews who had become rich during the inflation, when millions of marks could be bought for a few roubles.

"It was commonplace," Piers told Phillip, "that any film--struck young girl coming from the country and prepared for a camera test, found herself told to strip off her garments, thinking she was to act in a 'realistic' play until she was finally raped before the camera. I must admit that as far as I could see, most of the audience in a private house watching one such film were nearly all Germans, bald and middle-aged and biting their cigars as though they were nipples."

Phillip glanced at Melissa. "My cousin Willie told me about the destitution in Berlin after the war. I wish I'd been there to see it."

"You must come over and be my guest," said Piers.

"Thanks. My cousin told me that he saw in Hamburg small girls of six or seven offering themselves to sailors for a piece of soap. They must be clean, the Germans."

"Sign of a guilt complex," said Piers. "My father, a typical Etonian of this period, is always concerned to have clean hands. Believed in the birch as a good healthy corrective to lust between members of Pop and fresh-faced fags. Canes tied with pale blue riband hanging on the study walls of members of Pop. This mob here is out to kill."

"I should say that, individually, each man here is struggling for a better life for his children."

"Yes, with cosh, razor, and broken bottle. I'm afraid that most of your swans are geese."

The two men and Melissa went down the gangway kept by the police and, to the jeers of the crowd, got inside the building. There they were scrutinised, but on Piers being recognised, were smilingly led the way to their seats.

Birkin was late. The van bringing him had been held up by the angry mob. Individual faces had threatened the uniformed figure sitting inside, ignoring them as police pushed their way around the van, amidst cries of *Scabs, Blacklegs, Bogies, Bleeders.*

An hour after the advertised time the lights were diminished, and a procession of stewards holding banners of the many branches of the I.S.P. moved up the central gangway, followed by Birkin.

As he thrust himself forward trying to minimise a Byronic limp, all within rose to their feet the better to see the pale but smiling figure, now being greeted by cheers from those with raised arms and open hands, and boos from sections of faces below clenched fists. Phillip thought how eager he looked, rather as Willie had looked, but Birkin seemed more compact, more head than spirit. He might have been limping out of the first battle of Ypres in 1914 with a spiritual translation of all that horror and chaos into clarity and order, he thought, as the tall spare figure reached the platform erected in the middle of the vast floor and climbed up.

"Fellow Britons——"

At once renewed din made inaudible what the speaker was saying. It was clear that organised groups, each over a hundred men, were occupying strategic points in the arena, and the galleries above. Birkin stood still while spot-lights moved on these points, and grey-shirted stewards moved in upon one or other of the groups. Chairs were lifted, brought down on their heads, dodged. Comrades in other parts of the arena moved in to help comrades. More chairs were used, stewards were carried out, with bloody faces; comrades were pushed, shoved, and knocked down. While the members of one scattered group were being put out of the doors, fights were being continued elsewhere.

"Birkin! We—want—Birkin" broke out in chants about the building. As soon as order was achieved in one place, by the use of fists and wrestling holds followed by expulsion from the hall, disorder started elsewhere. This went on for the first half-hour, Birkin seldom being able to speak for more than twenty seconds. It continued for an hour and then another hour. Phillip wandered about, as he had done on the battlefield, watching events on his own. Rooms prepared for casualties were being filled as soon as bandaged, bloody-headed men were led away. The St. John's Ambulance volunteers were working continuously. One girl wearing a grey shirt was slashed from cheek to shoulder muscle by a razor. Motor cars outside were used as dressing stations, where broken noses, fingers and cheeks torn by barbed wire wrapped round chairlegs were patched and bandaged. One young Greyshirt lay deathly white on the floor; a great contusion on his forehead, his hair spikey with coagulated blood. Phillip moved down the hall. While he had been away Birkin had been speaking from the platform; to stop when his words, despite amplification by loudspeaker, could not be heard above the din. People were standing up everywhere to see the fighting. One woman near Phillip stood up and shouted something at a steward who was dragging a smaller man along the gangway by his hair. She was told to shut up by another steward. Her companion then stood up and shouted something at this steward, who went to him and was hit first in the stomach then on the shin. While on the ground the steward was kicked in the stomach when he rolled over. Phillip put his arm round the neck of the kicker and held him until two other Greyshirts came up.

"Don't hurt him," he said.

"You're telling us, guv'nor!"

The man was punched on the nose, he fell on one leg and held his face while blood streamed between his fingers.

"Damn you!" shouted Phillip. "We who wore army 'grey backs' in the war didn't do that to German prisoners!"

Upstairs, from the galleries surrounding the arena, another kind of guerilla fighting was going on. Two men with anti-Birkin pamphlets were climbing up the curved lacework metal rafters of the glass roof, followed by four Greyshirts. Up they went, hand over hand, slowly, looking down for toe-grips on transverse metal struts. The two leading figures were apparently making for the ridge of the roof more than a hundred feet above the arena. It was hard-going, because they were hanging all the time by their arms, it being impossible to get on top of the curved girder, since it bore the purlins of the roof. There was comparative silence as thousands of faces stared upwards, the uplookers dreading a fall by any of the six men clinging there.

Birkin's voice, powerful, controlled, and ironic was now audible.

"Now you can see for yourself what happens at our meetings. You can see how we try to break up our own meetings. You can see how we attempt to stop free speech, to prevent Britons from speaking for Britain, to tell you how Britons can create a greater Britain. You can see how we arrange sideshows to help keep you in your seats, such as the human spiders we train to crawl about over our heads, as a diversion. But enough of irony and sarcasm. Who are these people who come here to prevent the truth being clearly and simply told to you? I will tell you who are our hidden opponents. Funds for the buying of tickets have been traced to Jewish sources, and many of you have seen Jewish faces among our opponents today. We are not against Jews because they are Jews. We know many Jews are men of high achievement, and loyal to this country, and fought brilliantly and bravely in the Great War for their adopted country. We are not against Jews for being Jews, far from it. Our Empire is composed of many races, castes, colours, and creeds, and one of the main reasons for this meeting today is to try to bring our fellow countrymen to realise that, as things are going now, this Empire of ours, won by our forefathers, is not only being neglected, but destroyed by the forces of International Usury, called High Finance, which cares nothing for the people of this country or the Empire. Money cares only for Money, which can be made in this country and then put out abroad to undercut our factories and industries by employing cheap sweated foreign labour and so to undercut and destroy the home industries——"

At this point shouts of *Leave him alone! Stop it! Look out, mate!* arose urgently from the arena. Looking up, Phillip saw that one of the leading men had pushed his legs to the knees into a criss-cross of metal ties. By the way he was clinging, head bent, arms thrust through similar ties, he was dead tired.

"Usury, or International Finance, has credit organisations which cart round hired toughs in vans to cause uproar at our meetings. Why do these people, not of British stock, want to break up our meetings? Why do they want us to stop telling our fellow-countrymen the truth: that if the standard of living in this country is to be raised—if our unemployed are to be found work—if the Great Estate of Empire—one-fifth of the world—is to become truly great, our people educated after work has been found for them, and our vast resources of Empire opened up—then first the entire racket of the international financial system, largely controlled by Jewish banks, will have to be revealed for what it is, not only obsolete and inefficient, but unable, by its very nature of always seeking the greatest profit, to serve the will of the people awakened to a better life, to a state of welfare and service, to a Greater Britain where class prejudice based on money shall give way to a classless nation, where great talent and achievement in the service of our people alone shall receive great reward——"

The climbing Greyshirt, puffing with the clumsiness of his jack-boots and heavy tunic belted by leather, and his voluminous riding breeches, was now very near the man above him. This exhausted individual was seen to thrust his head between the two V-struts to ease the ache of his arms.

"Our party has declared war on every kind of anti-social activity, from the jugglings of international finance on Bourse and

Exchange down to the organisations of vice trades in the great cities. In so far as the Jew is identified with any of these activities, so far but no further need he fear the advent of our party to power. The Jew who conducts himself as a decent citizen—obeying the laws of the Corporate State—paying in accordance with the high-wage system required by every employer—conforming to price regulations, and putting the interests of Britain above those of international finance, will not in any way be molested. Jews or Gentiles who refuse to observe these requirements will be treated exactly as other enemies of the people will be treated, absolutely without racial discrimination."

Two nimbler Greyshirts were now almost up to the man clinging near the ridge of the roof. Suddenly a shower of pamphlets descended from the humped-up figure. Laughter rippled in the arena below.

"We have fought because we were challenged and because Britain was threatened. The Jew himself has created anti-Semitism, created it as he has always done through the ages, by letting people see him and his methods. Why, do you think, Edward the First banished the Jews from England, by Act of Parliament in the thirteenth century, the Commons playing a prominent part? Why did the King of France follow suit, and other rulers of Christian Europe? So grave did the situation for the Jews in Europe become, that the Sanhedrin in Constantinople was appealed to. The reply, in November fourteen eighty-nine, advised the Jews to adopt the tactics of the Trojan Horse: to make their sons Christian priests, lawyers and doctors, and so work to destroy the Christian heresy from within. And so on down the ages. But we are not against Jews who have served our country in the last war, or Jews who serve it well now. But we British will tolerate neither Jews nor Gentiles who put their own interests before Britain's interests as a whole. No! We do not persecute Jews, but we shall not tolerate persecution by those Jews who are our own opponents out to destroy us. It was when they came out into the open, when they marched recently to Hyde Park and tried to drag this country into war with Germany, when fear made them less cunning, when they revealed what they were to the British people. That is when anti-Semitism was born. But now these war-mongers have found a force, a power, and a spirit in Britain resurgent which money cannot buy. And thus we march forward to a victory which is inevitable, not by small illegalities or petty violence unworthy of a great movement, but with an appeal to the whole of the British people, by disciplined methods characteristic of a mighty nation, to give to our party power by verdict of an electorate which knows we shall use that power in the British way to challenge and break forever in Britain the power of International Money."

A man more nimble had reached the two men clinging there. A third man with a rope arrived to help while cheers for the speaker filled the great hall. The exhausted Communist was lowered safely to the ground.

Most of the Sunday papers carried the same story: Birkin's Greyshirts had aimed at suppression of free speech among members of the audience.

On the following Monday in Parliament honourable member after honourable member arose to protest that Birkin's 'thugs' had 'deliberately' turned a peaceful meeting into a riot by unprovoked attacks on respectable, law-abiding citizens. And although these stewards, as Phillip had seen in his area, had used only their fists, they were accused of using knives, coshes, broken bottles and razor blades carried by their opponents as offensive weapons.

The theme of *The Blind Trout* was formulating itself. Phillip wrote rapidly.

> In the stricken rivers of Great Britain, first the small invisible forms of life, diatoms and cyclops, deprived of oxygen, cease to exist, with the microscopic vegetable growths on which the underwater nymphs live. Then the nymphs—Olive Dun, Pale Watery, Iron Blue, Grannom, Green Drake—are no more. Trout eggs, laid in autumn in the gravelly shallows, are attacked by fungus disease. Gradually, as more sludge pours into the rivers, a creeping paralysis of death spreads down its bed, once alert with multitudinous life. There comes a period in summer when the heat of the sun takes what little oxygen the water holds in solution from the air: the moment of lifelessness, of asphyxiation, of untruth, suddenly arrives. Older trout, which hitherto have survived, thin and dark, turn on their sides, gape irregularly and drift downstream without poise. Pick one up, and you will see it covered with a grey mucus—the sweat of asphyxiation.
>
> The so-called coarser fish—carp, roach, tench, rudd—exist sluggishly, but as more oxygen is absorbed by the silt of decay, they, too, die. Last to remain are the eels, but even eels must breathe; and when the water is entirely dead, acid and sour, they are gone. Once a pure English stream, there remains now but an open drain, the divine life once within the living water destroyed by an uncontrolled industrialism.

Will all our English rivers die, or will the spirit of resurgence, now animating the few, spread until our nation is reborn? There is yet time. There is still hope. And there is faith. For in all those rivers of Great Britain which are pure in spirit the smolt are going down to the sea.

That to me is a marvellous thing, like the music of Delius, and green corn growing: like swallows nesting in the porch of our farmhouse, and the moon—the nightingale moon—rising over the marshes which lie to the sea; like the Rhine music of Wagner, when the lyric gold of life is safe with the Rhine-Maidens.

Smolt are little salmon which, born in the headwaters of rivers and their tributaries, and wearing the moorland red-and-black spotted dress of trout for about two years, suddenly become strangely excited, assume a silver sea-coat, and seek the ocean water of ancestral memory.

No longer than a man's hand at two years and weighing between two and three ounces, a smolt may return to its native river after two or three months in the sea, weighing four or five pounds, the length of a man's forearm.

Or it may remain in the sea two years, and return a forty-pounder.

For some reason unknown, many of the Wye fish stay two and sometimes three years feeding on herrings of the Greenland shoals, and prawns of the deep submarine ledges of Europe's end below Ireland; this has made the Wye the most famous salmon river in England.

I have stared at smolts jumping in a West Country river as they went down with the current, always head to stream in the clear water wimpling over the blue and brown stones at the tail of the pool; or, in the fast runs below, prickling the brown water as they dashed at the frail water-flies dropping their eggs at sunset.

I have seen hundreds dropping over the weirs of mill-ponds; while the turtle doves from Abyssinia were throbbing in the blackhorns, I have followed them down the valley, ever widening with its steep hill-sides of oak, spruce, larch, and rock-set grass, to the broader pastures which end in the marshes and sea-walls of the tide's head.

From western Wye and Irish Shannon, Tay, Coquet and Usk, Hampshire Avon, Scottish Tweed, Devon's Otter, Taw, Torridge and Tavy—from scores of fresh rivers in Britain, Germany, Sweden, and the eastern seaboard of Canada—the smolts find theirs home in the Atlantic; and from there they return in their season to their native rivers, as salmon, where, if they can escape their enemies during the months of spring and summer, when they do not feed, they will spend themselves for the spirit, or future, of their race; and, thus achieving immortality, will die, and so return to the Atlantic in dissolution; as salts of the sea to the great father.

Once upon a time before the pollutions of the Industrial Age, there were salmon in all our rivers. Romans saw salmon leaping in the Thames, and named them Salmo Salar—the Sea Leaper.

One day our children, or maybe their children, will see salmon jumping again in the Pool of London; and watch them rolling up, showing their square tails in play, below the piers of London Bridge.

One day our children, or their children, will save millions of pounds—the hundreds of millions of pounds' worth of factory waste, sewage sludge, and other valuable chemicals now cast into our rivers, and after treatment, put them on our land, our England—the great mother of our race.

Anciently the fish was the symbol of regeneration: as baptism is the symbol of the new consciousness of faith, of hope, of *clarity*. We are aspiring, struggling, learning—just beginning to believe we can build a fine new Britain. We are passing through an age of industrial darkness; but beyond it, I can see salmon leaping again in both the Rhine and its ancient tributary Thames.

Chapter 7

THE GARTENFESTE

Once again it was St. Martin's Little Summer, and time to plant trees—scores of little trees—in the field above Malandine which Phillip had bought for £100. With Rippingall's help, he marked out three triangular areas at the corners of the field, to be put out as wind-shields. There were two kinds of pine trees, the quick-growing *insignis* and the slow *austriachus,* for the front line defences. And a hundred beech trees, two feet high, with some ash, sycamore, and oaks. These were for the support line. Within their shielding were the reserves, mainly larches of two varieties, Japanese and the English. He imagined doves nesting in these, and perhaps a sparrow-hawk. Behind these three lines hawthorn bushes and silver birch would lighten the interior of the field.

Rippingall told him the village opinion: no trees would survive the blasts of the salt south-west winds in that high and exposed place. Certainly in the adjoining plantation in a higher field the beeches and firs had died out.

"I don't want to hear village opinion."

"I agree, sir, I was wrong to listen to 'the gossip of the servants' hall'."

Phillip told him he remembered when first he had come to Malandine, in the second summer after the war. Most of the firs were then leaning from rotted roots, their trunks bored by wood-peckers and old nests of sparrowhawks and magpies in their disverdured tops. Now all but one trunk was gone, cut and removed as firewood by the villagers during the General Strike of 1926. The one fir-tree that remained stood at the narrow end of the plantation, and farthest from the cruel sea-winds.

The epithet was not sentimental, he declared: the trees had suffered a slow asphyxiation from hard-blown salt upon the leaves by which they breathed. Slowly they died where they stood.

"Like the inhabitants of Sodom and Gomorrah, if I may be so bold as to say so, sir."

"Year after year after year their lung-cells have been blighted by Channel gales. A tree's life is a man's life, which, Conrad wrote, you may recall, has one basic theme: he was born, he suffered, he died."

The Gartenfeste—the Garden Strong-point—was the name Phillip had given to the garden room of his grandfather's house, where he had lived after the old man had died—an empty house, resonant with his own footfalls as he walked about, during those winter nights after he had left the army, excited by the scenes which arose before him while he was writing his first novel. That had been his true life: the life of the spirit. Now, thirteen years later, he must recapture the mood of that secret and exciting time of the first flowering of his spirit. The semi-ruinous linhay on the hill was to be converted to a studio, with a concrete dugout below. It would be lit by electric light supplied by a car-dynamo driven by a propeller on top of a pole. Here he would live alone, and keep, like Arnold Bennett, to a strict routine, with every morning and part of the night given to his writing.

"We'll have to sleep in the tallet over the linhay, Rippingall."

"Sir, I can sleep anywhere—on the ground under the stars, if necessary. At Mons," reflected Rippingall, "when we arrived on that Sunday afternoon, we all bathed in the Canal. What a relief after those Hommes forty, Chevaux Huit railway trucks. As I was saying, we were all enjoying ourselves in the canal, when suddenly, on the skyline, a row of horsemen was presented to our wondering eyes. The Alarm was sounded. Every man back to his unit was the order. There the Uhlans were, lances and flat-topped helmets, beating it back to Berlin. I slept that night under a G.S. waggon," he added, inconsequentially.

The first thing to do in the field was to make a map of it. With the leather-cased tape borrowed from Pa, Phillip measured the lengths of the hedge boundaries while Rippingall took bearings with the prismatic compass. The field lay almost due south, facing the Channel. Behind the northern hedge stood a semi-ruinous beech plantation. This he hoped one day to buy and replant with oak, the native tree of the seaboard country.

They had brought sacks and sleeping bags in the car, with kettle, trivet, and frying pan. It was cold in the tallet, the loft over the cattle shed. The fire below filled it with smoke. So they kipped down by the fire. At dawn Phillip got up and walked about the hilltop. Above the plantation Polaris shone, coldly but faithfully, six lengths from the beam-end of the Plough. The earth had revolved since he had climbed to the tallet, so that the constellations of night appeared to have moved from east to west. The moon, too, had come up from below Dartmoor, which lay north, and now was descending to the ocean whose great pulse came from the moon. How strange that the moon, captive in her own serene orbit, ruled not only the tides, but all phases of human life. As Richard Jefferies had written, the sum of all nature was maintained in the beauty of Eve, the great earth mother: in the tenderness and sympathy of woman extending far beyond her own species. If man was the essence of the sun, woman was the essence of the moon, which ruled the menstrual or monthly phases of woman—the 'flowers' of the Victorians, the 'curse' of the Georgians. Why the 'curse'? Was it from the Garden of Eden: the fall: the serpent's wisdom: or some visionary forecast or prophesy that woman would one day rule the world, as the female dominated in the lesser worlds of ants and bees? The innocent moon, that nothing does but shine——

He had brought the saplings with him from the weedy nursery of the Fawley Estates. Rippingall and he had dug them up at night. The War Department would only let them grow wild and then probably uproot and burn them.

"Good morning, sir."

"Hullo, old soldier. How did you sleep?"

"Mustn't grumble, sir."

Day after day Phillip and Rippingall dug holes for the saplings, stood them in, spread the roots, shook soil over them gently so that the rootlets would have no checking air-spaces. Then each hole was filled and trodden down firmly before the soil was tumped hard with a post to prevent evaporation.

Phillip was not used to physical work, of shovelling and bending down hour after hour. During the first days before the rhythm of body work was established, there was a confusion of mental dross due to the changing metabolism of the body. In physical stress it seemed that the world as he had encountered it was largely a mosaic of lies. Most of what had been told to him and said of him in the past was untrue. The figment of his old headmaster often reappeared to tell him he was the worst boy in the school; and now, ironically, according to a recent letter from the same source, his achievements in the literary world had added lustre to that institution which was proud to number him among its Old Boys. And the spirit of the school, unwittingly, had failed to recognise the talent which now was applauded.

But that was the dross of thought. Mankind learned painfully, by trial and error. It was a good life. The digging and planting cleared his blood, and so the mind. He became optimistic. The light had broken through the darkness of England, and of Germany too. There would never be another Great War.

"Time for tea, old soldier."

Every day was of the same pattern. Phillip made a fire of sticks and boiled the kettle. While the autumnal afternoon was absorbed in a dull quietude of solar decline, Rippingall made toast of brown bread, butter, and bloater paste. The tea warmed Phillip, sudden joy expunged the querulous fatigue-thoughts of the last quarter of an hour. Food was important. How fortunate he had been, how kind in intention his parents had always been. Likewise his old headmaster: how generous of the school to welcome him back as one of its *alumni*! And greatest of all he had the friendship of one whose faith was based, like Barley's, on pure intelligence. He imagined Melissa's face, calm and steadfast in its own beauty, a spiritual love like that of Matilda Wesendonk for Richard Wagner. Now he would be able to re-create scenes and faces passing through his mind no longer in fatigue like a much-worn and patched film through an old bioscope. The spirit of Barley had come again into his life. Here in this field, here on this very sward had they lain side by side, at this very place where the blue flowers of wild chicory bloomed every summer. And now her spirit was intertwined with that of Melissa, for both were of the same essence.

Ernest arrived one day at Monachorum to tell his sister Lucy that their father was dead. Since his bronchitis Pa had been sleeping in the glass-walled annexe to the sitting-room of Down Close. Ernest said he had found Pa lying on the floor when he went downstairs that morning. His eyes were fixed in a stare, his face had a look of suffocation. Had he tried to get to Ernest in the night? There he lay, having tripped over the thick cord of his dressing gown. There was a bruise on his forehead. His hands were half-shut with trying to claw himself up from the parquet floor of discoloured deal.

Ernest told Lucy these details in a voice unaffected by emotion. What was worrying him was not so much Pa's death—after all he was eighty-two—but what would become of himself now that 'those thieves' of the Legal Reversionary Society would have all the family money.

Three days later Pa was buried beside his wife in the small graveyard of the smaller Saxon church above the river. At least, Ernest thought his mother was buried there; her grave had no stone; the only mark was an overgrown flowering-currant bush. This bush also served for Pa, since brother and sister agreed that Pa would not want a stone on his grave either.

"What will happen now, to Ernest, Lucy?"

Phillip knew that Lucy's three brothers had sold their reversions years before. As for the house, which had belonged to Ernest, that carried a first and second mortgage. The family trust had provided the money for both mortgages. The trustees were members of the Copleston family, together with the so-called family solicitor; for the legal business, or firm, had changed hands twice since Pa's marriage settlement was made. Ernest having declared that he had no money, the mortgagees took over Down Close, with its two acres of garden and the Works which had been built on part of the land, and put it up for sale. Within a few days it was sold. Phillip asked Lucy how much Ernest had got for it.

"Nothing, according to Ernest," said Lucy. She went on to explain that the only offer for the whole lot was seven hundred pounds, which Ernest had accepted.

"But it's worth far more than that. What did Ernest mortgage it for?"

"I think Ernest said seven hundred pounds."

"But there is the second mortgage, of three hundred pounds, which you provided."

"I don't really know anything about it, Phillip."

So Phillip abandoned his tree-planting and sought out Ernest, who was reading *Cohen on the telephone* in the coach-house of Down Close.

"That was the only bid, so I sold it." He muttered, "I've had just about enough of those thieves."

"But, Ernest, you signed the reversion deed, after all."

Ernest would say no more, so Phillip went back to Monachorum.

"I think he means when the Boys sold their reversions, they signed away all and any moneys which might come to them, and now the lawyers are claiming the legacy from Aunt Andromeda which she promised to Ernest when her lady's maid died. The lady's maid had the interest during her lifetime, then the money was to go to Ernest. Her maid died a month before Pa, and now they say Ernest has no right to it."

"But a legacy isn't a reversion."

"I don't really know, but Ernest did sign for everything that might come to him, one way or another." Lucy looked flushed. Why could not Phillip let Ernest get on with his own affairs? It was Ernest's own lookout if he lost his money.

Phillip went into Shakesbury and saw the house agents who had sold Down Close.

"I must admit I was surprised when Mr. Copleston told us to accept the offer of only seven hundred pounds. He asked us to find a buyer some time ago, and the only offer was from Mr. Solly, the farmer down the lane."

From the house agents, Phillip went to see the farmer, who lived in the lane beyond Down Close. Mr. Solly weighed about eighteen stone although he was not very tall. He was jubilant about his good luck.

"I wor prepared to go to sixteen hun'erd, my bid was in for years, cor', wasn't I surprised-like when Mr. Ernest let it go like he did."

Phillip motored back fast to Monachorum. Ernest was staying there with Lucy.

"Why didn't you try and get the bid raised, Ernest? Solly tells me he was prepared to go to sixteen hundred pounds."

"Oh, I was fed up with the whole business. After all, that was the only bid."

"But the house was worth more than seven hundred, otherwise the trustees wouldn't have allowed that second mortgage of three hundred. And the money came from Lucy's share of the marriage settlement. The fact is, you owe her three hundred. What are you going to do about all that machinery in the Works? Those lathes and other stuff, as well as the gas engine, are bolted to the concrete floor of the Works, and so don't comprise landlord's fixtures. Would you like me to go to London, and see the family solicitors? I'm sure there must be some mistake about your having signed away any legacy from elsewhere, as well as the reversions."

"I thought about going up myself."

That evening Phillip and Lucy had the house to themselves. She told him that Ernest, who had always been considered a confirmed bachelor, had met a girl while following the local otter hounds. They seemed to like one another, for he had gone down for the week-end to meet her mother.

"Has she got any money?"

"I've no idea."

"I sound like a bad, acquisitive character out of Jane Austen."

"Oh no, my dear." Lucy smiled uncertainly. "But I do wish sometimes that you would not take on other people's troubles."

Ernest came back looking glummer than ever. Only when asked did he mutter, "If I lived to be a hundred years old, I'd never see eye to eye with those thieves."

"Ernest, will you let me arrange for you an auction of the machinery and other things not included in the mortgage?"

After a reluctant silence Ernest said, "Oh, very well." So the machinery, including a milling machine and a 3-inch lathe, together with the original wooden workshop, bolted on a brick sill, which Pa had built for his hobbies, went for auction and fetched nearly five hundred pounds. This sum, without a word of thanks, Ernest pocketed; and soon he was to be seen, by a surprised Phillip, coming down from his bedroom in Monachorum house wearing evening dress. For the first time in his life, at the age of thirty-five, Ernest was going to a dance; and a slap-up affair too, the County Ball. His partner was the girl he had met during the previous summer at a meet of the otter-hounds. More surprises were to follow: Ernest had bought a set of golf-clubs, and a jacket of Lovat tweed with plus fours.

"What about Lucy's money, Ernest?"

"Lucy did not lend me any money," replied Ernest, in an even voice. "What those thieves did with our family money is not my affair."

"But you borrowed three hundred pounds on a second mortgage. The money came from Lucy, via the trustees."

Ernest muttered, "I'm not responsible for what the trustees did."

When next Phillip went to London he called at the solicitors' offices. Yes, the trustees were, under the Act, personally responsible for making good any losses in a trust fund.

"So Ernest Copleston received five hundred pounds out of the sale of the effects of the place, did he? I'm glad you told me this. We can recover the three hundred from your brother-in-law, Mr. Maddison."

"Well, as I told you about the sale of the machinery in confidence, perhaps nothing more should be done about my wife's three hundred. Oh, by the way, did Mr. Copleston leave a will?"

The solicitor rang a bell. When the will was put before him he read it and said, ". . . the testator's property to be sold and the proceeds to be divided among the four children. Otherwise we must get a valuation for probate, I suppose? From what I can gather the old gentleman left very little. Would it be under a couple of hundred pounds do you think? In that case the estate will not be required to pay death duty." Then he said, "I am personally very sorry for your brother-in-law. He arrived at this office every morning for three days, and sat outside in the waiting-room, and refused to budge. All he said was 'I'm not going to go until those thieves have repaid me my money'."

"They are an unworldly family. Well, thank you for what you have told me."

"What will he do, have you any idea?"

"Oh, continue to live with us I suppose."

Ernest was not happy at Monachorum. He mooned about the house, his face showing no feeling, as ever. Once and only once Phillip tried to ask him what was the matter. Ernest stood still, then after an interval said, "Oh, I don't know. I'll tell you about it sometime."

Lucy told Phillip later. Ernest had fallen in love, but neither he nor the girl had any money.

Phillip found it difficult to write while Ernest mooned about: and after Christmas he returned alone to the field, where the Gartenfeste had been built by a mason, a carpenter, and Rippingall and himself as general labourers. The upper storey, the old hay tallet, had been replaced by an oak frame. Windows and new roof timbers and upper floor were of Canadian pine. The lower room, below ground level, was lit by windows just above ground level, like the splayed slits of a German pillbox in the Salient. The walls and floor were of waterproof concrete. For warmth there were rush mats on the concrete floor. The walls were plastered. This underground room was heated by an open hearth with a chimney back which was part of a cast-iron hot-water boiler, fed from a tank in the loft. The boiler gave water to the scullery and also to radiators along one wall. Phillip had fitted the lower room with book-shelves, and the dug-out, with its grass-level views of sky and distant sea, gave a feeling of freedom and light.

There were many rabbits in the field. They gnawed the bark of the saplings, so Phillip put up posts with wire-netting cylinders round the little trees.

One January night, when he was alone in the field, it blew a gale, and in the morning when he climbed out of the dugout by way of the Columbian pine stairs to the loft above he saw that many of the little trees were lying dishevelled. Walking among them he found that every other tree had been spun and loosened by the storm which, according to his portable wireless set, had raged directly across southern England, throwing thousands of great elm and oak trees all the way to London. Two days later the north-east wind brought snow, and in the morning the entire landscape was white, and the tops of the beeches in the plantation north of the field arose above a white cliff. The wind had carved it with flowing lines of sculpture. It was like the winter when he had learned to ski with Piers on the downs above Rookhurst: now a region, in memory, of defeat, scarcely to be recalled without the stillness of a sigh.

The skis were in the Gartenfeste. He took them down and ran beeswax over the runners with a hot iron. He was alone on the world's top, leaning on ski-sticks, the points of his yellow skis elongating his feet. It was the first time skis had been seen in Malandine. A local photographer took his picture when Phillip called at the shop for a bread loaf. Soon he was on the way back to the world's height, walking with plumping wooden feet most of the way, and up the steeper slopes nearly splitting himself as he made herring-bone tracks to prevent slipping backwards. It was good to feel fingers, numb with cold in the village, now glowing with warmth that filled his entire body with a feeling of being able to live for ever.

More snow fell at night. No stars were to be seen; he was entirely shut off in a world soundless but for the slight falling sighs of the flakes of snow. Towards midnight, while he crouched over flames in the open hearth of the dugout, the frozen winter of 1916, in the valley of the Ancre, came back in splinters of soundless terror, that those scenes were gone forever. He must go back to his home, to Lucy and the children, and sit with them around the hearth in the sitting-room.

The little trees, each about two feet high when last seen, had been hidden under humps of wind-streamed snow; but so heavy had been the second fall that only the top of the six-foot palisade gate was visible the next morning when he tried to open it. With rucksack on back he got through the hedge after some difficulty and ski-ed down the next sloping field in a travelling wave of snow until, attempting to skim over the hedge he was thrown over abruptly, one ski-point having caught in a twisted stem of furze. The ankle was painful. After disentangling himself he forced himself to trudge back to the sunken lane and follow the turns and bends down to the village. He went faster and faster, his head and shoulders well above the hedge tops of the lane which normally were more than a man's height below the fields on either side. In the excitement of gliding downhill with the keen wind thrumming in his ears, he forgot the pain in his ankle until, at the sharp bend at the bottom, it gave way and he slid sideways into a stone bank, with a snapping noise.

The ankle was not broken, but the point of one ash runner. Unfastening the rawhide thongs he abandoned both skis and started to hop to the village by the aid of the sticks. He spent the night in the cottage of Walter Crang, his neighbour of just after the war. The next morning he pulled himself into his open car and went home.

After a hot bath he sat by the fire in his dressing-gown, one foot in plaster, the other carpet-slipper'd. There was a glass of whisky untasted by his side, a writing pad on one knee. It was a remarkable moment. He had just written the first paragraph of his story of the blind trout. Suddenly the form had come to him!

The entire *locale*, or scene of the story, was transferred to that part of Kent, now London, which he had known in boyhood. The river was the Randisbourne, that once-fair stream which arose, bubbling and clear, from Caesar's well above Reynard's Common—the Randisbourne which had died as soon as it reached the hideous suburbs of County London. Weep for Adonais, he is dead. Here lies water whose name is writ in pollution.

The moment of inspiration, of shock, had been preceded by a mood of agitation due to apprehension, even fear. It was not easy to break the habit of years; and for years he had felt himself to be not sufficiently able to write such a book, despite the compiling of innumerable notes from other books by acknowledged masters, and every copy of the *Salmon and Trout Magazine* from the first number at the beginning of the century to the present time.

The pure water-springs that filtered through the chalk beds of the North downs—falling first as dew or rain from the drifts of moisture in air moving in from the Atlantic and forming into cumulus, cirrus, nimbus, and other cloud formations over the contours of the land. He was a spirit of water echoing with a thousand genetic records and impulses of colour and light; all was guided from his being by the Imagination. At two o'clock in the morning he closed the manuscript book and pulled himself by the banisters to his writing-room. He lay there, warm with thoughts of creation, withdrawn from ordinary living, at last; knees drawn up, left arm round neck, one cheek of his head lying companionably upon palm of one hand. Through the immense ossuary of the chalk of the North downs—only a few miles from polluted London—the gentle waters filtered, by trickle and drop finding their way through the flint beds deposited by floods which had abated millennia since—thus to congregate in dark water lakes which rushed from every spring-head to feed brook and rivulet born at the foot of each its hill.

He lay on his couch, seeing the stars through the casement until his imagination returned to water, flowing cold and clear past the green beds of waving crow's-foot, the flowers shut against the rising of the sun; and with a sigh of release that at last the spring had broken out of his being, even as a rill from the dark and immemorial chalk beds of the downs, he fell asleep. And when the morning came, and Lucy in her dressing gown brought a tea tray and he saw two cups in their saucers, he said, "Oh, you look so sweet," and later in the year she wondered, with hope, if she was going to have a baby.

Week after week he wrote with determination to allow nothing to stop the flow. Sometimes he took Rippingall to the cinema, a flea-pit with wooden seats and flickering silent pictures, for the talkies had not yet reached the small country towns of the West Country.

Rippingall was an unexpected help. Phillip read what he had written to him after every stint, thus to see the story in perspective, instantly to detect false or inferior passages. He was working against time, too: the publishers had announced the book in their preliminary autumn announcements to booksellers.

"God, how time has flown. Tomorrow will be All Fools' Day, Rippingall. That's us, old soldier. Now be a good fellow and take this chapter to the post-box."

The mail was due to be collected at the box near the road-bridge in an hour's time. It was nearly five o'clock. Billy and Peter were just home from the village school. David was shouting *Good-ni'—Good-ni'—Good-ni'*—which meant he wanted more milk. Rosamund in the kitchen was asking for her tea. Phillip was adding, in his new and regular Arnold Bennett manner, an entry in his Journal.

31 March, 1935

Although it is hardly spring, today is the first whole day of this year. It was fine on March 22 until 1 p.m. when the wind changed and rain fell. Peter saw a red squirrel in the holly tree at the bottom of the garden. Lucy heard a willow wren singing from the honeysuckle bines over the runner or brooklet where I saw the first olive dun of the season.

Gossamers are gleaming in the faintly misty upper air. Midges and ephemeral water-flies cross and float by my window in scores. The south wind has melted winter's ice upon the heart.

A greenfinch disappears into the top of the eastern yew tree on the lawn, a dry grass in its beak. Tortoise-shells on the flowers of aubretia, with bees. This morning I went downstairs to take off the clothes of Rosamund and David, and they ran about on the lawn singing in delight. Everything was in gleam: leaves of holly and box-hedge, budding branches of hazels, ashpoles growing over the brooklet.

Five o'clock has just floated over the deer park from the stable clock of the Abbey. I am sitting on the lawn, my old indoor winter self is shed like a pellicle. The sun enlarges me. Closing my eyes, I fancy I can hear the buds of the blossoms breaking in the espalier pear-trees on the wall.

There is wind on the downs, but none in the vale. For weeks the treetops seen through my study window have swayed to the mindless north wind. For months—Scorpion, Archer, Goat, Water-carrier, Fish—hope has been locked in the earth. And suddenly this morning the cream-coloured distempered walls within the house were glowing with light, a bumblebee was prospecting under the thatch, and the great titmouse was vigorously ringing a little hand-bell in the lichened branches of the apple trees.

Surely it is no fancy, or sentimentality, to say that Hope is in the vale. Hope is here in the sun-light. Daffodils which have drooped on the borders for days, bullied by the mindless north, now lift up broken heads to the southern glaze of the sun. During wind and rain and snow they have waited; then with the shining of the risen sun the green stalks and leaves glistened with renewed hope. Slowly their yellow heads turned to the heavenly fire.

All day there has been a delicious presence in the vale. Far away the cawing of rooks tells that they too are rejoicing in the new lease of life. That lease is not yet signed: the north wind may return, perhaps with snow and sleet to wilt the pear blossom, numb the bee, tatter the tortoise-shell wing, silence the little tinkling bell of Master Tit: but the lease is drafted. Now the fire of spring is about to rush with the south-west wind over this sea-board country. Voices of willow-wren and chiff-chaff call up a general bird-song: wallflowers smoulder in dark brown beauty: aubretia on the borders opens massed blue flowers for the bees' delight. The plashes in the lane are shrinking, the ruts under the limes—desolate daily sight for many months as I walked the same way in all weathers—will be trodden out, grass will gleam there again.

My eyes catch a dark flick on the wall beside me, near one of the many rusty hand-forged nails to which in the past pear-branches were tied. Or is it my imagination. Sometimes down my sight there appear zigzag lines, like electric flashes—these recurred at times during the war, ever since I was buried by that shell on Messines Ridge on Hallowe'en, 1914. The flashes seemed to be bombarding my brain when the mustard gas got me in April, 1918.

I think more remotely, nowadays, of the scenes and faces I have lived with during those nights and days of the war. If only death were a reabsorption into the sun again, beautiful as this present thought and feeling is. Ah, that flick again. It is not my eyes, it is a lizard. He has just moved behind a flake of plaster, partly cracked away from the limestone wall. He's come out again. His eye never blinks. His scales glint slightly with his swift and shifting dry-leaf movements. Each movement forward is a scarcely audible rustle. He is looking for flies to lance with that thin black tongue. He sees my eyelid quiver and flicks back into shadow. Come forth, little one, to the god of the golden sun. We shall not harm you.

10 April

I began and completed an entire chapter, starting at nine o'clock this morning, ending half an hour after midnight. It wrote itself. One is a medium in touch with forces of the imagination. Then I lay down on my couch, fully dressed under a rug. I awakened with a clear feeling of joy. A star burned brightly over the tops of the spruce firs. Wood pigeons had not yet awakened. A star? Such a steady shine surely was of a planet. It had not the soft lustre of Venus, which will soon be rising behind my head, in the eastern sky over the hills of the Chase. I have not looked at a star-map for years. This planet was, perhaps, Mercury?

During several mornings I have wakened into a blue darkness filtering into the sky, and watched this planet moving as though slowly toward the west. When I turned away for a while and closed my eyes, to breathe deeply of the cold air stirring to live again—for the airs of night and day are different—the planet was gone. By moving my head sideways I saw it glittering among the topmost branches of another fir.

Before songlight, mated birds begin to whisper to one another. The greenfinches which nest in the yew on the lawn immediately below my window start with a low and rapid under-twitter, surely the inflowing of mutual joy, like to my own. They have nested every year in that tree, I am told by one of the estate workmen; either the same pair or their off-spring. One small bird coherently revealing its essence to another small bird: what I feel, incoherently, when I am with Melissa, despite the clarity of spirit.

The feeling between paired birds is keen and uncomplicated. They have not the worries, stresses, fears of the highest mammals beset by conscience and transience.

While I have been writing this the star has gone from behind the spruce-top. Turning to look through the eastern window, I see a pale tide of light flowing up to the zenith. The dawn wind, a least stir of air, is passing from open window to open window across my face.

A flute-like sound from beyond the garden, very gentle, and repeated twice: an otter is going back to the river after travelling up the runner which tinkles now and then below the bottom garden hedge. About twice a year I hear that cry. It comes from an old dog-otter who during the day often lies on the mossy bough of an oak over the weir-pool of the grist mill down the vale. He goes up the runner after eels.

I must have floated off because when I next opened my eyes I saw a sky of azure, while cirrus spread high over the valley; rooks noisy and pigeons floating across the garden to rise and, just before the point of stall, clap wings and glide down again; while the middle of this house is filled with bumps and cries of laughter: the children having their early morning rough-and-tumble.

A south wind was moving up the vale. Phillip, freed by the writing of the trout book, felt that the grass was shining with joy. It was visibly growing. He could feel the temperature rising. And he knew what to write next—his chapter would be entitled *South Wind.* Soon those sensitive dwellers under water, nymphs of the olive dun, were swimming up the limpid surface of the river. Bulging rises showed up and down the water, the trout were taking them under water. As the current took the nymphs downstream they struggled to break from the pellicles and so to open new wings and arise into what to them must be a delirious dream-life. As soon as they began to hatch, the trout moved up to be just under the surface.

Staring down from the parapet of the bridge he saw only water a-swirl with the fishes' rises. They were moving gently up on their air-bladders and taking the swimming nymphs just as they reached the surface. After each take the trout returned to its stance to watch for the next nymph floating down. Each trout had its special place in the food-stream, its own sky-light window below which it watched. This window, or area of visibility, is forward and above it, and is limited by the angle of refraction, which means that all outside a fairly steep slant is blank in the fish's sight, he thought.

The bridge over the Flumen had three arches which stood on two piers built into the river bed. Each pier had a cutwater, the point of which lay upstream, to divide the force of current. From either cutwater there was a rebound, causing a cushion of water where all that came down in the current was momentarily checked.

These two cushions of water were therefore the best place to be in when any food was coming down, because a fish could stay there with the least effort. It could, while hovering, see any nymph arriving in either the right or the left stream of the divided current. So a big trout was usually to be seen there during a hatch of fly. The lesser fish got for themselves the next best places, in order of strength or size. If any fish dared to move into those places he was, if smaller, at once driven away.

Sometimes a small fish took up position in front of a big trout, but in swifter current beyond the big fellow's window, where it could swim forward to left or right and seize nymphs floating down. Then the big trout would go hungry. The black trout, which Phillip thought was blind, had recently taken up its stance just above the bridge, on the edge of one of the cushions of water by a cutwater. It had a whitish mark on one flank, as from the grip of a heron's beak. He thought it must be the original black trout, because there was no similar fish in the old stance farther up by the water-meadows.

Every day that spring the black trout was there, hovering as though wanly, waiting for nymphs to float down but seldom taking in food because three smaller fish were in advance of the cushion. It was blind, he decided, because its eyeballs had a greyish look about them. There it was, noon after noon during the midday hatch of fly, seemingly thinner and darker, a thread hanging from its vent, probably a link worm, part of a colony joined head to tail which absorbed, through the main head in the gut, most of the food the black trout took in its mouth. There it was, Trutta Niger, idling slowly with a split tail-fin, in the conventional best place although its economic significance, to use a dull business term, had changed. Had it sight, it would have been a cannibal, driven by starvation to feed on smaller fish.

He had stood on that bridge hundreds, even thousands of times. Today there were twenty-five unseen trout feeding in thirty yards of water; unseen because the water surface was reflecting white cumulus clouds an oar's length above the bridge. But he knew every fish by its shape, movements, and pattern of red spots amidst the predominating black. Among these residents were some mere flicks in the water: these were fingerling salmon parr, still in trout-pattern coats but with three inky finger marks on each flank, which small trout did not have.

Another rise of fly was on. Sometimes half-a-dozen bulges appeared together: these trout were *nymphing* as it was called. He stared and stared, and at last, as the low clouds thinned with rising thermals, he began to see one after another of the twenty-five residents in ghostly or shadowy outline, sensed at first rather than seen; a faint white line of dorsal fin; a group of spots within a phantom stream-line. He wanted to stay there during all the morning's light and grace, forgetful of time and place, forgetful of the urgent need to finish the book, because there was little money coming in nowadays: he wanted to become thoughtless with the Spring: but he must return and write about the fluorescent hues of crow's-foot bine, bankside flint, otter's spiky hair, duck's feathers floating down—all objects glowing with their own mysterious fluorescence in the darkness of the night.

The prolonged strain to force words on paper told on him. Often he had to leave the table and walk about to relieve constricted thoughts. The placidity of the Coplestons—Ernest and Lucy—emphasised the stillness of the valley in the heats of young summer. And feeling himself out of it—his master unable to continue the book—Rippingall went on the drink.

His tipple now was methylated spirit. This liquid was dyed blue by law, a horrid steely colour to Rippingall's dreaming eyes, so he changed the colour to brown by the addition of brown boot polish; to which was added eau-de-Cologne from the bathroom, and a dash or two of Lysol disinfectant from Lucy's Red-Cross cupboard.

From the summerhouse came snatches of song, all of a melancholy nature. And one evening Rippingall's bedroom was empty. In the morning Ernest found him stretched out on the compost heap. Ernest stared at the sight for about a minute; then deciding that Rippingall was probably dead, he returned to the kitchen to cook himself some breakfast. Later on, while having a second breakfast with the family, Ernest mentioned casually that Rippingall appeared to have had a heart attack beside the compost heap. Phillip ran out at once with Billy and the other children, but the corpse had apparently evaporated.

"Rippingall's a silly fool," said Billy. "He's his own worst enemy, like you are, isn't he, Dad?"

"As long as I don't become, in due course, *your* worst enemy, Billy——"

"You should not say such things," said Lucy, to the boy. Whereupon Billy, feeling snubbed, disappeared. He was later found in the stable workshop by Ernest, in a dark cubby-hole he had arranged under the pile of wood. His uncle fed him on bread and treacle, a tin of which Ernest had hidden on a ledge by the stable eaves. Only when Lucy became worried, lest the absent boy had fallen into the river, did Ernest say where Billy was.

Ernest lived most of his day in this stable workshop. There he ruminated before getting on with a bee-hive which was being made at Lucy's suggestion. There was so much honey in the lime-trees in the park, and why not get some of it? Ernest thereby would be helping to earn his keep. The honey would save sugar and jam, some of it anyway, off the house-keeping money.

Every morning as the hour of twelve was tolled from the Abbey stable-clock across the park Ernest walked with measured tread to the kitchen to fetch what he called his elevenses—an egg beaten up in milk and sugar. Returning to his workshop, Ernest added a table-spoon of port from one of the bottles of Cockburn '96 hidden from Phillip's eye. There had been nearly three dozen of this old and crusted wine when Pa had passed away. Ernest had brought them to Monachorum in his motorcar and hidden them behind some old doors and planks of wood in the stables.

Ernest had a chronic dislike of his brother-in-law's interfering ways. It was all very well, years ago (he wrote to his brothers in Australia) when Phillip had been trying to help get things going in the Works, but it should have been obvious to him even then that they had all been fed-up, and simply didn't care what happened once the Works had stopped when the money had given out. Now it was beyond the limit when Phillip had taken the furniture and other things which had belonged to Pa at Down Close and stored them in the building he had put up in his field in South Devon.

Ernest did not explain in the letter that he had allowed someone to take one of Pa's guns in lieu of twenty-five shillings owing for milk; or that he had let go a small Jacobean gate-leg table to another neighbour for a smaller bill of a few shillings. Nor did Ernest think it worth while to add that Phillip had gone to Mr. Solly, and then to Mr. Millman, the neighbours in question, and bought back the 16-bore Holland-and-Holland gun for five pounds, and the gate-leg table for thirty shillings, and given them to Lucy, telling her to keep the gun, and its fellow of the pair in the leather case, for Peter when he was of age. The pair of guns were worth forty pounds, since they had been fitted with new barrels, and the market value of the Jacobean table was five pounds. Ernest had not had any of the Down Close household goods etc. valued for probate, nor had he, as one of the executors, held the auction which his father's will had requested.

It was Ernest's lackadaisical attitude which had driven Phillip to hire a van and remove, with Ernest's help, the rest of the furniture, chest of plate, Waterford glass, china, pottery, pictures, and all the library, to be stored until such time as Tim or Fiennes might want their share, or its cash value, under the Will.

"After all, Ernest, Pa did leave a quarter each to the four of you in his will. And Lucy hasn't had a thing."

"Ah," said Ernest, thinking with some satisfaction that the interfering ass, as Pa had called him behind his back, hadn't got everything. Ernest had taken the gold studs and cufflinks, a bunch of crested seals, and what he considered to be a rather horrible amateurish painting in lurid colours of a religious scene, which Pa had once described as an ugly mess of libelled human figures verging on the ludicrous, which somehow had found its way among some other water-colours done by his father and brought from Oxon to Dorset when his old home was sold, after his respected parent's death during the Crimean War.

"Utter rubbish, if you ask my opinion," Pa had remarked on that occasion to his friend "Mister", a neighbour who, like himself, had never done a day's work, other than to pursue a hobby, in his life.

The offending water-colour had been thrown on top of the linen cupboard when Pa, learning that his father had left a private debt of £90,000 in addition to the mortgage on the Oxfordshire property, had moved to the small house called Down Close. There it had lain for years under the dust and spider-web wreckage of three decades; until Phillip, in a self-appointed clean-up of the kitchen before his marriage to Lucy, had brought it down. Having blown away some of the dust he saw the artist's name *William Blake* followed by the word *pinxit*. In some excitement he had run with his find into the garden to show her father.

"It might be extremely valuable, sir. After all, William Blake is a classic."

"H'm, that thing valuable? I take leave to doubt it. More likely to have been done by the village idiot, one of the under-gardeners' boys at my old home, and brought to the kitchen door for one of the kitchen maids he was courting."

Phillip had gone all the way on his motor-bicycle to Malandine, returning with a copy of the *Nonesuch Blake* and shown Pa some of the plates. "H'm, I must admit they all look equally horrible to me."

"Would you like me to take it to Sotheby's, or Quaritch, for an opinion, sir?" "Oh, I don't suppose it's worth the journey," and Pa had returned to his rockery. Later, doing the cross-word puzzle of *The Morning Post*, he had said to his eldest son, "Phil's an interfering ass."

Ernest, remembering that talk years ago, now had an idea the picture might be valuable. So he had rolled it up in brown paper and concealed it with the bottles of Co'burn port. So far he had not bothered to do anything about it, although he was always half-meaning to take it up to London. The thought of Phillip was ever in the way, so there the picture remained, the lair of a black spider with eight long, thin racing legs. This insect was a female, and had rolled her eggs within a ball of white silk and fixed them to the girdle of Nobodaddy, resplendent with crown and jewels and the staring eyes of a late-eighteenth-century British Jehovah.

Escaping from the mental mildew of Ernest's presence (as he thought of it) Phillip was mouching around his field one afternoon, happily and thoughtlessly greeting each growing tree with a touch of fingertips, when he came upon, less than a shoe's length from his advancing foot, two partridges squatting side-by-side on the ground. The birds sat in brief shadow of a *pinus insignis* planted two years before. One bird faced west, the other east. The variegated and dun dead-leaf feathers of their right wings touched. They continued to squat still, looking rather puffy while Phillip stood, left foot still raised, without movement.

He froze in that position, daring only to blink his eyes. At the shift of stance they would fly away. Were they two hens sharing a nest? If only he had brought his camera. He stood there while a horsefly settled on his bare leg; he was wearing only shoes and khaki shorts. Lowering a hand he rolled the fly, its proboscis boring through three layers of skin, shapeless. As it fell the birds burst into action with grating cries, while a shower of chicks fell from under their wings.

One bird—perhaps the cock—dropped down half a dozen yards away and began to scramble through the grass. It uttered cries as though it had broken a wing, which was trailing. Phillip, still standing still, watched the sunlight-dapple-pattern'd chicks clambering laboriously over long cock's-foot grass stems. Soon their cheeping ceased. They were invisible. He did not try to find them, he feared to tread on them, he dreaded to see one of them die of fear in his hands.

He lifted his feet backwards. The cock followed him for nearly forty paces. When Phillip turned away to the Gartenfeste the cock retreated to its look-out on an ant hill. It made no attempt to conceal itself. It stood there, head held high, looking at him. When he walked faster it flew up with loud beats of wings—like a clock-work wooden bird and—dropped into a hedge bank and with head still high on lengthened neck gabbled at him.

Phillip strolled away. The bird flopped off the bank and followed him through the long grasses. He walked on faster. The bird pursued him, half-running, half-fluttering through the wilderness grasses of the old summer. He stopped and said, "You should know by now that I am harmless, Perdix perdix. You are only showing off."

When the bird continued to gabble he whistled like a curlew, a cry surely familiar since these birds of moorland and sea-shore often flew over the hill on their way to pick up sandhoppers on the tidal sands below. Apparently the whistle was recognised, for the jockling cries ceased, and the cock partridge disappeared. Later it stood on guard upon its anthill.

Phillip went into the dimmed basement of the Gartenfeste and sat at his table, pen in hand. But nothing would appear in image before his mind. Silently he rested his head on his hands, feeling his life to be a vacuum. He sat there until he heard the clip-clop of iron shoes from the lane to the north, between the hedge bank and the dying beech plantation. Then into his mind came the image of Barley. What zest and calm she had brought to the sensuous world. Never for a moment with her had he felt weariness other than that of an earned relaxation. Writing was but a substitute for living, an escape from non-living. Still, the book must be finished: every word extracted from the wan shade of being, from the stored brain-cells of visible memory. He took up his pen. An idea came into his mind; he dared not force it; he got up and went outside, holding to the vague half-feeling which had preceded it, a voice crying in the wilderness of life.

He was lying on his back when he heard the clink of the gate staple. He listened. Slow taps of horse's feet. He lay still, pretending to be asleep while seeing through his eyelashes the outline of Melissa against the sky.

She waited. He ceased to pretend, and rising on an elbow

pointed to the cock partridge on the ant hill. "That old bird usually clucks at *me*, Melissa. But not at you."

"I expect he knows a horse is harmless."

She lifted a leg over the cob's neck and slid to the ground. She took off her felt hat, shook her curls free, concealing her slight discomposure. Many times during the fifty-mile trek from Monachorum she had imagined this moment of meeting, feeling his arms around her and his soft kiss upon her cheek.

"How is the book going?" She felt foolish as she heard herself adding, "Lucy told me you were here. I'm only passing by, hope I'm not disturbing you."

"I write a few words, then come into the sun to recharge my battery."

She unstrapped a leather-covered box from the saddle bow. "I brought some sandwiches. Have you had any lunch?"

"The sun feeds me."

The partridge's head was now down on its shoulders.

"Does he keep guard while you are writing?"

"He feels your innocence."

My poor boy, she said to herself, you're dreadfully thin, you need me to look after you. She had ridden along the coast, staying two nights on the way with some of her many family relations.

"I had supper with Lucy the other night. She and the children look very well."

"They feel free when I'm not there."

She ignored this, thinking, I must not react to his mood, he hasn't been able to feed himself properly.

"So this is your strong-point," she said, at the heavy-nailed oak door of the Gartenfeste.

"Do come in. You see these thick concrete walls below ground? They keep it cool even in the hottest weather. But it's a winter hide, really. I'm getting a propeller fixed to a car-dynamo on a pole to charge a battery for electric light. Then I can live underground 'hiding from the shock of day, like the tribes in Himalay' in Francis Thompson's *Mistress of Vision.*"

Looking at him steadily she said, "And William Blake wrote, 'Drive your plough over the bones of the dead'."

"Oh dear, am I about to hear that old word 'morbid'?"

She turned away. "I must see that Tortoise isn't eating your lettuces."

He followed her into the sunshine. "Melissa, I'm sorry. I was rude. I know what you mean. But it isn't that any more."

She put her arms round his neck and kissed him, holding her lips against his cheek. She moved away when he did not respond. He seemed to be afraid of her.

"I've been working rather hard, I'm still petrified."

"Shall we go for a walk?"

They went down to the sea-shore, leaving the cob in the field. He was no longer afraid of the absence of himself. With her beside him he felt to be one with the people bathing and playing games on the sand; that he, too, belonged to the sun and the happy faces. While she searched for sticks, he made the fire to boil the kettle.

"Daddy wants to live in East Anglia. 'Boy' Runnymeade's given up the Castle, too, driven away by the R.A.F. bombing range."

The news of her departure was a shock. He heard himself saying, "W-when my trout book's finished, I had an idea of m-moving, too." He dared to ask, "Will you go with your parents?"

"I thought of getting a job in London. I'll be living with Mummy, at first. Later on, I may share a flat with a friend." She hesitated before saying, "Where will you go, d'you think?"

"It depends, really."

People on the sands were pointing to the sky. They looked up and saw a silver shape moving slowly in from the west.

"The *Hindenburg*, from its Atlantic journey!"

He could see the red emblem, the black swastika. The great airship seemed part of the summer sky, a cloud phantom.

There was a man sitting near, blue reefer jacket and white flannels, panama-hatted.

"Isn't she lovely?" Phillip said to him.

"Shouldn't be allowed to come over British waters like that, in my opinion. They're only spying, taking photographs for the next war."

"Don't you think they might be feeling rather proud of showing their new airship to the English?"

"Rattlin' the sabre, I call it."

"But surely Hitler wants to be friends with us? Like all other ex-Service men who fought in Flanders and France?"

"Well, you ask my opinion, so I'll give it. I'm damned if I'd trust the Germans a second time. My father was killed in nineteen seventeen."

The man, who looked to be about thirty, sat down again with

his back to the grey shale rock, and picked up the picture paper whence he had got his opinion.

Melissa, observing the strained look on Phillip's face, said, "I read your piece in the *Crusader* about the Silver Jubilee drive of the King and the Queen in South London."

"Do *you* read the *Crusader*?"

"Why shouldn't I? You write in it, don't you? I loved your story about the little man and the King—'Put it there, George'."

"It was true."

"Aunt Cary told me H.M. wasn't at all keen on the drive, telling 'May' that people didn't really care whether they saw him or not. Aunt Cary was Lady-in-Waiting, and followed in a carriage. You must have been very near him."

"Oddly enough he remembered me, among the other reporters, from some occasion or other during the war."

"'Some occasion or other!' Is that how you think of a levée at Buck House? How did the King remember you? What did he say?"

"When the procession got to Nine Elms, the railway depot near Battersea, a row of coalmen was drawn up, in leather caps and shoulder guards. There was that small dark man, a Celtic type, at one end."

"Was that you, camouflaged?"

He drew a dried sprig of seaweed over her knees. "Don't stop," she said. "It gives me a thrill."

He dropped the sprig. "Well, I saw the little man staring at the King going slowly down the row, and when he came to the little man he stopped and stared for a moment at the little man's wide-open brown eyes."

"Are you sure they weren't blue?"

"Then the little man shot out his hand and said, 'Put it there, George'. It was absolutely spontaneous. The King held out his hand and shook his hand warmly. Someone heard him saying to the Queen as they got back into the carriage, 'That chap liked me, May. It's made my day'."

"'That chap liked me'" she said. "I wish that other chap did."

"That other chap does."

When the man in the dark blue jacket had moved away, she picked up the dried sprig of seaweed, and stroked the sand.

"Is the other chap sincere, I sometimes wonder. Does he *really* think that Hitler is not preparing for war? Does Hitler know himself? Or that one side of him is ruled by the death-wish of his destroyed childhood, or rather of his mother destroyed by his father."

"Are you talking about me or Hitler?"

"Both." She dropped the sprig and pulled a burning stick from the fire.

"I didn't think you were a disciple of Freud."

"I'm not. I see it all in my own father, the same contradiction, I mean. He would have destroyed Mummy, if she hadn't been strong and forthright, and chucked her marriage."

"I've wondered why Lucy hasn't done the same thing. Hitler's 'revolution to destruction' is only the macrocosm of my domestic microcosm. The loveless youth, self-built, driving himself hard, followed by prolonged dilly-dallying periods of idleness, which cause frustration, and destructive criticism . . . of others."

She looked at his face and was moved by its gentleness, and said, "Do you really believe that about yourself?"

He felt her warmth stirring in him, and thought, This young girl, whose mother trusts me—and yet, *can* I yield to her? What is there left in me to give? Perhaps I am physically impotent. He took the embered stick from her, and blew upon it, before returning it to her, saying, "D'you know the old saying, 'Remember, stir not a dying ember'," while keeping his gaze on the sand between them.

She felt herself swelling with pity for his thin, sharp look. She said casually, "I'm staying a few days with Aunt Flo at Turnstone, won't you come and have supper with us? I don't believe you get enough to eat."

"Well, thanks all the same, Melissa, but I must keep on with the book until it's finished. It's now or never. I know how a spawned-out salmon feels."

She longed to hold his head to her breast, but thought as she had told herself several times before, Keep your hands off this man you little fool. She got up. "I must get back to Tortoise. I hope he hasn't eaten any of your young trees."

The writing of the book, owing to long hours and a poor and irregular diet, involved so continuous an anguish that he spent forty minutes of every daylight hour of that summer loafing in the field, to renew the energy to continue. He left the field only to buy food, usually when he had gone a whole day without any. Never since Malandine in the old days—Malandine with its now crowded and almost alien sands—had his mind been relaxed. Long periods of idleness were nervous strains because he had not been working. He felt dread behind this drive to finish the book: the night was coming—the deep darkness of men's polluted minds making another war inevitable in Europe, and perhaps throughout the world. He had tried to reveal what this mental darkness was in the Donkin novels, but it had not been acceptable; he had failed; the feeling of failure was never far away from his being. He could never get away from that feeling. So there had never been any true enjoyment of life, because there had been no mental freedom. By August he was writing very slowly, on an average a word a minute. He began the day's work about 9.30 a.m., after wandering about barefoot in the field in his pyjamas, and stopped at any time between 5 p.m. and midnight. He was ill-organised, working sometimes until an hour past lunch-time, then eating bread and cheese which he did not want to eat. He sat in the sun, wearing only shorts and coloured glasses, typing nowadays because of cramp in his writing hand. Day after day he sat half-naked in the sun beside a young pine tree, tapping intermittently, ice-cold in the sun of summer. He made every excuse to get up from the chair—to watch spiders in the grass, to catch blue-bottles and green Spanish flies and put them in spider webs—these strong flies which would otherwise blow their eggs around the vents of sheep to become maggots in the hot sun and gnaw their way into and under the fleeces. Or he stared at lizards in the sere bleached grasses of cock's-foot clumps, or hoe'd the small lettuce patch behind wire-netting against rabbits. Then to return and type another sentence, writing against time: for the book, promised for publication that autumn, was already announced.

Edward Cornelian, Coats' reader, had persuaded Coats to pay an advance for the book which, to be earned, must sell fourteen thousand copies. Chapter by chapter since the late winter had been sent off without the author reading, let alone revising, what he had written. It was being set up, not in galley, but in page proof, without the manuscript having been read in the publisher's office in Bloomsbury. Each chapter, as received, had gone direct to the printer to be set up in page-proof to save time. This meant that no additions or alterations except literals could be made, otherwise the pagination would be upset.

Daily he sat by the little pine tree, while the sun moved from the constellation of Leo into Virgo, and towards the end of the summer he began to feel that if the trout did not die, he would.

The ending was accelerated; suddenly, it seemed, the story was finished; he sat at the green baize table, bewildered and vacant, while the cock partridge and his hen moved through the grasses near him with their growing covey, without fear as each bird moved tortoise-like through the tall and leaning grasses, plucking seeds while talking to one another.

The sun moved into the western hemisphere. Shadows lengthened. At last it was done. He unstiffened and got up, to shut the typewriter in its case, to gather the last sheets and clip them together, address the envelope to the printers: a free man now that the blind trout was dead, and all that remained was to post the envelope. He felt like crying, but checked hysteria, and lay in the grass, tears coming to his eyes despite all.

When he wrote to Piers in Germany that he didn't know what to do now that the job was done, Piers replied with an invitation to visit him in Berlin, and later to attend the Nürnberg Rally.

Chapter 8

HAKENKREUZE

The weather was calm and sunny. He spent the first hour of the short voyage from Southampton to Bremen trying to sleep on deck. On the boat was an Englishman who declared that the Jewish-controlled financial system was ruining Britain, and that he had been invited as the guest of the Führer to Nürnberg. When this man went below to get some pamphlets he had had printed, Phillip slipped away to his cabin, for the tense manner of the propagandist had given him a qualm of sea-sickness. On his bunk, all was well.

From Bremerhaven to Berlin by train, staring at herd after herd of pied Friesian cows on dark green marshes.

The hotel, where he arrived 4 p.m., Berlin time, was occupied by transient English film actors and actresses. There he waited until Piers arrived from the studio at 8 p.m. They went out to drink and eat in a large restaurant called Kempinski's, resembling the Trocadero in London. Phillip was surprised to see so many prosperous-looking Jews eating there. Piers said, "It's owned by Jews." This surprised Phillip, who, while knowing what he considered to be the distortional magnification of the newspapers, nevertheless had been affected by the reiteration of hostile criticism of the Nazis. He had thought vaguely of all Jews hiding in cellars, or being held in concentration camps.

Next morning he went to buy a shirt at a department store owned by Jews and found it thronged. Occasionally it was picketed, said Piers; Germans were asked why they bought from aliens and not from German tradesmen. Many other Jewish shops were open, it appeared. There were no beggars on the streets. There was work for all who applied for it. Nine million unemployed had been found work.

Next day, having been lent Piers' 1½-litre Aston-Martin, Phillip drove to the studios, about ten miles from the city, in a suburb among pine trees. He was anxious about making a possible traffic mistake, but soon felt he might be in London, so mild-mannered and easy was the policeman who came up to direct him.

"When Hitler came to power he ordered, against advice," said Piers, "that rubber truncheons be no longer carried by the *Polizei.*"

The drive to Neubabelsberg was along the Avus, a racing motor track with two steeply-banked hairpin bends at each end. Phillip went down it every afternoon. His mornings were spent wandering about Berlin. Everywhere he saw faces which looked to be breathing extra oxygen: people free from mental fear. What a difference from the strained faces in certain parts of London! Would there be another war, he asked again and again, and got the same reply, No: Germany was now strong, and would create her own destiny: no more crowd-hysteria or mass-panic. No more political parties were fighting for power—there had been forty-eight such parties between 1918 and 1933, said the young Party-member who spoke English. He had appeared one morning at the hotel to take Phillip around the city. Proudly this young man wore the small gold and red badge of the 1923 Party-member. He had been a boy during the 1914–18 war, he explained.

"You are an ex-service man. Good! You, like our Führer, are a phoenix from the flame and steel of those days!" He spoke in clipped, sharp tones, obviously copied from Hitler in his speeches, which Phillip had heard (but not understood until he read them in translation) over his wireless set in England. "I am honoured to meet a front-line soldier, like the Führer!"

One morning Phillip invited Martin to lunch, and took him to Kempinski's. While the two were sitting at a table Phillip noticed that his guest was looking uneasy. Martin's good manners as a guest had prevented him from telling his host that to be seen in a Jewish restaurant might mean expulsion from the party: a host, moreover, to whom he had had the honour of handing an Invitation from Der Führer to the Reichsparteitag at Nürnberg with accommodation in the Diplomats' Train only that morning, this invitation having come from Dr. Goebbels himself at the Propaganda Ministerium.

Immediately he knew of Martin's dilemma Phillip left the restaurant and the two men went to a smaller place in one of the side streets.

Martin, he perceived, when he came to know him better, had two distinct personalities. One was the grown-up small boy of the war period; the other animated by his built-up National Socialist will. This first appeared in the small restaurant when Martin's sharp eye saw, on the bill of fare, that pork was ten pfennigs above the controlled price. His face became stern, almost tense; he clenched his fist; his eyes set hard; his voice, though subdued, took on a deeper, rasping quality as he said, "I shall write to the Party about this man. This is a working man's place, a poor man's restaurant. It is wrong!"

Phillip said, "Why not tell the proprietor about it now? It will save trouble."

"We must not be personal in the Party, Phillip. It is a matter for the Party to see to."

"Yes, I suppose you are right, Martin."

He wondered if most of the persecution stories in the British press were based on isolated incidents, groups or individuals taking authority into their own hands. Did Martin think this was the reason for the discipline of reporting to the Party?

"Certainly, my friend. Some time ago a group of the Sturm Arbeitlung, what you call Brown Shirts, put on uniforms, which by then was forbidden, for Der Führer was then Reichschancellor, and getting into a lorry they went to a Jewish café on the Kurfürstendamm near where you are staying and beat up some old men who were Jews. The police looked on while this happened, for they were not to know it was not authorised. It was not the true Nationalsozialistischen spirit, and they were expelled from the Party and punished."

"I remember reading about it. But our papers didn't say it was a private and illegal raid. By the way, what happened in the nineteen thirty-four purge?"

"Roehm had his own private concentration camps in those days, and he stole a lot of money, what you call a private fortune, from the Winterhilfe, the Winter Relief street-collection funds. They found out about this after he was shot."

"Why was he shot, Martin?"

The young S.S. man spoke in a hard, tense Hitler-like voice, the change-over was startling, "Roehm was a traitor to Germany!"

"Please, Martin, you are not addressing a public meeting."

"I am sorry." The voice was quiet. "Hitler was in tears during the shooting of many who were in Roehm's plot to embody his S.A. into the Reichswehr. Roehm was an old comrade you see, and Hitler could not understand his treachery. The plot was to capture Hitler and take him away and gradually what you call in the cinema fade-out Hitler as mortally sick, a stroke, a breakdown of nerves. For days after the purge Hitler kept himself alone, brooding on this horrible thing that had been planned. You see, if the plot had not been stopped in time, Germany would have had civil war and would have collapsed into chaos again. But the foreign press, much of it controlled by Jewish money-power, declared that Hitler had faked the plot, to get rid of Roehm, who was a homosexual, and self-indulgent with younger members of the Party. He was found in bed with one when he was surprised late at night. Hitler gave him a pistol to shoot himself with, but Roehm did not think he could really mean it, and so was later shot as a traitor to the Third Reich."

"I had a cousin who had a great admiration for Hitler," said Phillip conversationally, to keep the other relaxed. "He was here just after the war. He saw Hitler as someone who could save Germany, and the world. Hitler, he told me, had perceived the root-causes of war in the unfulfilled human ego, and was striving to alter this by creating a new, truly human world. I wrote some novels about my cousin, calling him Donkin. Donkin embodied the view of the frontline soldier, a point of view that only the rankers and junior infantry officers would understand, but not the civilians at home who had not known what it was to live and die on the Western Front. Before he saw Hitler, my cousin Willie thought there was only hope in Lenin's philosophy. Life was based on a tangled-up frustrated human jungle before the war. I suppose Hitler, to my cousin, was one who would, as it were, replace the jungle by afforestation, with individual responsibility and rectitude."

"That is well put, my friend! That is our Führer, who is a phoenix from the chaos of the battlefields, a messiah! 'In the beginning was the Word!'"

"But Martin, and please don't take offence, I must admit I saw, in my cousin, a nervous strain, almost a fanaticism, which alarmed me, although I understood how it had come about. For it was the attitude of antagonism at home that I dreaded, Martin. It was the attitude of the Old Men, who put Money before human living, and used their newspapers to create fear and hate in the man in the street. I felt that myself, long before I had ever heard of Adolf Hitler."

"My friend!" cried Martin, giving Phillip's hand a painful clasp, "You are a true friend of Germany! There will never be another war! Hitler has said, 'Whoever lights the torch of war in

Europe can hope for nothing but chaos!' But we in Germany live in the belief, not in another war, but in the renaissance of the West for a thousand years of peace in which together the nations of Europe shall build the greatest civilisation the world has ever seen. Heil Hitler!"

Piers left the small hotel in the Soho-Oxford-Street of Berlin early every morning in the studio bus, leaving his Aston for Phillip to drive where he would. Phillip usually went down the Avus to Neubabelsberg in the late afternoon. The UFA studios worked a twelve-hour day. Of the trilingual experiment plays, Lilian Harvey was the star, making the picture first in German, then in French, and last in English. She was a small thin girl, said to be a Cockney, with a beautiful face and dark violet eyes. At first it was amusing to watch the various versions, the subtle changes of the conventional theatre-idioms of the three countries; but it was the sameness of each studio day, the waiting or rather hanging-about, at a dead-level of endurance and sameness, borne patiently by the stars, that impressed Phillip. At the same time, there was an easy, quiet, and friendly feeling in the studio which, said Piers, had replaced the tensions under former Jewish producers, who had had to think in terms of schedules wholly based on money. Under Hitler there were subsidies, which made all the difference. Even so, as in writing, the whole of one's life had to be given to the work. The dedicated star must feel empty, despoiled in her own life, for all her vital sweetness was used up in an unnatural medium.

The three friends, two English and one German, left Berlin very early one Saturday morning to drive in the Aston-Martin to Nürnberg. Once again down the concrete track of the Avus, with its twin roads divided by a strip of grass. They rushed into the faint mists of sunrise, smoothly at eighty miles an hour by the clock. They broke their fast at Leipzig, and then were driving into the direct rays of the rising sun. It was thrilling to Phillip to pass infantrymen in *feldgrau* on the march—long boots and limber wheels slightly dusty, each soldier wearing a flower in helmet or tunic. The flowers of the forest . . . for a moment he was back in the Great War, darkly wondering about the future. He remembered poignantly the march of the newly-mobilised London Highlanders through Surrey, long ago and 'sunk in the abysm of seas', that sweltering August month which was the end of the old world of golden sun and everlasting peace, as it had seemed then. That war existed in a lost continent of time: the gifts of apples and flowers from cottages, women in sun-bonnets and print dresses; grit on lips, boots, puttees, sweat of burning faces, damp tunics bedewed and shoulders aching with unaccustomed pack and rifle and seventy rounds of ball ammunition in khaki-web pouches under the ancient summer sun, so unreal, and always a little beyond a horizon of shadow-fear, of battle, of life lost for ever and for ever.

The small green sports-car stopped to let the soldiers pass, with their open faces and clear eyes, the ease of their long loping stride. Then on again, Martin in white helmet and black goggles leaning forward to tap Phillip on the shoulder and say, again and again, "We are to Nürnberg, yes?" his face ecstatic like a child's.

They passed over a level-crossing with its long barrier pole upright and its skull and cross-bones of warning below the picture of a child's puffer-train. They stopped again to look at a landscape of new peasant-cottages, white and pink, spaced regularly and built a quarter of a mile away from the main road. Each, said Martin proudly, had its four hundred square metres of land.

"They are for workmen, from the cities. There is an adviser for garden cultivation. Each man is encouraged to make and cultivate his garden to his own ideas. Our Führer does not want us to be like bees or ants, you see. Each man must be a leader to himself. The Party will always remain, but when all our natural ideas are learned, the direct control will wither away."

They passed a troop of boys in shorts, marching along under a taller boy. "Hitler Youth, see for yourself how open are their faces, my friends!" They certainly looked happy, and smiled to see the little Union Jack pennant above the radiator cap.

Southwards under the risen sun of the afternoon, the small low car cornering fast. And then, abruptly, they passed an inn with two low white racing cars drawn up, mechanics knocking on wheels as at a race-pit. They stopped, examined, admired. They were Auto-Unions, just back from the Dolomite races. With a wave of hands they went on, and were cruising along a straight bit of road about seventy-five m.p.h. a minute later, when Phillip thought the Anzani engine had blown up, or the chassis had fractured: such a clattering, iron-vibrating noise. He had his Rolleiflex camera open and held by the strap round his neck at the time, with 1/300 sec. speed, ready to take a photograph of the rushing road. At the noise he looked up: a white flash past, the clattering of an open exhaust with it. Then von Stuck in his Auto-Union was a quarter of a mile in front. Phillip had clicked the shutter involuntarily, and now cranked up another square of film: too late, the racing shell was gone, showing the Englanders where their Aston-Martin got off.

"Those Autos can do two hundred m.p.h.," remarked Piers.

Somewhere along the way they turned down a lane and arrived at the house of Martin's mother. It was a 'very German' house and lunch, said Piers later to Phillip. Martin's mother seemed to Phillip to be hospitable like the Americans, but somehow with deeper feelings: roots in the soil. The Rhine wine certainly added to the feeling of pleasure within the house. Martin was proud of his English friends; Phillip felt proud of being English, and also of having had a German grandmother.

Martin told Phillip that many young men had been disowned by their parents for joining Hitler's party during the ten years' fight for power. Hitler had been a comic paper joke, a monster, madman, degenerate to the middle class (it was, Piers had told Phillip, a lower-middle-class revolution). Everything to discredit Hitler had been tried by the press, such as checking up on every known lodging since 1919, to find out if he were a pederast. When nothing was discovered, Hitler became a sexless pervert, who got his orgiastic effects on crowds. Women at the climax of his speeches sometimes murmured as though in the transports of love.

Leaving behind the villa they drove on southwards, turning off the route to cross into Bohemia, for Piers technically to renew his permit. At the frontier the car was examined. Martin had to stay behind, having no passport into what was now Czecho-Slovakia, so he took charge of their German money. No cash or securities were allowed out of impoverished Germany, with its extremely small gold-reserve in the Reichsbank, the English equivalent of between two and three million pounds. The customs house had a coloured picture of Germany, with her 2,000-mile frontier, with Army and Air Force strengths of her neighbours massed all around her borders. The Czecho-Slovakian aircraft were within 40-minutes bombing of Berlin. German efficiency was revealed in the key to the lavatory: it was firmly secured to a wooden board fourteen inches long and nine inches wide.

Piers drove into the country which had been German before the war. The rule of the road was as in England, on the left. They stopped at a tavern, with a fat, jovial host. The place looked like a film-set with peasants in home-spun clothes. They drank peach brandy, then returned ta the frontier and patient Martin.

The way, continuing south, lay over roads as good, or as bad, as many British roads, with wrong banking on corners, surface of tar or bitumen on uneven and pot-holed foundation. It was obvious that the country was still very poor. Piers drove as fast as the safety of springs allowed, overtaking all other cars, and being pursued for the last forty miles by a Mercédès-Benz flying *hakenkreuz* pennants on bonnet and wings. Piers' Union Jack fluttered persistently; the German pennants were stiff. All motorists seemed to be smiling, this seemed to be the party spirit.

They stopped at an inn in Bavaria where Hitler sometimes stopped on his journey south. They heard two stories about him—One evening when he entered he invited all within to have a drink with him. Hitler was teetotal: his usual drink was *Fachinger* or tonic water. One after another the drinkers asked for *Fachinger* water. At last an old fat beer-drinker cried out, Beer! "Ha," said Hitler. "At last I meet an honest man." The other story was his reply to an enquiry about his chances of being shot—"Only from a ricochet from one of your pistols"—indicating his Schutz Staffel guards in black uniforms.

There seemed, Phillip decided, an almost universal affection and even love for Hitler, at least among those he had met so far during his short and limited visit. True, there was someone at the UFA studios who did not like der Führer. He was an arc-light man, small and wizened, who had insisted on telling him, with offensive gestures of the gutter, the difference between English and German girls. He was politically and mentally opposed to the Government; perhaps his unnatural life behind eye-destroying light helped to add to the effect of an unhappy childhood.

They went on, and at twilight came near to their destination. Flags and banners, all red with white circles containing black *Hakenkreuze* stretched from roof to roof of barns, cottages, inns, houses. Phillip knew they could not be far off when the horizon began to glow and dilate as though with gunfire. The illusion of driving up the line was intensified by many shadowy figures against this glow of fireworks. At last they were stopped by S.S. men, helmet'd, booted, holster'd. Delay. Martin announced to one, "Here are guests of *der Führer*!" At once the invitation cards were scrutinised. The men were alert and quick to wave them on. Fireworks cracked, banged, cast shadows of radiance.

"There will be a million extra people in Nürnberg for the Rally," said Martin, as the Aston's lights suddenly went low.

"Damn and blast."

"What's the matter?"

"My battery's dud, and I've got to be back at the studio first thing on Monday morning. Dynamo not charging."

He drove to a garage. Mechanics said it was impossible; it was the *Reichsparteitag*. Martin argued. No use. Then some Storm troopers came in. They looked like shop-keepers, or clerks in normal life. They acted immediately. They telephoned head-quarters in the Grand Hotel. Outside lines and lines of Mitropa coaches were drawn up. They were filled with military *attachés*, secretaries, journalists, lecturers, Oxford Groupists, industrial millionaires, and a great number of foreigners like themselves: a million human beings to be housed, fed, transported, and entertained: a place for every one and for each his allotted time: and Piers wanted a battery charged. It took about half a minute for a reply from headquarters. Thither they drove with a guide, amidst coaches, buses, trucks, cars, and innumerable men in uniform. They reported, were known immediately, and directed where to go. Yes, the battery could be recharged. Leaving the Aston in a railway siding they entered a Mitropa sleeping waggon and were shown their cubicles.

Soon after dawn Phillip was awakened in his narrow bed by the steady beating of drums and wafts of faraway band music. It was Sunday morning. The sky was red in the east, soon a spiky ray shot up. Switching on a light he read that Hitler was to speak in the Luitpoldarena and guests from the Diplomats' Coaches must be in their places before 8 a.m. They had breakfast at 6.30 a.m. and were led to a bus. It was, said Martin with satisfaction, "Hitler weather". Phillip wondered if, should it rain, it would be Bolschewismus weather, but stopped himself making so feeble a joke. They climbed steps to a view of a vast arena, above which miles and miles of tiers of concrete benches arose to enclose an oval. Banners stretched up behind them, each about a hundred feet high and eight wide, great red roller blinds each with the usual black swastika within a circle of white. There they sat, soon to take off jackets as the heat of the sun arose upon them. Phillip fitted a yellow filter to his Rolleiflex.

They had chosen a good place at the end of a row by a gangway. People were now arriving fast. He sat at the edge, sleeves rolled to just below the elbows. They had been sitting there about half-an-hour when a tall young man with vaguely good-natured face came up and stood in the gangway beside Phillip while anxiously watching towards the entrance. Phillip wondered why he did not find himself a seat; but soon a grey-faced man sharp-nosed and bespectacled approached, and the young man deferentially moved aside without hesitation. A bulky rump was pushed against Phillip's lean one, and thus the stranger sat down at the seat-end. Phillip turned and looked at this fleshy cuckoo.

The cuckoo looked straight ahead. Phillip had a feeling that he could see with his entire left-side through his grey flannel suit, with its hand-stitched lapels. He sat still, until the cuckoo consolidated his weight on the seat, thus squeezing his neighbour beyond the limit of his original place. Turning slowly to regard the thruster with controlled fury, Phillip saw that he was now holding in his pale podgy hands a large envelope, ostensibly displayed so that the name and address were visible. The words OXFORD UNIVERSITY had been cancelled by a squiggle of blue pencil, as though done with irritability. As Phillip looked sideways the hand uncovered the first part of the name: the words *The Rev. Frank* were visible. And as Phillip's ironic glance changed to one of curiosity the hand, as though sensitive to the change of mood, uncovered the surname and Phillip read *The Rev. Frank Buchman.*

Two tall blue-eyed young women wearing identical cotton dresses with a design of blue flowers walked down the gangway and seated themselves in one of the lower tiers. They had blonde hair. Piers recognised them as friends of his, two English girls often photographed in newspapers as 'the two Mitford sisters'. One, less slim than the elder girl, wore the gold badge of the Party.

Soon a stir moved round the miles of tiered seats. Faces near Phillip lit up. The grey-clad cuckoo on his right did not appear to share the mass animation. The feeling persisted that the originator of the Oxford Group Movement was aware of, but entirely indifferent to, what he was thinking.

> A flutter of cries and a stir moving, like a tide, round the oval. Down below a minute black car gliding, followed by another, another, another, a string of Mercédès-Benz open touring cars. People were now on their feet, a roar of HEIL HITLER!—no, not a roar, an eager gladness, everyone happy and welcoming that tiny figure on the dais below with outstretched arms and open palms. The self-styled Rev. Frank Buchman, of the self-styled Oxford Movement, standing beside me, held out a left arm somewhat limply.
>
> People were sitting down, like hundreds of thousands of friends knowing one another and equal with the same trust. I can only describe

it this way (he wrote to Melissa) picking each word objectively. For myself, I hoped to regain a few inches of my lost territory in the adjustment of sitting down again; but no, God had provided otherwise. The Rev. Cuckoo spread his knees and leaned comfortably forward. I thought I would take a photograph, so flicking open my camera top with its screened glass focusing plate I stood up and moved back the shutter. Immediately an index finger was pushed into my ribs, and a voice said with a nasal intonation, spoken as to the air before unmoving gold-rimmed spectacles, "Can't see through you." With an ironic apology I sat down quietly and slowly, furious yet amused, for now it was plain how this commercial adventure had been built up.

Piers told me (he speaks German) that Hitler was imitating his earlier self in his speech in so far as the white-heat of declamation was concerned. The fanatical prophet was now the cool and calculating head of the nation; in his speech (only in the manner of it) he was assuming, momentarily, his old mantle, or worn-out trench-coat. He paused to look at notes held in the palm of one hand. Sometimes his voice was ragged, as though a vocal cord had worn slack. I wondered what would have happened to him had he been born an Englishman: perhaps he would have become a Jimmy Maxton, with greater fire (perhaps not in England: for there was no urgent oxygen in England after the war to make a smouldering will for reformation into a white flame to fuse men's minds). Perhaps a poet, or an artist living in a vacuum of negation, painting surrealistic pictures in a loneliness of his own spirit, or composing a jangle of discordant sounds to echo the discordance of the times.

Or would he have rejected the town, with its pavement-ideas, this poor English wander-bird without mission yet entirely severing himself from a money-based civilisation which repressed all the best in children while creating an economic factory-jungle and pavement existence.
Three figures, Hitler in middle, walking in slow march up the white approach to the urns of remembrance, while softly the band below played *I had a Comrade,* that lament equivalent to our *Flowers of the Forest.* The tiny trio went past the masses paraded there below: helmets of the new Reichswehr, small and dark-grey, like poppy-seeds: clay-brown squares of the S.A.; blacker S.S. rectangles. These clerks, farm labourers, waiters, tram-conductors, newspaperboys, sons of generals and princes, poets, writers, labouring men, comedians and wounded soldiers—all who heard him in those early days and were shocked, rightly or wrongly, truly or neurotically, into a new way of thought, and gave up all for the Idea, and bound themselves together for their beliefs, fighting the forces of gold and disintegration and rival Ideas, meeting terror with terror and death with death, and driving the Communists off the streets until more than 30,000 Nazis (according to Martin) were slashed, cut, shot, blinded and finally killed in the struggle which has shocked the mind of the old Europe. I do not forget

the opponents, tens, hundreds of men in a rival cause, millions of communist youths believing that the only way to a new world was by total destruction of the old civilisation, while Hitler wanted to base the new on the century-old virtues which were maintained in what was Old Europe. Yet many Communists heard the fanatic, and were disturbed anew, put into self-conflict, and went over to what they finally decided was the clear light.

As for the opponents, what did they think, the older generations? More set in their ideas, stronger in their egotisms (or beliefs, or humanitarian concepts) obstructed and fought with words during the fifteen years—and lost. Hitler wanted to restore the old German fabric, to redesign it from its ancient foundations: the Communists said it must be razed to the ground, a new building must replace it in geometrical, concrete design.

The flames of remembrance are now breaking out of the far-off urns. In grave, as though meditative, step, the three are returning, while we all sit still, and the air of *I had a Comrade* makes our mood.

Later, towards noon, Phillip watched the reviewing of the Regional Banners from a stand in the Adolf-Hitler Platz. Before Hitler arrived individuals in the crowd hailed their favourites. A Falstaff-like figure appeared on the cobbled square fifty yards away, and all stood up, holding out arms in greeting, leaning forward like children eager to answer a teacher's question. Reichsmarschal Hermann Göring laughed and smiled, they laughed with him. He seemed to be popular, to be regarded as a jester; but they respected him, holder of the German V.C., the *Ordre pour le Mérite*. Goebbels was seen next, and also hailed, but with lesser enthusiasm. Then an old man walked slowly towards a lamp-standard in the square while a young S.S. man ran with a chair for him. They hailed him, too. Martin told Phillip that he was a veteran General of 1870.

Another S.S. man stepped forward and took Göring's photograph. Another came out with his camera. Göring turned, obligingly. Others left the ranks. He posed, or rather stood, for them like a film-star until someone with a hand-motion stopped it. Phillip had seen uniformed men taking snap-shots of Hitler in the Luitpoldfeld: all was informal and friendly, so different from the pre-war conception of German discipline.

Phillip grew more weary during the continual march-past of red banners, while Hitler stood in his car, arm out hour after hour, and leaving his seat wandered away to prowl about below. He noticed that many of the S.A. men had rows of ribbons: there were ex-colonels, majors, even generals of the 1914–18 army as volunteers in the ranks. They seemed to have the spirit of English gentlemen who had transcended class-consciousness. There was no arrogance, but a tranquillity about them.

But when he came upon a smallish dapper man in greenish-grey uniform, obviously regular army, eyeglass cutting a red rim in the socket of one eye, four rows of ribbons and a service cap upthrust in front, he wondered who he was, for he looked out of place. The face was somehow familiar: yes, it was General von Fritsch. What was he doing, as he stood before a row of private soldiers and speaking to one? Phillip moved closer. The General was rating, in cold-passionate tones, a private soldier standing to attention with eight others in front of a row of black Mercédès-Benz cars. Von Fritsch's tone was not furious, but a sort of cold-ash fury was in a voice almost deadly quiet. Was this homosexual reaction to inhibited passion or lust? Piers had said that homosexual practices were rife in certain sections of the S.S.; but these were men of the new army. They were tall, like guardsmen, red-faced, but not de-humanised. When von Fritsch turned away they exchanged quiet, amused glances. He was the old, they were the new, Hitler-Army, with most of its officers from the middle and lower-middle classes given a new and earnest self-respect.

It seemed that the spirit of the elderly *Junker,* or squire, was entirely apart from the majority: an isolation of the old world within the new. After watching that perhaps not insignificant episode Phillip wandered away, while the incessant beat of the drums seemed more insistent, wearisome, de-human.

They passed: group after group, banner after banner, (he continued the letter to Melissa) Hitler standing in his car a few yards from where I had insinuated myself among his Schutz Staffel, his S.S. Black Guards, personal to the Führer: they let me through when I smiled at them. March, march, march, pom, pom, pom. It was one o'clock, we had been out nearly seven hours. The other two were wandering about. The sun was very hot. I knew from experience that impressions made when I was tired were biased, weighted by fatigue. People talk about thinking: when they mean cogitation, which perhaps is an attempt to ratify the feeling-records of the past in one's brain. Just as most writers get their ideas and feelings from literature, so the minority of writers get them direct from life—their own lives. Their feelings and reactions are to them the truth. But when a writer is tired, or fearful, or surcharged with the moods and idées fixes of others, he may easily lose divination. How easy to write of soulless militarism and mechanisation of the individual German here today, robots of a totalitarian state based on regulated welfare. These were disciplined—self-disciplined—individuals of a resurgent nation. I did not see one piece of paper thrown down anywhere. The streets, as well as the Luitpoldfeld were clean, when the hundreds of thousands had departed.

I have thought that Hitler might never have come to power had the radio not been invented. The Idea of renaissance brought a living personality to every man and girl and youth of this nation. The radio is sensitive to personality. Any pretentiousness, nervousness, insincerity, or fear is immediately magnified for the listener. Without radio Hitler would be dead by now, exhausted, burnt out, beating in vain against what Arnold Bennett called *le bloc*. In the same way the wireless has done more than anything to bring to the British public the simple, sincere, and duty-exhausted King George V.

The dilemma of any resurgent industrial nation is that a high standard of living for all must be paid for by exports, to get currency to buy the necessary raw materials and food which the country cannot grow for all its people; or wither again to a lower condition than that from which it arose. But in Great Britain we have every raw material in the Empire, and hundreds of millions of many races all requiring our industrial products. Yet we are gummed up by a financial *idea* out of date since the beginning of the war in 1914. British influence, otherwise rule, extends to nearly a fifth of the surface of the earth. The new way has been shown by Birkin; but the old way clings to power.

Wandering about worried by his thoughts in spite of knowing that idealistic unselfishness often has its base in frustration, Phillip said to an S.S. man, one of thousands lining the street, not to prevent assassination but to keep free movement of both masses and vehicles,

"Aren't you tired, standing here hour after hour?"

He replied, "We've been here since five this morning, but if our Leader who is older than us can stand there hour after hour for us, we can do the same for him."

Phillip went back to the Diplomat's train. There he found Piers asleep. He was returning to Berlin after dinner. The battery had not held its charge. Even averaging forty miles an hour for the journey it would take eight hours. When the two had gone—for Martin had his job in a bank—Phillip felt lonely. The masses and movements had exhausted his eye-nerves, he thought, accustomed to grass, trees, and the sameness of valley life. That afternoon he had bought a book with about two dozen caricatures of the Jew as financier, politician, rag-and-bone man, critic, etc. Phillip demurred when he was about to buy it, and when he did,

Martin said with a subdued look of reproach, "Don't look at that, it is not very worthy." Phillip, however, had kept it as a souvenir: the type of thing one could buy, but never think of buying, in the shops off the Leicester Square district of London.

He went out again and made friends with an S.A. man who spoke English. Like all others he had spoken to, this man was most friendly towards the English.

"Not because England is rich do we want to be friends. But because we are the same sort of people. That last war was a terrible mistake, but we feel we have learnt from it."

"Will it happen again—for the same causes, fundamentally?"

"It cannot happen again. Every German knows war is hell, useless, destroying the best, leaving the worst to ferment destruction of the state."

"Are you afraid of France attacking you?"

"Certainly not."

"Will you ever be friends with Russia?"

Immediately the S.A. man assumed his Hitler-built *persona*. His eyes set, he clenched his hands, his voice was harsh. "Never again will Russia march into our Fatherland as in 1914, killing women and children and destroying our farms and our homes. One day Japan will strike with them in the East, and then, we shall strike the Jewish snake of Bolschewismus!"

This was depressing. He was a keen, dark young German from Franconia. He was reproducing gestures and speech which had entered into and made his thought in the past. He relaxed.

"Our Führer will never make war," he said in his normal voice. "Would you ever make war? You, a front-line soldier?"

"I am afraid of the idealists and pacifists, both the older and the present generation who were children during the war. The older generation of pacifists would support a war against Germany, to compensate for their withdrawn attitude when they were of military age. The younger intellectuals in England now wear the clothes many of my generation discarded during the war and certainly afterwards. They would cause trouble and enmity but if they succeeded in helping a war-psychosis they would go to America or into some Ministry of Propaganda and kill Hitler at the microphone. True idealists are rare, they are the dedicated workers, who would if need be, die at the stake. You know, if I must be truthful, many true Communists are like that. And Jews are often very brave men. The best General on our side in the war was a civilian when war broke out and became a Lieutenant-

General, Sir John Monash, commanding the Australian and New Zealand Army Corps. He was a military genius immediately recognised by Haig, who used his ideas to break your Siegfried Stellung."

"Haig was a soldier! Our historians call him, 'the Master of the Field'. Your Pacifists call him, what? The Butcher?"

"More or less that. But, you know, the war was bloody awful..."

"My friend! To Eternal Friendship between our Brother Countries! To the New Europe, which cannot endure without Germany and England and the Empire! Peace and the arts of constructive peace for a Millennium!"

"In the West Country, where I live, there is a saying, 'If you want good neighbours, you must first be a good neighbour yourself.'"

"My friend, you have perceived the problem. Our foundation is built on rock, not sand. The Germans are very friendly to Englishmen, yes? Our newspapers do not distort news of England, and so the young Germany thinks happiness of his neighbour!"

I heard it gladly, hopefully, Melissa. I wish I had been able to believe it with, say, the idealism of cousin Willie, who did indeed lose his life for peace, even if few, if any except myself, saw it like that. His pathway led to death: keeping his word to Mrs. Ogilvie, and she failing to keep hers, was the direct cause of his body being taken from the sea, like Shelley's upon the sands of Lerici.

Germany is boycotted. Germany will not break the idiom of money invested for the greatest profit, irrespective of human life. The free for all is dereliction and death for millions. Oh Christ if this boycott leads to war! There will not be a Jew left in Central Europe, there will not be a Germany, there will not be an Empire, England will no longer be Shakespeare's "precious gem set in a silver sea, this realm, this England!" Yet Hitler is now within an economic trap, isolated in the centre of Europe, dying not from individual Shylocks, for the Jews are splendid family folks, and created one of the first corporate states in the known history of the world, but from an obsolescent system which no longer serves modern world-needs. War is war. I have seen German prisoners, surrendered during battle, bombed in communication trenches when led to the rear, *and* this by a Battalion of Foot Guards. 'Truth is the first casualty in war.' As for Birkin able to rouse our people in time, he is making no real headway. The sad truth is that the great masses of people never feel keenly about anything outside their home and jobs, and that is good. They're usually too tired after the day's work to want anything but food, social life and necessary beer in their clubs (i.e. pubs). And the intellectual minority which formulates, indirectly, their destiny, is not prepared to struggle for peace. They are isolated souls, seldom prepared to be good neighbours first.

The next day I was invited to the Party headquarters hotel. I sat not far from Hitler in the drawing-room. He was talking to several people. Very quick head movements. His face, in happiness, has a luminous quality, his eyes particularly, being pale blue with a kind of inner shining. A Shelley self-driven by an inner tyranny to strike evil? Or a saint who will never draw the sword?

Among the guests were the two young Mitford sisters, no longer wearing blue print dresses, but tweed coats and skirts, with no hats. Hitler in their presence seemed light and gay. He spoke rapidly, but was also a courteous listener. I could see that his natural pace was much faster than the normal. He glanced at me several times, I could feel sympathy between us. He had the look of a falcon, but without the full liquid dark eyes: an eyeless hawk whose sockets had burned out in battle and later filled with sky. A man of spiritual grace who has gone down into the market place and taken on the materialists at their own selfish game. Has such direct action ever succeeded in history? Is it not the beginning of another corruption? I recall a line of Francis Thompson's—about a girl, but it applies to us all. 'Her own self-will made void her own self's will.' I am tremulous. Darling Melissa, reassure me.

May angels and ministers of light attend you.

During the review of the Reichswehr next day Phillip was down in the arena of the Luitpoldfeld, sitting on grass most of the time, peering between S.S. guards. During Hitler's speech to the Reichswehr, about fifteen minutes, he saw not a helmet move down the massed files of the soldiers. They were standing to attention, too, and not 'At Ease'. The helmets were immobile: grey masses with rounded blunt heads disappearing to the size and colour of poppy seeds. He thought there must have been at least an Army Corps on parade, well over a hundred thousand men. When the battalions went past for the salute, at *paradeschritt*—the goose step—the boots came down so hard on the tarmac that the flesh in the taut cheeks of the sword-carrying officers shook with each impact.

But it was the Luftwaffe which seemed to get most enthusiasm from the onlookers. The dais or box where Hitler and his entourage stood was behind Phillip, to one side, so that he was able to see the faces clearly. Göring beamed as the bombers flew past; Hitler looked mighty pleased. Well, thought Phillip, the standard of flying was just about up to that of the R.A.F. at Hendon which I had watched seven years before. The Luftwaffe was new, amateurish. Was this the vaunted, the dreaded German Air Force? The 'fearful power' was surely exaggerated in the London papers; the R.A.F. could give them points on everything. Part of the dummy factory collapsed before the bombers were overhead, to the amusement of the crowd. There was formation flying in the pattern of a swastika; the star-turn was Udet's lone power dive beginning from above the clouds. The onlookers were happy; Phillip got their feeling that the Army, Navy and Air Force were their protectors, so that they gave Germany equality and security. The tanks also looked to be 1928 standard.

In the evening of the day after my glimpse of Hitler, my honorary equerry in the S.A. escorted me to the station, where we parted as friends. Trains were packed with men going home after their annual beano. I promised him copies of my snapshots, but alas, I'd already lost the address by the time the train to Munchen moved out. Perfidious Albion once again. At Munchen (how do names become anglicised, this one to Munich?) I took a cab to the Hotel Vier Jahreszeiten, whither I had been invited to join a Presseabteilung tour conducted by an official of the Propaganda Ministerium. Found them at dinner, half a dozen British newspapermen. (There I learned that München and Monachorum both meant 'belonging to the monks'.)

One of the party was a star Liberal political writer. He greeted our host with these words, "I don't like Hitler, or your form of government, but all the same I trust this won't make any difference to our personal relationship while on this tour." To this greeting our host bowed, saying nothing. A charmingly old-fashioned hotel, luxurious to me, with a large bathroom to myself. I pinched a china ash-tray, advertising tobacco, as a souvenir next morning. An official souvenir was presented to each of us on departure, a small flask of a potent colourless liqueur called *Himbeergeist*, the spirit of raspberries. Our star Liberal journalist was given a full bottle. He seemed surprised, and did not know what to do with it, but looked at us, saying diffidently that he didn't drink much and murmured about customs duty on arrival in England. I suggested it was worth the duty, that it was rare and expensive at home. He hesitated; but under managerial bowing his manner changed, he accepted it with a little return bow saying, "Thank you very much, most kind of you, I'm sure." Then with a glance at us, "We'll drink it on the journey, shall we?" "No, you keep it", we advised. He began to look pleased, like an inhibited child with an unexpected Christmas present. He was born in a West Country town, the son of a reporter on a local paper; he turned out to be kind and friendly, and no doubt he was efficient in his own idiom of journalism.

We got into two Mercédès-Benz cars and went on to a new autobahn, once touching 50 m.p.h. I sat in the rear car, about five years' old and slower than the leading car. Our host, a curious German-American fellow who had served as an officer in the German Navy during the war, stopped about five times on the journey to give us wine and bread and sausage, and we finally went to bed a couple of hours after midnight at Friedrichshafen in an hotel by a great lake. I was relieved to get out of the car. The driving was mediocre; the driver braked on corners downhill; the hood was closed over us.

The next morning we walked over the aluminium frame of a new Zeppelin. Everything about it suggested lightness; e.g. the bed foundation was a single thin silk sheet stretched tight. I wondered what would happen if a razor were accidently drawn over one in flight. No photography was allowed here.

At Stuttgart we visited the German Institute, where every German living abroad was registered, after being contacted. The idea, declared an official in a surprisingly loud and rasping voice—he had been talking with us gently before rising to his feet in a small room—was that the Fatherland wanted to know everything done by Germans everywhere. How they lived: what their houses looked like. Every German was Germany. There were masses of snapshots.

"In the old days we wanted our undesirables to emigrate. Now we say, Every emigrant must be an Ambassador, and show by his work, whether plumbing, art, farming, or science that he is heart and soul in his work!"

Speech-making seemed to be catching. The star Liberal journalist, who apparently had appointed himself (the bottle still unopened) British Representative, got up as soon as the stentorian but good speech was over and said suitable words back, often mentioning Peace. Even he had partly succumbed like the Rev. Frank Buchman on the first day, who was soon heiling Hitler and shooting out his right hand.

At 2 a.m. the next morning I stood the camera on the window-sill of my bedroom and clicked the shutter open, having first switched off the light in my room. I left it there while I undressed, washed, and got into my pyjamas. Then I leaned out of the window beside my little black metal box. After a further 2 or 3 minutes I closed the shutter, hoping all would be well.

Everywhere we went we seemed to collect new people. Hospitality was unlimited. Hock flowed down our throats from straight swan-necked bottles. An American girl appeared at Garmisch-Partenkirchen where I spoke to a Herr Baron who in a low voice, when asked what he thought of the new Germany replied with a shrug and the words, "Is it wise to say?"

When the baron had left with his dancer friend, together with the husband of the dancer, a Dutchman standing at the bar said to Phillip, "*Belle amie, ja?* Der husband is what you call complacent, ja?" He made the motion of flicking banknotes with his fingers. "Money talks, do you Englische not know so? The Herr Baron still haf fife horses," as he winked heavily. "Dat is somethin' nowadays."

"Does he hunt, or are they race-horses, as in England?"

"The Herr Baron he used to hav' fifty race-horses, now it is only fife." The Dutchman then whispered wetly in Phillip's ear, "No good, eh? *He* make war, eh? No no, not de Baron. You do not understand. You know who will make annoder war? Not the Baron, he make water, yes, we all make water, ja, but not de war. It is come soon, yes? Money talks, and he has no money, it is true, ja?"

"Money does more than talking. It can send men to death. Hitler is only Napoleon over again."

"That is so. No money, no gold."

The Liberal star journalist had joined the two and was listening.

"Napoleon tried to divert the use of money as usury, you see, and so tried to create a self-sufficient and united states of Europe," Phillip went on hopefully. "That, of course, was not the British bankers' idea at all. They wished for trade, in order to lend, and so make more money. You know that, you and old Van Tromp with his broom to sweep the British ships off the seas."

"Ja ja, Van Tromp, he did some sweeping, too, my friend!"

"The bankers, or banksters, of Lombard and Threadneedle Street wanted a gold-based Europe, since they had the gold in their vaults."

"What's wrong with that?" asked the pipe-puffing Liberal journalist.

"Bad for trade, sir. Very bad." Phillip drank his tenth glass of champagne and said, "Zum Wohl!", before continuing with what he had read in Birkin's weekly paper. "You see, France after the revolution was bankrupt. So she could not afford to buy sugar and other commodities brought from the British colonies in British 'bottoms'. So he started a new system."

"And ten million died in Europe as a consequence."

"Yes, when England started to blockade Europe. If Napoleon's system had prevailed, Europe would have become self-sufficient, with a share in the trade from the East."

"Then why did not Napoleon try peaceful overtures? Shall I tell you? Because he had a lust for power. 'And all power corrupts, but absolute power corrupts absolutely.' Lord Acton said that, if you know your history."

"My history, sir, is not of the law, such as Judge Jefferies and those judges who said, or one of them, that Englishmen would not be able to sleep safely in their beds if children were no longer hanged for stealing anything to the value of half-a-crown and upwards. But the point is this, Lombard Street bellies would have to shrink if Napoleon and his system prevailed. He offered a prize for anyone who discovered a substitute for cane sugar. It was won by someone in Poland who cultivated a weed which became what today we call sugar-beet. He offered a prize often thousand francs for a substitute for bicarbonate of soda from sea-water. Someone made it. Cotton from America was substituted by silk from Lille and elsewhere. Europe was blockaded, Nelson burned Danish ships which traded with Napoleon——"

"But Napoleon used force. And found his grave in Russia——"

"Russia, under Alexander the King, double-crossed Napoleon, don't forget. Napoleon was promised Russian wheat, then Alexander bilked and accepted a bribe of four million pounds in gold from Lombard Street not to deliver in bulk. So Napoleon went to give Alexander a punch on the nose and was defeated by General Winter. And—no, don't interrupt me—I know your point of view, in a way it is mine too—cheerio." He swallowed another glass of wine. "In eighteen fifteen Napoleon said, 'These English will rue the day they refused to work with my system. In a hundred years there will arise a nation across the Rhine which will break the strangle-hold of gold in Europe. And he was one year out; for ninety-nine years later there was nineteen fourteen!"

"Who are you? Why are you talking like this in Germany, when very soon we are likely to be at war all over again?"

"My name is Phillip Maddison, and I write books."

"Phillip Maddison? You wrote the Donkin Tetralogy? That was a fine work, an idealistic work. What has happened to you since you wrote those novels, and that even better book, *The Water Wanderer*? Stick to your last, my lad, and don't try and play Hamlet."

Phillip was relieved when the entourage got back to Berlin and put up at the Adlon Hotel. Too much wine and food and late nights had brought on a kind of sciatica in his left leg, which bore the purple scars of two wounds on the Somme. He limped. The American girl telephoned him one afternoon as he lay on his bed and asked him if he wanted a nurse. Alarmed that she might want to offer personal consolation, he hastily replied that he felt much better, thank you. That night a casual flier from Athens joined the party round the table. Later they went to a tavern and sat drinking in the cellar where, it was said, *Tales of Hoffman* had originated.

Their host told Phillip that the night-life of Berlin had been cleaned up since the Third Reich had taken office. Beer stalls where rouged youths dressed in girls' clothes awaiting nightly custom were no more, together with halls where pornographic films had been shown. Now the vice was no longer open. In the same café rows of girls were sitting behind the bar, each one with a seat opposite her. What did one talk about, the weather? They went to dance halls, but the Britishers kept together, occasionally dancing with the American girl from Stuttgart. In one bar Phillip saw a blond youth with the most extraordinary weary face. There were deep wrinkles round puffy eyes. He looked as though he had not slept for six months, but was kept going by being filled up with pale pink wax half-dissolved in alcohol. He was a waxen effigy, dead but giving the appearance of mechanical life. At first Phillip saw him as a hangover from the inflation, corruption, and consequent disintegration from defeat in the war, and the influx of the worst elements from the ghettos of Central Europe and Poland; but then he reflected, This man is German, and has corrupted himself.

In some small hotels where he went with Martin at night notices were displayed that Jews were not wanted, as coloured men were barred in some hotels in London and New York. Once as they were passing a photographer's shop he saw a youth sticking a notice, about a quarter the size of a foolscap envelope, with printed words *Ich bin Jude.* An hour later when he returned that way someone had scratched at it with a fingernail. Nervously? Covertly? Timidly? It remained like that for three days. On the fourth day he saw that it had been removed. And that evening, sauntering down the Kurfürstendamm about midnight with Piers and one of the actors who was the juvenile lead in *Black Roses,* a large Chrysler car moved slowly, as though courteously by them as the three men crossed a sidestreet junction. Usually cars rushed across, having right of way. There was no speed limit in Berlin, and frequently there were tyre-squeals as drivers braked to avoid smashes. In the Chrysler were four hefty men with prominent noses. (Why, wondered Phillip, as they were about to pass by, were German Jews so much more Jewish than those born in other countries? Or was this, if so, a phenomenon of inflation: overmuch food, drink, cigar-smoking and consequent sinus troubles and need to clear nostrils by fore-finger winkling?) He was surprised to hear Piers, who had been drinking a fair amount of Schnapps, say,

"Jah, Juden!", for this didn't sound like the normally courteous man he knew. The sequel was also surprising.

The car stopped. Four heads turned and regarded him. For a moment Phillip thought they were going to get out to slug Piers; but after a quarter of a minute the Chrysler went on, slowly, silently as before, leaving Phillip trying to account for the taunt. Perhaps it was lack of sleep, and the strain of working long hours in what was perhaps the worst atmosphere for a writer: a film studio. Fatigue and consequent nervous overstrain caused his own manners to deteriorate, he thought: lack of sleep and too much travelling on top of writing the trout book had made him so impatient with Lucy and critical of Felicity that he had literally flung himself away to the Gartenfeste. Even the Liberal star journalist had shown fatigue on the tour: on six different occasions when they were tired of motoring, towards evening, he had said, "We must open my bottle of Himbeergeist sometime." It had remained unopened: his humanitarian or benevolent desire seemed to be fulfilled by the thought-expression, leaving him once more on his more commonplace level of caution.

Once or twice, Piers and I, accompanied by some of the English actors, went to the Eden bar, where various girls sat each at her table, awaiting men friends known and unknown. They were beautiful young women: cool, poised, impersonal—almost. In fact, I thought, too good to be what they were: I am an inhibited puritan with a subconscious fear of syphilis from early warnings by my father when pointing out the dreadful shambling figure of one of my mother's brothers.

In fact, Melissa, I am old-fashioned. My experience, slight, in the war-years in darkened Piccadilly with such women or rather girls was that they were—except one—hard, grasping, callous. From what Piers said this evening, the Eden scene is part of a rapidly vanishing Germany. Such girls apparently do not go off with just anyone: the first consideration is that they must take a fancy, then a liking for a man, who will entertain, then be entertained by them privately. Distinguished amateurism rather than professionalism. Films now being made at Neubabelsberg set a standard of graciousness and gentility—false though they are. But all good manners are a kind of falsity, in that they are calculated, or consciously so. I found from my visit to the Eden tonight that I still have an adolescent fear of female beauty awaiting male appreciation.

The Adlon is different. No-one sits at the few tables or at its somewhat grim and massive bar. I almost expected the Kaiser to walk at any moment into the drawing room where the Imperial Effigy stands in an alcove and induces the imagination to see heel-clicking, stiff-bowing, uniform'd men with shaven necks bulging over hard collars and glint of eye-glasses fixed deep into sockets above duel-scarred cheeks.

All that has gone with the war. The Adlon is now a period-piece, yet more solid-seeming than the present with its classless revolution and mental idiom of speed and of efficiency through speed, facing up to problems and solving them instantly through action.

I have to watch this in myself, again and again, and try to check it. My own built-up idiom or tempo inclines to sudden peremptory action, especially after periods of inaction and hesitancy and putting-off. I suspect this to be Hitler's Achilles-heel, too: with consequent partial devastation, even insubordination, (Röhm, and the 'night of the long knives?') But so far as I have seen this effect has not yet reached the masses. Proper education for the young will eliminate the need for exhortation and drive: every man his own leader.

Yes, the Adlon gives a sense of security which somehow I cannot entirely feel in the new Germany. I expected to find lavender saches in the cupboards and drawers (no, this is sentimentality, I didn't expect to find them) but the period is Edwardian, or late Victorian, with the old-fashioned telephone, massive bath, heavy furniture, vast looking-glass confronting a hollow-feeling me shaving a tenuous ghost staring from the reflecting film of hydrageum. (Quicksilver to you, my sprite my Ariel. I'll continue tomorrow.)

There is a haunt in Berlin of American and British correspondents called *Taverne*. I went there tonight with the retired naval officer who took us on the motor tour. There my remarks met with disapproval. On hearing me say to Herr Leutnant that our youth in Britain is generally speaking leaderless, ruled by the pre-war idiom from which nearly all the younger intelligentsia react with a sort of communistic humanitarianism, one young girl sitting with her mother at the reserved Press table leaned over and said, "You are a little Englander, and ought to be ashamed of uttering such remarks about your country in a foreign capital." Beside her mother sat a man who was the Berlin correspondent of a leading English newspaper.

We got into conversation, or some sort of argument, about mediocrity and that originality called greatness. She went to a school on the downs near Brighton and looked like the captain of the hockey team when she demanded across the table, "I suppose you think you are a great man?" "Oh rather," I replied lightly. It was amusing, she was a charming creature. There were, *The Times* had said, some grounds for the unfriendly attitude of most journalists to the Nazis. The system of news-reporting was wrong. All news collection is essentially a keyhole business; either that, or one has to rely on official hand-outs which, as *The Times* correspondent near me pointed out, might give several versions, some contradictory, at intervals of perhaps several hours, in reply to telephonic enquiries at the Ministry of Propaganda.

Exasperating for a newspaperman: the paper going to bed in London and his column still untelephoned.

The Times man also said, significantly, "Part of Hitler is dead beyond resurrection. He is neither homosexual, nor capable of loving a woman naturally." I said, "You mean a phoenix?"

He addressed an envelope to Melissa, stuck and stamped it—and then threw it aside. It was awful, naked, weak stuff about the girls in the Eden bar. And *syphilis*—it would repel her. He picked it up from the floor and put it in the bottom of his suit-case.

That day he was taken by Martin to visit a labour camp. Young men working with the slow but steady rhythm of the body unimpelled to quickness by thinking too many thoughts. Draining marshes, reclaiming heathlands. Living in wooden huts. They looked to be limber and healthy.

"If only Birkin's plan to make new motor-roads, Martin, some years ago, with our unemployed, could have been put into action, instead of the millions virtually rotting on the dole."

"And England rich, rich, rich with gold, despite the great effluent across the Atlantic during the war!

"Yes, Phillip! During the 'twenties, our Rhine was an effluent, all sewage and pollution. Now we do not waste the fertility of our German soil! Our Führer has got back the Rheingold! Siegfried has slain the dragon and rescued Brunhilde! The fertility of our German soil is saved, and put back on our good German farms!"

Martin might have been addressing a public meeting. Once again he was a self-built image of Hitler. But how did the opera end? Valhalla of the Gods in flames, the world drowning as the Rhine overflowed to sweep all away. Was it the wave of death prophesied by D. H. Lawrence, the honorary soldier of the Western Front, phoenix in his own right——

When his Reisechecks were spent he was given 150 RM for the fare home. 4 hours and 35 minutes to reach Croydon, 990 kilometres from Berlin. Oh, the change from lyric-restored Germany. The away-feeling in the faces of Londoners. Shabby suburbs. Soot-darkened buildings of the City of London.

Sitting in the Barbarian Club was a West Countryman who had made a considerable success by writing his autobiography

Farmer's Boy. He told Phillip that many banks, which after foreclosing on mortgages, and being forced to farm land themselves had lost money that year. Hundreds of farms in every county of Great Britain were being put up for auction at Michaelmas without reserve.

"Read my article in *Farmer's Life* this week. Land in England has never been so cheap since just before Napoleon tried to have a smack at what your pal Hitler may be bloody fool enough to try and do. Now's the time to buy land. This world slump is bound to lead to war, and then your blind trout will be growing gold scales on both sides of his body."

When Phillip got home Ernest was in the house alone. Lucy, he said, was at the nursing home.

"What, ill? Or the baby?"

"Oh, it was the baby."

When Ernest said no more Phillip cried, "Is she all right?"

"Perfectly all right."

"Ernest, please let me know. What happened?"

"I told you," replied Ernest, distinctly. "Lucy went into the nursing home to have a baby."

"But *when*?"

"Oh, soon after you left."

"What is it—boy or girl?"

"A boy." He added, "It weighed seven pounds exactly. I weighed it myself, on my father's spring balance."

"I left my address, you know. The Stefanie Hotel, Kurfürstendamm."

"Ah."

"Is Rippingall here?"

"He is not," replied Ernest. "He absented himself the day after you left."

Chapter 9

OLD ORDER

"Lucy, although it's lovely to have you back again, I don't think I can stick another winter in this valley. Anyway I've missed the 'bus—the war-book boom is long over—Graves, Sassoon, Blunden, Manning, Barbusse, Jünger, Duhamel, Aldington, Edmonds, have all written their stuff. Remarque scooped the pool, writing with the tensions of imagined dread. They told me in Germany that he was too young to know battle, but I knew it after reading sixty pages."

Lucy was looking through several years' accumulation of Christmas cards, wondering which to keep and what to throw away, while half-listening.

"All I seem to do is newspaper articles. Chettwood of the *Crusader* wants some more about animals. I'll have to imitate my younger self, I suppose. I'm getting on for forty-one, and nothing done of my *real* life's work."

His real life's work. The words remained in her mind. What *was* his 'real life'. His hopes, perhaps. Well, she was more fortunate, being a woman. She had her baby, darling little Jonny. If only Phillip could be happy. Then there were Billy, Peter, David, Rosamund, and—Jonny. He was such a darling, with dark eyes and sensitive face like the photograph of Phillip's cousin Willie. If only Willie had lived—— Perhaps Jonny would grow up to be the friend he needed. Piers was good for Phillip—up to a point. Thereafter they were different. Poor, lonely Phillip.

"I think I'll go to the Gartenfeste, Lucy."

"Yes, you go, my dear. You're happier there really, in your Sanctum, aren't you?"

In the pale blue October air a sparrowhawk was wheeling, cutting an arc through the lens of the Zeiss glass with wings which shone at the turn like the yellow grasses in the low sunlight. It was so quiet on the hilltop that the cries of swallows dashing at the hawk seemed to come from just above the clump of beech trees behind the north boundary of the field. But even with the eight magnifications of the lens he could not distinguish the whitish patch on each swallow-breast. My eyes are not what they were. The delayed action of mustard gas, perhaps.

He focused on the hawk, deciding it was not the bird of prey that excited the swallows, after all. They were *playing* through the empty corridors of the sky—but not empty for them, for the birds were feeling the tribal message to migrate.

The sparrowhawk returned, and cut spirals against the candent blue of the sky. The swallows, fleeing back, rose up to another mock attack. They wheeled around it like a German fighter *geschwader* keeping the ring for their ace aircraft, circling in tight turns above, to dive out of the sun and pour tracer into a lone enemy. There was a continuous singing twitter while calmly the hawk soared, tracing a flat spiral (so it seemed, but of course it was losing height) upon the sky. Sometimes one of the winged specks seemed to hurl itself upon the hawk, but to flick up again hurriedly to join the agitated throng above. Phillip watched until the birds were out of sight behind the dingy-leaved beech trees.

He sat in the calm autumn sunshine, trying not to think how in a few days his poor trees, cut by Atlantic winds to the shape of a porcupine, would be black and bare as their topmost boughs already killed by incessant salt blasts. Soon the last brown leaves would be streaming away in the wind. And the swallows, which roosted in thousands among the reeds of the lakes behind Malandine sands, would be on their way to the African sun.

A hopeful grasshopper was risping in the grasses, fiddling away with his hind legs for a last chance of love. No blighting Puritan conscience about that soulless little harlequin. He, too, was born to die, as one of the inscriptions over a German youth camp declared—'for Germany'. All things pass away. That marvellous psalm, ending in 'dust to dust' . . . The Abelines would soon be gone; masons, carpenters and plasterers take over for the new co-educational school to be run by a refugee from Germany. How had he got the capital to alter the place, since a refugee was supposed to have come out with no more than ten shillings, owing to currency regulations?

When he returned from the Gartenfeste, Lucy said, "Melissa was over yesterday, Pip. She didn't know you'd been to Germany."

"I did write to her, but didn't post the letter."

"Oh, why not. She would have appreciated it, I'm sure."

Phillip had read it to Lucy in the nursing home. "It was clear, and very interesting, at least I thought so, but then I'm not really capable of judging. Did you see Piers while you were in the field? He rang up, and I told him you were there. Oh, before I forget, there's an *Urgent* parcel of proofs for you, from Plymouth."

"*The Blind Trout!* Now I'll know if the prose is any good!"

He tore open the parcel, and read at random. The prose was hard, it was true. He felt a glow. "I'll go through them later. How are the children?"

"Oh, just the same. Peter likes going to school with Billy. They walk across the deer park every morning, and back again in the afternoon. Melissa is staying for a few days, she said, to pack up her things."

"Is George there?"

"I think she said he'd gone to Norfolk to shoot partridges. Why not give her a ring, I'm sure she'd like to see you."

Melissa opened a side-door before the main entrance to the Abbey.

"I saw you from my room. Come on up, chuck your coat anywhere."

She had a flat in the east wing, once the land steward's quarters. A gramophone, a piano. Cut-out pictures on the walls. On the chimney shelf, part-covered by displayed telegrams, photographs. Her school; hounds, horses, yachts, friends and relations. Fourth of June occasions. Offered him her armchair, then sat at one end of the sofa.

"What was Germany like?"

"Quite different from the newspaper stories."

"Did you see that photograph in the *Crusader* of five hundred Opel cars all lined up at Southampton docks?"

"No."

"They were imported by a Piccadilly firm to be sold here at sixty pounds each. I saw it in *The Daily Crusader,* with the caption, *All going back to Germany*. The boycott, I suppose?"

"It looks like it."

"Lucy showed me some postcards you sent to the children. I didn't know you had gone there."

"I did write a letter to you, but thought it was pretentious, so didn't post it."

"May I see it?"

He pulled the addressed envelope from an inside pocket. The stamps bore Hitler's profile.

"He looks determined enough to get what he wants," she said, then lifted her eyes to Phillip. "I like a man who knows what he wants."

"Regardless of the consequences?"

"As long as they don't hurt others."

He began to feel insubstantial. She recognised this feeling, and said demurely, "May I keep the letter for my birthday present?"

"I wondered what all those telegrams were for. Congratulations, and many happy returns."

"I'm twenty-one. My own mistress, I suppose."

He thought of her father's remark at the hunt dance. She sensed what he was thinking, and moved beside him. "Aren't you going to kiss me on my birthday?"

He held her and stroked her brow. So tender, so clear-feeling. He kissed the dear head, so vulnerable now that he held it. Generous Melissa, O, he must protect this frank and impulsive child. "Poor you, all alone on your birthday."

She diverted, playing with his mood. "Will you bring Lucy and the children to my tea party on Saturday? Daddy will be back then, probably bringing his new wife-to-be. Or do you object to pre-marital relationships?"

"Only my own, I suppose."

"How is Felicity?"

"She's very happy now."

"I heard about the monk by the river. Someone said it was her father. What's he like?"

"They get on very well together. All three of us do, in fact."

"Why not join them, if that's the case."

"The *affaire* is over. We are now friends."

"I thought she was a nice girl, but not right for you, if you won't object to my saying so. Why do you move away from me? Do I stink?"

"You smell only very slightly musky."

"Really!"

"A very rare scent. Do you know that the musk flower lost its scent everywhere in the world in nineteen fourteen?"

"I was about to bathe when you telephoned. D'you mind if I do now? You can come and scrub my back for me if you like."

"Do your guests usually do that for you?"

"Depends on who they are. You might like to amuse yourself

with this book." She gave him *The Kreutzer Sonata* and went into her bedroom, taking the letter. Then to the bathroom. He heard running water, and sat still. Double noise of water, cold running in. Fear troubled him. If only I could feel ordinary. Is part of me, like Hitler, 'dead beyond resurrection', as someone in Berlin said at the *Taverne*? The bath water was still. Was she reading the letter? Time seemed to hiss silently in a vacuum. At last, noises of sluicing. More stillness. He started at the words,

"Are you reading Tolstoi?"

"No."

"Come and scrub my back if you've nothing better to do."

He went into the bathroom. She was lying on her back and smiling like a small girl a little unsure of herself. She sat up, leaning forward to conceal her stomach, breasts hanging a little, ready for her back to be soaped. He rolled up his sleeves and, kneeling by the bath, worked the ball of ivory soap round her shoulder blades then up and down the nobbles of her spine. This was pleasurable, a service of devotion. Her hair roughly twisted at the back of her head, showing the long neck, and pink ear-lobes. He knelt to press his cheek against the back of the neck, loving her, but not with passion. You are my child, he thought, feeling the tenderness of Barley upon him.

"I've read your letter. *Most* interesting!"

When she stood up he saw she was in proportion, a Rodin girl in flesh. He held a towel around her as she got out of the bath. Folded it around her, pressing and patting. When she was dry she stepped out of the towel and put on a peignoir, pushing her toes into swan's-down slippers. She seemed to have forgotten him as she went to her bedroom. A minute's silence, then she called his name. She was standing by her dressing table, the gown hanging slightly open in front. He saw her belly, with the little bush before she put her arms round his neck and with half-open mouth kissed him, so that he felt the tip of her tongue. He felt shame that he could not respond, and went slowly out of the room.

She followed him, her face pale. "You are a sadist, aren't you?" He did not know what to say to her.

During tea she showed him some photographs taken by her father. "George likes to take young girls in what he calls the buff. Here are school friends of mine, taken some time ago."

She put several sepia studies on his lap. "I've read the letter you wrote to me in Germany," she went on, while he looked at the photographs. "I wonder if *The Times* man is right in what he said in the *Taverne* about Hitler being neither homosexual nor heterosexual?"

"Until he finds the right woman I suppose he'll remain what Churchill said of T. E. Lawrence. 'A rare beast: does not breed in captivity'."

"*Was* Lawrence of Arabia a pederast?"

"When I met him I felt he was a disembodied spirit."

"Not even a repressed pederast?"

"What is a repressed pederast? A spinster? A man so natural that he isn't a fornicating womaniser? One who waits for love with his or her own sort—the supreme attraction of that rare thing, 'likeness of thought'? When that happens, the scent returns to the musk blossom."

"Oh darling, forgive me for calling you a sadist."

"Melissa, my flower, everyone has an atavistic streak. I was a proper little sadist when I was a boy. I had a stronger boy with me, whom I got to do my fighting. I used to urge him on to fight. It gave me a limpet-clinging feeling between my legs. But the often bloody results filled me with alarm—and the anguish of pity."

She sat beside him, and leaned her head on his breast, to be gentled.

"You were releasing tensions that your father put upon you."

"I suppose a girl can feel the same?"

"Possibly." She was giving no more of herself away.

"Also, Melissa, when one uses the imagination, and drives oneself with it, 'much power has gone from me', as Jesus said of himself."

The telephone bell rang. Lucy asked Phillip if he would like to bring Melissa back to supper, since she was alone. He gave her the receiver. She said, "I'd love to come, dearest Lucy." She put down the receiver and going over to Phillip put her arms round his waist, pressed her cheek on his chest, closed her eyes and said, "You are a sweet man."

At supper, among the children at the long candle-lit table, she told them that her father had bought two thousand acres of light land in East Anglia, at three pounds the acre including all buildings—four farmhouses, with all service cottages and premises.

"I'd like to farm again" said Phillip. "Perhaps, if my trout book sells, I can manage it."

"Will you farm down here, d'you think?"

"I did think of somewhere in East Anglia—land seems cheap there."

"What fun, we'll all be together."

She helped Lucy bathe the children. She carried David to bed, thinking that the little boy was of Phillip's flesh and warmth, and told him a story. She looked at the baby in its cot, and began to ache with longing. So much so that when she was leaving, and he said he'd run her back, she said she would walk across the park.

"I love walking at night, and it will be my last chance to see the river in starlight."

"I'll come with you, in case you fall in and frighten the spawning fish."

On the way into the park, hand in hand, she said, "You won't think the worse of me, will you, for this afternoon?"

"I was hoping you wouldn't think that of me." When it was time to part she said, "You will write, won't you?"

> Dearest Melissa,
>
> Orion bestrides the southern sky, and signals that it is night. Lucifer arises in the cold mirk of dawn, and a far voice says it is day. Is that frost in the grasses around the Gartenfeste, or heavy dew? My partridges are calling. I am a spectre moving with the last of the night. Waves beat on the sands of Malandine. The sun is fuming below the line of the moor, Lucifer a bead of red gold beyond the Abbey.
>
> At every step the long grasses in the field, uncut for two years, scythe my ankles. I am a spectre, confronted by an apparition with two feathery horns above a mad staring face floating over, the spirit of silence. It shows no fear of me, this lone owl which lives in the dark pinewoods of the valley and sometimes calls a melancholy and vain *Who?* from my roof ridge at night.
>
> I wander over the next grazing field, as light flows full and wide. Ruddy vapours over the Chase have quenched the morning star. The sun's rim gilds the tracks of sheep distinct among grasses, and the narrower trails of rabbits. I look back at my own braided steps, and imagine Melissian tracks beside them. And through the air I come to you.

The sun was declining from Libra to the star-group of Scorpio, and the book on the blind trout was published. To the author's surprise the critics greeted it on the day of publication as a small masterpiece. Just before Christmas the publisher wrote to say it had beaten all records for his firm by selling 3,000 copies in one day, in addition to the subscription of 7,000. Two reprints were on order.

In the New Year the vicar of Flumen Monachorum said to Phillip at the Badminton Club in the old stables, "When are you going to give us another book like *The Blind Trout?* You should always write that kind of book, you know, and not attempt any more novels."

Die Schwarze Forelle, as it was called in translation, was published in Berlin in due course. Phillip was able to return the 150 RM (he hoped without offence) to the N.S.D.A.P. official who had given him money in the Adlon Hotel.

The repayment, made as an act of chivalry to a poor nation desperate for currency, altered the course of Phillip's life during the years that were to follow.

> Nearly two thousand pounds in royalties is due for *The Blind Trout*, not including America and translations. If Birkin comes to power, farming will take its rightful place in the life of the nation. If Birkin fails to come to power, then farming will be a priority in defence of the nation.

Towards one dark winter night of the New Year at 6 p.m., while listening beside his wireless set, Phillip heard the words,

> "The condition of His Majesty shows diminishing strength"

and at once ran down to tell Lucy and Ernest. Then he called in Rippingall to listen.

"May I bring my cocoa, sir?"

Rippingall had come back with the frosts, penitent as usual.

"The following bulletin has just been issued. *The King's life is moving peacefully towards its close.*"

The voice from the aether ceased. There followed the dull tick-tock of a metronome. It went on and on. Lucy and Ernest went quietly to bed. Phillip remained with Rippingall. They lay on the rush mat, playing draughts, as in a billet—a good dry billet, thank God. At 10.45 p.m. the same words as before. They prepared for an all-night watch. Phillip fetched a bottle of whisky. They stood up. Phillip drank silently. Rippingall said, "In duty, sir, I drink my Sovereign's health," and threw the whisky between his teeth.

"Draw up that armchair, old soldier, and make yourself at home. After all, this is your billet as much as mine."

Each man lay back in a padded leather armchair.

"We must keep vigil, Lance-corporal Rippingall."

"Very good, *mon capitain*."

At eleven p.m. the same voice, the same words.

"Have another drink, Corporal Rippingall. Help yourself."

Rippingall stood up. A tear dripped off his chin. "We've all got to come to it, sir. Maybe in the next war." He was thinking, If it comes to that I'll dye my hair black and 'list in the footsloggers. He raised his glass. "Cheerio, Major." Having jerked back the liquid he remarked. "Chesterton once said, 'Cocoa's a cad.' I fancy that was at the time of the Belgian Congo scandal."

Phillip thought to telephone the features editor of the *Crusader* and ask to be allowed to cover the funeral procession through London. No: it would be bad form to ask this before the King died.

A single candle burned on the shelf below the chimney piece.

The hands of the grandfather clock tick-tocked towards the roman figures XII.

"Why don't they have great music at a time like this? Beethoven's Ninth Symphony. They could fade it out as the voice repeats the news more humanly, more intimately, while omitting the preliminary 'The following bulletin was issued', and simply repeating the phrase, which is beautiful, 'the King's life is moving peacefully towards its close'. I'm tired. I think I'll go to bed. No more whisky, Sergeant Rippingall."

"No, Colonel."

Rippingall stood to attention. His moustachio ends were waxed and spiky and each spike was nearly three inches long. It looked bloody silly. He must have seen that photograph in the *Crusader* of some bogus old sweat with six-inch spikes.

"Sir, with permission, I'll remain on guard. For soon Death the Antic with his little pin, bores through the castle wall and—farewell King."

Phillip was hardly in bed when a discreet tap came on his door. He crossed over the polished oak slabs lying unevenly on their joists. Rippingall, making his voice steady, whispered, "Sir, the King died just before midnight, I 'eard it just now. And I could hear the guns at E-priss." Tears ran down his cheeks.

"You are right, Sergeant-major Rippingall. War is coming, I'm very much afraid. Goodnight, old friend."

"God bless you, sir," sobbed Rippingall, going to bed with the bottle.

The features editor of the *Crusader* replied that staff reporters would cover the funeral from various angles, but would Phillip write a personal-impressions article? They would pay fifty guineas for a thousand words.

Phillip took Rippingall with him to London. He wanted a full-dress scene for his novel series to be started one day. The time was not ripe for it; the spirit of the people, which Wagner had written unconsciously gave strength to artists of their time, was against withdrawal. One must remain part of turmoil.

At 4.30 a.m., of a morning threatening rain, the two men left an all-night café near Leicester Square and walked down Panton Street, making for the Circus where Eros, the winged archer, delicately paused after drawing his bow. Recalling Thomas Morland's mere reference to Queen Victoria's funeral procession in one of the novels comprising *The Crouchend Saga*, he was determined to make notes of all he saw. He told Rippingall to make a night of it. Walking up Piccadilly, they passed silent rows of people squatting on the pavement edges, feet in the gutter. Some had rugs over heads and shoulders; newspapers were wrapped round some legs, children among the adults. All were trying to doze.

He decided to stand at the corner of St. James' Street. Rain fell steadily and towards dawn he began to feel peevish. Hadn't he had enough wet and sleepless nights in the war? He led the way onwards, to find a less unsheltered place.

"There's a hotel with a portico and pillars giving shelter farther on, Rippingall."

"The Ritz, sir."

"Oh, is that where it is?"

"Captain Runnymeade and I, Sir, in the old days——"

Phillip hastened on, looking for a stance. Every square foot was taken. They stopped beside a man wearing a bowler under an umbrella. Water dripped from several spoke-ends upon them.

"With permission, sir," said Rippingall, to the owner of the gamp, "I would suggest that an umbrella is an unsocial instrument in a crowd when it is raining."

The stocky man under a bowler ignored Rippingall. Phillip wondered if he were a detective mingling with the crowd. For it had been announced that the heads of many foreign countries would be in the procession, including a German general in uniform and coalscuttle helmet. Strings of a steady downpour continued to plop on Phillip's hair, coat shoulders, and sleeves. Rippingall addressed the stocky man again.

"My gentleman is getting extremely wet from your umbrella, sir."

The stocky man remained still. Sideway pressure and sway increased with the rain. A newspaper seller walked among the moving people in the street crying, "Morning Post. A newspaper, a tent, an umberella—all for one penny."

Rippingall bought two, and put one over Phillip's cap and another over his own. They moved towards the Green Park. Kerb-huddled children were beginning to look like dirty bundles in the indifferent light of dawn. The crowds were thickening fast. Phillip said to Rippingall that the place to be was inside the railings of the Park, with freedom to move about. They went through a gateway and walked under plane trees dripping mournfully upon those leaves which had detached themselves with the extra weight of rain. Strolling about, Phillip decided the thing to do was to transport a seat to the railings and stand on it to see over the heads of those packed on the pavement.

"Come on, Rippingall, lend a hand."

The seat, of wood and cast iron, was heavy. Rippingall accosted a man and two girls hurrying out of the murk, and offered them a part-share in return for part-haulage. They had dragged the seat about a hundred yards when a fat walrus-moustached keeper trotted up.

"You can't do that here. You put it back at once."

"We'll take care of it, officer."

"I can't help that, it's against regulations."

"Come on," Phillip said to Rippingall. "We'll put it back."

Then the keeper spied someone getting up a tree.

"Hi!" he cried. "You can't do that here," and went towards a white-faced and swift swarmer, who reaching the first fork appeared entirely deaf to all threats from below.

When the keeper disappeared the team returned to the seat and having secured new partners, they dragged it to within fifty yards of the railings, then the keeper reappeared.

"Didn't I tell you . . ."

Phillip admitted the crime. But now, three other gangs were hauling seats. The keeper hurried after them.

"I don't think we need take it any further."

So they left it and went to stand on a slight mound about twelve yards back from the railings. It was now light. The rain was lessening.

Soon many people were up trees. Others were dragging seats. The crowd on the pavement was now immovable.

Phillip and Rippingall found that the mound was not high enough. Then a voice behind them said authoritatively, "Now then girls, all together. I shall say *One, Two, Three, Heave.* And again, *One, Two, Three, Heave—Monica, pay attention—and again, as before.* Now then, all together. On your marks! *One, Two, Three, Heave*"—and the seat moved towards the railings not as ordered, but heaved easily over the grass by many long black-stocking'd legs, under blue mackintoshes topped by red-banded hats.

"Well done, girls, just a little farther. Here we are, well done, well done."

The front of the seat pushed the back of Phillip's knees. He moved forward. The seat followed. It now stood on the little mound.

"Madam, with respect I must inform you that you have put the seat on the rise my gentleman has chosen to stand on," said Rippingall, raising his bowler hat to the mistress.

"Take your seats, girls," she replied, turning away.

"What school are you?" Rippingall asked a girl. She said Saint Someone's in a south-eastern suburb.

"My gentleman is the Editor of the *Morning Post,*" said Rippingall. "He will no doubt give your school free publicity in tomorrow's paper."

Looking round Phillip saw that the mistress was listening to what had been said. She looked anxious. He felt sorry for her and was about to tell her not to worry, when all trooped off.

It was 7.30 a.m. Along the route were purple and black banners and poles draped with those colours. Phillip remembered the pomp of pre-war funerals, horses with brush-like head-dresses and purple canopies—bad taste nowadays. These purple and black drapes were proper cockney stuff: perhaps the last time they would be used for an English King.

Every moment the line of spectators inside the park railings was doubling, trebling. The crowd beyond was static. More groups were hurrying over the winter grass, some dragging seats. The crew of Phillip's original seat felt secure. They munched chocolate, smoked, got up, moved about, individual places guarded by the other occupants of the seat. Once when Phillip came back an argument was going on: the rest of the crew were resisting a boarding party.

"Fair play," "Be British," were two of the terms used.

After a while it became apparent that the craft was foundering. The iron leg, with cross-piece supporting one end, was now nearly a foot deep in the dark, soot-acid ground (they ought to lime that land to sweeten it, thought Phillip). The outside ones kept over-balancing and hopping up again. Mounted police passed up and down the street; human figures were at all the windows opposite; others were on the roofs, among chimney-pots or sitting nonchalantly on copings, legs dangling sixty feet above the pavement crowd. Meanwhile the sloping back of the seat was swaying. It had become a lever of wood-battens screwed to and held by slots in the solitary unbroken pig-iron arm. Stray individuals would stop near it, move in close to it, then, after obvious hesitation, try to get up. Rippingall was firm about these would-be boarding parties. "This is Government property," he warned them.

It was a timeless morning. Craft and crew had been there for ever. At last from the distance came the sound of a brass-band. A man on horseback appeared out of nowhere. He was followed by troops, officers of state, more troops. Then a blank. Minute after minute, nothing. (Phillip heard afterwards in the office of the *Crusader* that the crowd had broken across the road at the St. James' Street corner.) More music approaching, drums. The bier must be very near now. Four civilians in black, valets (Sergeant Footmen, Superintendent of Wardrobe, the news-editor told him). A naval gun-team hauling a gun-carriage with the coffin draped in a faded Royal Standard; sun shining through regalia—Crown, Orb, Sceptre—glowing, clear, immortal-seeming. A large tough-looking W.O. of Household Cavalry carrying the new Royal Standard before Edward VIII, followed by his brothers York, Gloucester and Kent. Curious how Edward looked to be the youngest of them: Gloucester, by far the senior. Edward, in the uniform of an Admiral of the Fleet, strode along desperately, as though tired, dragging himself along, very boyish and decent-looking. Phillip observed that a child fainted on the right of the road opposite as the King passed. He saw him take a step aside as though to help—he recovered himself and walked on behind his Standard-bearer. The Pragger Wagger is much troubled, Phillip thought.

Now other Kings were passing—Norway, Denmark, Roumania, Belgium, Bulgaria.

A cockney standing on an iron water-hydrant nearby was giving a running commentary to those behind who could not see. Phillip caught a line of monologue.

"There goes King Carol—'is foters flatter 'im, I consider, but that's only my erpinion, ladies and gents——"

Several girls giggled. Phillip noticed that Carol of Roumania, alone of all the immediate followers, was turning about to look at the crowd. The white cock's-feathers in his hat made this action conspicuous. Coaches followed, Queen Mary with the Queen of Norway in the one leading. More soldiers, then a German general who limped and was wearing a steel helmet. He was followed by high-ranking Japanese officers.

By now half the crew of the seat had left. The cockney who had been giving the running commentary from the water-hydrant suddenly hopped up beside Phillip. He wore a choker and had the hoarsest voice.

"Ole King worn't a bad bloke, was 'ee, guv'nor?"

"No, indeed."

"Now 'e's gorn where 'e can't take no krarn or jools wiv' 'im, can 'e? 'Member ve old song, guv'nor?"

Then in a hoarse whisper, the tatterdemalion sang,

We all come in vis world wiv' nuffin'
Noclo's to wear
When we die, bear in mind
All our money we must leave be'ind
Finish up, wivout ve slightest daht
The same as we began,
For—
We all come in vis world wiv' nuffin'
And we can't take anyfink aht!

"Too true, mate," said Phillip.

The Silver Eagle had been left in one of the side streets off Pall Mall. Phillip drove to Fleet Street, and having given Rippingall money for breakfast, and told him to wait at the Barbarian Club afterwards, went to the *Daily Crusader* building and sat down in the features editor's room to write his story.

Each page was taken away to the comps' room as it was written. Damp proofs came back within a few minutes. Someone brought him a cup of tea, which turned cold. At last it was written; subbed; proof'd; corrected; reset; matriced; plated; bolted to rotary machine; and the special late edition ripping off into the van-yard. Phillip saw a copy and ran his eye down his stuff. In the column beside it was another story of the dead King's maxim which had been pinned to the wall of his study at Sandringham, written in the Monarch's own hand-writing.

Teach me not to cry for the moon, nor over spilt milk.

It was the sort of *cliché* my father would think in terms of, thought Phillip, himself using a Victorian *cliché* as he left the office to get breakfast.

It was a winter of discontent.

At the beginning of March Hitler reoccupied the Rhineland. Photographs appeared of relaxed German soldiers, mounted and on foot, crossing a Rhine bridge.

Phillip sub-let his beat on the Flumen.

He never went near the river now.

"Lucy, how would you like to live in East Anglia, on a farm. With Ernest? He could look after the machinery. He's a first-rate mechanic, as you know. Shall I ask him? No, you'd better. We could form the nucleus of a community. Felicity could milk cows and also act as book-keeper and secretary. Brother Laurence knows about bees. He's tough, he worked in the Congo. The children would love it, especially Billy. What do you say?"

Lucy remembered how writing and farming had clashed when he had been a pupil-labourer on Uncle Hilary's estate. Would not Ernest be to Phillip what Phillip had been to Uncle Hilary—rather an irritation?

"I'd like to think it over——"

"You are thinking of the past, and the trouble over the Boys' Works. Ernest is first-rate in a machine shop, and also a good carpenter. We'll all work on a profit-sharing basis, now I've got some capital."

Lucy said again, "Well——" and then, flushing with semi-desperation that she had to decide, "—if you think it would work——"

"Would you like to be a farmer's wife again?"

"Oh yes! I like an open-air life, you know."

The agent agreed to the sub-letting of Monachorum. He confirmed that the Abbey and all lands and hereditaments were in the market.

The summer wasted away.

As Old Michaelmas Day approached, Phillip said, "Let's give a party, shall we, Lucy? Better send out the invitations at once, time is short."

Together they compiled a list.

Heath Vale Nursing Home. S.E.3 October 11th, 1936
Tuesday.

My dear son,

As you will see from the address I am here for a rest and a minor operation so please do not be alarmed, there is nothing whatsoever to worry about.

How are the little ones? Do send me a line won't you, if you can spare a moment. And don't forget to let me know how Billy is getting on at school, and Peter goes with him by now, I expect? Also my love to dear little Rosamund, and to David as well. And kiss the baby for his Grannie, I do so long to see him. I am lying down and must not sit up until the doctor's examination is complete, so Miss Lewis, my nurse, is kindly writing this for me.

Give my fondest love to Lucy, and to yourself, my very dear son,

from Mother.

Lucy had a letter, too.

"Father-in-law asks me to tell you that when next you are in London he would be glad if you would go and see him. He says that the doctor in the nursing home has decided that he must get another opinion for it may mean a major operation, but you are not to worry——"

Phillip took the envelope and saw that it had been posted in London at 8 p.m. the previous night, and then looked at the circular post-mark on the letter from the nursing home.

"Posted at noon the day before. I'll go at once."

Three hours later he arrived at the nursing home, one of the larger Victorian houses below the Heath. He waited. The Matron came.

"Is my mother very ill?"

"She has an even chance of recovery, Mr. Maddison. Yes, you may see her, but you must be prepared to find a change in her. I need not tell you that it is best not to remark on it. Your sister Elizabeth is with her at the moment. Would you like to go in straight away?"

"I think perhaps I'll wait outside, Matron."

He drove the Silver Eagle round the corner, and sat in the cockpit, trying to calm his thoughts. An even chance. It must be cancer. Was cancer the effect of a psychological condition? The disintegration first taking place in the mind? First the mind in distress—the breakdown of the spirit—the mutiny of the body's cells. The condition began in her early years, in the dark fear she had of Thomas Turney her father. And in marrying my father she exchanged one object of self-suppression, of fear, for another. This fear has haunted all my mother's life. He lifted his feet over his head and got out, pacing between one lamp-post and another, trying to keep his mind calm. Let the mind rule emotion. Yes, she was going to die, like D. H. Lawrence's mother. He returned to the house. The nurse on duty said that he might have five minutes but no longer.

"Has my sister gone?"

The nurse nodded. He followed her into a large square room where a fire was burning in the grate. He saw his mother's face looking small above neat sheets. Her cheeks were flushed, her eyes bright as though with pain. Having drawn up a cane-bottomed chair he took her hand, thinking it was as delicate as the clenched foot of a bird.

"How are you, Mother?"

"Oh, I shall be all right soon, dear. Have you seen your father?"

"Not yet. I came across Thornton Heath, and down from Brumley to avoid traffic on the Great West Road."

"Phillip," she whispered presently, her eyes shining with pain. "Could you pay fifty pounds into my banking account. The dividends from the Firm's debentures are due next month."

"Of course, Mother. I'll pay it direct into your bank as soon as I leave here."

Pain puckered the face on the pillow. After a muted sigh, she whispered, "There's no need to tell Father."

"Of course not, Mother."

She tried to smile, but the wrinkles on the yellow skin of her forehead revealed pain. He held her hand between his palms, willing her to get better, while a sombre thought came that if it were possible to transfer her condition to himself, he would accept it with resignation. He smoothed her brow, seeing with pity that the wispy white hair had been tied with black ribbon into a small frayed plait.

Matron came into the room and said quietly, "I think you Mother should rest now."

He bent down and without any feeling kissed her forehead.

"I'll attend to that matter with the bank immediately. Lucy asked me to give you her love, and the children send their love also."

"You are a good kind son, Phillip. One more little thing, dear. Will you, without troubling your father, bring me my aspidistra fern from the front room? I miss it, I had it before you, my little son, were born. I don't want Father to know, because it may remind him of a pair of his old boots I gave away to the rag-and-bone man. They were too small for Dickie, really, and he was always saying he must get rid of them, so I gave them in exchange for the aspidistra."

Having dropped the envelope with the cheque for his mother's account at the bank, Phillip went to Hillside Road to see his father, who said, "Well, old man, this is a surprise. I am in the act of writing a letter to you about your mother's condition. She is not here you know, but gone into a nursing home for an examination."

"I've just been there, Father. She wrote to me." They went into the garden room. Phillip saw, through the french windows, that the elm tree at the bottom of the garden was dead. Here he had climbed on sunny afternoons during the summer holidays, with cushion and book, to hide among green leaves near the top, where his nesting box had been tied to the trunk. Here he had read away many dappled hours of those unending summer holidays from school.

"I'm afraid I cut it back too severely last year, Phillip. Either that, or it was the Dutch disease."

"Healthy elms can stand a pollarding, Father. It's dank down there on the yellow clay." He thought, How like mother, cut back from a true flowering all her life. But I must not blame my father, my sister, or myself.

"How did you think Mother looked, Phillip?"

Sulphurous fogs, dank yellow clay, mists and smuts from the factories on the marshes of the Thames. What a life his parents had lived. "I thought she needed a rest, Father."

"More than that," said Richard, with an earnestness only partly suppressed. "Look at this letter, it came only a few minutes before you arrived. Only I must warn you"—he went on, retaining the letter—"that it may be a shock to you."

"I had a feeling that Mother was very ill, Father."

"I'm afraid so, old man."

Phillip saw misery in his father's eyes. "Better read it for yourself."

A condition of carcinoma exists . . . Yes, it was psychological. Distortions from the truth had distorted first the spirit, then the body.

"You know what the word means?"

"It is sometimes curable, isn't it, Father?"

"I know only what this letter says, Your mother is to have treatment from the surgeon in Harley Street, beginning with radium needles."

Richard imagined a cure: Hetty would be back again to play chess with him, listen to the wireless, and prepare the meals. It was awful to be alone in the house, simply awful.

"It can be cured, you know, Father."

"Why yes, your Mother will benefit for the rest, I dare say." His optimism was checked by the memory of what his elder daughter had said to him the previous evening.

"Would you believe it, Phillip, your sister Elizabeth had the effrontery to call here for the sole purpose of asking me what money would come to her after your Mother's death!"

"Elizabeth was shocked as a child, I think, Father——"

"I do not know what you mean."

"Well, Father, that's only my idea, when she ran away one night and was found on the Hill shivering and exhausted. It was all my fault. It was after my horrible act in getting Peter Wallace to fight Alfred Hawkins, who used to talk to her over the garden fence. It was an innocent idyll, that was all. I was a horrible little bully, as you so rightly told me at the time."

"But you were only a bit of a boy, Phillip. All small boys are bullies at times. It's part of their nature."

"What I mean is, Father, that shocks in childhood often reveal themselves in strange ways later on. Elizabeth's mania for new clothes, for example."

He remembered how Father had told Elizabeth that he did not love her any more, so she had first withdrawn into herself; later came the fits, and the need to keep up with new fashions.

"I'm afraid I don't follow you."

"I may be quite wrong of course." He thought it best to change the subject. "By the way, Father, Lucy and I are thinking of taking up farming again, perhaps in East Anglia this time. I hear that some land is so cheap that one can buy a farm with a house, premises, and all service cottages for less than five pounds an acre."

"You will lose your money if you buy land, Phillip."

"If war comes, won't farming come back?"

"War, you say? That's a new idea for you, isn't it? You were always sticking up for the Germans, I seem to remember."

"Of course I hope there won't ever be another war, Father. But some people say that the obsolescent financial system will go to war to preserve itself. I mean, as things are now. If there isn't a war, the general unrest in this country will lead to rioting, and direct political action——"

"You mean those rascals of Socialists will force a General Strike again, as they did ten years ago, to get into office?"

"Not Labour, Father, which cannot govern, it's the international money system which governs. I mean the Communists. Then Birkin's party will strike and seize power from the Communists."

"Oh well, I'm afraid all this is beyond me, old chap. Would you care for a cup of tea? Do stay awhile if you can. I find it pretty lonely here without your Mother, you know. You don't play chess, do you?"

"No, Father, but I can play draughts."

Richard brightened at the prospect. After a couple of games he played the gramophone, and put a decanter of sherry on the table. Phillip went down to the fried fish shop in Randiswell, to return with a double portion of cod and potatoes. It was the first time that Richard had tasted such food, which he pronounced to be capital tuck.

Phillip had only intended to spend a few minutes at his old home, but he had stayed nearly three hours.

At last he said that he must be getting on his way.

"Won't you stay the night, old man?"

"Well, thank you very much, but I must see someone in Suffolk tonight. I'm thinking of buying a farm on the East Coast. I've had some prospectuses from a land agent."

"Well, you know best I expect, old man."

"Oh, by the way, Father, I wonder if it would be a good idea for Mother to have her aspidistra fern with her? It means a great deal to her, I think. I can easily take it in my car, and I have to pass there on my way to the Blackwall tunnel."

"Are you sure it won't be any trouble, old chap?"

"None at all. May I tell her the fern's from you? I am sure it would please her."

"You do what you think is right, Phillip." Richard added a little ruefully, "She will listen to you."

After delivering the fern—"With Father's love"—Phillip went through the tunnel under the Thames and through docks to Romford and the road to Colchester and Ipswich.

There was one place on heavy Suffolk land which he wanted to visit for an ulterior reason. In the vicinity of Little Ypene lived a girl who had written to him several times. She had an extraordinary surname of Wissilcraft. In her last letter she enclosed poems which seemed to him as beautiful as they were strange and rhythmical, reminding him of the poems of the dying D. H. Lawrence; but these verses were no mere imitation of that poet's mood. Was this another Emily Brontë, a girl Shelley? She wrote that she would meet him in the village of Ypene, near Skarling, at the Wooltod Inn, and come on a bicycle, with a red riband tied on the handlebars.

It seemed a queer way to ensure recognition. Would she take the bike into the pub with her? The name of Little Ypene was an added attraction. Ypene—Ypres—hadn't refugees from the Low Countries come to Suffolk at some period of persecution? Huguenots? Ypres was the centre of the Flemish cloth trade. Perhaps Suffolk wool was imported in the Middle Ages, and a colony of merchants had decided to settle there, calling the place Little Ypres, now corrupted to Ypene? There were probably *kabarets* called after wooltods—big bundles stitched in hessian sacking and loaded high on waggons—in the Salient before the war. By 1917 the walls would have been used as shuttering for those massive concrete and steel fortresses called mebus by the Germans and pillboxes by the British troops, ringed by calcium flares at night and tempests of fire by day while the battles for Passchendaele were raging. They would have names like Vampir, Kronprinz, Von Tirpitz . . .

The fancy was not dispelled when he came to the Wooltod Inn. It was little more than an ale-house for passing carters and waggoners, with a few regulars among local farm labourers. He had written to ask for a bedroom for the night, and supper to which he had invited a guest, he said. The room he was shown into was overcrowded with furniture, pieces bought at local auctions because they were cheap. Pictures and steel-engravings hung on the varnished walls. On entering he thought that she must have left the room—a bicycle, less red riband, was outside—but seeing booted feet under a cracked Chinese screen, he thought she was having a joke with him, and said, "I spy, with my little eye, your pedal extremities, Laura Wissilcraft."

She made no reply, so he peered round the screen and saw her in an armchair upholstered in black horsehair: a nondescript young woman in dark clothes, with red hands which she did not try to hide, and wearing a black overcoat which might have been her mother's.

"I expect you're tired after your bicycle ride," he said, wondering how he could get out of the place and continue his journey north, to find a proper hotel. She did not reply.

"What happened to the red ribbon? It wasn't on the handlebars."

"I put it on the war memorial."

"Yes, it will be Armistice Day soon. A fine gesture for a poet."

The sitting-room apparently adjoined the public bar. Loud voices ceased when supper was brought in, eggs-and-bacon and strong tea with home-made bread and butter. She would not eat, but sat in the chair.

"No need to feel shy with me, you know. Authors are ordinary people who usually start to live apart, in the imagination, because they don't fit in with normal healthy people."

In that half-moribund hamlet, in the museum stillness of the inn, now that hobnailed footfalls had passed away down the lane, in the light of an oil-lamp hung from the ceiling, she was unable to arise from out of her environmental self . . . winding lanes overgrown with thorn hedges; water-logged arable and meadowland black with wilding thorns; broken field-gates, waggons and carts unpainted, half-rotten; decaying thatch on cottage roofs growing nettles and grass, sodden woodwork of doors and window-frames with broken panes stuffed with sacking and paper—all this visual decay had made her passive with frightening nihilism. Her silence wore out his resistance, he heard himself being rude to her, angry that she could think only of herself, of her own pessimism and misery. Had he not been like this in his own formless past, before he had reformed himself into some sort of rectitude on paper? Blowing black smoke in other people's faces? The root of pessimism lay in loneliness, then despair.

He tried to explain her to herself: she the effect of causes which must be rejected: the heavy Suffolk clays, ditches fallen in, tile-drains choked, thorns spreading over fields which no one would buy at any price, tall thick hedges which kept the drying winds from the small thistly sheaves of August; threshed-out samples unwanted in the Corn Hall, wheat grown for nothing——

"I know it all, truly I do. Beans grown to feed bullocks which cost more to fatten than the market prices the beasts fetch. Barley for pigs that don't pay. Drip of thatch, fallen bedroom ceilings, green mould inside the putty-rotten, loose panes of glass——"

"Why are you talking like this?" she cried wildly. "You don't understand! You haven't had to sleep with a snoring grandmother since you were three years old!"

"I've tried to sleep in a military hospital with men snoring because they were shot through the head! Or burned by phosphorus bombs," he added, suddenly quiet.

"You took part in that war! You helped to keep it going on!"

"I must go outside for a moment. I'll be back."

The air was frore, stars glittering. The loneliness, lovelessness, deathfulness of an ardent spirit snored over in a feather-bed, suffocated in the death of a hundred hens with broken necks or cut throats; this girl's fertility encased in the black beetle-shard of a living death. This spirit a clear stream which had written the poem on the Saxon brook, this dark Ophelia seeking a water-death to carry her spirit through eternity...

How to move her from the darkness of a lost self? Could she share with him his feelings of Mother dying of cancer, that great sooty crab walking sideways out of polluted Thames to confront office and factory workers . . . despair and inner struggle of the young to escape from the death, death, death of a dying civilisation, whose only freedom was in war, the enemy of Carcinoma.

"Laura, you can arise out of yourself if you try. But you must *start.* You are like a tree embedded in peat."

"You don't understand!"

His star-renewed sympathy was leaching away. Damn this could-be pretty girl who would not respond, who wouldn't help herself. Her spirit wasn't strong enough, which meant clear enough. She preferred to drown. "You are polluting the clear stream of yourself. You prefer to drown. You're like a blind, black trout——"

His supper was cold, congealed in fat. He sat down with knife and fork. "Come on, eat up. Be a pal, Laura. Make your craft whistle!"

"Food! Who wants food!"

"I do. I've come over sixty miles from London to see you."

"You haven't seen me yet."

"I can't help you if you won't help yourself. I'm going to pay for my bedroom, then go on to Yarwich. How far away do you live? Three miles? And you haven't got a lamp on your old bone-shaker."

"I can see in the dark."

"Right you are. Now I'm going to pay the bill."

She sprang up and stood with arms spread across the door.

"Let me pass, please."

"No. You must not go."

"Laura, be a good, kind girl."

Her face was different. She had beauty, her mouth quivered into a gentle line, her eyes had become blue he saw as he stared at them.

"Very well, I'll stay here for tonight. Are you expected home?"

"My mother said it would be good for me to see you. She understands me."

"I'll see if they have another room for you. It's freezing outside."

He saw the landlord. "This lady is tired. Have you a spare room for tonight?"

"I'll ask the missus, sir."

Candlesticks to the cold rooms. At her door, "Well, goodnight—see you tomorrow." He went to bed in a room with coving ceiling and sloping floor, and lay sleepless. After a fume of negative thought he got out of bed and listened at the open door. Silence. He went back to bed; got out again and went down the passage, opened her door and got in beside her. He was shivering. She lay passive.

"I hope I won't make you cold, Laura."

She was warm. He put an arm round her, laid his head on her bosom. Her breasts were firm. He felt them, his hand moved down to her stomach. It was hard, she was rigid. If only she would respond to tenderness. How old was she? What would her parents do if she did not return? Bang on the door and find him in bed with her? Then up with the old rusty gun? He began to laugh to himself, a little hysterically.

"How old are you, Laura?" She might be any age between twenty and thirty.

"Eighteen."

"One day you'll fall in love naturally, then all your thoughts will change into happiness. Now go to sleep, and rest your weary head."

He got up quietly and opened the door, and went back to his smothering feather-mattress. In the morning, at breakfast, it was the same again. "Food! Who wants food!"

"You do. Now eat and be sensible. Don't be intransigent. It's a long word for a long process. It means you will not come halfway to meet me."

"Nor will you."

When he said goodbye on the main road, out of sight of the

Wooltod Inn and started to drive off, she sprang on the running board and with desperate eyes stared into his face and cried, "I love you!" He stopped lest she fall off.

"I wish you did love me, but you do not. Everyone needs tenderness."

"It is you who are afraid of love, not me."

She jumped on the running board crying, "Take me with you", clung to him. He wanted to hit her. He stopped the car, and said quietly, "Laura, I must go. I've got three farms to look over, then I must go back to London tonight. My mother is dying."

"You'll write, won't you?" She was pale, her eyes tragic.

"I'll write. And you start writing a novel."

All that day passed in near-hopelessness. His sense of failure was deep. He had already given notice to leave Monachorum at Christmas. Where could they go? Fawley: no, that was out-worn, like Monachorum. Did he really want to farm? To have the old conflict between 'pen and plough' all over again? Yet it would be a good thing for the family. And he could earn money writing about the family's adventures. So, with mixed feelings, Phillip bought three hundred acres of waste and wild land beside the coast of the North Sea for £5 an acre. Subject to contract, he told the land-agent. It would take several years to get the land back in heart. The farmhouse, once an Elizabethan seigneurial manor, was in a state known as dilapidation.

Chapter 10

VALE

"Lucy, ought we to cancel the party?"

Lucy could feel the underlying tension of his thoughts. She divined what he was suffering over his mother, and that his stoicism had grown out of a life-long despair. She knew, too, that he was worrying about the farm he had bought.

"Oh, you know, I feel sure that Mother would not want us to do that."

"But can you make all the arrangements? I can't really face the idea of taking on anything more just now."

"I am sure I can manage, Pip."

"Shall we ask Felicity to come early, with Brother Laurence, and give you a hand?"

"Yes, if you like."

"And I'd like to ask the Channersons down from London. He's the war painter, I've met him in the Club, his wife is jolly. He isn't really appreciated, so I'd like to give the party for him."

"Well then, I'll write to her, shall I? Oh yes, Becket Scrimgeour, the vicar's brother, is staying at the vicarage. You like him, don't you?"

"Yes, he's quite amusing. But a little too cynical for my taste."

"He called here yesterday, while you were away, and played all the afternoon with Billy. I don't think," she added, with a smile, "that he and the vicar exactly hit it off. But then Becket is artistic."

"If we ask him, we'll have to ask the vicar and Mrs. Vicar. That will make twelve. How many can our table hold?"

"Twenty at least." She saw distress held behind his eyes. "Don't you worry, we'll manage."

"I'm thinking of Father. No, of course he couldn't come."

"I suppose there's no hope, really, for Mother?"

"When I went to see Father yesterday he said to me, 'Phillip, the Harley Street specialist told me to expect the end within ten days. She has the smell of death, the specialist told me,' I asked Father if those words had been used. 'Yes,' he replied, 'they are exactly what I was told.' I suppose the specialist has seen so many like it that, for the moment, he forgot he was not talking to a colleague."

She thought how kind Phillip was really, how he understood others. Poor Pip, few *really* understood him. "How was Father, Pip?"

"Oh, he was in one of his tense moods which we all, especially my Mother, found so tiresome in the old days. But there was a reason for his distraught condition. You see, every morning at the same time he walks over the Hill, and down past the dead Randisbourne, which held trout and roach when he was a young man. A hopeful, clear stream of bright water, now cancerous under the spread of civilisation, otherwise unplanned drainage. But I'm wandering into my book! The point is, that morning he was late, and he knew Mother would worry when he didn't come——"

Lucy had a busy morning ahead of her, but she did not like to interrupt the flow of his thoughts, knowing that often he got ideas while talking to her.

"Father said to me, 'I left an envelope, which came addressed to your mother, on her drawing-room table, Phillip. Now I cannot find it. I have looked everywhere, upstairs and down. I suppose my memory is failing. Wait until you get to my age, you will then know how life wears one away. The only way by which I can account for the missing letter is that your sister, Mrs. Willoughby, called this morning, but why should she want to take such a thing? As you know, I have forbidden her the house, owing to her abrupt and withdrawn manner towards me, her downright rudeness in fact. Well, I must be off.'

"I offered to take him in the car, Lucy, but he said exercise helped to clear his head. So when he had gone I went round to Doris' flat in Joy Farm, on the Gordonbrock fields, which I knew as a boy, with my cousins Bertie and Gerry Cakebread, both killed in the war. All the hedges gone, it's now a mass of yellow brick houses surrounding the seedy farmhouse. Doris had the letter. And what do you think her explanation was? That Mother had asked her to put a florin on a horse with Chamberlain the butcher in Randiswell, and the horse had won nine to one and Mother had won a pound. Mother didn't want Father to see the envelope because he disapproved of betting. So she asked Doris to go to Hillside Road and ask for a book which she had left there years ago, and get hold of the envelope. Which Doris had done. When

I told Doris that it was wrong to have taken it she went stubborn and said curtly that I was always on Father's side nowadays, and was growing just like him. I tried to explain, but she was adamant and said, 'I do not wish to hear anything more about it.'"

"Poor Doris," said Lucy. "She does rub people up the wrong way, doesn't she?"

"I got to the nursing home in front of Father, and asked Mother why she had proposed to Doris such a thing. She cried, and said she had done it for the best. And the ironic part of it is that when, later on, I told Father that Doris had taken it out of loyalty and a feeling of protection for Mother, I put my foot in it, as Father used to say. 'Are you, too, against me?' he said, with a return of the strained voice. I said I was only trying to put Doris' point of view, while well aware of her gaucherie, which came from a single-mindedness at times amounting to rudeness. My God, Lucy, it's as tragic as a play by Tchekov. He said, 'My dear boy, I have known for a long time that your mother bets on horses, but she does it with her own money, and what she does with her own money is not, and never was, my affair.'"

"Poor dears," said Lucy. "Oh well. Now I really must get the washing ready, the van will be here any moment."

"I've hindered you. Let me help. Give me your orders. Shall I write down the items while you call them out? Anyway, talking about Mother's money, Father got on to Elizabeth. 'She's a vulture,' he said. 'She goes down to see your mother nearly every evening after her work in London solely to get money from her, in order to dress herself up in all her finery. I've known for years that she has bullied your mother for money, but now, with your mother lying helplessly there, your sister so plays upon your mother's feelings that in the end she has to give way.' It is tragic that Father cannot see that he is partly the cause of his daughter's alienation."

"I suppose she has little to live for, only herself really, and so tries to keep her end up by how she looks."

"I remember Mrs. Neville, my old friend of before and during the war, telling me that women like nice things to wear, not to attract men, but to give themselves pleasure. To boost their morale, in other words. I suppose the root of the matter—or rather the effect of the injury to the root—is that Elizabeth has never been able to *lose* sympathy for others, because she has been striving desperately ever since adolescence to maintain her own life. I'll go and get a pencil."

"Don't you bother, Pip. I'll soon get these out of the way."

"Are you sure? Yes, Elizabeth is so depleted by her psychic wound draining her spirit that she lives in a vacuum, which she is always trying to fill. Well, thank you for listening. I'm becoming a bore, I'm afraid."

"It's rather a trying time for you, isn't it?"

11 Hillside Road,
Wakenham 12 November, 1936

My dear Phillip,

This is a stand by notice for you. Last night while trying to raise herself up on her pillow, poor Mother fractured her left thigh bone. This, the Doctor and Surgeon attending her say is a very serious and dangerous complication, and because of her bad condition it will be a most difficult matter to deal with. Mother must have an anaesthetic for the setting of the fracture, which may prove fatal, and in any case the accident will lead to an earlier demise. The operation will be this afternoon or tomorrow morning and I will let you know tomorrow how things are.

Greetings to all and love from
Your affec. father,
R. Maddison

Tranquil Vale
Blackheath
Monday

My dearest Son,

Father thought I would upset you by saying I have broken my leg whilst in bed but I am alright.

My love to you all. Write to me when you have time.

Nurse is writing this for me as I am unable to do so.

Your loving
Mother
p.p. J.M.L.

Dear Mr. Maddison,

Your Mother lives for the post, it would be kind if you would send her a letter. She is so devoted to you.

Yours truly,
Jane M. Lewis (Nurse)

Dearest Mother,

You are brave in your suffering because you cannot help being brave. This courage is the spirit of life, which endures and is never lost. No love is ever lost. There is a great reservoir of love which has created life in this world, in many forms which must maintain themselves. You live in me, your son, and in your two daughters, and we live and always shall live with you, and with Father, and in our children and our children in us. Among the Semitic desert tribes this vision of love was before Jesus, but he clarified it and made it real in a way that scientists may, in time to come, accept as proved 'reality'.

We are all with you, Mother dear. Your spirit shines with a clear, steady flame. I owe what gifts I have to you: not from your words, but from your essential being. I am with you, Mother, always. And I shall look after the two girls, and Father, in due course.

Soon you will be seeing Grannie, and your sister Dorrie, and your brother Hugh. Do you remember one morning, years ago, when you dreamed that you saw Grannie and Dorrie by your bedside, and Grannie said to you, We have come to fetch Hugh? And later that morning we heard that Hugh had been freed of all earthly pain exactly at the time, six o'clock, that the vision of beatitude came to you. There is a paradise, and all true artists work to the glory of its existence, even if they do not always believe with conventional or organised faith. Be happy, Mother, in this vision which was always your vision.

He sat at his desk in dejection. It was something to *say* to her: not to be written. He cast the second page, and took another line.

And I shall look after the two girls, and Father, until you are well again, and return home. I know how hard it is to endure pain after an operation, before one heals up again. The aching and throbbing of a wound always gets worse before it starts to heal. So keep going, Mother dear. I shall send you a letter every day, you can count on that. Billy and Peter and Roz all send their love, and look forward to seeing you spend your convalescence with us, so hurry up and get better. Ever yours in love, dearest Mother,

Your son, Phillip.

His letter might arrive too late, so he set off for London a few minutes later. On his way up, without breakfast, he found it hard to control his thoughts as he imagined her lying in the tree-shaded room of the nursing home, thin, wasted, refusing all drugs, pretending she did not know what was wrong with her——

If only she did not *pretend*, the truth could be between them. But she pretended for the sake of others—pretending all was well, otherwise what would happen to Doris whose husband Bob Willoughby had left her unsupported for some years now, and Elizabeth so dependent on her, highly strung and liable to fits, all due, so the doctor had said years before, to the shock at adolescence when the father she adored had turned against her. He spoke to his mother in imagination, begging her to believe him, that she drop all pretence and allow the spirit of truth, of true understanding and compassion, to come between them. Sometimes he shouted as he drove. Mother, why did you always try to suppress the truth when I was a boy, always hushing me, distorting the truth through fear of Father's wrath. And yet—was he not like her in this weakness? Never doing what he truly wanted to do—forever censoring his own nature. By the time he reached Blackheath he was exhausted.

"Your mother is very weak, not more than two minutes, Mr. Maddison."

She lay still, only her eyes moved, her nose like a beak without power to peck any living or dead thing, a beak which would never open to sing but go down into the earth, into darkness deeper than the deep blue of the Bavarian gentians of which D. H. Lawrence wrote while dying under the pale blue Mediterranean sky.

He kneeled beside the bed, and took a hand like a claw and pressed it between his hands and heard the slow whisper, Do not worry about me, dear, hardly heard even with his ear close to the yellow lips, I shall soon be well again, Phillip.

There was a respite to summon strength. It is Father I am thinking of, the faint words came again.

Was she dying? He willed her to live, eyes wide open. Take all my strength, Mother. God, help me to give all my strength. Help me always to do the right thing.

Who will look after him when I am gone—he is a very lonely man, Sonny—he has been lonely ever since his mother died——

Yes, Mother, hold on to your truth—I am with you in spirit—do not worry about the girls—I shall look after Doris and Elizabeth.

She seemed to rally. Yes, dear son, I shall be all right soon.

Then the drawn yellow skin that was her face wrinkled with pain and she said as though the very last dreg of life were being burned away within her, It is the nights which are so terrible.

She seemed to die away, then murmured to herself that she would soon be seeing Mamma and Papa again, and Dorrie and Hughie.

When he had to leave he said goodbye which was all he could say until he got to the door when he turned round and said I have forgotten to kiss you, Mother, and the wisp in the bed said in a whisper, It does not matter, and then he knew that he would not see her alive again. How false he had been in thinking that she deceived herself. She was held together by faith in her recovery because there was no alternative but to give up and die selfishly. Mother was unselfishness itself. God in heaven, she would need no purgatory, her life had been a pure flame of the most gentle courage.

With the help of Rippingall and a flash-lamp, rows of dusty bottles in the cellar under the dining-room floor, where the main rat tunnels were, were brought up. The bottles were not old; the dust came through cracks in the dining-room floor boards, which were of mixed wood and all hand-sawn some centuries before. So far as Phillip could determine there were lengths of oak, beech, ash, sycamore, and poplar. Ancient colonies of the death-watch and furniture beetles had long ago abandoned their mining in the sap wood of the planks.

The bottles varied in shape and colour, being bought as oddments from bins advertised in *The Daily Telegram,* which was the paper Rippingall took in order to add to his knowledge of racing form. And having few glasses in the pantry, Rippingall had suggested that the Backwoods party should be given in the Norwegian style. This style, he explained, was to partake of many kinds of wine to be drunk in rotation during one meal, with cries of *Skol!* glasses being raised to shoulder level, and all wine to be renewed after each toast in the same glasses. The meal would start with sherry, he declared, and followed by a dry white wine, then red wine, then white madeira or champagne according to whether the guest were lady or gentleman, after which, he declared, "Anything and everything would be quite all right. They do it just like that in Sweden, sir."

"But Norway isn't in Sweden, old soldier."

"With respect, sir, I suggest that one bottle should go round all the company, followed by another kind of bottle. Of course, sir, there will be scarcely more than enough for each guest, in a manner of speaking, than to wet his whistle."

"But don't some wines mix ill with others?"

"Sir, with all those bottles in our cellar, there will be enough for the blithest singing bird, if you follow my meaning."

Rippingall had a weak sort of grin on his face. His moustachios were waxed by *pomade hongroise* to horizontal pieces of stiff string. A bluish tinge about his chaps might have come from methylated spirit.

"What can we feed them on, Rippingall?"

"For a real Backwoods party, I recommend a single game pie which would not disgrace Captain Runnymeade's best at the old Castle, sir. Moreover, I have taken the liberty, as your butler and major domo, to make enquiries in Shakesbury as well as in Colham and Smotheford of the leading pastrycooks, and also took the precaution to see what dishes were available."

Rippingall unfolded a crumpled piece of paper and gave it to Phillip. On it was written the word *Everything* underlined several times.

"That, sir, refers to the ingredients. Leave it to me, sir."

Now a great oval china dish was sitting on the larder slate. Under the crust, moulded with a design of wheat-sheaves and a reaping hook, were two pheasants, a hare, a brace of partridges, a wild duck, two widgeon, two teal, all ordered to be set in aspic with the best chopped Aberdeen Angus beef, with onions and hard-boiled eggs, and sage and thyme and other herbs. Surely it was the pie of a life-time, an historic pie.

Unknown to Rippingall and Phillip, the pastrycook in Smotheford had spent many hours taking out all the bones and rendering the various meats into little shreds, all to be stewed or baked democratically together and combining to one taste and appearance. This Utopian dream of equality was indeed tasteless. The aspic had not set, it was watery. So was the underside of the crust. As for the wine service *au Norge,* the mixed guests did not appreciate the mixed wines, and Rippingall became upset by the number of hands placed over glasses as he was about to pour from a bottle. And at this juncture there was a wambling of the front door-bell on its wire to the kitchen, which adjoined, and wondering who it was Phillip went to the door and there stood Cabton the writer and a young woman.

Before he could speak, Phillip was offered an outstretched hand while Cabton with a friendly grin said, "How are you? Surprised to see us, aren't you?"

Phillip took the hand and received a knuckle-grinding grip which made him pull back his hand. He had never felt easy in the presence of A. B. Cabton.

"Hardly the way to welcome a guest, is it?" remarked Cabton. He was dressed in a black leather coat, like the girl.

"We went to Fawley, and were told you were here. Aren't you going to ask us in?"

Phillip moved aside and the two moved in.

"I suppose you're touring, Cabton? How goes the writing?"

"Oh, slowly as usual. We heard that you were having a party, so we came along. Quite an affair, isn't it, to judge by the lot of people we saw through the window. If we're intruding say so and be done with it. I've bought a dozen sheepskins from a fellmonger, so we can sleep anywhere."

"Would you like to wash?" for Cabton's hands looked as though he had been changing a sparking plug in darkness.

"No thanks."

"How about your friend?"

"You mean my wife?"

"I'll fetch Lucy. Come into the sitting-room."

"My God," he said to her behind the larder door. "It's Cabton, turned up, as usual, without notice."

"Leave them to me, I'll manage. You go back and eat your supper."

Lucy found a place for them. Cabton looked with an amused air at Rippingall. The house-parlourman was dressed in tail-coat and boiled shirt, with Edwardian high collar and white tie, patent leather boots, and his cuffs—for the suit had belonged to his former master, 'Boy' Runnymeade—stuck out a good three inches from the sleeve ends. To fatten his moustachio spikes Rippingall had added tow from an old rope-end and rolled it in with wax.

Cabton made a note on a cigarette carton. *Butler looks like a dolled up old rat.*

As time went on Phillip noticed that Rippingall was filling glasses while the owners were busy talking to neighbours. Mrs. Scrimgeour, the vicar's wife, observing her rising glassful, said, "I say, what are you doing?"

"Trying to make the party go, Ma'am," said Rippingall wistfully.

Having swallowed several glasses of mixed wine in quick succession, Phillip tasted the pie and at once cried out for everyone to hurl their platefuls out of the window. Polite murmurs of how good the pie was. Twenty-two people were sitting at the refectory table when the four nearest the window, including the Cabtons and the vicar's wife, suddenly subsided. Part of the floor-boards, reduced to frass by boring beetles, had given way under the pressure on the long oaken form. Rippingall got to work at once, and with the help of George Abeline, Piers and Phillip, soon reset the legs standing on planks laid cross-wise upon the broken places.

Other unexpected guests arrived. In the middle of the meal, which was illuminated by a row of candle flames blown and guttering in the necks of bottles base to base along the middle of the twelve-foot long oak table, the door half-opened and Billy peeped round. Invited to enter, the pyjama-clad figure instantly fled. There was giggling and whispering outside the door, and then Peter looked round. He came straight in, solemn-eyed, and sat on Piers' lap. Meanwhile George Abeline had slipped away and was dressing up as a woman in the kitchen, to the fluster of Mrs. Rigg and two other women who were waiting there. Mrs. Rigg had come down from Rookhurst to help, and stay the night. "Oh my dear zoul, vancy that now! Here be Lordy like one of us in the back-house!"

The door opened and George Abeline reappeared rouged, bewigged, and simpering at the Vicar. Phillip saw the Vicar looking puzzled, as though he was thinking, *What* sort of party *is* this? Then the other door opened again, a coiled brass *cor-de-chasse* was thrust in, and shattering bass blasts came from the circular trumpet before it was withdrawn and the door slammed. That was Billy's joke. Phillip, who had been drinking everything poured into his glass by Rippingall then decided to play the part of irritable host, and throwing down knife and fork he exclaimed to Becket Scrimgeour across the table, "I heard what you said I said. I did not say it! You're a bloody liar!" and while faces were turned to regard this astonishing outburst Phillip seized one of the bottles and struck the guest on the head with it. The bottle was an Abeline joke; it was made of black cardboard. A pair of men's braces fell out of it. During the laughter, Rippingall, turning his back momentarily on the guests, threw back his head and swigged a champagne glass filled with brandy.

Phillip had put Channerson, whose paintings of the war had won him a fugacious fame—in that, the war forgotten, Channerson was considered dated by the fugacious critics and art dealers—opposite Captain Runnymeade. Both men, after the introduction before dinner, had not said a word to one another since the conventional how d'you dos. 'Boy' sat at table next to Melissa, who knowing of the painter's fine work from Phillip, had spoken across the table to him. When this had happened, 'Boy' had withdrawn his head a little, as though remotely in protest at her lapse of manners, but really because he felt he was out of his element. He drank only whisky-and-soda, and nibbled boiled bacon specially prepared by Lucy for him.

Channerson, attracted by Melissa, began to speak of his reception in New York on his second visit to that city, when he had found that he was already forgotten.

"They drop you as completely as they take you up when the newspaper reporters push past you at Ellis Island, seeking the latest 'celebrity'" he said, ironically. "But then the Americans are the only nation in history to have achieved decadence without civilisation", and his hearty hollow laughter broke out as his eyes roved around the table.

"My Mother," said 'Boy' Runnymeade, heavily, "happened to be an American."

"Young American women are the most beautiful in the world," replied Channerson.

"Apparently not when they grow up, Mr. Channerson?"

"Some remain beautiful, I dare say. But those who grow into what Arnold Bennett called *le bloc*, no. What do you think?" he asked Phillip.

"I think that your war pictures are already classics, 'Channers'."

"I've never seen them," said Runnymeade, and took no further interest in the party. He withdrew from the conversation and left soon after supper. Channerson went to bed. His wife stayed down for awhile, then quietly said goodnight to Lucy.

"I don't want to disturb the party, so I'll go up now. 'Channers' has only recently recovered from an operation, you know."

Becket Scrimgeour, who was a composer of music, and a journalist, said to Phillip, "Channers didn't like your praising him at supper to the company. He said to me, 'Nobody's heard of me'." He drew Phillip to a corner. "I say, what a little tick Cabton is." He glanced around. "I like that girl Felicity. Who is she? Do you sleep with her?"

"No."

"Where's her bedroom? She's too good to waste."

"I've no idea."

"Who's that friar?"

"He's her guardian."

Ernest had not spoken more than a few words during supper, or afterwards. When he had disappeared to his bed in the disused loose-box, George Abeline said to Phillip, "What's the matter with Ernest? He's not all there. That branch of Julia's family was always a bit odd. Is Ernest half-witted, or what?"

"He's very unhappy. He's in hopeless love with someone."

"Like you, then, my boy!" George poked him in the ribs. "Groping for trout in strange waters, what?"

"Speak for yourself," Phillip retorted. "You and your bathing belles."

After the Vicar and his wife had left, and the Cabtons had taken themselves off to bed, the party became intimate. Kippers were grilled on the trivet over the embers, a heavy cast-iron pan sizzled with eggs and bacon. Billy was the toast boy. Felicity, Melissa, Brother Laurence and Phillip sat together, talking. Becket Scrimgeour joined them, with George Abeline, who said,

"Tell us what it was Phillip was supposed to say to you, Scrimgeour, that he denied? For a moment I thought he was really going to knock you on the head with a bottle."

"I'll tell you," said Becket, snorting. "I told old Phillip that my brother was once chaplain at Strangeways gaol, and that he'd been present at many hangings. Phillip asked him if the men were frightened, or upset before the drop. My brother said that, on the contrary, all of them had been calm and even joyous at the idea of going to Heaven. Phillip thought a bit, then he said, looking my brother in the eye, 'With all due respect, Vicar, you are not only a bloody old liar, you are also a bloody old fool!' Ha-ha, that was a bit of wit, wasn't it? Dear old Phillip, you'd think butter wouldn't melt in his mouth, wouldn't you?"

"Did you say it?" asked Melissa.

"Well, not exactly in those words."

"It's too good a story to be denied, anyway."

Rippingall came in with a bowl of punch. He stood above them, a figure spirituous and euphoric, and enquired, "Everything all reet?"

The glasses having been topped up, he raised an arm in a Roman salute, saying, "Up Birkin!" and with a grin of amiability turned and put the bowl on the sideboard. Then lifting the bowl to his mouth, he drained the contents.

"Needs a lemon," he announced, and disappeared into the kitchen. He returned at once to say, "My lords, ladies, and gentlemen—the wireless says—the Crystal Palace is on fire!"

Richard was walking up to the crest of the Hill, feeling that now he was old he was lost and had no purpose at all in living, when he saw a glow in the southern sky. Reaching the summit he saw what appeared to be a Zeppelin fallen and on fire. As he stared, the urgent notes of a fire-engine arose from the darkness below. A succession of headlights was moving along Charlotte Road. Then from behind, in the direction of Deptford and Blackheath came other urgent bells, and he realised that the Crystal Palace was burning.

Striding now with some purpose down the gulley, he went home and wheeled his bicycle from the lower lavatory room where it had always been kept. The tyres needed pumping up. The wick of the silver-plated King Dick colza-oil lamp burned steadily. He had recently overhauled his faithful steed, as he still thought of the Sunbeam.

Bicycling along Charlotte Road and then to the left up the Rise, he remembered the many times he had pedal'd up and down that way, Oh, forty and more years ago now. How had he come to be old? He was still the same man, except for a mental load of experience which had been in the nature of slavery for others, he reflected. The unaccustomed exercise soon tired his leg muscles, but he kept on, for endurance was now his main feeling, endurance and loneliness. Many motorcars passed him, he began to feel excitement in the air, as the red glow over the roofs before him increased in the north-west wind which had got up when the sun went down on the late November afternoon.

At last he was pushing the Sunbeam up the hill, one among hundreds, nay thousands of people awheel and on foot. He arrived within sight of the top of Sydenham ridge in time to see the great lunar chrysalis, as he had thought of it in his youth, glowing like a gigantic lobster being boiled to death. Then flames burst through the thin shell of the lobster, and became Valhalla on fire, as in *Götterdämmerung*.

It was now impossible to get farther up the hill. Already, two hundred yards away from the building the heat of the flames could be felt on his face. Police were trying to clear a way through the packed masses of people for the fire engines to go on up. It was now eight o'clock: there must have been nearly a hundred fire-engines either at the fire or on their way there. Someone told him that the water pressure w r as poor, that the only thing to do was to concentrate on the south tower and the low-level railway station. The flames from the transept were at their peak. Glass was everywhere melting and forked flames waved high above the iron flame. At half-past eight the glass was all melted, the iron frame was twisting in the heat.

From the terrace of the House of Commons the rise and fall of the flames were reflected in the tidal river. Hundreds of thousands were watching from high ground around London. Hampstead Heath was black with figures. People living in Brighton and Hove left their houses and tramped up the Devil's Dyke on the downs to watch the fire fifty miles away. But from South London came the greatest numbers. Smoke and gases made eyes to smart, and caused coughing. Soon only the south tower, three hundred feet high, and the framework of the other tower, was left. The south tower held a thousand tons of water. What would happen if it fell? As in a dream Richard heard this being discussed. He stood there, knowing that wherever he went it would be the same situation, his life was now nothing but consuming memories. His life was already gone, like that of an old person who has died after prolonged pain and disease. The face of Hetty was fixed in his mind like a land that was eroded, the soil exhausted, desiccated and dead. The fertility, the life, was drawn out of everyone inevitably.

The crowd was thinning. People were returning home. He pushed the Sunbeam nearer the crest. There he saw a familiar figure standing bare-headed near a motorcar, where a chauffeur held a fur-coat. He recognised Winston Churchill. Going nearer he saw that tears were running down his face. Could this be the arrogant turn-coat after the Boer War, who had pleaded for the lives of the Boer generals to be spared? A hero to his sister Theodora, who had once said that a phrase in Churchill's speech in the House of Commons was worthy of the ancient Greek poets. Richard remembered it well, for somehow it had not fitted the character he had formed from reading *The Morning Post*, and later *The Daily Trident*. What was the wording now—ah, he had it—*The grass grows green again upon the battlefield; but upon the scaffold, never.*

Overcome by memories of himself riding to and from Hetty's house in Cross Aulton, and of himself and his dark lantern searching for moths at night upon the Hill, Richard broke down. Tears ran down his cheeks. The discredited politician moved beside him and said in a growling voice, "An age is passing away. I see that your eyes, too, are dropping their tribute salt. And when we cease to weep, we cease to live." He walked back to his motorcar.

Richard was being watched by a youth with a girl. The youth said, "Fancy crying because this old pile of junk is burning. It's had its day, hasn't it?"

The girl did not reply. She was moved to pity by the old man's staring eyes

The quartet, now joined by Becket Scrimgeour, Lucy and Billy, was sitting on the floor and in chairs before the fire listening to the midnight news when from the hall came the shrill notes of the telephone bell. Billy went to see who was calling. He came back and whispered to Lucy. She got up murmuring, "Do forgive me, won't you." Then the door opened and she beckoned to Billy. Meanwhile Phillip was trying to look calm and easy. Billy came back and whispered in his ear. Phillip got up and went outside, closing the door behind him. Lucy stood there, he heard her saying in a low voice, "Here he is Gran'pa." In the light of the oil lamp on the hall table her face was grave, her eyes downcast.

"Mother?"

She nodded. Father's voice was higher than usual.

"Phillip, it's been simply awful. It's like Wagner's *Götterdämmerung*. Poor Mother, like Brunhilde, is at rest. The whole sky is still glowing."

"Yes, we heard on the wireless that the Crystal Palace was on fire. I'll come to you at once, Father."

"No no, my boy, it's far too late for that. I've been expecting poor Mother's death during the past few days. I shall write and tell you of the funeral arrangements. Are you there, Phillip? Can you hear me?"

"Yes, Father. Mother is now free. I'll come up tomorrow."

"Wait until I can let you know the time of the funeral, my dear boy."

Before he went back to the sitting-room Phillip said to Lucy, "Don't let anyone know what's happened." He sat by the fire with his arms round Billy.

Becket Scrimgeour said, "What was it? *The Crusader* wanting you to describe the ruins? They say in Fleet Street that you get a hundred pounds for an article."

"You're mixing me up with Arnold Bennett, aren't you?"

"Anyway, you could do it better than Bennett. He said in the *Standard* when reviewing your *Blind Trout,* that he was outclassed as a descriptive writer."

"All great writers are over-generous to their juniors at times."

Melissa kept her eyes away from Phillip. She felt, as often before, to be swelled with frustration that she could not comfort him. Later on, when he said he must take a sleepy Billy to bed, she went with him. At the door she said, "Felicity, do let me see Edward."

The three went together up to the night nursery. There she

brooded over the sleeping young ones. "Oh, he's the dearest little boy, Felicity!"

Lucy joined the two women, to arrange beds for the men. Billy, Peter and Rosamund were carried asleep to her bedroom, placed in a row at the foot of the bed, and tucked in. It was a fairly large bed, five feet across. Lucy occupied the other end. She asked her cousin Melissa if she would like to stay the night with her, the bed was big enough.

"I'd love to, Lucy, you're sure I shan't be putting you out—literally."

Melissa felt some satisfaction, but without a sense of guilt, that Phillip no longer shared the matrimonial bed; even as she was now unperturbed about Felicity, since he had told her that the affair was over. She believed everything he told her. Had he not opened her eyes to the beauty of the world? She owed everything to him, even her new attitude towards her father: an acceptance of what George was.

When she was in bed beside Lucy an awful thought struck her—how cynical her words must have seemed to Lucy about 'putting her out—literally'.

At three o'clock in the morning, Rippingall brought in the last litre bottle of Algerian wine. Phillip was reading aloud from Shakespeare's *The Phoenix and the Turtle.*

Beauty, truth, and rarity,
Grace in all simplicity,
Here enclosed in cinders lie,

Death is now the phoenix' nest:
And the turtle's loyal breast
To eternity doth rest,

Leaving no posterity:
'Twos not their infirmity,
It was married chastity.

Truth may seem, but cannot be——

At this point Becket Scrimgeour broke in with, "Of course Shakespeare was in love with Southampton."

Phillip at once closed the book and left the room. There was a short silence, then the friar said, "How do you deduce that from this poem?"

"Southampton was a nancy boy. And Shakespeare was pure artist, all his sex went into his fantasies. You can see a self-portrait in Hamlet. He was obviously an invert, a masturbator, like Hitler."

"Why do you think that, Becket—may I call you Becket?"

"I'm honoured, mon père. All Hitler's rages are signs of chronic masturbation."

"But don't you think," replied the friar, gently, "That the poem Phillip has just read is the spiritual essence of the poet? Shakespeare was surely apart from the world of so-called reality. As a youth and young man, possibly not altogether, but when his poetry welled up like spring water, he experienced a metamorphosis. The Old Adam in him died."

"That's evident in lesser forms of life," said Phillip, returning. "The mayfly is pure poetry—pure love. Its mouth is sealed, it neither eats nor drinks after its wings are grown. It dies for love, literally."

"You'll be singing 'All things bright and beautiful' in a minute," scoffed Becket. "Let's have some of that Algerian wine. It sends the Foreign Legionaires *cafard*. I've never been *cafard*. Have you, mon père?"

"Oh yes. I was a scout pilot in the war, and towards the end some of us were blotto nearly every night."

"Good for you, brother!" and Becket slapped him on the back.

"Shakespeare," said the friar to Phillip, "may, as your analogy of the mayfly suggests, have been entirely sublimated, owing to the hard grind of work."

"Don't forget he had a mistress, the Dark Lady of the sonnets," put in Becket.

"Yes indeed, Becket. But I doubt if she gave Shakespeare any feelings of self-esteem, or that confidence a man needs to keep even a liaison going, much less a marriage."

"Don't I know it," snorted Becket, and sang a bawdy song about dilldolls and whips.

Phillip put on a record of the third act of *Tristan,* saying to Brother Laurence, "Here is the equivalent—before the deaths of Tristan and Isolde—of *Phoenix and Turtle*. The immovable essence of honour that was Tristan struck by the irresistible force of the love potion."

"*Tristan* is all unfulfilled sexual desire and yearning for death," said the friar. "All the *leitmotifs* illustrate psychic states of unfulfilled longing incapable of resolution."

"Hear, hear," said Becket. "Nietzsche saw through Wagner, and bloody well showed him up!" He filled his glass with the rough wine.

"I think Wagner's music is heavenly," said Phillip, sitting on the floor beside the gramophone. "I love his sense of the endless melody of life."

"Heavenly my arse," retorted Becket. "Wagner's *unendliche Melodie* is certainly endless but not all melody! There's a bit of wit for you!"

"But Nietzsche was never disenchanted with *Tristan,* surely?" said the friar. "He rejected the *Ring,* certainly, but never Tristan, I think you will find. The trouble with Nietzsche was his puritan conscience, he felt that the music of Wagner was wrong, aesthetically and morally."

"Nietzsche had syphilis, and was suffering from G.P.I. Anyway, *Tristan* is a carpet-bag of emotional tools," retorted Becket.

"One can analyse music to destruction," said the friar, "and in doing so, one is perhaps in danger of missing 'the singing, the apple-blossom, and the gold' of Euripides. One must surrender to music—*musique bain chaud*—and abdicate self-will. Have you come across Berg, Mr. Scrimgeour? I heard his Wozzeck about ten years ago. The effect of greatness still remains."

"Did you, as a Catholic, surrender to that orgy of defeatism, lust, despair and murder?"

This remark did not surprise Phillip. With him, Becket Scrimgeour had been frank to the point of exhibitionism about his own private life. In London, among other activities, he taught the pianoforte to young women of seventeen and eighteen years. And when mistakes were made, Becket used to spank a pupil on the bare bottom, having put her across his knees. Ah ha, my boy, don't I just enjoy it! No, I don't have them, like you do. What, you don't have lots of girls? Of course you do! Everyone knows you've had an affair with Lady Abeline, and now you're having one with her daughter. I have a mistress, that's the only woman I have. I'm faithful to her. The smacking of bottoms doesn't count. But I must say it gives me a hell of a thrill.

"Well," replied Father Laurence. "I thought that *Wozzeck* was a great work, and I still think it is. It has compassion which embraces, and thereby transmutes, all the acts so frankly shown to us."

"You can't improve on Mozart and Bach."

"Ah, there you have pure music, Becket, before the slide to the fall."

"The fall? What fall?"

"One might say, the Faustian fall of Western Man. Mozart and Bach represent the flower of Western civilisation at the height of its splendour, as *The Ring,* and even *Tristan* reveal the beginning of Europe's decline. Art mirrors the age, don't you agree, Phillip? Today we see art, as in a glass darkly."

"You talk like Hitler, with his Museum of Decadent Art at Munich. Hitler will go to war to try and put the clock back, but all he'll succeed in doing will be to smash up the whole bloody caboodle."

Becket Scrimgeour turned to Phillip, and by the snorting half-laughter Phillip knew that some bawdiness was coming,

"Did you notice Cab ton's trousers? He bought them in New York, he told me. He said he saw them advertised in *The New Yorker* as 'The Manhatten Sportsman's Pants with the Fly-by-night Talon Zip-i-addio defence machanism'. He'll need them, on those sheepskins. This house is full of rats, my reverent bloody fool of a brother tells me. I hope they bite that bloody little squit Cabton!"

Stars glittered over trees. Dead leaf upon dead leaf was dropping in the deer park. The grass was white with hoar frost. Phillip had no bed to sleep in. He walked by the river, he would keep watch by his mother's bier. He felt in balance with himself, as upon the frozen battlefield of that Christmas of 1914, a star-like presence bearing him up under the bright orb of the Flanders moon.

The Cabtons were sleeping in Phillip's writing-room. He had explained to them that as Becket Scrimgeour and Brother Laurence were in the only spare room, he hoped they would not mind that his room had only a single couch-bed. Cabton, taking charge as soon as he had looked around, had removed the mattress and put it on the floor. Then he had piled the bed-frame with sheepskins brought from his motorcar. "Gert and I are used to roughing it."

Phillip had thought to walk about under the stars and see the dawn in, keeping vigil for his mother; but the image faded, the late November night soon dragged without purpose, like any ordinary sleepless war-time night; so he returned to his home and, wrapped in his grandfather's coaching greatcoat, tried to sleep on the landing carpet.

It was cold, a draught was coming from under the closed door of the boys' room. Rats began to trip up and down the bare oak treads of the stairs. They must have smelt the uncured sheepskins. They came through the broken floor above the cellar. There was a second colony of rats which entered the house by way of the bathroom hole under the waste pipe. Usually the bathroom rats went exploring on the ground floor, while the cellar rats went outside in the garden below the children's night nursery for biscuits. Now both colonies were apparently after the sheepskins. Which was which, he wondered. One lot seemed to be playing, or courting, on the landing; the other lot to be running races above the ceiling.

He could not sleep. His brain, part-poisoned by the blood-stream polluted by the mixture of drinks in belly and gut, began to churn up past mortifications, miseries, thwartings, work undone, misjudgments: all the compost of the past which only by writing and transmuting would, he knew, move away out of his mind. The two grandfather clocks downstairs wheezed and struck four within a second of each other. This was a coincidence, for he had not wound them for years. Once they had been his pride, in those days of solitary living followed by the blissful year with Barley. He had washed their flower-and-bird painted faces twice a year, at the summer and winter solstices, and oiled the worn brass wheels and cogs, pinions, bearings; pulled up the weights before breakfast every morning. Rippingall had wound them up, after days of stagnancy, for the party. Mother was dead. He had longed for her death, to free himself; but death had brought no relief. Now, lying cold and sleepless, he entered the coffin to lie beside her, seeing but a brittle relict of herself lying there, part of the eternal patience of the earth's suffering before its final dissolution.

Oh, Mother, I have been a bad son, I have not been kind to you: even the nurse had to write a line to me asking me to write to you. O Christ Almighty, even when she had moved ever so slightly in bed she broke her thigh-bone, which was rotten with the rays of radium needles used on a hopeless case. He saw her groins pocked by burst tumours: Passchendaele craters in miniature, the water turned yellow by British lyddite shells, the Salient pocked and re-pocked beyond the death of every worm and beetle as the shells spouted and respouted every ounce of putrid soil and flesh and litter of the parade grounds of Europe. That is true, anyway, for all wrong living in Europe erupted into the Great War. Oh, Mother, are you with those spirits of love and grace which are called angels?

I must not think of the letter of reality. One day I shall write a novel about your life and Father's, I've been thinking about it for years and flinching from the task. At least it will not be critical and satirical as once I intended. If only I can write the simple natural truth it will be understood by everyone in the world. But shall I ever be free to write it? Mother, I hope I get cancer, I feel you want me to be with you in the grave. No, no, I am allowing myself to be possessed by bad spirits. I shall write my book with love and understanding, I swear to you I shall.

The vision went out of him as the clocks raced one another to be the first to strike six times. It was that damned Algerian wine which had given him such gurgling turmoil in his guts. It was what Becket Scrimgeour said the Foreign Legion drank before going *cafard*, or mad-smashing-killing. No more poison, wooden case of six bottles delivered free from a firm at Ratcliffe Docks for ten shillings.

Becket Scrimgeour was groaning and coughing downstairs in the children's day nursery. Phillip thought of getting logs for the fire in the sitting-room, which seldom went out in the autumn and winter on its foot-high bed of ash, but he lay still, half-asleep, cold in the small of his back, clammy hot in legs, after many turnings over, enwound by the Ulster coaching coat which he had found, surprisingly mothless, in one of the big black coach-trunks in the Fawley lofts. At last the grey lifeless light of dawn. He got up, soused cold water on face and hands, and went down to the sitting-room fire. He got some logs, passing Rippingall curled on sacks in the kitchen. Two empty Algerian bottles lay beside him.

At nine o'clock Lucy, Felicity, and Melissa had breakfast on a polished refectory table. Brother Laurence had already shaved and bathed. Becket came in tousled, red-eyed.

"How did you sleep, Becket?"

"Bloody awful."

"What happened?"

"Those cushions fell on the floor, leaving me jangling all night on the wire mattress."

"I thought you were composing after the manner of Schönberg," said the friar with a smile.

"How did you sleep, Cabton?"

"Not much better. You want to get rid of those rats."

"Which ones?" asked Becket Scrimgeour.

"The trouble is they come in whenever they fancy the idea," said Phillip.

"I was hardly asleep after the rat race when you put on the gramophone—this place is a madhouse," said Mrs. Cabton.

"And when you stopped playing those records, I could hear you snoring," added Cabton.

"Your rats seemed to be remarkably tame," said the friar. "One sat up at the foot of my bed and washed its face."

"That's more than some of the guests here do," remarked Becket.

"That's the rat the children call Dippy Dan, mon père. Dippy Dan originally came after Garibaldi biscuits. He tried to take one whole down into his tunnel, which is too small. He spent a lot of time trying to drag it down, until gate-crashers came up and helped him, and themselves."

After breakfast Melissa, finding Brother Laurence alone, asked him what he thought of Phillip's books. The friar divined that she meant Phillip himself, and replied, "He has great natural faith, and a terrible honesty that his occasional sophistry or doubt cannot destroy, and a kind of child-like simplicity that is the only thing that saves us all from being downright wicked. And I have a steady respect for his work and faith in his future."

"I am so glad to hear that, Brother Laurence. He needs friends more than most men, I think."

"Friendship is the word, Melissa. He himself is a loyal friend, I know."

Brother Laurence, driving an old Renault car which he called the Toad, left later with Felicity.

"That friar is bogus," said Becket to Phillip. "I asked him what Order he belonged to, and he said 'Laurentian'. I've never heard of it, nor has anyone else. I bet he sleeps with Felicity. I saw him kissing her this morning, in the sitting room."

Yes, thought Phillip, all we say about others is a revelation of ourselves.

The Channersons departed after breakfasting in bed. The Cabtons remained for lunch, and stayed on for tea. Once again the old routine was to be heard from Phillip.

"What are your plans for your holiday, Cabton?"

"Oh, we never make plans when we are on holiday," replied Cabton, with a lazy smile. "We believe in taking things as they come. Why don't you try doing that, Phillip? You're screwed up half the time. Why don't you give yourself a break?"

"I think I'll take your advice."

Over the Gartenfeste a drift and delicacy of sleet was wandering down the wind. There was an expressed letter from his father forwarded from Monachorum, telling of the day and time of the funeral. With this letter was one from his sister Elizabeth who wrote that the doctors had experimented on poor Mother with radium needles although she was a hopeless case from the first. The specialists' fees were nearly a thousand pounds: she hoped that Father would not try to get the bills paid out of Grandfather's trust, which would now be shared by the three grandchildren. Would he speak to Father about it when he came up for the funeral, as 'you are the only one of his family he likes. You are his favourite.'

He motored at once to London. Cousin Polly Pickering that was, turned up from Beau Brickhill. Her mother was too frail to come. Mrs. Bigge looked sadly out of her window as the coffin was borne to the motor hearse. Cousin Arthur and his sisters from Surrey came with their father, Uncle Joe. The large white face of Mrs. Neville was at her window in the flat below Hillside Road. The sides of the grave were smooth yellow clay. Phillip dropped the first handful of soil on the coffin. Mother was now with her father, her mother, her sister Dorrie, and Uncle Hugh. Uncle Joe, the last of that family, stood beside Phillip, looking humble and gentle. His sister Elizabeth wore the new black coat and skirt, payment for which she had demanded, Phillip thought, from Mother which he had covered by paying his cheque into Mother's bank. He thought no more of it; obviously how to pay such respect to Mother had worried Elizabeth very much. Anyway, the money was only a slight return for all Mother had done for everyone in the family. He took his father aside afterwards and said he would like to help him pay the medical expenses; his father said, "Thank you, my dear boy, but it is my duty to do that. Will you come and have lunch with us at Beeveman's in the High Street?"

"Father, I am so sorry, I must go back to London, do excuse me. I have some work to do. Thank you for inviting me, but I must go."

He walked back to London along endless streets, thinking that he should have gone to lunch with his father and sisters, and not deserted them at the time of their distress. I might have drawn them together, now it is too late.

He went home the next day and learned that Rippingall had

wandered off. The emotions of the past weeks had exhausted him. He had drawn out his savings from the Post Office, and got drunk in Shakesbury, where he had been taken in by a war-widow. She had a pension, which she would lose if she remarried; after some hesitation and doubt she agreed—according to a letter from Rippingall to Phillip—to marry him.

Phillip wrote and wished him luck, and sent him £10 as a wedding present.

115 San Remo Parade,
Westcliff-on-Sea.
2 December, 1936

My dear Phillip,

I was indeed pleased and surprised to get a letter from you. You say you only got my address when I wrote to your father after the funeral, about which nobody in the family told me. I think if you had wanted it Dickie or Elizabeth would have sent it to you at any time.

Your letter is most interesting, but I read between the lines that you are a disappointed man in your family life, more or less. I am very sorry whatever the cause. You know we must give and take, and make allowances in every way. Dickie and your dear Mother never got on well, he was selfish and very exacting, then he was of a most jealous nature, and he resented strongly the attention Hetty gave to her babies. He said she neglected him and he was very sorry for himself. Poor Hetty had a sorry time when Dickie left the office and for some reason I could never determine he went to bury himself in the country, where we had all lived as children, not very happily I fear, since Papa was of a spendthrift nature. My poor mother could never say anything to please Papa, just as Hetty failed likewise with Dickie, and she did try, she told me, with tears in her eyes.

He had no sympathy if she was not well, so naturally she kept any ailment to herself, including the last and fatal illness, until it was too late. Poor fellow, Dickie is now a very sad man, and misses her greatly, as I expect you know.

I hope your new venture is going to be a success in every way. At first it will be hard, uphill work, but I am sure it will pay in the end. I hope your books will bring in plenty of money to fill the gap while you are reconstructing the farm.

With my love, and every good wish that 1937 will be a great blessing to you in every way,

Your affect: Aunt Belle.

There was a note from Brother Laurence. He wrote that Phillip had undertaken a great physical task on the land, but this was good, because it would help to clarify and simplify a greater spiritual task that lay before him: a clarifying of values that the peoples of the Western world needed.

> Even in the terror of ordinary living we are wrung and rent and scorched and temporarily destroyed by the emotions whether of love or hate, anger or ecstasy, fear or resentment, but we can have all purged by the pity and terror of great art, and thereby find ourselves, like the phoenix, living in the spirit once more. You know this, you always have known this, and with this knowledge you have a strong spirit that will lead you past calamity, derision and despair to the Faith.
>
> All great art is grown out of the predicament of man. All creative effort destroys the peace of the flesh, the warring of the flesh, only to clear the way for the flowering of the spirit of creation. D. H. Lawrence knew this, while he rode on the crest of the wave of death. Shakespeare knew this, and Beethoven, Bach, Michelangelo, Mozart, Homer, and all the major poets. You know it, you have always known it. You cannot escape the presence of these values, the presence of what is sometimes called the Holy Ghost.

It was a winter of grief and dismay in a world decaying. An issue of Birkin's weekly newspaper arrived from Piers in London. In big black type STAND BY THE KING.

Under the winter stars of the western hemisphere many voices were encircling the world. Among them was that of the abdicating King of England. His voice was preceded by another voice—the same gruff, wreathing voice which had announced the results of the General Election through loudspeakers during half the night at Mr. Gordon Selfridge's party.

"This is Windsor Castle. His Royal Highness Prince Edward."

Phillip wondered if the voice that followed would break; but he knew it would not. Three—four—five words. Then the voice had to pause to gather fortitude, like a man alone climbing a Himalayan Peak.

Afterwards Rosamund, sitting on her father's knee and examining a half-crown, asked what the words meant round the head of the old King.

"George the Fifth by the grace of God King of Great Britain."

"And the other side, Dad?"

"Defender of the Faith and Emperor of India."

"Why has the new King gone, Dad?"

"He grew up on the battlefields."

And now nearly time to pack up and pull out for East Anglia. But first he must see his father off from Southampton on his world cruise. Richard had bought a ticket in the *Arandora Star,* together with a new wardrobe of clothes, including his first dress suit.

"It's rather a tumbledown house on the farm, Father. Lucy and the children will remain in a Dorset cottage she has rented until I've got it more or less in order."

"Will you be on your own, old man?"

"Ernest, Lucy's brother, may come with me."

"Well, I hope you won't lose on the land what you've made from your books. Au revoir, Phillip. Thank you for coming to see me off. I'll write to you."

Ernest said to Lucy, "I suppose I may as well go with Phil, as remain here." He added, "At least until I hear from Fiennes and Tim about joining them in Australia."

Richard wrote, while lying nauseated in his cabin during the crossing of the Bay of Biscay, *Never again, old chap. I am returning overland from Gibraltar. I will never find my sea-legs at my age.*

"One more for the community, I suppose, Lulu. He'll make a good gamekeeper. There's a lot of wild birds on the farm, also a duck decoy."

The gamekeeper didn't last long. At Gibraltar the sun was shining, the gale had abated. Richard made friends with other passengers. A postcard of the Rock, with a large monkey staring in the foreground, said, *I am a new man, this is a wonderful life.*

How Mother would have laughed!

The Abelines had gone, masons' trowels rang in the Abbey, the Yacht Club was empty, yellow willow leaves lay resting on the bines of crowsfoot endlessly weaving in the cold spring-water of Flumen Monachorum.

Part Three

WAIFS & STRAYS

Chapter 11

'DENCHMEN'

Phillip and Ernest had arrived with a caravan, but owing to the cold weather were living in what was called the Old Manor. At night the east winds echoed down the halls and passages, for the seventeenth-century house was ruinous in one wing. Indeed, the entire building was in a condition nearing dilapidation.

From 1915 to 1918 it had been occupied by soldiers. Compensation for damage—floors pulled up and doors taken off hinges, panelling ripped off for firewood; smashed plaster, broken lavatory pans, fallen ceilings—had not been used to restore fabric or interior. The owner, believing that England was finished, and that the future of the white man lay in Africa, had departed with all his capital, to farm in Kenya.

The Old Manor and its lands had been bought by a group of local speculators—clerks and lesser tradesmen of the decaying coastal town of Crabbe. What remained of the interior was gutted. Doors, panelling, fire-backs, fire-dogs, the chimney-piece of the main hall, an Italian plaster ceiling were sold. When Phillip bought the property the Old Manor had been standing empty for a decade.

Phillip's billet, as he called it, was in one of the smaller rooms of the second or top floor. This room had been chosen because of a small open hearth, upon which had been heaped, when he first saw it, the remains of many seasons' jackdaw-nests. Sticks filled the fire-place, sheep's-wool, grasses, even paper spread out across the floor of heavy oak planking. When all this rubbish had been stuffed into the hearth, on the principle of kill or cure a match was applied one night; smoke poured out, dimming the stars. Flames in the chimney thundered. They had pails of water ready for any falling carbon crusts.

These were soon dropping, to slide red-hot across the floor. Ernest dealt with them expertly with a wet mop. The accretion of wood-oil and soot was thick, probably from oak-wood smoke at the beginning of the century. At one moment Phillip feared that the house might burn down, so great was the thunder of flames in the chimney. While Ernest remained on guard with his mop and pails of water, Phillip hurried by the light of an electric torch to a passage window whence the north wing stack could be seen.

Red flames arose from one twisted-brick chimney, sultry in billowing smoke. As he watched the flames became more urgent. They began to stab the darkness, they were changing colour to pale blue and lilac, there was no more smoke. The chimney was a huge stub-exhaust of a bomber aircraft at night. He thought of the rockets the Germans were experimenting with, some attached to racing cars. He had seen a group of young men in a forest clearing while going round labour camps with Martin a year ago. Martin had gone past without looking, saying, "We have seen nothing, yes?" Phillip had considered himself to be a guest, he had not mentioned it to anyone in England.

While he watched, the pale flames rose higher and there was a burst of sparks which swirled and fell with red fragments. And at that moment there was a banging on the heavy oak door below. He remained still. The banging came again, together with faint cries. He waited. The fire in the chimney burnt out, only a spark now and again whirled away in the darkness. Then there came an irregular tolling of the courtyard bell.

"What the hell is all this about," Phillip said to Ernest who had opened his door.

"Ah," said Ernest, and closed the door.

"Someone in the village must have thought the bloody house was on fire. I wish to God it was. Not really. It doesn't belong to me, but to white owls, and bats," and Phillip went down the stone stairs and through the kitchen to the courtyard door.

A shadow stood there. "Hullo," it said, and then cleared its throat. "I know you, but you don't know me," it continued. "I thought I'd see how you're getting along. Everyone in the district knows me, I live in the yard by the Cross."

"Do come in. My name is Maddison."

"I know that."

"Oh."

"I saw your house was on fire, so I thought I'd come and insure it for you."

"That was kind of you."

"No-one need know I didn't sign the cover note this morning. I'm an agent, you see."

Phillip went into the courtyard and looked up. "I rather think the fire's out now, but thank you for coming round so promptly."

"That's all right. I like to help a neighbour if I can. Everyone hereabouts knows me. I'm Horatio Bugg. I don't need to work, you know, I do it for a hobby. I live on the interest of my money. Your bell rope is rotten, do you know that? I can supply you with a good second-hand rope if you like. I've had it some time. I bought a lot at the auction of Yarwich old prison before it was pulled down and made into flats by the Labour government, robbing the savings of decent people to give it to those who had lived in slums all their lives. They only use ropes once to hang anyone, did you know that? They're as good as new."

"Well, thank you for coming. I'll let you know if I want a rope to hang myself with."

After playing the torch around the kitchen, rather in the mood of a criminal returning to the scene of his crime, Phillip went upstairs. He felt near to despair. That great rusty range, put in what once was an open hearth thirty years before, when a dozen servants were employed in the house—that horrible old hot-water tank, resting on a diagonal beam, and going up to the ceiling—the pipes solid with lime deposits. Mere fossils. All to be taken down and an entirely new system put in. And a water-softening plant. Then the electric light wiring was perished, where it hadn't been pulled out of the wall plaster in which some genius had buried it. Everything about the place tumbled down, or rotting—the coach-house with its conked-out oil-engine, said by Ernest to be one of the first ever made. That enormous flywheel weighed about half a ton. Ernest had tried to draw the piston. It had seized in the cylinder, the skirt probably cracked, the rings broken. Value as old iron, eighteen pence a hundredweight.

He wandered into the larders, then to what had been the servants' hall. Sweating flagstone floors. Damp brick floors of pantry, larder, apple-room, scullery, outhouses. Narrow Jacobean bricks, worth something as antiques for some rich business man wanting to build in the country, according to the agent, who had had the farm on his books for several years.

He flashed his torch-light on hanging, obsolete spider-webs, rat-holes, fungoid growths on damp wood.

Ernest was in his room, reading *The Model Engineer* by the light of an oil-lamp. He had fitted out his room as a workshop. There was a small treadle lathe held by carriage bolts screwed into the oak floor. He had bored holes first, and filled them with soft wood, without permission. It was a good floor, or had been. Still, he had made a fair job of the lorry they had bought for ten pounds at the diddecais' field. The diddecais were not true gipsies, or Romanies, but odd family groups dealing in scrap metal. Ernest, having repaired the lorry, was making a model of a traction engine, to scale.

"Someone wanted to insure us against fire."

"Ah," replied Ernest, examining a slide-rule.

"He also tried to sell me some old rope."

"Ah."

Phillip went back to his room, and turned up the flame of his copper oil-lamp. Greyish-black lumps of wood-tar lay on the oak planks of the floor. Ernest might have swept them up. Odd lumps were still dropping down, perhaps he had been unfair to Ernest. He swept the floor and then brought in a wooden box, filled with selected twigs, to light a fire. The box had been taken outside for safety. A cord of logs, tied-in at each end by header-stretcher, stood against the far wall. When the kindling was alight, he built logs around it, leaving air-spaces. The flames climbed. No smoke came out, thank God. The flames rose higher. Still no smoke billowing out. The chimney was clear of two decades of jackdaws' nests.

He settled almost happily to write.

> My farm is known locally as the Bad Lands. It consists of woodland, meadow, river, and arable beside the North Sea. This country is the homeland of the wild goose, pheasant, partridge, and, in one great park some miles to the north of my holding, a flock of wild turkeys. It is an arable country, growing malting barley, sugar beet, oats, wheat, and hay for fattening bullocks in winter boxes in the yards after grazing on the marshes in summer. My house and my farm premises are near ruinous. My farm, like many others in this bankrupt granary of East Anglia, is mortgaged to a bank.
>
> The villages along this coast are peopled by a mixture of racial types. Dark South Folk, sensitive, easy, and untidy; fair-haired blue-eyed North Folk, descendants of invaders from across the sea, as were the red-haired Danes whose ancestors came in galleys to burn and kill, and seize women and cattle; salmon-eyed people from Iceland.
>
> To me, coming from the West Country, this area of England is a wild, remote, and betrayed country. There is a great arable tradition half-lost in its weedy fields and rotting barns, in its shabby hamlets where live many men who have been without work during the years when it was said that only fools farmed land because they weren't smart enough to get out in time to put their money into industry of the

towns, or even smarter, into industry abroad in backward countries, where factories employ sweated labour to produce goods with which to undercut the home market and so put British people on the dole.

The fields of arable, with their subsoil of chalk, lie on ground a hundred feet and more above the level of the sea and the coastal marshes to the north. The sea used to flow at high tide up to the farm buildings. Even so, in periods of heavy rain, when the river floods over its banks, water comes very near to the farm premises; but when the sea-wall was built on the coast-line, the saltings and flats became meadows. In the mildest winter the meadows are water-plashes, the haunt of snipe, and an occasional bittern. Duck fly across the North Sea from Holland and farther east, and feed in the grupps, or dykes, between the meadows. It is a sporting country.

Phillip raised his head. Down the chimney came the noise as of a brass band beginning to practise somewhere. He listened at the open window, looking up to the stars. The geese were flying in from the North Sea. A sound remote, romantic, inspiring! When the flock had flown inland to their feeding ground, probably some clover field, he shut the window and went back to his writing.

My four-hundred-year-old premises stand in the valley, the arable fields lie a hundred feet above the premises. This means that everything has to be brought down steep hills, and much of it taken up again later in the season. As a farm it is not, I have been told by my professional valuer, an economic unit. But I did not accept this valuation by ordinary standards. I have other ideas for this farm. I believe that nothing is impossible and nothing therefore is inevitable. I intend, by new ideas and methods, to create a yeoman farm for my family. This time, my second attempt to farm, I must not, shall not fail.

The casual eye of the rambler or nature-lover would see in summer, from the high fields, a world of beauty lying before and below him. I can imagine an enchanting prospect, while sitting on the grassy Home Hills near the pine wood, among plants of ladies' bedstraw and eyebright, wild thyme, cowslip, and pale July harebell swaying on delicate stalk, while before and below one, the river winds through the meadows, beyond the woods and coverts. Afar lie the marshes and a sunlit line of sandhills below another line of azure sea flawed by a remote whiteness of waves breaking on the shoals of the shallow coast. It is a view beautiful to behold, in rare moments when the mind is free of business details; but to the farmer's mind those meadows are water-logged, the dykes choked, the trout stream is polluted; while the flowing slopes of arable make the farm so costly to work. Every tumbril of muck from the yards—I am told two hundred and fifty loads, more or less, every year—each load weighing about three-quarters of a ton—has to be hauled up to the high lands, if the fertility of the soil is to be maintained. Every load of straw has to be brought down from those fields, to be spread as litter for cattle in the yards during the winter to tread into muck—to be hauled up once again. Hence the local name of my farm—the Bad Lands.

It is a question of great frictional loss in haulage. I watched a stack being threshed this morning. The day before, the tackle arrived to be set in. Up the steep slope the lumbering traction engine, drawing drum and elevator, had to puff and chuff—relic of the age of steam box and engine and grasshopper-like elevator on wheels weighing well over twenty tons. For every ten acres of corn there is a stack to be threshed; and for every stack, four hundred gallons of water has to be lugged up to those Bad Lands—nearly two tons of water slopping about an iron coffin on wheels, journey after journey down to, and up from, the river below. The corn, too, must be brought down those loamy hills so slippery in winter, and shot in the Corn Barn. I reckon that one hundred and more sacks of corn from every stack—1½ cwt. of oats, 2 cwt. of barley, 2¼ cwt. of wheat per sack—had to be lifted into the tumbril, eight to a load because one horse could not manage more, and brought down, and tipped out on the asphalt floor of the barn; then all the way up again, to fetch another 16-cwt load.
To bring down the corn from one stack means twelve tilting journeys sideways down the grey slippery clay of the hillside, while the old wheels of the tumbrils in the vast puddled ruts look like being wrenched off. It may be better with the old-fashioned waggons with their thin iron wheels, although the pull would be greater than with modern rubber-tyred tumbrils. I helped as an unpaid hand with the nondescript threshing team of twelve men, to gain experience. The result is that I have determined to cut a road up the hillside of the field called Steep to the arable above. How does one build a road? I have made a rough survey of where the route should lie, along the lane under the pine wood and so to a hollow or bottom under a steep slope rising to the skyline field one hundred and fifty feet above. I would need to fill the bottom with a raised road, or causeway, starting at a gap in the hedge: a new opening with a wide curve of entry, for the second-hand lorry I have bought, and big green trailer I have ordered, to turn in easily. Mechanical speed across a causeway and up and down a new cut will solve the horse-breaking problem of the centuries! When I mentioned my idea to the steward—until I came to the district he had been a teamsman—he asked anxiously if it would pay. Meanwhile we are making up the old roads and I drive the lorry and also work in the stone-pit from 8 a.m. to 5 p.m. daily. I am more or less fit, but not too well fed—cheese, brown bread, apples, bully beef, and tea—rather monotonous, but better than Flanders in 1914. *And I can sleep dry at night.*

My woods are now, in winter, a-wing with the grey, or hoodie, crow

> from over the North Sea. The grey crows are larger than the native carrion crows, and even more wary. The villagers call these 'foreigners' Denchmen (Danishmen), the old name for the invading Vikings, a name which possibly has been in use on this coast for a thousand years and more.

Phillip was being paid £25 by the *Crusader* for a weekly article of 850 words describing his adventures as an amateur farmer working towards the idea of community. These articles appealed to many young men and women who worked in offices all day and longed for a life of adventure, by which they hoped to become changed not only in their circumstances of living, but in their natures as well. A number of letters were forwarded by the Features Editor every week.

One letter was from a young man called Hurst. He stated that he had been educated at one of the 'better known public schools' and that he had worked for three years in a private bank of the City of London. As a cypher clerk he read and coded all outgoing cables and decyphered those coming in from the foreign branches of Schwarzenkoph Brothers. 'It is like being behind the beak of a great octopus, sucking power after squeezing whole areas of economic death by foreclosing on loans and mortgages.'

The letter went on to say that, having read *The Phoenix*, he felt it to be his mission in life to write and say that he, Phillip Maddison, was the revolutionary prophet Britain was waiting for. Might he come down and visit him on the farm? Phillip replied by letter that there was a chasm between the inspiring word and the hard reality of a political party. The young man was persistent: Deepwater Farm, he declared, might be the centre of what he had long awaited: 'the protoplasmic dot of an upsurge, a Renaissance'. It was his duty to say so. He was arriving the next day, and would make his own way to the farm. All he required was food and lodging and somewhere to lay his head.

Phillip and Ernest had been alone for the past month. Ernest did the cooking, which too often was fried slices of bully beef and hot pickles. Sometimes it tasted of paraffin; but there had been no dissension. Phillip had given up trying to alter Ernest, and thought of him as the tortoise. He himself was the hare. But when Brother Laurence and Felicity came, it would be different. They had been about to set off in the Toad from Reynard's Common when Felicity went down with scarlet fever. That meant six weeks before she was out of quarantine.

The hare was dejected. Overworked, underfed and thereby depressed, he became obsessed by the idea that the farm would never be ready for Lucy and the family. With this was another feeling: that the farm was the microcosm of the European macrocosm: it was a race between resurgence and death, otherwise another world war. He knew this was a fantasy, like passing a lamp-post before a car overtook you, otherwise you would have bad luck. Perhaps the young man from Schwarzenkoph's bank might not be so bad as his letter seemed? He must not be afraid of his coming. After all, he would be going back to his job at the bank.

The young man arrived. He wore in his button-hole a founder-member badge of the N.S.D.A.P. This was surprising, for how could he have been one of the original party-members of 1923, at the time of the Munich *putsch* by Hitler?

"I had it copied," explained Hurst. He was dark-haired his pale face was too often clouded by perplexity. "I wish I could get you to see that Birkin is a fraud, Captain Maddison. I know many men who were in the Imperial Socialist party, and were expelled for no reason other than that they were advancing the cause too rapidly."

"What does that mean?"

"Well, Birkin's director of propaganda, Frolich, is a brilliant speaker, and drew the biggest crowds to his meetings. Then Birkin sacked him. And no reasons given. All Frolich had done was to advance the cause."

"What cause?"

"The cause against the Jews, the cause Birkin is supposed to be standing for, but isn't." Hurst went on,

"There is a tremendous dissatisfaction with Birkin as the Leader. Frolich, after five years with Birkin, was simply kicked out, but he wasn't the only one. Jock Kettle was another. Jock can prove that, whenever a branch looked like being a success, and grew in size, the 'Iron Ring' around Birkin automatically closed down the branch."

"Really."

Hurst looked distressed. His white face took on a look that was almost ugly. "Please hear me, Captain Maddison. I know Jock Kettle very well. I also know Frolich. A Yid at one of the meetings tried to cut his throat with a razor, but only succeeded in slicing his right cheek. Frolich has a scar from his eye to his mouth, so he can hardly be accused of other than devotion to the cause. But if you listen to Jock Kettle, who is coming to see me soon, he will tell you the same thing. Jock brought in over seven hundred members when he was in charge of the Houndsditch branch, and then he was given the push. The same thing has happened to all the other branches which were increasing membership."

"But why should Birkin work against himself like this? It doesn't make sense," said Phillip. "Now look, I must get to work. I've got to drive the lorry, we are short of a driver. A friar called Brother Laurence, who served in the war, was due to come up, but couldn't. Can you drive?"

"No, but I can learn. You will give me a job then? You see, I've already resigned from Schwarzenkoph's."

Hurst was taken down to help dig chalk to spread on the pot-holed farm roads. Gravel was to be brought later to cover the chalk. Phillip was about to leave him working under Luke the steward, when the young man, dropping his pick, ran after him and said, 'Just a moment, sir, I must tell you this. No doubt you've heard of Captain Bohun-Borsholder, one of the biggest landowners in Kent? Well, I know him. He too was a member of the I.S.P. and is now completing evidence that Birkin is deliberately sabotaging any attempt to form a real national socialist party in Great Britain, by discrediting his own party in the eyes of everyone in this country. Major Borsholder told me the reason. Birkin is in the pay of the Jews!"

On his return Phillip said to Ernest, "Hurst is a crank."

"Ah," said Ernest. He was designing an alternative to a duck's-foot cultivator. Phillip intended to plough all the arable of the Bad Lands; to let the fields lie fallow, and when weeds—chiefly thistle and charlock—sprang up, to cut them below the furrows by cultivation, and to follow this with finer cultivations by replacing the duck's-foot tines on the spring-loaded tine-holders with new tines shaped like spread wings of a bird. These would slice all roots and eventually the arable would be weedless. Nitrogen and sun would restore the fertility. The fields would then be rolled by a heavy Cambridge roll, and mud and rotting rushes, dug from the choked dykes on the meadows, spread with other compost from weed-heaps.

There were nearly two hundred acres of arable. A thousand tons of compost would, he hoped, be available in one year's time for this purpose.

It was a 30-cwt. lorry. With chalk to be spread as well, at the rate often tons an acre (half the cost to be borne by a grant from the new Land Fertility Scheme) this job would take some time. Three thousand tons in all to be transported and spread by the steward, Brother Laurence, and Hurst.

The hare became a tortoise, and after the day's roadmending got on with the job of decorating one of the rooms in the Old Manor. He broke off to revert to a hare, his mind racing to write an article about the farm's progress. He was still the hare when towards midnight he finished a script for the B.B.C. in the weekly series, *English Family Maddison*. Then to blind the next afternoon, after digging all the morning, to London in the Silver Eagle, and return in the small hours. The work must be done, it must be done, it must be done, cried the hare with staring eyes.

Jock Kettle was taken on as a community member. For a few days he worked with pick and shovel, loading and driving the lorry. Then he drove only, refusing to help load. His driving every hour to and from where the chalk was being laid on the roads was less than half a mile.

One afternoon Hurst suggested that they should hold a meeting in Yarmouth.

"Jock will help to spread the idea of the regeneration of the soil of Britain, beginning with Labour Camps for the unemployed. We can establish the first one here."

"Well, he might also shovel some chalk for us occasionally. What else will he say?"

"Oh, he will know when he gets the feel of his audience."

They drove to the market place in Yarmouth. There Jock Kettle got hold of an empty herring barrel.

"You'll see how he uses it, Phil, to get a crowd." Jock Kettle was a slim dark man with thin humorous lips. He spun the barrel in a tight circle, causing passers-by to watch. He changed to a figure-of-eight, skilfully flinging the barrel at the arcs of the figure. Then checking, he set up the barrel, climbed upon it, and opening a packet of chewing gum held it up to look at it, shook it by his ear, tossed it up and caught it in his mouth. After chewing with exaggerated face movements he pulled out a long string, and wound it back with his tongue.

"I see some young men before me, young men of the greatest fishing port on the East coast of Old England. I see trawlers tied up in the basin, rusting away. Gulls are the mourners at the funeral of Yarmouth fishing. I see older men in threadbare coats.

rotting on the dole. In my journeys about so-called Great Britain I see the same disease in all our once-great industries. We all know that East Anglian men have the hearts of lions and are the first to volunteer in a war. Are they to die upon the battlefields of Europe, to preserve the same rotten, worn-out system that enriches the few, the fat men that control this country with their millions, while we rot on their dole? And what is this dole but something to keep us quiet, and remain in virtual slavery, until war comes and you exchange your freedom to rot on the dole for another freedom to die under machine-gun fire and rot on the battlefield as your fathers did before you. While at home the old folk and the little ones burn up under bombing by aircraft at night?

"Ah, I see some comely lasses over there! Ladies of the herring industry—what is left of it—because it does not pay the moneybag men to keep it going—they bring in cheap tinned fish, caught and processed by sweated labour, paid one third of even the miserable pittance you lasses get here in Yarmouth. Yes, ladies, you should be the mothers of bonny bairns instead of the unmarried mothers of the dead! I tell you that unless we rise up in this country, war will come, and for what reason? They will tell you it will be to preserve your homes and parents and children. Who are *they*? The men who control this country, who have most of the money, the Jews! They will drive the goys to the slaughter, in order to tighten their hold on world finance! Down with the Jewish commissars! The Yids! Down with the moneylenders! All history reveals the Yid to be the yeast that ferments revolution, who turns one Christian nation against another Christian nation. The Yids are orientals whose god is the Golden Calf, the graven image of the moneylender with his sixty per cent interest! God help anyone who gets in a moneylender's clutches! Who financed the revolution against Charles the First—executed by Cromwell—where did Cromwell get the money from, to pay his soldiers? Shall I tell you? From two Yids in Holland. And what did they get for lending the money? A promise to let the Jews return to England, after being expelled by Edward the First three hundred years before. Nobody in Europe wanted the golden tapeworm of Judah in the body politic——"

"What are you, a Communist?" shouted someone. "We don't want your sort here!"

"Nor do we want any Facinists!" cried another voice.

"Well, well, well," replied Jock Kettle. My friend over there thinks I am fascinating! Thank you, sir."

"One of Birkin's lot I meant."

"Birkin? The Bleeder? Nay, don't let's spoil an honest session with mentioning the unspeakable in pursuit of the ridiculous, as Shakespeare says. Any more questions?"

"Is that your lorry over there?" asked a policeman. "It's after lighting-up time. May I see your licence, please?"

"It's my lorry. I've got the licence," said Phillip.

Particulars were taken. In due course he was fined ten shillings. By that time Kettle had returned to London. He left without notice. He wasn't in his room in the morning. Later in the day a police van stopped by Horatio Bugg's petrol pump. They went into his house. A desk had been forced open, a number of pound notes had been stolen. Dusting revealed no fingerprints. Bugg declared that over £79 was missing.

"The Old Manor is a thieves' kitchen in my way of thinking," he remarked to all who stopped to speak to him.

As was to be expected, Hurst's attitude changed when he had to hand over his ill-kept account books. His manner became critical. He derided the community farm idea in the Hero—one of several pubs so-called in the district after Lord Nelson of Trafalgar. Horatio Bugg was only too eager to tell Phillip what 'the Denchman' had been saying. Phillip ignored the gossip. Once Hurst pointed to the words painted by Ernest in small white letters on the left side of the lorry, and in sardonic tones read them aloud slowly, in Phillip's hearing, "P.S.T. Maddison *Esquire*—ha ha—Deepwater Farm, Crabbe. They say in the Hero that Phillip is bogus."

"My brother-in-law," Ernest replied in his slow distinct voice, "has held the King's commission, and since he is also Lord of the Manor, either condition qualifies for the style of *esquire*."

"I was only joking," said Hurst.

Soon after Brother Laurence and Felicity arrived, Ernest said he must return to Dorset, giving the excuse that he must go and pack up some things for Australia.

"Well, come back if you have to wait for your passage," said Phillip. "Your help will make it all the sooner for Lucy and the family to join us here." Ernest had done some good work in what was left of the kitchen. A new sink now replaced the heavy, chipped, and cracked earthenware horror. The bathroom would have to remain as it was, and be filled by water-carrying until the pipes were either cleared or replaced.

"I shall miss you, Ernest, my dear old fellow."

"Ah."

By its appearance that bath had been put in about the time of the Great Exhibition of 1864. The tiled floor was laid in a pattern of swans and nymphs. Every tile was bashed and cracked, presumably by the conscripts of 1916–1918. The bath itself was deep and badly chipped, too. Green water-drippings from the taps disfigured it. Its large cast-iron lion-paw supporters rested upon sheet lead which had a rolled parapet to retain splashes and lippings-over upon entry of rotund and sporting bodies—now mouldering somewhere in the churchyard.

On returning from the railway station, Phillip went down the road to get some petrol, Felicity sat beside him. She was to take over all accounts from Hurst; and one of her new duties was to get a signature from Horatio Bugg, in the *Petrol Book*, for every gallon used in car and lorry.

"You'll probably find Bugg very curious," he told her. "He's like a village dog, ever on the lookout for something interesting. 'Ah, here be somp'n, the foreigner with a young maid.' That's Bugg, by his pump. Notice how he throws out his chest and metaphorically cocks his leg on my near side front wheel. Squirt-squirt, his thoughts pass behind his *pince-nez* spectacles."

True to form, Horatio Bugg peered at Felicity, then he asked, "Are you an actress?", as he unhooked the hose-pipe.

"Yes."

"Where do you act?" as he inserted the nozzle in the filling column of the tank.

"Oh everywhere."

"Then why don't I know your face?" as he worked the rotary pump.

"I usually wear a wig on stage."

"Ah, Shakespeare I suppose?"

"How did you guess?"

"'Tom Fool knows more than Tom Fool tells,' isn't that what they say?"

"Do they?"

"I could tell a tale or two, you know, if I wanted to open my mouth."

"Now will you sign my petrol book, please, Mr. Bugg?"

"Ah ha, now I know you're the new secretary, I guessed as much when I saw you. I hope we'll be good friends and neighbours."

Not long afterwards Horatio Bugg made a formal call.

"Here is our friend from the village," remarked Brother Laurence, standing by the caravan door one morning.

The caravan rested among the pine trees growing above the chalk quarry. Below were the premises. Jackdaws were nesting in old rabbit-holes in the top subsoil above the chalk and flint layers.

Phillip and Felicity sat inside the caravan. He was reading the typescript of an article. She writing in the farm diary.

"Mr. Bugg is a fly," said Phillip, reading on. But he could not connect with the words. He waited for the visitant to arrive. He tried not to feel aversion to the weak face, badly shaven, *pince-nez* spectacles, shapeless cloth cap with greasy band, dirty white rag around neck which failed to conceal a goitre.

"Hullo. Thought I'd come to see how you're gettin' along." Without waiting for an invitation Horatio Bugg climbed in and sat down.

"You bought that lorry too dear, did you know that?" He paused to fill his pipe with thin hair tobacco. "Those diddecais are out to do anyone. We don't like them around here, you know." He took matches from his pocket. "Or Denchmen, for that matter."

"Captain Maddison is rather busy at the moment," said Brother Laurence.

"Busy, I can see he's busy," replied the intruder, lighting his pipe. "Don't let me interrupt you," he said to Phillip. "I'm always ready to do anyone who's stowed up a good turn."

Phillip had written his article beside a dead pine tree while Brother Laurence had been getting breakfast. It was a description of a tree-creeper which had made its nest in a branch split by lightning.

He folded the article and gave it to Felicity. She put it in a foolscap envelope and was addressing it to the literary editor of the *Crusader* when the visitor spoke again.

"They say you are going to turn the Old Manor into a Roman Catholic community or somep'n. Is that right?"

"We're roadmenders at the moment."

"Well, I know that, I've got eyes in my head. I hear most of what's going on in the district down by my yard, you know."

He puffed contentedly. "There's a rich lady living in the village, a titled person, and she came to ask me what you were going to do here, and how it would affect the wild birds she likes watching. You may have heard of her, Lady Penelope Carnoy. She prefers it all wild, you know, like the other birdwatchers who come here to study on the marshes and roundabout."

Every suck at his pipe now made an uneasy bubbling noise. "As I was saying, now your lorry is broken—what, didn't you know? Mr. Hearse come to me to get him a second-hand gearbox saying the old one gave out."

"Damn that fellow," said Phillip, "I told him not to tip off any more chalk that way."

"So I thought you might like to buy my motorcar to carry on with. It's in perfect condition except for a dud battery and four flat tyres. These can easily be replaced by second-hand ones. It's a Chevrolet and used to belong to the Ranee of Sarawak, who came here to stay with Lady Penelope to study wild birds."

When there was no reply Horatio Bugg turned an ear, augmented by a hand, listened awhile, then exclaimed, "I can't quite hear you, I'm a bit deaf."

"I must go to the post," shouted Phillip, waving the envelope. "No need to shout, I'm not that deaf."

Horatio Bugg seemed to have trouble with his pipe. The split bowl was enwrapped with adhesive rubber tape. He stopped sucking to say, "I suppose you know all about that Invisible Ray working on this coast to stop German aeroplanes coming over to spy out the land? It stops the magnetos of all motorcar engines, too, did you know that?"

"Is that why your car won't move?"

"I told you it needs a new battery, that's all." Horatio Bugg sucked hard. No smoke issued from between his lips. "I suppose you can't lend me a pipe cleaner, can you? No. Well, I can sometimes clear it by blowing." He blew hard, and a shower of sparks dropped out. "What did I tell you? That's cleared it."

"Mind you don't set fire to the caravan, it isn't insured."

"Not insured? I can arrange a policy for you. I'm an agent, as I told you when you set fire to your chimbly."

"Well, we must be off," said Brother Laurence.

"Where are you going, anywhere in particular? If not, I'll come with you. I've got nothing to do at the moment. Is that the German eagle on the radiator?"

"Brummagem."

"Hey?" said the other, cupping an ear. "Speak up, if you don't mind. Just a minute," as he struck a match to try to relight the gurgling compost of ash, wet threads, and nicotine poison left in his pipe.

"I said 'Brummagem'!"

"Well, that's hardly polite, is it?" He turned to Felicity, "And in a lady's presenqe. I suppose you help him as secretary, don't you?"

"That's right. I'm the dogsbody."

"You found a dog's body?"

"Yes."

Horatio Bugg began to ask more questions when he saw the two men going towards the "German" motorcar.

"Is that monk with you a well-known order, or what?"

"He's a Laurentian friar, devoted to poverty."

"Poverty, eh? Well, he's come to the right place. Where did he come from?"

"From God."

"Oh, so you're religious, I see."

"That's right."

Phillip was removing the green canvas covering the sports car standing under a pine tree. He took his usual care to get the canvas straight on the ground before walking round to fold it precisely section by section. It had belonged to his uncle Hiliary, who had sold it to him with the caravan before going to live abroad with his wife.

Horatio Bugg watched the ritual of folding as he stood by the splintered stump of the dead pine, tapping out his pipe. The tree-creeper's nest was in a crack in the wood. Phillip saw with concern that the mother bird had flitted off her eggs.

The heavy cloth, impregnated with preserving chemical, took some time to be folded. It was half-done when Horatio Bugg, seeming to come out of a trance of tobacco juice, went forward and said, "Let me give you a hand."

"That's very good of you."

When the cloth was folded Phillip started the engine on the handle. He ran the engine to warm up the oil, and then got in to wait for Brother Laurence, who had returned to the caravan with the 2-gallon galvanised water can. There was about a quart left in the can, and the friar returned to empty it into the kettle.

"That's a rum'n," said Horatio Bugg. "You save even water."

With Felicity beside him and Brother Laurence in the tonneau, Phillip drove slowly in reverse over the hump at the edge of the wood. Buried under the turf lay the remains of an old wall which, he had been told by Lady Breckland, was the remains of a Roman fort or look-out against Viking invaders. Lady Breckland had recently called to ask him to join the Imperial Socialist Party. Phillip had demurred at first, then had agreed out of politeness. He had demurred because he was overworked and at times his mind was near distress at the thought of all the work that had to be done. Now Hurst had broken the lorry and road-making would be held up, he thought as he drove slowly over acid-thin grass to the top drift which led to the road a quarter of a mile away.

The letter was posted, the water can refilled. They returned; covered the car with the green canvas; and opened the caravan with all windows to clear the interior of a shaggy smell.

Brother Laurence said, "Would you like me to give a hand to the men remaking the lower road to the premises? We can use the horse and tumbril. Or, I can dismantle the broken gearbox."

"Oh, good man! Will you remove the gearbox? As soon as we've finished the lower road, we must start the New Cut. Perhaps you'll see Horatio Lord Bugg about a second-hand gearbox for the lorry, as soon as you've got particulars of the old one, will you? Thank you, mon père. What should I do without you?"

The idea of the New Cut was to bring down swiftly the corn loads of all future summers to a stackyard site planned in the quarry near the Corn Barn. The steward had objected. He didn't want the boss to do a silly thing like spending money on a new road. He believed, from his late master's experience, that every penny spent on a farm was a penny lost.

"But on a level road cut there, Luke, there will be no accidents, as last year."

The steward had protested that carting corn so much farther—up to half a mile from the field—to the premises down below—would mean a lot of waiting about for the men building the corn stack.

"A hoss-drawn tumbril load would take ten minutes or more, after leaving Great Bustard field, to get to the stack yard."

From his experience at Fawley, Phillip realised that the margin between profit and loss even on good land was small; while on the Bad Lands—as his farm was locally called—any profit on a field of corn would easily be lost in the scores of hours while the stack-builders were idle.

"The Flying Column will save time, Luke. Also a level road will make muck-carting easier for you and your horses, at the back end."

"I don't think it's necessary, that I don't. But you're master."

Phillip tried to get Luke to see that the large green trailer, drawn by the tractor driven by his son Billy, could gather a second half-load, which would not need to be roped in the ordinary way, for the wooden rails and lades of the trailer would keep the sheaves from falling out.

"The lorry and the green trailer together will comprise the Flying Column. This will keep the men at the stack 'going'. Each stack, holding ten acres of corn, will be built in one instead of two days. And winter threshing in the new stack-yard only a few yards away from both water and Corn Barn, will be simplified."

"Well, if 'twas mine, I'd keep my money in my pocket."

When Phillip arrived at the farm premises, he found the men standing idle, while Brother Laurence was removing the broken gear-box.

Hurst had devised, together with the steward, another way of dumping loads of chalk. The chalk, which was being put out in heaps for later spreading on a field, was moist. It had clung to the sheet-iron floor of the lorry even when the body had been raised on the hand-screw tippers at a high angle.

Instead of getting it off with shovel and muck-crome, Hurst's idea was to shoot it off in one avalanche by putting the engine in low gear and suddenly letting-in the clutch. So the engine was revved up to its maximum and the clutch let-in abruptly. The gear-box was churned into nuggets of crystallised steel.

"It was worn out," said Hurst. "Like democracy," he added sardonically.

This was the second vehicle to be put out of action. The steward, using the large green trailer for a load of straw when littering the bullock yards, had backed the trailer while attached to the tractor. Phillip had often stressed that the trailer never must be backed: if backed, he said, the automatic brakes went on hard and wedged the brake-shoes against the drums. This locked the wheels, which were liable to shudder and cause a half-axle to break under the pressure of more than a ton thrust from the tractor. If a half-axle didn't break, the springs might be torn from the shackle-bolts.

"We won't be in no muddle," said Luke. "Horatio here says he can get you a gear-box cheap to replace this one. An' he can get you an old spring to put in place of that worn-out one on the green trailer what broke itself. You don't hev to worry. We won't be in no muddle."

"You're quite right. We're in a bloody muddle already."

That night in Horatio Bugg's house the steward said, "You know, I reckon our boss may be going bust."

"In my opinion," replied Horatio Bugg, "that man Hurst what gave your boss notice today is a Denchman. He scowls like one, an' he wears that Swass-tika badge. I shouldn't be surprised to see the whole lot picked up one day as spies. There's always a beautiful woman among spies, and that Felicity is her, I reckon. As for that monk, whoever saw a genuine priest ever do any work?"

Hurst had already arranged to work for a man who owned a considerable landed estate. This country gentleman was trying to rouse his neighbours to the evils of what he called the coming Bureaucratic State, or British Stalinism. It was a relief when Hurst was gone. Phillip spent the evenings re-decorating the interior of the Old Manor. He must not drive himself too hard, repeated Brother Laurence when the New Cut was completed: he was on the land most of the day with the tractor, or helping the men to pull mud from the grupps or dykes and to cut overgrown hedges when it was fine weather, or working on the premises when it wasn't possible to go on the land; at night writing articles for the *Crusader,* and scripts to be broadcast from London once a week.

These articles had brought several more strangers to the farm, most of them young. Phillip also had many letters, for the tone of his writings was light-hearted, idealistic, and at times passionate for the land and its renaissance. Old acquaintances and pests were attracted for varying reasons. One morning Phillip saw an old saloon car smoking along the drive, then Cabton got out with a walking-stick gun under his arm. Forewarned by memory of Cabton's indiscriminate potting at anything that moved on land, in air or in water at Fawley some years before, Phillip got in the first shot. "Have you a gun licence? The local bobby is very hot on licences. Also a syndicate has the sporting rights over my land."

"How are you," replied Cabton, holding out his hand. "Are you in the syndicate?"

"No."

"In that case, why worry? You haven't seen me, that's all."

Cabton and his wife were dressed in rather smelly sheepskin coats. She carried a small flat wooden box. "We brought you a box of kippers from Yarmouth."

"Thank you. Are you touring round?"

"We never make plans, as I told you when I saw you last."

"He asks us that as soon as we arrive," said Mrs. Cabton. Turning to Phillip, "I wonder you have any friends left, if you treat them all as you treat us, when we come to see you."

A red touring motorcar turned in by the broken gate, and came towards them with a coughing roar. With joy Phillip recognised Bill Kidd. At the same moment the driver saw him, and the klaxon began to stridulate in Morse the dots and dashes spelling out MY MAD SON, ending as the car stopped on the gravel.

"How are you, my Mad Son? You old scrounger, you? My God, if it isn't little old Cabton with his blasted poacher's gun! How are you, Masson old boy? Salaams!" as Bill Kidd got out, hatless, and bowed to Mrs. Cabton. "Who's that bloke at the window? The family ghost?"

Ernest's face at an upper window was at once withdrawn. He had come back to give more help, urged by Lucy, and was making a model of a traction engine for Billy.

"The ghost of an old retainer, Bill. Pensioned off. He died in seventeen seventy-seven."

"I suppose you think that's funny," said Cabton, turning the handle of the walking-stick gun and opening the breech.

"Now look here, my lad," exclaimed Bill Kidd. "Don't you load that bloody poacher's gun here. That's not funny! Bill Kidd's telling you, mind! I remember when you nearly shot Masson's little boy, you had your hand on the button, remember? Your life may or may not be of any value, but mine is, see? How's the missus, Masson old boy? Is she here?"

"Still in Dorset. Her brother and I are getting the place more or less habitable first, then she'll come with the kids."

"I've got a fine boy, you remember my nipper? Hell of a chap. No nonsense about the coming generation. Tells me to go to hell if I get on old man whisky. Quite a wheeze, what, tellin' off the old man, what?" and Bill Kidd's head shrunk into his shoulders with the wheeze.

"Like to see the house?"

"Of course I would. That's what I came to see, with you, you old leadswinger! Just to check up on what you write, and see if it's all Sir Garnett."

"Would you like to see over the house, Mrs. Cabton?"

"I think we'll go. We know when we're not wanted. Come on, Cabton."

"The scrounging bastard," said Bill Kidd cheerfully. "Had the nerve to bring out that walking-stick gun, without so much as a 'by your leave'. Those bloody dagoes never were any good. Miserable bastards."

Bill Kidd had all sorts of ideas for improving the house. One was hens.

"I've seen it in Lincolnshire, where I'm living now, Masson old boy. Fill the rooms up with hens. Laying White Wyandottes. Tons of eggs. This place will cost a packet to put in order. Get some incubators, hatch off some pedigree eggs, and next time Cabton comes he'll look up and think he's got dee tees, thousands of old gels in white lookin' down at the bastard!"

Another of Bill Kidd's ideas was to get the hot-water system cleared. With acid.

"Sulphuric acid, old boy. Fill the blasted tank with H_2SO_4. Then light the fire and get it circulating. Keep all taps open, let the water work up the pipes followed by the acid which has a lower specific gravity. I used to be with the Chemical Warfare Department, old boy, and know my stuff. The acid will reduce the lime to hydrocarbonic acid, CO_3HSO_2. It's simple. I fixed it up for my wife's uncle's place in Sussex. Stenning Towers. Cost you a fortune to replace all the pipes otherwise. I guarantee the result."

"Will you do it by contract, and then give me a guarantee, Bill?"

"Spit in my eye and choke me if I'm a liar, my Mad Son. From now on I'm O.C. Petrified Waterworks of the Old Manor. I'll buzz off in the old boneshaker and get half a carboy of acid from the garage in Crabbe, where the bloke tried to sell me a Railton Terraplane. Offered me fifty quid for 'Otazelle' my old 'bus. Damned impertinence! I wouldn't sell the old gel for five hundred quid. She's an ancient monument. Now I'll go and get that carboy. It won't take a brace of shakes to get your bathroom working again."

It took a lot of screw-wrenching and tapping of nuts with cold chisel and hammer. Then the hot-water tank was drained; the screwed metal plug replaced; another plug removed at the top for the acid to be poured in by glass funnel. Acid must never be poured into water, but water into acid, said Bill Kidd.

"Otherwise it will blow up the whole caboodle. My tactics are to infiltrate, like the Boche did in the Bird Cage on the twenty-first of March, nineteen eighteen. This acid will bomb down the whole system of pipes, until the garrison cries *Kamerad!* and ups with their hands. Leave it to Bill Kidd, old lad."

He seemed to know what he was doing . . .

. . . up to a point (wrote Phillip the next evening to Lucy). Bill Kidd lit the fire under the boiler and we went for a walk by the river, looking for trout. We didn't see any, for the east wind was blowing, and that put down what few fish are left after the slow pollution of years. The regulator must have been left full on, for while we were having tea in my Jackdaw Room on the top floor there was a rumble and a roar, and when we went down we saw steaming water and acid all over the floor and a great hole in the wall where the boiler had stood. It is a rubble wall, mainly of round flints, and they had cascaded down with half bricks and mortar. In short, Bill Kidd not only cleared the lime deposits in the boiler and pipes, but the whole of the archaic hot-water system as well.

More damage was apparent after he had departed. A beam which had apparently been shored up by the wall and was eaten to frass by furniture and death-watch beetles—an elm beam—gave way and the floor above caved in during the night. The whole house is rotten, and I am thinking of having two cottages at the end of the garden beside the road converted into one, for a new farmhouse. It will cost much less than having the Old Manor put in order. So I am afraid you will have to wait down there a little longer. I'm going to have a local builder estimate for the job, and not buy any more experience from these glorious amateurs.

The next visitors, Phillip wrote to his faithful Lucy, were a little more conventional. He saw one morning an elderly woman accompanied by a man in a city suit and black Homburg hat walking among the weeds of the drive. At once he recognised Mrs. Ancroft and Felicity's guardian, Fitzwarren.

He went to meet them. Mrs. Ancroft stopped, and put a hand to her side. Fitz said something to her.

"How d'you do," said Phillip, who had not the least idea what to say next. Mrs. Ancroft said, "My charwoman reads the *Daily Crusader,* so I was able to find you here. I will come straight to the point. Is my daughter with you?"

"Well," he replied, "she is in the house somewhere, I think."

"You only think?"

"She may be with the goslings. She looks after the incubator, Mrs. Ancroft."

"Is your wife here?"

"No."

"Are you being divorced?"

"Not that I know of. Lucy is coming with the children as soon as we've got two cottages put more or less in order."

"Who is 'we', may I ask?"

"My brother-in-law, Ernest Copleston, and—let me see—well, that's about all at the moment. And Felicity. Oh, and an older friend of mine, who served in the war and is now a friar."

"A friar, did you say?"

"Yes, then there's Edward. He goes to the village school, and is what is called a 'first-class infant'."

"And you are living with Felicity as your mistress?"

"No."

"Then why is she here, may I enquire?"

"She is secretary and book-keeper of the community farm."

"You say your wife and the children are coming from the West Country to live here also?"

"Yes."

Mrs. Ancroft turned to Fitz and said, "Thank God Felicity will not after all be marrying a divorced man. Fitz, give me your arm."

"Do come into the house," said Phillip. "It's a bit of a ruin, but all we have at the moment."

Mrs. Ancroft saw a hall which went up halfway to the roof, with doors going off into other rooms, and at the end of the hall a broad staircase leading up and round to a landing with a heavy oak rail supported by twisted banisters.

"And what do you think you are going to do with a community?"

"Farm land and make a profit, Mrs. Ancroft."

"But do you think, having failed once, that you are likely to succeed a second time?"

"I have an idea that the depression won't last. Do come up into what was once, and we hope it will be again, the drawing room."

Here was a trestle table, a pail of ceiling whitewash, an old pair of dungarees, and some kitchen chairs.

"Do sit down, I'll go and find Felicity." And warn mon père if I can find him, he thought.

The warning was unnecessary. Felicity's voice was heard saying, "I'll make your favourite herb omelette for your lunch, mon père. Have you seen Phillip? I thought I heard voices. Some more of his fans, I suppose."

She looked round the door. She saw who the visitors were and went forward to greet them, saying, "This *is* a surprise! Where have you come from? Edward's at school, he'll be home shortly. It's only just up the road. I suppose you've read about our community effort?" She kissed her mother. "How are you, Fitz? How's publishing?"

"Oh, much about the same."

This was a different Felice, she made him feel uneasy. He hadn't wanted to come with the old girl, there was nothing left but habit between them, and latent antagonism.

Phillip came upon Brother Laurence in the courtyard. He had been ploughing the Steep with the hydraulic tractor, an innovation in the district. Even the steward had said, when he saw Phillip creeping up the one-in-five gradient without turning over and without digging in, "Blast, I like that patent. It'll beat hosses, won't it tho."

"Visitors, mon père. Felicity is looking after them quite happily. My word, that girl has acquired poise since you turned up from the grave." He looked steadily at the friar. "It's my illegitimate mother-in-law, with Fitzwarren, an old family friend, I gather."

"I saw them, Phillip. Nora has a weak heart." He walked up and down, dissolving. "What shall I do?" he said, weakly.

This was a pierced Brother Laurence. We all lose form with some people, it is wrong to think of them as fools, for we ourselves may be fools to them. One must abdicate from the little ego in their presence, one must not hurt their feelings.

"Let Felicity tell her. I'll call her down. You stay in the apple room, mon père."

"Phillip—don't think me callous—but I could never return——"

Phillip nodded several times, as though he were a puppet. He felt levitating tears. Lucy would understand. You looked such a poor one, she said once. What generosity, what quality of spirit in Lucy . . . and he had called her stupid, unimaginative, dull . . . killing him. Killing the devil in him, not the gleam he had inherited from little Hetty Turney. Now he understood the tag, used of Suffolk—*saintly* Suffolk, which was also *silly* Suffolk, said to be due to misspelling.

Let workaday wisdom blink sage eyes at that
Which towers a hedgerow high, poor bat.

"Felicity, this is what you must do. Take your mother into the rose garden. I heard the first nightingale there this morning. Rather shrill in the east wind, but a nightingale. Sit down on a rug, hold her hand, tell her how you love her, as your sister. Tell her you are a whole person, and why. Tell her it is a miracle, but your father wasn't killed after all, a mistake was made. Only that—a mistake. Tell her what a good man he is now. Leave it there. Meanwhile mon père will be in the apple room, out of the way. I'll go and get Fitz, and invite him to see the premises, while you're with your mother."

Fitz laughed when Phillip told him.

"Nora always said he'd turn up like a bad penny, sooner or later. So he's here, is he? She always regretted telling Felicity that her father was dead. You know, the old gel's had a rough time, from the start. No, she won't die of shock, she half suspects it, as a fact. This will help her, as it's helped Felicity. She's a different gel. What's the boy like? I haven't seen it since it was a baby."

"Edward is like Felicity."

"That will please Nora. She has a lot of pride in her family. Your wife took the baby's coming very well, I thought. I'd like to meet her one day."

"Do come and stay when we are settled in. Everything is a bit rough at the moment."

"Still, you've got it in you to succeed. And you bought on the ground floor. The war's coming all right. You'll see. Oh, I know how you view things, but the war psychosis is in the air. Hitler can't stop. It's happened before. It's the pattern of history. No man, no system can alter human nature."

"Then we're all doomed."

"Of course we're all doomed. Hitler's only a child of this age. When he's gone it will break out all over the world. First Asia, then Africa. We haven't had Armageddon yet. You're wise, you know, to get back to the land. 'Only a man harrowing clods' will still be there when these modern dynasties have gone the way of all flesh."

"Yes, I see you have the scholar's perspective. Now I must leave you for a bit, I must fetch Edward from school."

While Mrs. Ancroft was enjoying Felicity's omelettes with water-cress from the pond below the clear-water spring in the garden, Phillip made his way back to the apple room, holding Edward by the hand, and thinking of the last walk with his father on the buried Roman road across the downs. And Mother had feared an awful row! It was like that first Christmas Eve in the war. Go straight out to the German wire, levitated by the opposite of fear, and you are walking on water.

"Now, mon père, this child will lead you, I've told him what to do. Follow him."

"Grannie, Grannie, I got you, an' I got Grandpa, an' I got Mummy, I got Lucy, I got Phillip, an' ever so many brothers, and I got a sister as well! Aren't I a lucky boy?"

When the blossom was on the white-thorn, and the turtle dove was come from Abyssinia to the Home Hills, the cottages were ready for the family. A bathroom had been built on, electricity installed. Four bedrooms, three rooms downstairs, and a kitchen. It was beginning to look like home.

"I think you are fairly well settled now," said Brother Laurence. He looked calmly at Phillip. "Perhaps now you should have a rest, so to speak, from too many apprentices. You will be able to settle to a rhythm with your little family. Felicity and I both feel that you should be an undivided farmer, not hampered by amateurs. After all, you have learned your job, and we haven't. Felicity must be with her mother, to help and comfort her, now that she has made a new relationship with her. For myself, I hope to become a lay brother with the Carmelite Friars in Kent.

"But let us not lose touch, my dear friend. Do not look so sad, Phillip."

Chapter 12

SUMMER, SUMMER IN THE GRASS

"It is so lovely for the children on the marshes, Pip! We went there with Lady Penelope, who took us part of the way in her motor. She called here just after you had gone to do your broadcast in London, to ask if she could help in any way. She left this note for you. I think she is just a little worried that all your plans may disturb the wild birds. Such as the draining of the meadows, and afterwards ploughing them up. I told her that you loved birds, too."

He opened the crisp blue envelope. The writer declared that she had been inspired by the books of W. H. Hudson to watch wild birds. She had also read what he, Phillip, had said about Richard Jefferies, but (she wrote)

> I prefer Hudson who is calmer. I wonder if you would allow me to walk as in previous years over the fields of your farm, among the wild birds which are my chief delight in life. I shall of course be most careful not to disturb any game with my dogs, which I always keep on a lead, as they have their freedom on the marshes.

He replied saying that she must not allow his coming to interfere in any way with her walks, and hoped that the bare-fallowing of the arable would not spoil the wildness of the place for her: that the idea of ploughing and re-seeding the meadows depended on a resurgent Britain and a long-term policy for farmers supplying the home market. Then he referred to what she had written in her letter about Hudson.

> I, too, admire the writings of W. H. Hudson, but Jefferies felt deeper, and saw clearer. His efforts to alter the entire thought of mankind were as vain as those of all the great seers and prophets. Of course he had an awful life: Sisyphus.

Lucy tells me she enjoyed the picnic on the marshes greatly, and may I add my thanks to hers for the wonderful time you gave her and the children while I was in London recently.

Yours sincerely,
Phillip Maddison.

Occasionally he saw her aloof figure wandering over the farm, leading two large Russian wolf-hounds on a leash. Once, while he was writing in the caravan within the pine wood, he met her startled gaze through the window: instantly she looked away, and changing direction, disappeared slowly among the trees. Sometimes he caught glimpses of her by the grupps adjoining the meadows—dykes thickly overgrown with reeds, where warblers and other birds nested—and always accompanied by the narrow, white, angular borzois held in leash and one day they became friends.

Phillip's friendship with Penelope became one of the reliefs of a strenuous life. It had its basis in warm camaraderie, in confidences he could share within the oasis-like security of the little boudoir room where usually she sat, or more usually reclined, on a couch by the fire. It became his habit to drop into her house after the day's work, to be greeted by the graceful prancing of dogs, and, after calling out at the bottom of the stairway, *May I come up,* to be invited into the small upstairs room with its open window and view of bird table, apple trees, and pantil'd roof. The invariable hospitality and graciousness with which his appearance was greeted—whether straight from work on the farm or from the compressions of the writing desk—was one of the stable things of his new life. The room, its walls azure as a starling's egg, was the retreat of a quiet spirit which loved wild birds, and which above all else desired to see children free and happy as those very birds which flitted with such pure instinctive movements about the bird-tray on the window sill. Here was sanctuary, wherein the unspoken rule was, Be thyself.

Penelope at her best, which was nearly always, was unselfishness itself. For many hours she had listened to the diverse view-points of people sitting in her boudoir. Penelope was the resolver of disharmony. Never, since his friendship with Mrs. Neville, the mother of his boyhood friend Desmond—not heard of, or from, for nearly sixteen years now—had Phillip felt so at home, so free to talk exactly as he felt. The past dissensions with Lucy's brothers; the loneliness of Lucy; the sale of the family property in the West

Country and the migration to East Anglia to make a fresh start—he had told Penelope everything, including his relationship with Felicity, and his views upon the condition of Europe; his visit to Germany, his admiration for the spirit of happiness and resurgence he had found everywhere there.

"*Everywhere*, Phillip?" had been her only comment to his enthusiastic descriptions.

"Well, everywhere *I* went, Penelope."

She changed the subject. "Let me ring for some tea for you," and when the tea came, with his especially large cup, they talked about the farm.

She realized that he must justify himself by achievement; was he always hearing, unconsciously, his father's critical voice in childhood? She was glad he could expand in her presence: he had an audience; he could tell her about his plans to write a series of novels one day, when the farm was in order, and Billy would be able to run it for the family and he would be free to return to his hilltop eyrie in South Devon.

Sometimes Phillip wondered if it was a one-sided friendship: if he were taking for granted that what interested him was of interest to Penelope. Certainly she always seemed pleased to see him. Was he a bore, he asked her one day.

"That is the last thing I should say you were, Phillip, provided you always remain yourself."

Penelope never spoke of her own marriage, beyond saying that she had been unhappy and that was all over. She was happiest in the open air, where the freedom of birds was as her own. She lived quietly in the old house with her dogs and her birds, looked after by a housekeeper, a cook, and a parlourmaid—to Penelope a simple household after the conventional orderliness of an ampler life in her father's home.

Once, talking in the rattling sort of way she usually did when referring to her past life, she said, "My father was in the gutter when he started," which he took to be a comparative understatement, since he had inherited the family cement factories; and from what she had said at other times, her father lived in a country house with a variety of gardens; and served by a model Home Farm with chromium-plated machinery and walls of white-glazed tiles. Its timbered park was grazed by a herd of pedigree, tuberculin-tested, agglutinised Ayrshires; the gamekeepers on its surrounding farms, and its lodge-keepers, wore livery. Penelope had mentioned peacocks, water-garden, a dovecot, a gazebo—near none of which, apparently, could she breathe.

Anyway, she had run away from it all, to find happiness and a sense of freedom in that very wilderness of nature which in Phillip induced a feeling of loss of freedom: the Home Hills overgrown with tall and ragged thorns where the turtle dove throbbed in high summer noons: the eroded arable where happy flocks of goldfinches—the scarlet and yellow King Harrys—fed among the forests of the thistles: the swampy meadows: the ragged woods and coverts: the ruinous Old Manor, home of owls, daws, a kestrel, and every year a pair of redstarts.

To Penelope those meadows slowly reverting to bog were a delight.

"Do you know, Phillip, I think I heard a bittern there last winter? It was a strange note, not at all 'booming', as most writers say it is."

"I heard it, too—the blare of an invisible bull with parchment lungs."

"That is exactly what it *was* like! And have you heard the trilling chatter of sedge-warblers and reed-buntings in those wildly-growing osiers?"

At such moments Penelope's face had the light of enthusiasm, while Phillip's heart sank as yet again he thought of all the work that had to be done. The very things that she loved to see were to him at times the cause of near-desperation. Of course he could have written of more beauties than she saw herself; but he would be imitating his earlier self.

Where the thorn-hedges had spread, untouched by steel hook or slasher for twenty years, Penelope could listen with delight to the sharp rattle of the shrike, and watch a family of longtailed titmice swinging in loop-gossamer flight from twig to berry-cluster red against the pale blue sky of early autumn. Every walk on the decadent farm was for her an adventure: for on the meadows might she not see the slaty flap of the harrier when the sycamores below the hanger cliff were turning yellow. In the spring there was the happy bleating of snipe to be heard as they dived over the water-plashes amidst the rush-clumps of the meadow.

"In fact, Penelope, the Bad Lands in the days before the coming of the reformator was a wilderness in which you found your happiness—or consolation."

"In freedom *only* is happiness, Phillip. And I prefer the farm's true name—the Deepwater."

"Do you know why it is called Deepwater?"

"Because it overlooks the only deep-water harbour on the east coast north of the Thames estuary. I'm told that Napoleon considered an invasion here because at all tides there was anchorage for his transports."

Penelope's small daughter went to a school where the choice of work or not to work was left to the pupils. Apparently these pupils called the masters by their Christian names and in all things pleased themselves. In summer time boys and girls slept side by side in little tents about the grounds. The community made its own rules. There were few private possessions, inhibitions, or repressions. No discipline other than that imposed by general agreement of the juvenile community was enforced.

Lucy visited the school with Penelope, and returned with a desire that all her children might go there. She said it was the kind of school she had dreamed about, there was real freedom and everybody looked happy.

"How about the founder and headmaster?"

"Well, he did look rather sad."

"I don't wonder at it. All his workshops mucked up by kids."

"He looked as though he were not properly understood."

"You should read Strindberg's *The Father*."

On the first occasion that Phillip met Penelope's child, during her holidays, she had looked at him with hostility as he peered in the doorway of her school-room where she was painting on a table.

"I suppose you come here after Mummie's money?"

"On the contrary, your Mummie has invited me into her house in order to get mine. She keeps a Crown-and-Anchor board."

"Soppy," replied the child, continuing her angular painting. The next time they met Phillip gave straightforward answers to her questions, and found her friendly.

Lucy's little girl, Rosamund, went to quite a different sort of school. The fees were one-seventh of those paid by Penelope for her daughter's schooling. Rosamund's school had only eighteen pupils, all small girls. The school was in a private house in a side-street of one of the coastal villages. It was run by two nuns who were dressed in light brown clothes. They were elderly spinster sisters. The children were not allowed in the garden except to work there. It was a small garden, but the playground, with a gravel surface, was smaller, and enclosed by a rusty iron-spiked fence. The fees were £15 a term, which included board and lodging. The main meal of the day was almost invariably bully beef. Once when passing the village in his car Phillip had seen a wan face looking at him through the rusty railings, a dark little girl dressed in a brown uniform. With surprise he recognised Rosamund. So that was where she went to school. Usually merry and lively, this mite looked positively woebegone.

The nuns were dumpy and their vitality withdrawn by too many interior ruminations. Just like himself, in fact. His feeling was to avoid them when they approached as he was talking to Roz behind her cage, but summoning up an impersonal manner, he spoke cheerfully to them, saying that the fine keen air of the coast was so different from the relaxing atmosphere of the West Country. He shook hands with both through the railings, and then blowing a kiss to his small daughter, left with mingled feelings of regret, relief, and despair that he was so neglectful a father.

The visit had a sequel later on in the year. Through Lady Penelope, Lucy met a parson's wife, Mrs. Frobisher, who invited them over, saying in her note that her sister was a great admirer of Phillip Maddison's books, and all at the rectory would be honoured if they would dine with them one evening, with Penelope. Thither the three went, in Penelope's motor.

Phillip enjoyed the party. He thought, I must take part in the social life of the district in future. The rector had been an athlete in his youth, a triple blue of Oxford University, Penelope had told them on the way there. He asked Phillip if he played golf, and offered to put him up for the local club, with its links beside the sea, near 'Boy' Runnymeade's cottage. All was friendly, the young daughters were pretty, the older folks lively, the saddle of mutton had the flavour of the aromatic plants growing on the 'mashes' beyond the sheep-walks along the coast. The talk came round to the possibility of war, and Phillip's opinion was asked.

"Now listen, my dears, very carefully to what Captain Maddison has to say," said the aunt to her nieces. "In years to come you will be able to tell your children of this evening."

No war, said Phillip, and heard himself giving the reasons which few had accepted hitherto.

"Birkin will be speaking at Fenton soon. Do please go to the meeting, Mrs. Frobisher, and give him a hearing."

A silence followed this request. Then a young doctor, husband of the rector's daughter, said to Phillip, "I hear you have a daughter at school in Staithe. There used to be a sanatorium there, and many of the villagers now have tuberculosis. In fact, it's in most of the cottages. If I had a daughter, I wouldn't send her anywhere near the village."

At home Phillip said, "I think Roz ought to leave at the end of term, don't you? I wish I had the money to send her where Penelope's daughter goes, but all my capital is now laid out on the farm. Anyway, I'm not in debt, thank God. She'd be better at the village school, for a year or two anyway."

Lucy was alarmed. Her mother had died of tuberculosis. She telephoned the school and gave notice, saying that the district was known to be infected by tuberculosis.

"What? We happen to have lived here for some years now, Mrs. Maddison, and have never before heard that said!"

"Well, my husband heard it from a doctor last night, I forget his name, but he has just come to practise in the district."

"You mean that young man who lives at Staithe rectory? Then it may interest you to know that he is the junior partner of the school doctor, who is also Medical Officer of Health for the district. And he has always given us a clean bill of health!"

Unaware of what had been said, Phillip learned of it in a letter from a solicitor. The matter was settled by payment of a small sum, in addition to a term's fees in lieu of notice. He asked Lucy to write a letter explaining to Mrs. Frobisher that it was not he who had used a private conversation which surely must have involved the young doctor in some trouble with his senior.

"I can imagine him saying, 'I thought Maddison was a gentleman, and would know better than to use a private conversation like that.'"

"Oh, I don't suppose he will think any more about it, do you?"

Phillip left the farmhouse without eating his breakfast and when he returned it was late afternoon. Something had gone wrong on the farm, he said. Things usually did go wrong with poor Pip, thought Lucy, who had heard his voice shouting from far away. Once again Luke had backed the light green trailer, the brakes had locked, the shackle-bolts holding one spring to the body had been torn off.

"Do you really want me to write that letter?"

"It doesn't matter."

There was now between Phillip and Penelope a partial constraint; a matter of literary importance had to be resolved: a point which he felt sometimes as the sharp thorn of injustice. It was this: in his reply to her request for permission to walk over his land, there had been, said Penelope, a sentence which had startled her on beholding it in a letter from a stranger.

"We can agree to differ about a matter of personal taste, Phillip, but you must not try to argue me out of what I know to be true."

The letter he had written to her, she maintained, *had* ended with the phrase, *Of course Jefferies had an awful life: syphilis.*

"But I could not have written such a thing about Richard Jefferies! It is untrue."

But no: Penelope maintained her sweet calm and repeated that he had written exactly that phrase.

"Might I see the letter, then?"

"I'm afraid you can't. I threw it in the fire."

Penelope pressed the bell. Immediately her housekeeper, who must have been waiting outside, he thought, entered with a tray.

"Do help yourself to a peg before you go, Phillip. No, I won't have anything, thank you, I've given it up. I was getting too fat. Give my love to Lucy. Good night."

Penelope lay on her couch, and took up *The Daily Telegram* but she did not read it. The problem of Phillip, his isolation from Lucy his wife, was often in her mind. He had undertaken a task too much for him, that was obvious; but he had ability, knowledge of farming, tremendous vitality—how he managed to do all the physical work he did all day, and write at night as well, she did not know. Obviously he was driving himself too hard, and his men were duds. She liked them, having been acquainted with them for three years, but they had been left to themselves all during that time, the former tenant having taken the land for the shooting. Then there had been that friar flapping about the farm—what use could a man like that possibly be? No: she could not be sure how far Phillip was an effect of all the muddle about him, or the cause——

There was his constant frustration. Sometimes his voice came across the river from the Old Manor. At least he never shouted at others; only when alone, and in what he called the Jackdaw Room, where he wrote. Of course he needed help with figures and Lucy had no head for business, but she was a worker. He was kind to his children, but treated them as equals, which was a mistake. Children should be left to develop their own personalities, not be *forced* into patterns against everything of what their father chose to call the 'old decadent order'. They were untidy, certainly, but children should be allowed their own untidiness, which was natural.

Penelope could not bear people who shouted. Her husband, whom she had divorced, had shouted; Daddy shouted, alone in his own rooms. Just like Phillip. Daddy had built himself up into something that threatened to destroy him. Mama was partly to blame, of course; and she herself could sympathise over all the difficulties of a marriage gone wrong; but she had seen clearly how the responsibilities of money and position had weighed on Mama, as they did on Daddy—and how social ambition could, and did, spoil human life. Had not Stevenson written, *It is better to travel hopefully than to arrive?*

Poor Daddy. Where had ambition brought him? She saw his kind face, always so humorous and gentle with her, as she had last seen him: Daddy standing up in the library at home to greet her, his whimsical smile as he went forward with arms outheld to embrace her. The sudden stagger, the recovery, the hand on the table to steady himself, the fixed smile as he tried to show her that he had not been drinking.

For awhile Penelope felt sad. The corners of her mouth drooped. Then she caught a movement outside the window, and her eyes became bright with interest as she watched a nuthatch pecking at the nut kernels strung on a string across the bird-tray. A flicker of wings, a scolding chitter: and a blue-tit had driven the nuthatch away. She watched it pecking with tiny furious power, then it danced aside, raised its blue crest as a robin arrived. The robin stood still and regarded it with wings held down, as though it had a sword ready to draw. Suddenly it stabbed forward, the blue-tit vanished. The robin regarded her with full gaze for a few moments, then flitted away into the dusk beyond the pantiles. He knows me, she thought happily.

Penelope pressed the bell. The housekeeper entered.

"Oh, Mrs. Treasure, might I have the lamp, please? And I won't be down to dinner, I'll have a tray. And let the dogs come in now, will you?"

At her words the door, which had been left ajar, was pushed open, and the borzois, each like the half of a hairy hoop, curved into the room to lay their heads side by side on the sofa, to receive the evening blessing of two hands stroking in unison.

"And my spectacles, please, Mrs. Treasure. I think I left them on my dressing table. Thank you, Mrs. Treasure."

The curtains were drawn, the fire mended, the housekeeper left as quietly as she had come. When she brought in the tray she said, "Mr. Maddison has just left this note for you, m'lady."

"Is he waiting downstairs, Mrs. Treasure?"

"No, he said that it did not require any answer, and left at once."

Penelope put it aside until she had eaten her dinner. The envelope was still unopened when Mrs. Treasure came to take away the tray. When she was alone again, Penelope opened it.

Dear Penelope,

Forgive me being a bore, by bringing up the case of Richard Jefferies again, but I felt I must explain the position. I wish you had known my cousin Willie, who was drowned in 1923, in the estuary of the Taw and Torridge in Devon. He could make things much plainer and truer than I shall ever be able to do. I was given his books afterwards, and his copy of Jefferies' *The Story of my Heart* was for many years never far from me. I mention this because a passage in that book seems to me to express what, in the spiritual sense—'First there was the Word'—is everywhere being countered in Britain today.

Jefferies is the seer and prophet of a new way of life which can come about only when it is generally accepted that 'the whole mode of thought of the nations must be altered before physical progress is possible'.

I know that Hudson, who loved Jefferies (though they never met) thought that Jefferies in his *Story* showed 'strange unnatural feeling', and that he was a tormented man, but the forces of negation and reaction that wore Jefferies out 'before his time', as Hudson wrote, are the same in the world today, equally powerful, and actively intent on destroying another man of genius. If history is any criterion he will fail; but at least he will have made the attempt.

This is what Jefferies wrote:

'I would submit to a severe discipline, and go without many things cheerfully, for the good and happiness of the human race in the future. Each one of us should do something, however small, towards that great end. At the present time the labour of our predecessors in this country, as in all other countries of the earth, is entirely wasted. We live—that is we snatch an existence—and our works become nothing. The piling up of fortunes, the building of cities, the establishment of immense commerce, ends in a cipher.

'These objects are so outside my idea that I cannot understand them, and look upon the struggle with amazement. Not even the pressure of poverty can force upon me an understanding of, and sympathy with, these things. It is the human being as the human being of whom I think. That the human being as the human being—nude—apart altogether from money, clothing, houses, properties—should

> enjoy greater health, strength, safety, beauty, and happiness I would gladly agree to a discipline like that of Sparta. The Spartan method did produce the finest race of men, and Sparta was famous in antiquity for the most beautiful women. So far, therefore, it exactly fits my ideas.
>
> 'No science of modern times has yet discovered a plan to meet the requirements of the millions who live now, no plan by which they might attain similar physical proportion. Some increase in longevity, some slight improvement in the general health is promised, and these are great things, but far, far beneath the ideal. Probably the whole mode of thought of the nations must be altered before physical progress is possible.'

Penelope stopped reading. Sparta! It was a cruel system, producing only evil. She did not want to read further.

This was the Phillip of the strained look, who girded against so much; and for what ultimate goal? To be harmonious and happy? Of course. What then was stopping him? Hurst, with that abominable swastika badge, had long ago departed. Phillip had complained when Hurst was with him; he had complained when Hurst gave notice. If only Hurst had been this; why wasn't Hurst that? Phillip had wanted Hurst to be something that Hurst definitely was not.

She hesitated. She sighed; then with resolution let the pages float into the fire, where the coal flames twisted the paper and turned them red. One charred fragment quivered, and remained. For a moment the written words seemed to stand out greyly before the heat took the fragments up the chimney. She leaned forward, and read the calcined words.

> The life of Hitler, the 'unknown soldier' of the 1914–1918 war has so far been lived in the belief that the divination of European genius will, by his efforts, be followed by the union and resurgence of the West for a thousand years of peace.

Lucy said: "I've written the letter to Mrs. Frobisher. Would you like to see it?"

"How very kind of you, Lucy. And you have so much work to do—literally all day and half the night. No, I can't read it. What a tyrant I am—no, don't post it. Yours was a perfectly innocent remark to the headmistress. My attitude to you was self-willed and petty."

The work entailed in the making of the New Cut had been easier than anticipated. Phillip kept the details in his Journal.

61 ton-loads of lump chalk picked from the quarry by the premises laid the foundation; 40 tons of gravel spread on the chalk—and there was the causeway across the bottom corner of the Steep.

Reaching the grassy side of the hill, grown with little thorns, they cut a way through the marl and shovelled the marl direct into the two horse-drawn tumbrils, emptying the loads into heaps on the field below, where the soil was sandy, and inclined to be acid. Thus they made two improvements at the same time.

When finished, the New Cut was a fine sight. Lorry and trailer ran up easily; the old back-breaking problem of inaccessibility was solved: and all for a capital expenditure of £25. He found satisfaction in thinking he earned this money by writing an 1,800-word script for the B.B.C. It meant an hour of writing between eleven o'clock one evening and midnight; and early the following evening a hundred-mile journey to Broadcasting House in London, arriving back in the small hours. He thought he could do that sort of thing for years, so why worry about capital, he told Luke the steward.

Having chalked some of the acid land, why not finish that hollow of nearly four acres? So by the top of the New Cut they opened a small quarry, digging loam for spreading on those areas which had not already been covered. Half the cost of digging the sweet, thick marl was met by a grant from the Land Fertility Commission. It was reassuring to feel himself becoming a regular business man.

One morning he had a surprise—a letter from Ernest, written when he had arrived at Sydney, whither he had sailed in a P. & O. liner, working his passage among the steerage passengers, all emigrants like himself. Ernest wrote that he had spent eighteen hours of every one of the forty-seven-day voyage in washing-up dishes, and concluded, *If I live to be a hundred, I shall never see eye to eye with the chief steward, the purser, and the captain.*

Chapter 13

'THE WHEAT WAS ORIENT——'

How quickly the time had passed. Could it be a year ago that the New Cut had been made, and then the bare-fallowing of the twenty acres of the Steep? How pleasing to see green, sappy heads of wheat waving in the breeze of early morning, beside the neat design of the New Cut leading up to the skyline.

He sat down to enjoy the sight of a weed-free field, pleased with himself that he was able to get free of worry for a moment. Could this be the same field upon which he had looked with such despondency from Pine Tree Camp in his first year of farming, to see what appeared to be a silver-grey mist lying upon a lake in the early morning? But it was not the foggy dew of morning before a day of great heat that he had stared at on that occasion, but twenty acres of seeded thistles which had completely overtopped a dwarfed crop of thin barley stalks: a grey mass of one burst cardoon touching another burst cardoon extending to the distant trees of the Great Bustard Wood. And the yield of barley that season, sown merely to add to the sum to be paid for ingoing covenants—hay, straw, standing crops, etc.—had been about two sacks, and the yield of thistle seed about four sacks, an acre. That was the Steep in the year of his taking over. Luke, and Matt his father, had been the only hands working on the farm.

Phillip had, the winter before, watched Luke ploughing the slippery slopes with two old horses. The single-furrow plough had barely scratched the surface. The horses had been under-fed. At its steepest part the field had a gradient of 1 in 4. And during the subsequent harvest, of almost entirely thistles, he had watched a Fordson tractor drawing an old Albion binder jattering and slewing about behind it, and sometimes rearing up, while the binder in mechanical panic hastily jettisoned a string of unbound sheaves.

"You can't do anything with this land," the driver had declared to Phillip. "It's a thistly old sod."

The grass seeds he was supposed to have sown in the young barley the April before, to restore a permanent pasture which had been ploughed up by his master, simply hadn't come up. No wonder, in a seed-bed consisting of dried strips and lumps of sulky clay held together by weeds, and scratched about by harrows.

That was the Bad Lands system of farming before he had taken over.

What a difference today! Sitting at the edge of the wheat he felt a flow of happiness: for he had, by insisting for once on having his own way, changed the surface of the field. Luke had objected to a bare fallow, so he had ploughed the field himself, with reliefs by Brother Laurence. Still, one must be fair: neither Luke nor Matt had seen working the new and unknown make of tractor Phillip had bought without seeing after reading about it in *The Daily Trident* by the farming correspondent whose daily *Countryman's Diary*, under his initials, Phillip had read in his youth. The tractor had an hydraulic attachment by which twin plough-shares could be lifted out of or put into the ground by a lever. Plough and tractor were designed as one. The machine was a very light affair. It could walk up steep hills while ploughing, without digging-in its wheels or overturning, a fault in old types of heavy tractors which merely lugged heavy-framed ploughs.

Phillip ploughed twenty acres of fatty loam, up and down the Steep, in the month of May, happy on the new tractor. The furrows dried out. Then rain fell, and soon through the crumbling furrows arose a green luxuriant crop of thistles.

"Mygor, what hev you done?" asked the steward's father.

"Raised millions of eager thistles, Matt."

"Harn't yew a-goin' to cultivate them?"

"I'm going to let them grow."

One June morning he replaced the greased plough-breasts with seven shining cultivator tines fixed on an iron frame. These were the tines designed by Ernest, who had made a mahogany prototype, which had been taken to a foundry, and a dozen mild-steel tines pressed out.

Behind Phillip on the tractor seven tines winged like down-slanting terns moved eight inches under the furrows. Up and down the slopes the driver went, cutting roots of thistles. Soon their green luxuriance was wilted in the sun. Within the shine of another day they had turned to bronze. By the third day they had lost colour. Within a week all were withered away.

The stirring of the soil, making it friable, pleasant to crumble in the fingers, had stimulated another form of life. All over the Steep little dark green spots were breaking from out the loose soil. Kneeling upon his bare knees—for in the hot sun Phillip wore only shoes and khaki shorts—he stared at the blue-green kidney-shaped leaves of the charlock, hundreds of little plants to the square foot, thousands to the square yard, trillions to the acre. Each tiny seedling appeared to be dark-green because of its sharp shadow thrown under the high noon sun. Behind the shining tines of the cultivator the sun burned them to dust, even as it burned Phillip's flesh to the colour of dust. He was happy, he could feel virtue coming back into the soil, and so to himself. No more decadent living, no more cramped hours with the pen, shut away from the sun, living entirely in the imagination, to warp the outlook! How glad he was he had risked all in buying the Bad Lands!

When the thistles came up again the gleaming winged tines once more rustled through the earth, crossing their previous course. Underground they severed stalk from root, leaving behind a mould to feel which he must dismount again and again to hold in the hand, letting it fall through his fingers lightly, a lovely mould, the 'marther' by which all things came to being. That was Matt's word—he supposed it came from 'mother'. The Steep was no longer a thistly old sod: it was reborn, it was alive, it was fertile.

And now, in this summer of 1938, it was growing a first-rate crop of Squarehead II wheat.

Leaving the wheat on the Steep, he went on to the Great Bustard. This field had not been bare-fallowed. It had been sown down to barley, at Matt's earnest request; and then 'seeds' had been drilled, for the following year's hay, when the barley plants had three or four leaves.

The Great Bustard field adjoined the wood of that name. In past time those birds, now extinct, used to nest in the wood.

There were twenty acres of hay which looked to be not too bad. True, there were many docks, but these when cut could be collected by the children, and burnt. The hay was from a seeds mixture of cowgrass, alsike, Dutch white clover, and trefoil. Above this green 'bottom' swayed delicate stalks of rye-grass. Purple bells were hanging on the awns of the Irish rye-grass, but the pollen was not yet come to blow.

It was time to cut, said Phillip.

"I shouldn't cut if 'twas mine," replied Luke. "I'd wait and cut for bulk."

"Bulk means woody stalks. The sap is gone from the clover leaves into the flowers."

"But if we cut now, there'll be little more than a ton an acre to carry," replied Luke, anxiously.

"We can't expect a good shear while the land is still exhausted after all the corn you and your late master took off it, without putting anything back."

"But what will father's stock have to eat next winter if we cut now? That's what worrying me and father."

"Last winter the cows gave poor milk, didn't they, Luke? The hay was little more than fill-belly. There were three reasons for this. In the first place, it was cut too late, and was what you call 'woody'. Then it was left after cutting until it was bleached, which means it was unpalatable to stock. Thirdly, there was a thin 'shear' because your small seeds had been sown on a cobbly seed-bed."

"That was the weather, you can't help the weather."

"Yes we can, if we do things at the right time."

"But you put us on all that other wark, guv'nor," said Matt, who had come up silently on worn-out rubber gum-boots.

"True enough, Matt. But this year we mustn't make the same mistakes. Hay when 'fit' should not be brown when put into the stack, but a grey-green colour."

"Then 'twill go mouldy," objected Luke.

"Not green-sappy when carried," Phillip insisted, "but grey-green in colour. Dry hay—sun-bleached—all the sap gone out of it—all the volatile oils which make the scent of it—what is called chlorophyll, or green colouring matter—without this, hay is really no good."

"Theory," exclaimed the stockman.

"I know you distrust theory, Matt, but I wish you would trust what I say. Was that a quail?"

A liquid quipping note, several notes in quick succession, like the Morse code *dash dot-dot, dash dot-dot* repeated, came over the grasses swaying to the breeze in silky waves.

Father and son exchanged glances. They knew that Horatio Bugg had been paid four pounds for a pair by the old gentleman who collected and had rare birds stuffed, and who lived in a neighbouring village.

"Quaquilla the quail," said Phillip. "That's what the Romans called him—quaquilla—after his liquid note. He flies from the deserts of North Africa, all the way up the Rhône valley. *Wet-my-lips, wet-my-lips*—do you hear it? It will be dreadful if we slash through the nest."

"That's what I mean," said Luke, strain in his voice, "if you was to cut now."

"Perhaps if I found the nest first——"

Phillip felt his mind dissolving. So much to do, so little done. He forced himself to remain calm.

"Hay must be dry, of course. But like a good girl's hair, never bleached. We had a rick on our land in the West Country—a stack as you say here in the East—of dry, greenish hay, which beasts fought to get at when it was put in the racks."

"You can't beat brown hay that's heated a bit in the stack, guv'nor."

"Ah yes, I know what you mean, Matt. It heats in the stack and becomes like a kind of silage. In fact, if it is put in sappy and trodden hard when being stacked, so that the air is shut out as it settles, then it wads and heats and becomes almost cake. But if the air gets in, then you get your mouldy hay, Luke. Or perhaps a fire. But the best hay is wind-dried, green and sweet-smelling. Then see how the beasts eat it. All farming books emphasize the value of hay which retains chlorophyll, the essential oils."

"Theory," said Matt.

"You can't beat brown hay," said Luke.

Phillip knew that to be too keen was a fault when that keenness cut across slower minds or natures; but he did not realise what offence he was giving by his insistence.

"What I say are proved facts."

"Theory," repeated Matt, with scorn.

"The men what write those theories have never done a proper day's work in their lives, Master. How should they know?" Luke's dark eyes held a hint of pain.

Even so, thought Phillip, there is no hope for the farm unless it is different from the old one. That means altering the minds of those about me. The war of ideas on the farm is like the greater looming continental war of action and reaction.

"Of course I know last year's crop was brittly stuff, but I won't have it about green hay," repeated Luke. "You can't beat brown hay."

"You can beat it with grey-green, *sweet* hay."

"Then 'twill go mouldy, so I harn't a-goin' to do it. What will they say in the village——"

"Is the village running this farm?"

"You're master," said Luke, quietly. "If you order me to cut, I'll cut."

Not wanting Luke to continue feeling hurt, and also thinking of the quails, Phillip said, "Well, let's wait a bit shall we?" while knowing that the hay, for the best feeding quality, should be cut now, before the seeds ripened.

He felt relief as he left the Great Bustard behind him: at least he would have two or three days clear before haysel, and so he could do some writing. It was nine o'clock. Luke had been horse-hoeing between the sugar-beet ridges when Phillip had asked him to take a look at the hay. The other two men were scoring sugar-beet—the final hoeing of weeds between the plants. It was contract work, they were their own masters, and happy.

He waved to them, and returned by way of the Steep. How time was passing! Only last week, it seemed, the swallow-winged tines were decimating for the third time the growth of thistles underground. Again the sun killed them. Yet once more they arose, yet once again were slain. Thereafter in August nothing had grown on the bare fallow. Hares squatted there, partridges had the dusting baths to themselves.

In the following October Juliana wheat was drilled, ten pecks to the acre; and now the June slopes of the Steep were thick with wheat: the plants had tillered well, each plant had several stalks with thick long ears, every one identical, soon to curve with its own weight, to rustle with its fellows in the sea-breeze of late July and August mornings. It was a sight wonderful to behold. All those corn-heads uniform and close together, brother and sisters in a dream of resurgence: not one thistle or dock or campion or charlock plant to divide them. The soil at the base of the tillered stalks showed neither red pimpernel nor blue speedwell, but only the little plants of rye-grass and clover which he and Billy had drilled across the harrowed rows in April.

It was his first wheat. While he was biting a milky head, Matt appeared under the walnut tree by the steep chalk slope. What did he think of it? Matt snatched a couple of heads, rubbed them out, and went through the motions of biting with his brown teeth.

"They're full of milk." He looked at Phillip. "Yew did a good job up here, guv'nor."

The honest brown eyes regarded him kindly. It was a generous admission, since both he and his son had declared it to be impossible.

"Yew don't want to cut wheat too late, else 'twill shill out," he went on. "An yew won't go wrong if yew cart wheat when it's raining. D'yew know why?"

"No. Do tell me."

"The wind blows through wheat straw, guv'nor. So it don't heat in the stack."

"I've learned something, Matt."

Sitting on the bank at the top of the New Cut he looked down the valley. He saw the sky-gleaming river, and the red roofs of the farmstead amongst the trees. Then his eye strayed to the sprawling and overgrown thorn-hedge below: and for the hundredth time a feeling of dullness overcame him. When, oh when, would they start to cut those 'great old bull-thorns', those interlocked masses of brambles, those clusters of nettles growing eight and more yards out into the arable? They had grown like that ever since the repeal of the Corn Production Act in 1923. Their shadows poisoned more than an acre of ground. Enough sandy soil had been thrown there by rabbits to fill a dozen tumbrils. Thousands of rabbits, grey verminous rodents, were living in the woods and on the Home Hills, though nearly two thousand had been sent to market during the past two winters. From the hedges the restless mind went to the undrained meadows, and to other tasks which burdened the imagination; and trying to put them away, he got on his feet and walked down the Cut, the pale blue sea unseen through the trees below.

The wood was the haunt of pigeons to hear whose cooing was but to think of the flocks of a thousand and more that had eaten bare the tops of three acres of swedes, grown for the small ewe-flock the previous winter. Then there were the adjoining gardens of his cottage and the farmhouse—nearly an acre of ground between them—to be cleared of litter and rubbish and weeds. His own cottage damp as a dungeon, to be reconditioned. Seventy acres of arable must be spread with seven hundred tons of chalk, first picked from the face of the quarry and carted up to the several fields, as soon as the corn harvest was over.

A rutted cart-track led to the premises. He felt tired. He had been writing the previous night until the small hours. By the last tree in the wood, a wildling elderberry, he stopped. He had rested there many times before. He had a feeling for the tree-spirit, which was old; only part of it was alive; a clutter and wind-rattle of old yellow bones: a tree damned like himself. No wonder elder was the black witch's tree, supposed to have supplied the wood of the cross on which Jesus was nailed. Some bird had squitted out the seed there, and the elderberry had grown. Its berries fed the redwings, migrants from Scandinavia, in winter.

"Hold on, old tree. I'm your friend," he said aloud, with a wave of the hand.

The rough cart-track led to the farm premises, of Jacobean red brick and flint. The first building was the Hay Barn, with double doors tall enough for a loaded waggon to enter by. It was the haunt of doves. Several pairs of these gentle birds nested on the tops of the walls, and upon the wooden platform on which sacks of barley and oats for the grinding and rolling machine below were hauled up on ratchet and chain. Whenever he looked into the Hay Barn a score of white wings fluttered.

The doves were sprung from a couple which had made a nest during his first spring: strays perhaps from some race, birds tired and lost. Now he stopped at the open door, admiring the birds in a remote way—for his mind was fixed upon the needs of so much to be done. He saw herring-bone pattern of the narrow red bricks on the floor. Chinks of light entered by the pantiles of the lofty roof. The rafters were worm-eaten; all must be renewed.

He stopped on the bridge over the river, dreading what he might see of this semi-polluted chalk stream. The water ran clear over a foot or so of quiescent black mud, detritus of organic decomposition from scores of open drains and pitless sewers. Often the water ran murky, a-prickle with bubbles of deadly carbon-dioxide, the inert gas of asphyxiation and death. The stain of the mud-pulling higher up had not yet come down with the stream.

From the bridge a footpath led to the door in the courtyard wall, half fallen from its rust-thin hinges. The courtyard was green with weeds growing between the cobbles. He looked around before continuing his way to the new farmhouse. There from under the porch swallows dived and fled softly dark blue past his head. Their young were perched on a purlin, beside the nest above.

"Aren't they darlings?" said Lucy, coming out to look. "Breakfast is just ready."

He sat at the long oak table. It had been polished. Silver

gleamed. Sprays of Sweet William stood in a bowl, beside another bowl holding deep blue gentians.

"Penelope gave them to me. She's just returned from the Black Forest, where she has been with her father."

"I remember that blue, or its shadow of blue, in the Pantheon—Napoleon's tomb in Paris. That blue light coming down upon the dome. Do you know D. H. Lawrence's poem, written as he was dying, *Gentians*. Of course I've read it to you before."

An hour later, while he was writing upstairs, he heard voices. He retreated from his table by the window. Then Lucy came round the path by the new bathroom building and called out, "George Abeline and Melissa have looked in for a moment. They're on their way to see 'Boy' Runnymeade. They hope they're not disturbing you."

He ran down the stairs to welcome them.

George Abeline said, "I suppose this is a call. You've got some fine coverts, Phil. Melissa and I saw them from the road. There should be some high birds, from a stand on the meadows. You must come and shoot with us in the autumn." He laughed dryly. "That's a lead, Phil, for you to ask me over for a day with you."

Soon they must be going. "'Boy' Runnymeade has arranged for us to go mackerel spinning. By Jove, I must take your photograph, Lucy. You look like a young queen."

Phillip had to go to the blacksmith, to get spare blades for the cutter. Melissa went with him. And then it was goodbye. What could he do? He thought to look at the meadows.

On arriving where the coastal road ran beside the river, his heart sank to see the thistles on the meadows, the choked dykes, the inert flow of the river, now dark-clouded with suspended mud. The sight was too much, he returned and walked down the street, to speak to the bricklayer about repairing the courtyard wall. Seeing him, Horatio Bugg hurried out.

"That was a pretty girl you had with you just now, when you went into the blacksmith's shop," he said. "Who is she?" presenting a hand-enshelled ear for reply.

"That's right," he called into the hand.

"Her name was Wright, you say? Where does she come from?"

"A rose by any other name would smell as sweet."

"I don't know what you mean."

"Nor do I," said Phillip, walking on. Looking back, he saw Bugg tapping his forehead. Phillip tapped his, then pointed to Bugg.

"No, you!" shouted the dealer, tapping his brow and pointing at Phillip. Phillip gave him the two-fingers' sign, as he went to call on Penelope.

Under the monkey tree in the carriage sweep a black Daimler was drawn up. By the open door stood a chauffeur in uniform, rug on arm. On the threshold Penelope was talking to a stout oldish man of medium height dressed in a dark overcoat obviously made in Sackville Street or Savile Row. Here was part of the financial strength of Mansion House and Guildhall; here was Penelope's father.

As Phillip walked through the gate without hesitation the chauffeur continued to attend the slightest want of his master, whose round pink face under a bowler hat looked in the direction of the visitor. Penelope's chin went up a little higher, her amiable face moved only its Cambridge-blue eyes. He imagined her assembling words as he came level with the bole of the monkey tree set with its arboreal shark-teeth. No monkey-man catchee Penelopee, he thought absurdly, to the pink face.

Whatever Penelope's father might have thought, nothing of it showed in his manner of greeting Phillip, who was impressed by his modesty and charm, which showed itself immediately in the interest the noble visitor assumed to have in what he, Phillip, had done and was doing. His courtly manners were most impressive, as he referred to the most interesting and inspiring newspaper articles pleading for a virile peasantry, and for the unemployed to be used for the draining and reclaiming of idle acres.

"As you will have already imagined," went on the Earl of Skipton with smiling deference, "I am one of your innumerable town readers who looks regularly, and with anticipation, to your country writings. Penelope has told me how well you are doing your land, too. I am a farmer in a small way, and envy you your work in the open air. I would like to be your pupil, but alas, my dry-as-dust duties call me. I am so glad to have met you at last."

"I am the one who is honoured, sir."

"If I get an opportunity during the debate tomorrow in the Lords I shall refer, Maddison, if I may have your permission to do so, to what you wrote about the salmon smolts and the pollution of the Thames. Do you know, the value of waste products cast upon the waters of Spencer's Sweet Thames—you know the quotation, of course—below the Pool of London is in the neighbourhood of two hundred million pounds sterling annually? In Yorkshire we have perhaps learned to do things a little better.

From the reclaimed and treated sewage of the city of Bradford alone, enough polish to shine all the boots and shoes of the Midlands is made. Out of this waste our West Riding Transport lines grease all their omnibuses. Also a valuable compost fertiliser is prepared, and we make a substantial annual profit after the seven percentum interest on the Corporation stock is paid. So you see your article, my dear sir, is both practical and poetical, as, I would venture to say from my most limited knowledge, is the classic literature of our nation."

Thereupon he held out his hand, and shook Phillip's warmly, while the chauffeur awaited the exact moment to help his Lordship into the car and put the rug over his knees.

"I've just remembered something," Phillip made excuse to Penelope. "Do forgive me running away," and he left father and daughter together.

Horatio Bugg, like a dog, was still on the look-out for anything interesting.

"Didn't stay long, did you? I could have told you who it was who come there if you hadn't been in such a hurry to pass me by. He's just going now."

"Do you buy pig-meal sacks?"

"I pay eightpence a dozen."

"They pay a shilling in Crabbe."

"I have to take them in to town, see."

"So do I."

"How many bags have you got?"

"About a hundred."

"I'll take them off of you. Will you be going to Crabbe soon with your lorry?"

"Possibly."

"I've got some old iron I want taking in. It's up a shilling since last year. Half-a-crown now. They want it for armaments. The diddecais only pay me half a dollar, so if I can get it in to Crabbe, it will pay me, see?"

"What will it pay me?"

"You'll have to go in anyway, you said."

"Who's going to unload your old iron?"

"I'll ride in with you, and be company for you. We're all neighbours, aren't we? Here," he lifted his nose, "Come in here." He led the way into a tarred and decrepit wooden shed, wherein hung sacks and rabbit skins above a heap of broken implement parts and other rubbish.

"Is it true what they say, that you've sold the Old Manor?"

"Ah."

A retired industrialist from the Midlands had sold his interest in his company, together with all his stocks and shares—to avoid all taxes—for he would have no income if he lived on his capital of £300,000—and bought the Old Manor, together with the four acres of the grounds and gardens in which the house was set. Phillip had got £600. This sum had cleared off the bank overdraft, guaranteed by a form he had filled in, and signed, relative to the live and dead stock (tractor, implements, etc.) he possessed on Deepwater Farm. So while Phillip owed nothing, except the mortgage interest to Lucy, he possessed little ready cash.

"What did you get for it. Next to nothin', I reckon."

"How do you know so much about everything, Horatio?"

"Ah, I have ways and means, you know. Here!" His nose jerked towards the darker end of his shed. "I can see you are scared of Lady Penelope's old man," he said. "You got reason to be, I reckon," he added, winking at Phillip. "Nice bit of skirt Lady Penelope, eh?" His elbow dug into Phillip's ribs. "You have a way with the ladies, I can see that, y'know. I admire you for it. That was a choice bit of stuff you had with you earlier this morning, and no mistake. But you're so good looking, you can get away with it. I can't," he said, rather sadly.

"Still," he added, drawing himself up, "I live on the interest of my money, I do." He squared his shoulders, and hastened indoors to tell the latest news of the sale to an old mother and elderly sisters, who habitually wore black clothes of an age not yet bygone in that district of Old England.

Chapter 14

'BIRKIN FOR BRITAIN'

Lady Breckland telephoned to say that a meeting of the Imperial Socialist Party was being held in the Corn Hall at Fenton on the following Sunday night.

"Do come if you can, and bring your wife to see us afterwards, won't you? I do so hope that Sir Hereward Birkin's words will be heeded. He has the only realistic policy for putting farming on its feet, and the whole country and Empire as well; while the alternative is an increasing depression. It is all so simple if only people would believe it——"

Phillip knew all that Lady Breckland was saying about Birkin; their minds ran in the same groove, literally upon the same grooves of Birkin's idealistic words on the gramophone record, the deep almost mystic voice concluding with the words:

> *Together we have lit a flame which shall burn through the ages. Guard that sacred flame, my brothers, until it illuminates Britain, and lights again the pathway of mankind.*

"I look forward to it, Lady Breckland. I'll bring my wife, and fill the car with some of my men. Meanwhile may I have six tickets?"

"Wonderful news," he told Lucy. "Birkin is coming on Sunday. We'll ask Penelope, shall we?"

Phillip had already met Birkin Hereward at Lady Breckland's house. He and Brother Laurence had been invited to dinner. Felicity had found Phillip's dress clothes in a trunk, and hung them up to dry and uncrease in the kitchen of the Old Manor, where they were then squatting.

During the day both men had worked with the concrete mixer; at night, weary but hopeful, they had found their way across unfamiliar country, sometimes stopping by sign-posts, while Brother Laurence struck matches and Phillip examined his map in the glow of a side-light.

Birkin and his adjutant arrived during dinner. They had made a long motor journey from the North, where a meeting had been held in the Free Trade Hall, Manchester. Birkin gave Phillip an immediate impression of great and controlled strength. He was tall and of powerful build, dressed in a grey suit, and looked tired. There was a ragged red scar nearly two inches long in his left temple, where he had been struck by a stone a few months before and knocked unconscious.

Phillip had read about that meeting; but the impression given by the newspapers was that Birkin's thugs had been beating up working men, and in the mix-up Birkin had received a blow. In fact about three thousand roughs had gathered around the loud-speaker van, many with missiles, including safety-razor blades pushed into potatoes. Such missiles on striking were capable of making superficial cuts in face and hands. Another common weapon was an old chair-leg enwound with barbed wire. Knuckle-dusters also were used, visible when the Communist salute of a clenched fist was given.

The man who had flung the stone which knocked out Birkin on that occasion had been arrested by the police, together with some of Birkin's bodyguard; but the assailant was let off at the Court of Summary Jurisdiction, there being no evidence given against him by Birkin, who had regarded him as a misguided Englishman, victim of semi-starvation and slum conditions.

Half tree-trunk, as long as a man but thicker, burned on the hearth of the dining room of the Hall. Phillip's waistcoat was tight; two years since he had worn it. Digging flints and making roads had increased his chest expansion. He sipped champagne and ate roast duck and felt he was enjoying himself after the dullness of workshop nights, making up accounts, writing articles, and trying not to feel that the undertaking was too much for him.

Lady Breckland was saying, "I asked the King why de Laszlo, who had painted more royal portraits than any other living artist, had not painted him. 'The fellow's a cad', replied the King. 'A cad, sir?' 'Yes, he's a cad, and I won't be painted by him.' 'He's supposed to be a very good painter, sir.' 'Possibly, but when an escaped German prisoner went to him in the war, the fellow gave him money.' 'Wouldn't you give an escaped prisoner money, if he appealed to you, sir?' 'Of course I would,' said the King gruffly, then he added, 'That fellow gave him money—then he rang up the police and told them. He's a cad, and won't paint my portrait'."

Phillip saw Birkin's face brighten at this story, while he thought that the painter, being a naturalised Austrian, would have been in two minds about his duty, first to the escaped prisoner, then to his adopted country. Also he would have suffered fears for his family in those days when feeling ran so high. Looking across to Birkin, he saw that he was reserved within himself once more. Had he seen two sides of the story, as well?

The talk at the table changed to racehorses, then to farming. At once Birkin showed interest. Lady Breckland began to declaim against the general apathy, so many on the dole, the land losing heart everywhere, a few old tenant farmers carrying on and doing things properly to keep the soil in good heart, and coming to ruin thereby.

"It's all so tragic. They won't help themselves, and turn away when I tell them the only way. They believe everything they read in their wretched newspapers, although they say in the next breath, 'Of course, 'tis all lies'. What *can* you do with such people?"

There was silence. Phillip felt that the other guests were wondering how the conversation could be maintained with a light touch, for he suspected that Birkin's ideas were not accepted by them.

"What do you think, Sir Hereward?"

Birkin said evenly, quietly, "They will know the truth soon, Lady Breckland."

"How soon?" asked an Irishman, who had been talking about Arab horses.

Birkin seemed to take a deep breath, before moving his head forward and saying, very quietly, with his eyes fixed in the centre of the table, "Within two years, at the outside. The system must crash within that time—or save itself by war."

On that occasion during the first few months on the land, Brother Laurence had come with Phillip because he was anxious on Phillip's behalf. He had heard so many contradictory things about Birkin. He found Birkin withdrawn; but then he was tired after the long journey from the north in a small car. He thought that Birkin had certain powers in him, and no-one could deny his courage; but was it only the spirit of English bone, stubborn and indomitable in war? How sensitive was he behind his reserve? Was there an awareness of the still small voice within? Certainly, by all accounts, Birkin had a voice, which was used loudly and powerfully. At times he worked himself up into a frenzy, like Hitler; was this in imitation, or due to an interior frustration from his early years? There had been trouble with his father.

"Phillip, do you remember telling me about your old Colonel, and how he dealt with the little mutinies, in many camps of soldiers returned from the front, owing to the delay in demobilisation? You accompanied him on his tour, you said. And how Lord Satchville's fame was so great that men of units who had never seen him listened to him when they had boo'd the Generals of Eastern Command?"

Phillip had told Brother Laurence how Lord Satchville, the great bearded blue-eyed Viking, never raised his voice in speaking to any of the thousands of officers and men of the Gaultshire Regiment: he was invariably equable and courteous.

"But the conditions weren't the same, mon père. Birkin has to shout at his open-air meetings to be heard above the din of Communists trying to wreck those meetings. Also, isn't the use of loud-speakers forbidden by law?"

"Only in certain parts of London, such as parks and places of recreation, Phillip: otherwise it would be Babel."

"I know what you mean about shouting. I shout. And I know in my case that it's due to weakness."

After dinner the two friends were standing talking quietly, apart from the others, in the drawing-room, when Lady Breckland led up Birkin. He listened attentively while Phillip spoke of the formation of a farming community.

Birkin said that it might well be a beginning of a renaissance, a return to the old values of true service to the land. "Such values are our greatest need today. The soil is the base of all life and culture. It is something the towns must be brought to realise. I have read your articles, Maddison, you are doing splendid work."

Birkin went on to say that men of action who were also poets and artists had always in history been an inspiration to men of good will, who put service to others before themselves.

"We in our party believe in a classless state. Wherever talent be found, whether in cottage or castle, it must be used in the interest of the community."

"Would an artist in such a state be free to express himself, Sir Hereward?" asked Brother Laurence.

"How else could he express himself truly, except in freedom? We believe that great reward should come to great talent. This does not mean money only, in the sense of the values of the old parties. The state will provide opportunity, as in the age of the Medicis. Our aim is nothing less than a great efflorescence of Western civilisation, based on true values of the human spirit. We go with Nature, but we aid her. We believe in the fostering hand of the Creator, above all."

Brother Laurence asked, "Would you say that the great travellers and colonisers of the Renaissance were able to do what they did because they were alienated from themselves?"

"You mean that they were driven in protest against the material values of the age, before the birth of the new idea of leadership by the Florentine princes?"

"Not altogether, Sir Hereward. Did not the men of the Renaissance subjugate primitive worlds by the force of cannons? And, in so doing, added to their own confusion and alienation from the true light of the spirit?"

"I mentioned the Medicis in reference to the need for a new flowering of the spirit in this country, Brother Laurence. We British do not need to expand our territories. We do not require to find living room for our people, by the aid of force. We have in our Empire a great estate comprising one-fifth of the world, and, as we see it, it is our duty, and our privilege, to serve our fellow men, of many creeds and colours, in that Empire. There we have resources which are unlimited. These resources will enable us to withdraw from the cut-price of world trade, in order to build the greatest civilisation the world has ever known—not by alienation, but by service. Our party works for the transcendence of the little ego which cowers within all of us at times, a feeble spirit blown hither and thither by every gust of transient political manoeuvring. Men so alienated are rendered nervously anxious by every little upset in the jockeying for office and self-advancement. But when we of the Imperial Socialist Party come to power, the first thing we shall do is to forbid the export of British capital abroad. Then we shall command the means, which is the finance, to develop our great inheritance. Our opponents who control the Money Power know this, and employ every device to discredit us as a party of thugs and crooks."

"You would nationalise the Bank of England?"

"This is the next step after we come to office. Then we shall impose a gradual ban on the export of British capital, except within the Empire."

"Then it is material advance that you would put first, Sir Hereward?"

"Certainly, Brother Laurence. Man does not live by bread alone: but starving millions first must have bread. Until the body is looked after, spiritual progress to an ultimate social harmony is not possible."

"I have recently been reading about the Desert Fathers of the Fourth Century, Sir Hereward. As you know, they lived in the deserts of Palestine, Arabia, and Egypt, and were perhaps the first Christian eremites totally to forsake the values of the market-place. They had the example of their Master before them. Jesus retired to the desert to find purification from direct action against the money-changers—the first and last political action He took, as far as records reveal."

"I wonder—and I say this with the greatest respect—if the world is not too far gone to be saved only by the gestures in retirement, of a relatively few great and noble souls, Brother Laurence? What do you think, Maddison? I have read your novel, *The Phoenix*, and found much in it which has helped me to clarify some of my thoughts."

"I think that in avoiding further direct action against the usurers in the temple, Jesus of Nazareth—for a while anyway—saved Israel. Many of His followers expected direct action at the Passover. And in remaining silent before Pilate, Jesus did not really 'pull his punch', but took the longer view, of going down into history as a living force in men's minds. That at least is terrestrial immortality."

"Bernard Shaw says much the same thing in one of his plays, if you remember," replied Birkin. "'Had Jesus of Nazareth taken to the sword, he would have gone down to history, with Mahomet, as a bloody-minded tyrant.'"

"Perhaps only the greatest leaders can be detached from the market place," said Brother Laurence. "One such must also be detached from himself to a degree that is beset with terrors, not least among them that of loneliness. I do not mean aloneness. There is a distinction. Such a one cannot risk attachment to his own ego, or the destructive ecstasy of self-will. He must shed all identification with his superficial, transient, and self-built self. For the true self is not self-built, or self-willed. The true self is transcendent, mysterious, the source of all strength, all harmony, *eirene*, the soul of the ancient Greeks."

With eyes downcast, and voice nearly inaudible, Birkin said, "Our aim is nothing less than the spiritual revolution of our people. We do not go against the Church, we aid the Church. We believe that all will be achieved by the ultimate triumph of the European soul, based on two millennia of the light of Hellas, reinforced by the Christian ideal of service."

"The means provide great difficulties, and terrors, Sir Hereward."

"The means are at hand, Brother Laurence. Our Empire awaits its efflorescence. Yes, there will be great difficulties," he said. "We do not ask those to join with us who have obligations to family, or who may suffer loss by working with us. Indeed, we can promise only the hardship of the narrow way. Many of us learned what true comradeship was on the battlefields of our youth. I believe that you served, Brother Laurence."

"Yes, Sir Hereward. I served on the Western Front, then transferred to the Royal Flying Corps, and was shot down in Palestine by the Turks, and taken prisoner."

"Then you will know what hardship brings out in a man, so often the best. Thus we survivors of the war generation count it a privilege to live in an age when England demands that great things shall be done—a privilege to be of the generation which learns to say, What can we give, instead of, What can we take. For thus our generation learns there are greater things than slothful ease—greater things than safety—more terrible things than death."

That was in the past winter. Since then Birkin had made no real progress, Phillip thought as he lay awake in the caravan, seeing the stars above the dark pines. Which was the true way? Action, and the market place: or inaction in retreat? The farm as it had been—a nature reserve reverting to wildness, a wilderness so beloved by Penelope?—or the farm civilised: brought back to culture, its wild flowers to be seen as weeds to be destroyed: the snipe bogs to become meadows for milk: the reeds pulled from the grupps, and the reed-warbler homeless?

When the deserts of the world were all irrigated, to grow fine crops as in California, where would the eremite, the hermit, go?

Tom Cundall, his old schoolfellow, who had recently died of t.b. following war-time exhaustion as a Camel pilot in the R.F.C once wrote, *The world is too far gone for saints*. Would the last saint become a militant saint, and go down into history as a bloody-minded tyrant?

Should he write to Brother Laurence, and ask him down for the week-end?

"Well, to be frank I don't particularly want to hear what Birkin has to say," said Penelope briskly. "Daddy says he is a wild man." She went on, "I saw some duck on your meadows this afternoon. That may mean hard weather coming. I fancy some were eider. They come down from the North, don't they? And there was an all-black little fellow with a wispy black crest. I've been trying to identify him." Volumes of Gould and Thorburn lay on the table. "It was too small for tufted duck, or scoter. And as I said, completely black."

"Could it be a smew?"

"I hadn't thought of that, Phillip."

"I thought I saw a marsh harrier on the end meadow, Penelope."

"Yes, I heard one comes there. That frightful man at Bly collects rare birds, you know. Beast. Mrs. Treasure tells me that he paid that wretched poacher at the inn at Durston four pounds for a pair of quails under your Bustard Wood last summer."

"He puts down currants with bamboo splinters in them, to choke them."

"Who told you?"

"Jakes, who wants the rabbits."

"Don't you let him have them. He's a poacher, too."

"So I'm told. But Conger, at Durston, is honest."

Mrs. Treasure came in with tea. "Help yourself, Phillip. I must identify that black duck." She took up a heavy volume.

"No, I don't think it could have been a smew," she said, after some minutes' search. "Is Lucy going on Sunday?"

"Yes, she wants to hear Birkin. She asked me to say that she's got a ticket for you, if you want to come."

"That's another matter, of course. Before, I did not think it right for you to be seen with me."

During tea the telephone rang. "If it's Daddy, please don't speak. He's rather concerned about any men in this house. No need to go—Oh, you know where the throne is, don't you?"

Phillip, having made this excuse, came back some minutes later.

"Daddy wanted to be reassured that I had not bought that land," she said. "Apparently he saw an article of yours, about land being the cheapest for a hundred and fifty years. He was anxious, lest I should have seen it. He asked to be remembered to you."

"Thank you. I thought he was charming."

Penelope was gay, she looked so young. "Daddy runs a bank, among other things. People calling to see him throughout every day, at precisely fifteen-minute intervals. He has no other life, poor darling. Well, Phillip, give Lucy my love, and thank her for asking me for next Sunday. I simply can't stand the cold in an open car—Ninian sold my saloon as soon as we were married, and bought one of those huge Bentleys, and I've never been properly warm since. So tell Lucy I'll take my car, and if she cares to come with me, it would be fun. Goodbye, and don't work too hard."

Phillip had three tickets to spare, so he telephoned several acquaintances, but all refused. Finally he asked Matt and Luke if they would like to come. They demurred.

"Birkin isn't the devil, you know, and there are points of view other than that of the *Daily Herald.*"

"I know that, master," said Matt. "But I got to be up five a'-clark tomorrow to feed me calves. I ken take two more good'ns when you go to market. Cherry's got a good bag yet."

"How about you, Luke?"

The steward made no excuse like his father but said simply, "I dursen't."

"Why not?"

"It's what they'd say down to Yard"—otherwise by the petrol pump owned by Horatio Lord Bugg, as the dealer was now called among the family.

"I've half a mind to ask Horatio."

"Tes the night we do football pools," explained Matt. "Horatio comes to ours."

"What, on Sunday? Gambling? You ought to be ashamed of yourself, Matt."

"Now look-a you a-here, Master——" began Matt seriously, but Phillip cut him short by hugging him and saying, "I'm only joking, you know that. Enjoy your little Sunday flutter, Matt."

"—there be a God above, and there be a Devil here below," said Matt, not to be put off. "An' I don't see no more wrong in football on Sundays, than in going to church or chapel," and he gave Phillip a full look of his dark Brythonic eyes.

Lucy said she would invite Felicity and her father down to spend a few days with them, and telephoned to their cottage on the coast near Chelmsford. The next day they motored up in the Toad. Felicity said she would be quite happy to look after the children.

Early on the Sunday evening the four set out, Lucy beside Penelope within her cream saloon car; Phillip driving with Brother Laurence, both enjoying the feeling of an open cockpit with the stars overhead, well-wrapped in leather coats, goggles and flying helmets. The windscreen was flat, for the night was frosty.

In the dim light of stars in a black sky they passed the aerodrome with its hangars housing the new dark green Blenheim bombers, its windows of the officers' mess and men's quarters lighted up. Through huddling villages, the headlights illuminating flint and brick walls; past fields of plough and stubble and great heaps of whitish-yellow sugar-beet beside the road: a winding road, rising and falling in gentle undulation until the straight with the woods and coverts of Sandringham, and so to the long carr-stone wall enclosing Breckland Park. Turning right-handed they entered the main road to the town, and were upon the straight and fast stretch leading away through trees to a hill-crest whence could be seen the lights of Fenton spread out below. Phillip had been there once or twice by daylight; the place gave a feeling of having been partly submerged in the floods, and then left to dry again, but with the damp and water-marks remaining. Like many another little port on that coast, it had a feeling of failure about it, despite its rows of modern houses and sporadic new industries run, he had heard, on overdrafts. As for agriculture, seventeen million pounds were owed by the farmers of the county to the banks.

The Corn Hall stood back from the Square. Motorcars were parked irregularly before it. The Hall shared the obsolescent look of the town: too big for the shrunken modern harvests. Two or three dozen policemen stood near a gathering of about a hundred people waiting outside, hands in pockets and collars of shabby overcoats turned up.

The two men waited for Penelope's car, and went into the hall with the two women. More people than Phillip had anticipated were sitting on benches and chairs. He felt exhilarated. There was a feeling of life, of excitement in the air. As they walked to the reserved seats in front he got the impression of many mixed stocks or races in the audience; round-faced Dutch, dark long-headed Huguenot, ruddy big-faced Dane, small-sized Saxon with fair hair, fair-haired Scandinavian, square-headed Teuton, thin-necked Celt, small round-headed, black-haired ancient Briton. Interbreeding during the centuries since the Nordic invasions, augmented by immigration of continental fugitives had cast clear a minority of racial types, while diminishing the hybrid majority, like the smaller grains of tail-corn which came through the sieves during threshing. Here and there sat a man or youth with more assured glance; the head corn.

"I think you'll be surprised by what you hear," he said, with happy confidence, to Penelope.

She did not reply, but wrapped her chinchilla coat about her. Phillip had brought a rug to tuck round the feet of the two women. "Don't you feel something in the air, Penelope?"

"Only the cold so far," she replied, with a faint smile.

"You wait till Birkin speaks."

"Oh, I've heard a lot about him."

"What the newspapers say about Birkin is entirely misrepresenting."

"I seldom read newspapers."

Lucy smiled at Phillip. "I'm quite excited," she whispered.

The clock on the wall of the Corn Hall pointed to ten minutes to eight. Stewards with armlets of red, white, and blue were moving up and down the aisles, selling pamphlets and party newspapers.

"I'll be back in a moment," said Phillip as he got up, having seen 'Boy' Runnymeade in the front row. "Come with me, mon père."

"Hullo, Maddison. I thought I'd see you here," said Captain Runnymeade in his drawling, slightly thick voice.

"I'm glad you could come."

"Who's the blonde beside your wife?"

"Lady Penelope Carnoy, a friend of Lucy's."

"Bring her over to the cottage one day and we'll have a party. Is she one of Birkin's lot?"

"No. She is only really interested in wild birds." Seeing Runnymeade's eyebrows lift he said, "Have you met Birkin?"

"I knew his father in the regiment. He was a bit of a waster, so I'm not surprised that his son is a bit of a bolshy."

"May I introduce Brother Laurence."

"How d'you do. Sit down a moment, and tell Stefania all about your boy friend, Maddison, while I talk to Brother Laurence."

Phillip remembered Stefania Rozwitz at the Castle, *ballerina assoluta* with the Russian dancers. Now she was choreographer and producer with a London team. She had changed. Her voice had a gruffness about it. Her once-dark hair was brass-coloured, drawn back over her brow and held by a kerchief. He supposed her to be about forty-five. Slight dark hairs sprouted on her upper lip and chin. She looked strong, compact, and vital in a confused sort of way. He felt on the defensive in her presence.

"So you are now an admirer of Fascism are you, 'Farm Boy'?"

"I'm for Birkin and a Greater Britain."

"And you?" Runnymeade said to Brother Laurence.

"I'm here as an observer, Captain Runnymeade."

Phillip moved away to talk to Lady Breckland, who introduced him to a woman wearing the same sort of grey silk blouse under her coat, with the small silver badge of the party in the lapel. She bore a name which had ruled the East Anglian farming world, by prestige of two great ancestors, since the land-reclaiming days of the eighteenth century.

"Mrs. Cheffe has just started a school for young children," said Lady Breckland.

"You must come over and see my school, Mr. Maddison. Do introduce me to your wife, won't you?"

When the two ladies had gone and the four were seated once again Penelope said to Lucy, "Mrs. Cheffe's husband is selling off some of his land. I do so want to buy ten acres of it, but Daddy won't let me. He says that land is the worst investment. I was telling Lucy, Brother Laurence, about a house I want to build. My father is the solid banker, and never speculates. Phillip, when is your man coming? It's ten minutes past eight. Is there a committee? I don't see any chairs up there."

The platform was empty but for a table with a glass and jug of water. Against the wall behind was draped a large Union Jack rising almost to the roof. Without warning the tall figure with a slight limp walked out of the door beside the platform. Immediately the floor of the hall seemed to rise with many people on their feet, waving arms in salute, and cheering. Phillip turned round to watch them. Their faces were alight with happiness. Birkin climbed on the platform, smiling and acknowledging their cheers. He stood quite still in front of the table, thrusting out his chin, and breathing deep, as though to take the feeling of the people. Then under the cheers and the clapping there was a growing roar, hard and deep, and at this Birkin drew himself up and, with one hand clasping the back of the other before him, stiffened to immobility. His face was set, looking to the back of the hall.

Meanwhile other heads were turning round, towards the massed booing. Stewards began to move slowly down the aisles. At length the noise died down, and Birkin shifted slightly to begin his speech. "Fellow Britons——" he cried, when someone yelled from the middle of the hall, "Smash his head, make a proper job of it this time, the enemy of the proletariat!" and the booing began once more.

Pointing an arm towards the din, and standing erect, Birkin said, "The people come here to listen to me, and not to you. You can ask any questions you like after the speech, but you will keep quiet while I am speaking, or you will go out."

The outcry started up again, a voice roaring, "We've as much right to free speech as you have, you bleeder!"

Raising his arm again, Birkin said quietly, "Put them out."

The stewards, most of them small men, ran down the hall, one muttering as he passed, "You're telling us, guv'nor." Then began a new noise, which was at first puzzling. It was a continuous clattering, as though hundreds of muffled fire-crackers were exploding. Still never having moved from his position on the platform, Birkin said in an easy voice, "All right, keep your seats. This happens every time, though it is very rnild tonight. You have an opportunity of seeing how badly we behave, according to the papers."

There was a wave of relieving laughter. The clattering in the middle of the hall continued. Then two stewards passed up the gangway, dragging another steward by his armpits, his head down and covered with blood. The toes of his shoes were scraping on the floor. He had been knocked unconscious by a chair.

The clattering noises were made by chairs used as weapons against the stewards. Gradually the noise grew less. Phillip heard the sound of large double doors being unbarred and unbolted. There was a noise of scuffling, then oaths and shouts, with banging and kicking on the door from outside. People began to clap and cheer. The statuesque figure had looked straight to the back of the hall while the injured steward had been dragged to the room behind the platform. Phillip saw the white-banded caps of St. John Ambulance men.

The speaker began by saying quietly that the Government elected by the people must have the power to rule. That was denied them at present, because Parliament did not rule. The Money Power behind Parliament ruled. What did the Imperial Socialist Party intend to do when it came to power by the will of the people? The first thing it would do would be to pass an emergency measure to prohibit capital going abroad. Then all foreign holdings, gradually would be realized, and the money brought back in sterling, to Britain. This would be done gradually in accord with the rise of new productivity at home. Gradually Britain would withdraw from World Trade—which meant International Finance—and have a ring fence of sterling around Britain and Empire. Every raw material needed for modern industrial civilisation was lying in the Empire. These raw materials would be brought to Britain, to be returned as manufactured goods. Thus Britain would have no price-cutting competition to drag down the living standards of the people. The genius of the people, the work capacity of the people would create the new wealth by which to acquire the raw materials to be returned as manufactured goods to the peoples of the Empire.

But what was stopping them doing it? International finance, which exploited where it saw the biggest profit. Britons were enslaved. For a thousand years unconquered by any foe without, they had been subdued by the foe within.

For an hour and a half most of that audience of between two and three thousand people believed that it was possible to create a modern Britain which would have fine new roads and rebuilt villages, with water, light, and drainage; towns with a population partly educated in the countryside when young and believing that the work they did afterwards was truly and directly for their country. Everyone would work, great reward would come only to great talent, and privilege would end. They saw fine housing estates and no more building speculation, they saw their children glowing with health and vitality, their young people natural in sexual impulses, without furtiveness or the corruption of shame and repression. They saw ships going to the colonies with motor-cars, tractors, machinery, and other fine English things, passing ships bringing grain and fruits and raw materials from the finest Empire on earth. Those ships passed other ships, flying other flags, and saluted them in friendship; for the financial interests that directed them were not international, but nationally controlled and therefore did not clash, but existed side by side in harmony. No more consumption crises, factories idle and men out of work because there was too much for people to buy, and therefore no more work, and therefore no money to buy the too-much. No more trade-wars between rival industrial groups called nations!

The only rivalry would be that of the works of peace, for art would truly serve the peoples of the earth, each with its authentic national inspiration, and therefore of a natural truth and beauty. All this was possible, if only people believed it possible, and set themselves in the resurgent modern spirit to make it real.

Birkin ended in a frenzy of appeal, calling on them to believe that what their fathers had died for in Europe a generation before was not only possible, but indeed inevitable if only they would themselves move out of the twilight of an obsolescent economic system into the sun and the truth of national resurgence. For while they hesitated, divided among themselves, the more they would continue to be subdued by forces which, in the end, would bring about their ruin, and the loss of that Empire for which their forefathers had striven in the glory and faith of Britain everlasting.

The passionate power of the speaker brought many to their feet, singing the National Anthem with fervour. When it was over Birkin went to inquire after the injured steward, who was a shop-assistant at thirty shillings a week.

As they went out of the hall, Phillip heard someone say to Captain Runnymeade, "Same old speech!" while Runnymeade replied, in his thick and slightly mocking voice, "I've heard some balderdash uttered in my time, but never such demagogic rot in all my life. I came to look at him because I knew his father, but——" and then people came between him and the back of Runnymeade's check coat.

In starlit darkness hundreds waited to boo and jeer. In small packs to enclose around one or another of the known party men, pressing around him, to assail him with obscenity, and if he seemed to quail, to strike with fist, or knee in the groin, then to stamp on his face. The women were the more dangerous, Phillip could see, for against them there was no defence. They knew where to give a man the sharpest pain.

He lost Brother Laurence, Lucy and Penelope. Moving about, Phillip realized he was the object of a shout, "He's one!" Immediately pale and distraught faces began to press around him. They aroused no fear; for he did not feel any evil in them, only weakness. He waited as though nonchalantly, hands in pockets, and they moved away. How sad, he thought, that the man who had given much of his great inheritance to the poor, was taken by them to be their enemy. The women looked to be overwrought, like the men, their very words and expressions and faces and bodies corrupted by poverty and the very things from which he would save them, and millions like them.

But not all of them were of the local poor. He saw an alert bunch of men, most of them dark, with horn-rimmed spectacles, and foreign-looking faces, jumping down from a lorry. Spread out like a rugger forward line before action, they made for Birkin's waiting motorcar, police helmets around it.

He pushed his way to the car, to get a sight of Birkin moving with bent head through the human gangway of his followers standing two deep with arms linked against the pressure of the crowd, led by the lorry-load of dark men now in full insult. There were cries of *Turn the car over* and *Fire it,* but the police were pushing and thrusting; and amidst cheers and boos and shouts the small M.G. car drove away.

He saw Brother Laurence standing by Penelope's motor. Lucy said, "Lady Breckland asked us to a small party to meet Birkin, and I've accepted. I do hope you will come, Penelope—it won't be very late."

"Well, I shall have to leave early, I have some letters to write."

"What did you think of the speech?"

"I found it most interesting, Phillip, but I can't bear people who shout. Brother Laurence is coming with us, he knows the way, and I'm much slower than you."

Phillip let the oil warm up before he drove away from the Square through narrow streets leading to the long straight road up to the ridge from where, in daylight, the sandy heaths and forests of pines stretched away for mile upon mile to the south and east. There he stopped, for a cylinder was missing.

When he got out to change the plug he saw that the sky to the north was glowing with colours of red and green and yellow, shifting and changing, as he stared, into zones of light shot through by spokes and rays arising from the rim of the sea. A wonderful sight; a portent; a glory of the heavens to match the resurgence that seemed to be waiting upon the world!

He found a detached lead, fastened it to its plug, and getting back into the car, raised his arm in salute to the flushes of light among the zones of copper-green—"Hail, Dawn of the Winter God!"—and putting the sports-car into gear, screamed away down the road in full-throttle acceleration, until he saw the cream-coloured car half a mile in front of his head-lights.

The hall was of dark oak, and lofty, with exposed beams, purlins, kingposts and rafters. In the light of candles in sconces and branched silver upon the tables gleamed suits of armour, pikes and halberds, lances and swords, among them a tin-hat and gas-mask of the Great War.

In the hall stood a number of people all seeming to know one another, by the animation and amiability of each face. Through the mêlée of talk, as sandwiches were munched and cups of tea and coffee sipped and held expertly, moved Lady Breckland, with Sir Hereward Birkin in tow, making introductions at the rate of two or three every couple of minutes. To each in turn Birkin gave his sudden smile, flash of eyes opening wide, hand clasp, and ready appropriate words about each, from what Lady Breckland said. "Lady Penelope is most interested in watching our wild birds——"

"We must see, with Maddison's help, that they remain a national heritage, no more glass cases. How the old-style sportsman liked to shoot and stuff everything, Lady Penelope."

"Mrs. Maddison, with such a fine family of sons, Sir Hereward——"

How like Daddy, thought Penelope, before an audience turning on the charm.

"All keen to follow their father, about whose work of reclamation I read with the keenest interest. How are you, Maddison?"

A firm handclasp, a feeling as of rare poured wine, words that were not heard by anyone else, "You can write, I can speak. Let us go forward together into the Age of Renaissance."

Phillip felt he must not monopolise Birkin. He saw Melissa, and went to her.

"How are you? Did you like the speech?"

"I think he's up against too much. He's like Sisyphus. The stone is eternal. How are you, Phil?"

"Oh, getting along—rolling my little stone up and down the Bad Lands."

Lord Abeline came to them. "Hullo, Lucy, you look prettier than ever! So do you, Lady Penelope. Lucy, why didn't you see that Phillip invited us to shoot your high birds? What about this high bird, Birkin, are they going to shoot him down? You look out for yourself, my boy, or they'll get you, too. Come on, Melissa, we must be getting back. Do come over, Lucy. And bring Lady Penelope. Au revoir."

Lady Breckland was saying, "I do hope it will have some results. You know, I don't think any good can come from our class, they are so static, they are—impenetrable. It *was* so good of you all to have come."

Phillip wondered if anyone had told Birkin how good his speech was. Heavens, he had taken it for granted. He went to him. "I didn't want to bore you with praise, Sir Hereward, but your speech was tremendous. If only you could get back into Parliament, and have a platform there."

"All the old parties are tied to Money, Maddison. And I don't think I would stand a chance of being elected. No, we prepare ourselves for the smash. It is bound to come. The Tories will scuttle as soon as they see the depression deepening, and get out, leaving Labour to face the music. Labour will not be able to do anything, for all the old parties are tied to the financial system. Labour will lose control, three million unemployed will go out on the streets, and one small incident will start off a condition of mob rule. The Communists will try to take over; then we shall step in, smash them, and seize control. That is what we are organised for."

Phillip saw Brother Laurence standing near. The friar was going with Penelope and Lucy in their car, Phillip to follow.

"I mean, it looked serious last September, until Munich, didn't it?"

"It is still serious. Hitler has kicked out Money, and Money wants its revenge. The economic war is on now, the bombing war may follow. The Germans are trying to barter; finance is trying to frustrate every export move they make. Ah, Brother Laurence, must you go? How good of you to come." Birkin had seen that the ladies were waiting for the friar. When they had gone Phillip said, "We used to have on our farm a young man who worked in one of the richest private banks in the world. Hurst was in the London branch, which had a staff of about a dozen clerks, all Gentiles. They knew only about the current accounts of customers. The real business was done by the two Schwarzenkoph cousins. They kept their ledgers, with details entered in their own handwriting, in a safe within the vault. The young man, who chucked his job and came to me because of some book I wrote, had to code and decode cipher telegrams, and he said that literally millions of pounds sterling were moved down one line, transferred from this country or that country by another line, by means of short-term loans or their non-renewal. It made me feel quite ill, to think that such masses of money could depress an industry, causing the ruin perhaps of an entire community, by the calculated thought of two men of inherited desert genius, working in the religious belief of their service to their jealous God."

Birkin's brown face, with its long bony structure, giving the idea of inheritance from some Florentine Renaissance forebear, seemed to smoulder with controlled life.

"Yes, it is their religion, the Golden Calf. But there are as many Gentiles as Jews involved in the money racket. It is not exclusively the Jewish banker we are up against. It is the obsolescent world-finance system which we strive to get altered, by the will of the people at a General Election."

"May I ask you a leading question, Sir Hereward? I have met two men who have left the I.S.P. One was Frolich, the other Jock Kettle. Why were they expelled?"

"William Frolich was appealing almost exclusively on an anti-Semitic platform. As for Kettle, we found out that he was a burglar in his spare time, and used to crack cribs when we took him with us to our big meetings up north. Also he is rabidly anti-Jew. Our party was not and is not anti-Semitic. We have said again and again that, just as our Empire consists of many races and creeds, so we are not concerned with what might be called racialism. But if any man or group of men, such as Communists, act in such a manner as to cause division we shall, when we come to power, give warning that any disloyalty to Crown and Empire will bring expulsion, by withdrawal of passport. We all know that many Jews fought for Britain and Empire in the Great War. How then can we, ex-service men ourselves, be against our old comrades-in-arms?

"Maddison, I will say this. If war is declared on Hitler it will not be because he wants Danzig, which is German, to return to the Fatherland; nor will it be because he demands the Polish Corridor, which is Silesian and therefore German. These places are no concern of the British people, or of the British Government. If war is declared, it will be a war of the Moneylenders' Revenge."

Chapter 15

COMPLICATION

One morning in late July of the year 1939 Phillip was standing in the weedy garden of the empty, dark and damp cottage which he intended to recondition and live in by himself one day, when Lucy appeared by the open farmhouse door a few yards away, and said that he was wanted on the telephone.

"It's Rippingall asking if you would speak to Captain Runnymeade. He sounds *very* reformed, I suppose it's his marriage."

Rippingall was back with his old master once more. Mrs. Rippingall cooked.

With a feeling of dread, of one more weight upon his mind, Phillip picked up the receiver lying on the refectory table, and listened to the voice of Rippingall asking him to hold on a moment, he would fetch the Captain.

He imagined the ruddy-faced, pepper-and-salt trousered figure pulling itself out of an armchair beside a silver tray holding decanter of whisky, glasses, and syphon of soda: saw him moving, slightly bent-backed, through the doorway to the telephone on the wall of the passage outside. Soon he heard footfalls and breathing; a pause while the figure seated itself beside the little table: then the familiar slow and somewhat drawling tones were asking him if he would care to bring the children over to a party that afternoon.

Phillip hesitated; and his hesitation communicated itself, for the voice said, "Leave that goddam farm, Maddison, and give yourself a break. A friend of yours tells me she is looking forward to seeing you."

"Thank you very much for the invitation," Phillip replied, with forced joviality. Was it Melissa? He forebore to ask. "I'd love to come. All the children? There are five, you know."

"Bless my soul," the voice was slightly mocking. "Very well then, at three o'clock this afternoon. Bring any friends you like." The receiver went down abruptly at the other end.

Oh, why am I so weak always? I *don't* want to go. He saw himself surreptitiously pouring away most of Captain Runnymeade's over-generous drinks into the hearth. He hadn't been there since the early spring, when there had been a fire to conceal his furtive act, for the flames of the seasoned logs of split ship's-timber had been of the same hue and lambency as those of the alcohol leaping up the chimney.

While he was trying to arrange in his mind all the jobs that needed to be done as he sat on the stool by the table, Lucy came into the parlour from the kitchen. She carried an armful of clothes, for she had been ironing the shirts, pants, vests, and other smalls belonging to the seven individuals of the family. There were two little daily maids, but since they were untrained the burden of the general work fell upon Lucy.

"Did I hear something about the children and a party?" she enquired lightly, as she put down the clothes on the corner of the table.

"I shouldn't have accepted! I *must* go to Yarwich market today! I don't like those rich social fritterers at Staithe. They're idling while the country is declining into war." There was the worried look on his face that she knew so well; and dreaded. "Why *must* you carry the ironing in your arms? Haven't I bought you a special basket for the job? They look so higgledy-piggledy, carried like that."

To help lighten Lucy's tasks he had bought several wicker baskets of differing shapes and sizes; one to carry the ironing, others for egg-collecting, shopping, clothes-pegs, picnics on the marshes, kindling wood for the fire—but, like most good intentions, this one had gone awry.

One or another of the baskets was as likely as not to contain such varied objects as a cat with kittens; a heap of old magazines and papers; a mass of rotting weeds left in the so-called garden, or worn and patched shoes belonging to the children.

The shoes were usually old, for Lucy was economical, keeping each pair, as a child outgrew them, for the next child. Some of them were almost heirlooms, with the clothes. Thus Jonathan, the youngest, wore, when he came out of the bathroom in the evening with David, the old faded blue dressing-gown, with faint suggestion of yellow stain that no amount of washing would remove, which had been made with such loving care for Peter, her first-born, twelve years before.

"Yes, of course a basket for these clothes is proper, but I had to come in here so I grabbed them without thinking."

"Today is Saturday, and I'd planned to go to market and buy two calves. Also a new stackcloth, as corn harvest is near. I bought a good cloth at auction two years ago, now it's lying in the Corn Barn, ripped and near-useless, after flapping for two days through a half-gale last season on one of the barley stacks up by the Great Bustard Wood."

To prevent it flapping loose on the stack in that exposed place he had taken up a heavy rope for Matt and Luke to tie round the stack. To this heavy girdle the lesser cloth-ropes were to be secured, he had told Luke; but when he had gone up the following day to look at it in a high wind, he had found the new rope unused, while each of the guide-ropes of the cloth had been tied to a heavy lump of steam coal. These weights had torn the ropes from the cloth in places, leaving eighty square yards of jute to thunder and beat with the wind under them. In two days the cloth had flapped itself to tatters.

"Also I must get some shackle-bolts to set-up the torn-off spring of the green trailer. This is the fourth time they have been torn off by backing the trailer when it is hitched to the tractor. But I don't suppose I'll find my tools in the workshop, to do the job. The men take them without authority and never put them back."

Lucy waited beside the pile of children's clothes. She looked pensive. She was waiting for Phillip to stop talking, before getting on with her work. She tried to be patient with Phillip, knowing that he could, when tired, talk himself into desperation.

"It's all very difficult, I know. But you've done splendidly, considering what the farm was like when we came." She made to move away.

"But we haven't *started* yet! There's no change in the mental outlook on the farm, so there is no material change. Look at the pigs! I've asked Matt again and again that the used sump-oil from the tractor, which I put in a special can, be used for rubbing on the pigs' backs to kill the ticks. But day after day, week after week, the pigs' backs remain studded with grey rivets, sucking away all profit. 'What do yew want to do that for? Nobody else does it about here. Pigs always have ticks, 'tis nature,' says Matt. I've proved that the ticks die when the oil is squirted on them, too. It's the same in the cowhouse. Never a cow washed before milking, and water laid on from the artesian well by Brother Laurence."

Lucy said gently, "I think you should try to get another cowman."

"You know very well I can't. I haven't a service cottage! You know I let outside people have them, when they come with their hard-luck stories. Luke lives in a council house, I have no service cottage for another cowman. Do you know, the splashes of dung dropped by cows belonging to the old tenant, who left bankrupt all those years ago now, are still on the concrete floors! As for germs, they are 'book-squit'. 'Whoever saw a garm,' says Matt."

"Yes, I know," said Lucy, wearily. "But you must take Matt as you find him. He says to me, when he brings up the milk, 'I'm always serving the master's interests, but I don't seem able to please him.' He's good with young stock, you know, he's splendid. But he *is* afraid of innovations."

"Of course I realize that Matt works hard, that he has a lot to do, seven days a week—stockman, shepherd, pigman—looking after forty ewes, all the young stock, cows, and pigs in the yards generally, and helping with haysel and harvest. But I don't want a farm like that of the late tenant. That failed because everyone on it was what he was. I want a new farm. So we must start with the human beings. If we are to do better, we must all change in our minds first. The mental blue-print of the present is no good. Listen to what Runnymeade and nearly all of his sort say about farming—only a fool or a crank would put his money into it. Every bloody time I go over there, he says the same thing! 'What beats me, Maddison, is why you waste your time and talent on that goddam farm. You don't get anything out of it, as far as I can see, except worry. Then why do you go on with it? You're an odd fellow, Maddison. And why the devil do you listen to that fellow Birkin?' Then like a fool I try and explain that Birkin is attempting to do on a national scale what I am trying to do on a small scale: a sort of desperate attempt to avoid the coming smash. Then the hunt is on. Runnymeade throws in remarks to cause a row, which he enjoys, as he sits back, stimulated to help himself to more whisky. You know his Polish mistress, Stefania Rozwitz? He likes to see us arguing—he tries to get me to make her lose her temper—he's impotent, his desire for stimulation and excitement covers a hollow man, so he cannot bear to be quiet. Or it may be, 'Tell us about your pal Schicklgruber, Maddison, you met him at Nürnberg. Is it true he's a pederast?' Like a fool, I run, trailing his aniseed. The hunt is up, Runnymeade fills the glasses, and before long I am the fox, or the aniseed-dolly on a string, doubling all the time to answer his questions, his provocative damned silly idle-bodied bloody questions, while knowing all the while that he is hoping that Stefania will turn on me and make a meal of the hunted fox."

"Still, perhaps at a children's party it will be different."

"Great Britain has become either Prolonged Dole, or Great Cocktail. Talk, talk, talk, nobody taking off his coat to do anything, Idlers and sots, indifferent to the truth that the soil of a nation is its mother, that the fertility of the mother of Britain is going down the metropolitan sewers into the sea, polluting the rivers——" He unclenched his hands. "I'm sorry, Lucy. You've heard all this rant before. Mental to physical, and physical back to an occluded psyche—the minds of the people polluted with money-based ideas."

Yes, Lucy had heard it all before, many times, so many times that she had come to accept it, together with his chronic complaining and increasing irritability.

"I'm an interfering waster, not Runnymeade. Oh well—if war comes, I'll dye my hair and rejoin my regiment—*if* they'll have me."

He went out. His eye took in the garden. Hours of hoeing needed to kill the weeds. And, fatally, he peered inside the adjoining cottage, which was called the Children's. It was chaotic like the farm. Toys broken and flung about anywhere. Draw-leaf table stained with spilled tea and cocoa. Boots, shoes scattered over the floor. A feeling of anguished desperation came over him whenever he saw it, for it seemed to him that his hopes of a family strongly and truly based on the land—order, neatness, strength—were being infected as by spores from the decadent past. And lately his thoughts had taken a dangerous trend: that the Copleston pattern was visible in his children. Thank God that Billy was like his mother, the nonpareil Barley. If only Billy were four years older, and eighteen. Oh no. Billy would have to go into the army!

Yes, he would dye his hair, and get away in time. Then Billy would be in a reserved occupation.

Lucy was upstairs, tidying the children's night nursery and making the beds. Phillip went up to her.

"Lucy, please help me. I feel that if you don't *insist* on tidiness it will wreck both the family and the farm, if order is not insisted on with each of us. Look at your two maids in the kitchen. You allow them to leave the sink dirty after washing up. Can't you see that they clean it, and wring out the mop, and stand it up to air, and that they keep the soap-dish clean? And those lower shelves in the cupboards—they're an awful example for the children—there is no good in the old broad and easy-going way—

it will bring the family to ruin—where is the four-thousand-acre estate of your family——? Stop! What did I do with the Fawley land? I behaved in such a way, with my silly little bits of writing, that I virtually threw it away."

Utter weariness overcame him; words ceased. He leant his head against a wall, feeling that the *mortmain*, the dead hand of Copleston, would inevitably reduce him to failure.

"I do *try* and get the children to be tidy," said Lucy, desperately. She thought that Phillip's remarks were utterly unfair; *she* had never been the one to squander money. She remembered what Penelope had said to her, and how *true* it was. *Isn't it better for children to be happy, even if they are a little untidy, than to be subject all the time to restraint, and perhaps fear?* That was what Phillip was always telling people, and also had written in the Donkin novels —when she first knew him.

"Don't heed what I say. I'm using you as a scapegoat, Lucy. Please forget it all."

He returned downstairs to the parlour. Even so, why won't she pay the shop bills weekly? She promised she would. I bought her a book for the grocer's account, I give her the housekeeping money regularly. Now she owes four weeks' account at Dodman's. It isn't fair, those little people have to pay on the nail for their goods. I had to pay for those four weeks yesterday. No! She is overworked. She is kind. She forgets, as I forget—what I——

He sat by the telephone, trying to persuade himself to telephone Runnymeade and make his excuses for not taking the children to the party.

While he was sitting motionless on the form Jonathan, the youngest, appeared in the doorway. At first the child did not see his father. He was four years old. He resembled Phillip at that age except for the colour of the eyes, which were brown. He reminded Phillip of his cousin Willie. Recently he had fallen and broken an arm between wrist and elbow. It was now encased in plaster-of-Paris. Several of Jonathan's street friends among the village children had written their initials and made crayon drawings in various colours upon the cast.

When he had broken his arm the boy had been taken to the cottage hospital, accompanied by the entire family in the Silver Eagle. The children all sat in the tonneau nursing and reassuring the 'baby', while Lucy sat in front beside Phillip. The 'baby' had sworn at the surgeon who had set the bone, striking at him with his free hand, his eyes flashing and his cheeks flushed. He had used such phrases of abuse that David, standing by with Billy, Rosamund and Peter, all four trying to soothe the 'baby', exclaimed in a mock-shocked voice, "Jonathan! Such words!"

"You shut up, you bloody fool," cried Jonathan. "You bloody idiot! You half-wit! Don't grin at me, you bastard!" And he had tried to strike his six-year-old brother with his broken arm. Billy enjoyed it all with an aloof and sardonic look on his face. Billy had felt for a number of years that his father did not like him. He felt, at times, apart from the others because his 'real mother' was dead.

"My youngest son sometimes gets upset," Phillip had explained with assumed geniality to the white-coated surgeon. Thereupon Jonathan had given him a mournful, wounded look, uttered a stifled reproach of "You be quiet, you old man," and broken with tears. His mother soothed him, sensibly; and on the way home, sitting in the back of the car with Rosamund, Billy, Peter, and David, all five eating an ice-cream ("Don't throw the paper away," said Peter, "keep it for Daddy's compost heap, see, Jonny dear?") the little boy had recovered his equanimity. And he had faithfully carried down the paper to the compost heap and buried it. A rat, unfortunately, had dug it out again and bitten it up, since it, too, liked ice-cream.

Jonathan slept in the big bed beside his mother in the largest of the three bedrooms of the two cottages made into the farmhouse. In the next room slept Rosamund and David, a table with their treasures between the bed-heads. In the third room Billy and Peter had their beds. The so-called Children's Cottage adjoining had one large bedroom at present unoccupied, used as a spare room, and the playroom downstairs. Phillip slept in another cottage up the village street, where in the evenings after the day's work he kept the farm books and accounts; and when they were done, sat in an armchair and wrote articles for the newspapers, his eyes usually smarting with weariness.

Jonathan, thinking himself to be alone with his mother, became imperious. Phillip, sitting quietly out of sight on the form running the length of the table, heard him say, "Mother, I want my other shoes on, my sand-shoes! Be quick! Where are they? I can't find them!"

"Oh, I put them away in one of the baskets, now which one was it?"

"Not the proper one, of course. Be quick, I say! I want to plant this pea I found, in my garden."

"Hullo," said Phillip.

The startled child saw his father sitting beside the telephone. His imperious and anxious expression changed to that of a boy a little awed before the presence of his father. Phillip, who knew that his own interior balance was disturbed because of the disharmony of his own parents, was determined not to let Jonathan grow up as he himself had grown up. Jonathan loved his mother dearly; but he needed the animal warmth of a father.

"Come here, Jonny."

He sat him on his knee, an action which the child resisted slightly; but before he could struggle Phillip spoke in a confidential whisper by his ear, while nuzzling the soft warmth of the dark hair against his own cheek.

"You didn't come to our horkey in the Corn Barn last year, did you? We had twenty candles in empty bottles all down the table, and the flames bent one way when the sack dropped out of the broken window and the white owl looked in, screeching with dismay. We were all so happy that we went home long after midnight, forgetting all about the food left on the table—the ham and the mince pies and the Stilton cheese and the plum cake. And do you know, when we had all gone away, and it was quiet, first one cat, then another cat, and then a third and a fourth and fifth cat, all crept through the broken window, and had a party. And when the cats were gone the rats crept through their holes in the walls and had a party. And after the rats had gone away with full bellies the mice came and nibbled away all the rest of the night. And in the morning the table—this same table beside us, we took it down on two carts—was littered with bones and crumbs and little rolls of mice money, which they issue whenever they feel the need for deflation. O, 'twas a wunnerful horkey, Jonathan. And do 'ee know, midear, just now Captain Runnymeade telephoned, and invited you and all the other children to his children's party this afternoon. Won't it be fun?"

He stroked the dark, Celtic head, tenderly smoothing the imaginative bump at the back. Jonathan was amenable now, his affronted selfhood dissolved by imagination.

"Shall us wear our horkey hats, Dad?"

"Of course we shall."

"I have the Dixie cotton-picker's cap you gave me tidied away in the bottom drawer of the tallboy over there, Dad," said Jonathan eagerly. "Mum, Dad said we are going to a party tomorrow. And we'll all wear horkey hats. And I shall wear my cotton-dicker's hat Dad gave me."

"What fun," murmured Lucy. "Jonathan is so good," she said to Phillip with a smile. She looked so young, he thought, remorseful for all his beastliness and sneers at her family. Except for a shared love of the children there was no flow between them. There never had been, really. Oh, he must try and be kinder to Lucy, who was kindness itself. He turned away his face, lest tears come, as he gentled the child on his lap.

"Yes, Jonathan is a boy after your own heart, Pip. You ought to see his garden. That will please Dad, won't it, Jonny?"

"My bean is coming up, Dad! And now I have got another pea a boy gave me, to plant!"

"You'll make a good farmer one day, Jonny."

"And I shall always put old oil on my pigs, Dad, like Billy did this morning to the Large Whites. Coo, he made them scrap!"

"Oh, Billy did that, did he? Good boy, Billy."

"He squirted with your squirter, Dad. Then he squirted Matt, and Matt chased us, Dad!"

Phillip felt the warmth of the child's head through his cheek. The warmth spread through his body. He began to feel happy that he was a farmer, farming his own land. It would become the family land. Oh, things would one day be different.

"Now I must get on," said Lucy, in happy voice. "I have rather a lot to do, but I'll get through it. And we will try and make the place nicer for you," touching Phillip's head as she went past. "You and Jonny are so much alike, you know. He likes everything to be neat and tidy, just like you. Won't you have your breakfast now? It.'s nearly eleven o'clock."

"I can't spare the time!"

When he had done his business at market, hurrying from place to place as usual, he found that there was no time for a proper lunch. After a cup of coffee, beef sandwich, and cheesecake he felt easier; and when clear of the town, fastened the windscreen flat, pulled on flying helmet and goggles with curved Triplex glasses, buttoned coat to neck and put his foot down. The revolution counter was showing 4,600 r.p.m., the speedometer needle 77 m.p.h. along the straight nine miles out of town.

And quietly drove down his new road to the farm premises shortly before three o'clock. There he eased each calf out of its sack—all but the little creatures' heads had thus travelled warm—and put them in a cowshed box for Matt to find at 4 o'clock milking time. He tried to avoid the sight of tiles fallen off; of unswept concrete roads through the yards, cluttered with pats of dried dung; of dead rats lying about fly-blown; of patches of uncut nettles (he had imagined, a hundred times, wallflowers replacing them one day) growing out of the bases of the flint walls. But he did, against self-exhortation, look over the bridge into the stream for trout which he knew had already died of asphyxiation in the warm, sluggish waters bubbling with gases from the black silt of pollution covering the once-sandy bed. One day he would see to it that that chalk stream was de-polluted. The Effingham All Saints Rural District Council allowed—or permitted—or took no notice of the fact—that the drains of over two hundred cottages and new bungalows poured their sewage direct into the stream, thus ignoring two Acts of Parliament and their own by-laws. One small part of the decadence into which Great Britain had fallen. Poor Birkin, what a load he was bearing...

He returned down the new farm lane to the gate, and so to the main village road—the tarmac stained with and faintly odorous of dried sloppings from the weekly Night Cart—and drove to the cottages used by Lucy and the children.

"Hullo," said Lucy, coming in with a smile. "I've got the children to tidy their room. They've gone down to the granary to fetch the horkey hats. They won't be long."

"I must give the car a rough wash, and polish the radiator. Is there any metal polish?"

"Yes, I'll fetch it. Have you had lunch?"

"I had a snack, and some coffee."

"We had a roast cockerel. It was such a nice luncheon, I did hope you would be back in time. Would you like some now? I put back a plate——"

"I don't think there's time, thanks all the same."

"But you had no breakfast."

For all his fancied knowledge, Phillip did not know that lack of food and sleep were the main causes of his depression. The delay that morning, and the consequent missed breakfast, had been due to his discovery that the grass-cutter was broken. The men were to snatch time before corn harvest to cut the thistles and rushes which almost covered the meadows. The cutter had lain broken, unknown to him, in the hovel since hay-cutting at midsummer. All breakages were supposed to be reported by the steward at once, so that they might be remedied immediately, and the implement be ready for action at any time. That seemed common sense. Luke had objected. Why set about repairing anything until it was needed, he argued. That was what they did everywhere else.

"I see, it is to remain the old farm here, even as the old firm in Threadneedle Street."

"I don't know what that means, but we won't get in no muddle," said the steward. And the broken cutter had not gone to the blacksmith.

There were two fairly old horse-drawn cutters on the farm—one a Samuelson, the other a Bamford. Phillip's plan for the morning's work had been to draw one cutter by tractor, the other by horse. The spare cutter was found to be without a knife. During the June haysel its spare knife had lost several shark-teeth blades. Phillip had arranged for spare blades to be in their place in the workshop, upon the Spares Shelf. The whole set had been taken during haysel and left somewhere under a hedge. The rivetting-hammer also was missing. So was the box of rivets.

It was 11.30 a.m. before the cutters had left for the Saturday morning's work of thistle-cutting on the meadows. One man had left his scythe half a mile away in a thorn-tree, three weeks before. By the time he had returned with his scythe it was time to go home.

"Do let me give you some chicken, Pip. Or will you get something at Captain Runnymeade's?"

"Do roses like gin? Or is it hydrangeas that turn blue in the face? There won't be a merciful fire in this weather."

Soon with pails of water, brushes, wash-leather, polish and rags the Silver Eagle was being groomed, as befitted its visit to a retired dandy of Edwardian refulgence. The children waited silently—hushed by Billy—holding their hats while Father worked in grim haste, swabbing, drying, cleaning, polishing. It was half-past three when he went to wash and change his clothes. He had a cold tub, and immediately felt to be glowing with life. His legs were hard, so was his belly; he could still wear riding breeches made in Cundit Street in 1917: what fun, what foolishness it had been in those days, he thought as he rubbed himself down. An impulse came to him to wear the breeches in honour of those days, and of his host: but no, all eccentricity of dress must be confined to the children. And feeling much refreshed he went into the parlour wearing only a towel, and there on the table was a mug of milky tea and a plate of buttered brown bread spread with honey. He ate this, and the party seemed to be a thrilling possibility. Would Melissa be there?

"You'll have missed some fun because I am late," he told Billy, Peter, Rosamund, David, and Jonathan standing quietly in that order before him.

"It doesn't matter at all, sir," replied David, smiling, where before he had been serious of face. "Really it doesn't. Your pigs look ever so nice now," he added.

"They're ever so streaky, sir," said Rosamund.

"Good. I'd like to tether the sows on the meadow, and let them have sun and fresh air. They need to snout about for roots and things which their natures require. But Matt is afraid they will stray. Well, thank you, Lucy, for the honey. It's power; the best kind of food. I wish we could all be vegetarian."

Jonathan looked serious. "Dad, sir," he said, thoughtfully. "Are pheasants vegetarian?"

"Ha, ha," laughed David. He was the second youngest, and looked just as Phillip's father had looked as a boy, according to an old photograph. At times David had a poignant appeal for Phillip because of that likeness.

Jonathan scowled. To avoid him feeling that he had asked something silly, Phillip said, "That is an interesting question. Pheasants eat almost anything, including corn, worms, beetles, apples, mice, small snakes, grasshoppers."

"I know what they eat, Dad, I mean sir, but are they vegetarian food for us?"

David rolled laughing off the arm of the leather chair on which he had been sitting. He collapsed and hid his long thin face in a cushion. Stifled laughter came from the cushion. Billy remarked sardonically, "Are pheasants vegetables?"

Jonathan's eyes showed mortification.

"I know, darling," said Rosamund, going to the rescue. She was Celtic, dark like her small brother. She sat him on her lap. "You see, Johnny, pheasants eat clover and peas and corn, and when we eat them, we also eat what they have eaten, so in a way they are vegetarian. Vegetarian food means things like milk, butter, honey, and nuts. Figs, too, and dates, then there's apples, potatoes, beans and peas, oh, lots of lovely vegetable food."

"Jolly fine grub," said David, his toothy grin reappearing for a moment over the arm of the brown leather chair. "I want to be a vegetarian." With a merry glance at Jonathan, he hid his head again.

"Shut up, boy!" cried Jonathan. His dark eyes showed his hurt. Phillip made a sign to David not to pursue the joke further.

"Now then, how about these horkey hats? I guess we won't wear them through the village, or they will think the Corney Band Boys are going to play somewhere."

The Corney Band Boys was a family joke, an imaginary dance band made up of children, cats, pigs, foxes and mice all playing musical instruments together in the Corn Barn where the harvest horkey had been held on a September night of the previous year —the year of Munich.

Chapter 16

EXTRICATION

That was the month when British corn prices suddenly dropped over 100 per cent in price, because much of the corn harvest of Central Europe had been bought by a group of financers in the City of London to prevent it going to Germany by barter. Before that year's N.S.D.A.P. rally at Nürnberg Hitler had cried, *Germany must export or die; and Germany shall not die!*

The corn was yellow in the fields beside the winding coast road. Over the flat windscreen the heated air rushed with the smell of sap in stalk and leaf. The barley was topped with the hail, the oats were in jag, wheat berries were already hardening. Phillip rejoiced in the colour and light of sky and field and line of sea; he told himself that he was a farmer of this famous malting district where on the light soils and in the foggy dews of early morning some of the finest light-ale samples of barley in Britain were grown. His spirit rose buoyant in a sense of freedom because the harvest was not yet; there were two weeks, perhaps three—or even four weeks clear before the barley stalks would bleach white in the sun and the prawny heads hang down dry and brittle—sign that it was fit to cut. The wheat would be earlier than the barley, and the oats too; but Luke had said there was no need to worry. And the reaper-and-binder had been serviced at the blacksmith's; and the shackle-bolts could be refitted to the frame of the green trailer; and a broken wooden lade repaired by a village carpenter. If only he hadn't worried!

"We won't get in no muddle," Luke had said. "And if there's war declared, you'll see, your barley will fetch a good price. You'll see I'm right."

"I wish we'd bare-fallowed all the arable last year."

Phillip's plan had been to grow no crops at all for the first two years, but to concentrate on restoration work, including meadow drainage and reconditioning of farm cottage buildings; the arable to be ploughed and cultivated only. Thus weeds would chit. Further cultivation would then kill them. Phillip meant to keep on doing that, killing crop after crop of weeds, throughout the second summer. The special wing-shaped tines on the tractor cultivator covered ten acres a day. There were two hundred acres of arable: twenty days a month, for one man, during three months.

The next season they would have started with a new farm. But he had allowed himself to be turned away by the earnest pleas of Luke and Matt. Without pressure, in their own time —a whole clear year—they would have built pigs' houses, repaired the roofs of stable and cowhouse, made a liquid manure tank, drained the meadows, bridged the dykes, even planted new spinneys of larch and oak in the centre of the largest field; and in that spinney, a crowstarver's hut, like the one he had seen in the Big Wheatfield, with cousin Willie, during his boyhood.

But, not to hurt their earnest beliefs that the farm ought not to miss a year's cash-cropping—(had he been too frank about the smallness of his capital?)—he had sown barley against his own judgment, because he did not want to discourage Luke. They had sown a hundred acres; and after the following harvest of 1938 had met the greatest slump in British corn prices for many years.

Phillip had offered samples of his barleys in the Corn Hall. The best bid did not cover the costs of fertiliser, seed, labour, depreciation, and rent. His chronic weakness: Oh, why did he always consider other people's wishes? It made him bad-tempered; he was always denying himself. No pigs' houses or liquid manure tank; meadows remaining undrained and the old dyke-bridges fallen in; no trees planted. There would have been hardly a weed left by now on an arable revitalised by exposure to sun and nitrogenous air.

It was an old-fashioned English summer, like that golden year of 1914. There was to be, in years to come, another illusion of summer of dreaming sunshine and of life everlasting.

A drift of Painted Ladies was crossing the North Sea. Many butterflies were dancing over the seeded flowers and brambles of the hedges lining the wide extent of arable susurrating with the wind in the corn, the wind drawing a different sound from sprays of oats, from braided heads of wheat, from yielding sweep of bearded barley.

Phillip stopped the car. "My father would love to see those butterflies."

"Why don't we ever see your father, Dad?" asked Rosamund.

"I've never seen him," said David. "What is our grandfather like?"

"According to photographs, he was exactly like you when he was a boy. But he never had a decent chance."

"Why don't we see him?" persisted Rosamund.

"He never answers my letters. He's worn out, I expect, after fifty years in an office, and no-one to look after him."

"I'd love to look after him," said Rosamund.

In brilliant clear light for which the coast had long been esteemed by landscape painters, the open car, holding five children in its seats, passed through little coastal villages of flint and brick and pantile, to arrive at the end of a narrow lane, overset by thorn hedges, where at the edge of marshes azure with sea-lavender in bloom across their wandering flats and channels stood Captain Runnymeade's cottage, behind a tall garden wall of round grey pebbles.

There the children got out, whispering to one another to be quiet while they adjusted their horkey hats. They wore their blue working overalls, washed and ironed for the occasion. There was a last-minute flurry while the hats were taken off, exchanged, tried on, rejected, and the originals handed back again.

In addition to the hats, the children had brought several instruments capable of producing sounds and noises. These were, indeed, the instruments of the Corney Boys Band. The master-instrument was a French *cor-de-chasse,* eleven feet of tapered brass piping curling like the shell of a wentletrap, but, unlike that sea-snail, capable of uttering when blown a range of notes, said Phillip, of an historic gravity of tone.

"For a thousand years in Europe, long before that, indeed, in Charlemagne's time, the wild boar has quivered and grunted to hear the echo of these notes, even as the horn of Roland in the Pass of Roncesvalles. Pay attention, Billy. I am giving you priceless gems of culture."

Billy was laughing, but not at what his father had said in a mock school-master voice. He was thinking of Captain Runnymeade as a wild boar, quivering and grunting with rage at the sight of them all hurtling into his garden party.

"The small and crumpled bugle you carry will perhaps detract from the majesty of my salute on the *cor-de-chasse.*"

"It won't," said Billy, pouting a little. He looked defiantly at his father, not sure whether he was being got-at. Billy had a great but concealed admiration for his father, mixed with sighful perplexity for some of the things he did, one of them being the mobbing of Mum, otherwise complaints and sometimes cross words.

"Well, you can hardly help it, on that battered object, Billy my son. Anyway, it's all supposed to be a joke. Peter with the cuckoo pipe, Roz the quail, David the wood-pigeon, Jon with his water-whistle."

"Dad," said Jonathan, anxiously. "I haven't got any water, so I can't be a nightingale."

Billy and Peter doubled up with silent laughter.

"Shut up, you bastards," cried the child, his eyes flashing and his cheeks flushing. Rosamund put her arm round his shoulders, but he wriggled away.

"We can't really go in playing our instruments, you know," said Phillip to Roz.

The children waited, watching the play of feeling and indecision on their father's face. "I knew he'd change his mind," whispered Billy to Peter. Phillip heard him, and looked with a flash of anger towards the boy; at once softening as he saw a look of Barley on his face. "Well, Billy my son, it's Captain Runnymeade's show, and I don't think we ought to gate-crash it." So the horkey hats were removed, and hidden with the instruments in the car.

Docile now, the children prepared to follow their father as he opened the postern gate in the garden wall to see, framed in the doorway, a lawn upon which two figures were posed, and before them a score and more of children sitting in a polite arc, and behind the arc a dozen uniformed nursemaids and an elderly nanny or two.

Of the central figures upon the lawn, Captain Runnymeade was sitting with nonchalant ease upon a chair; while the other, pale of face and sombrely dressed was standing at a table, and holding in his hands a wand, a large red handkerchief, and part of a lettuce. It seemed to be a moment of climax, so Phillip motioned his children to remain still.

Chapter 17

PHOSPHORESCENCE

The lawn was desiccated and shaven, a sandy mat of withering grasses studded with dwarfed plants of dandelion, plantain, and daisy, lookingas though, for too long, they had had to endure the cruel knives of a mower. And there sat the tyrant of their decimation, lord of the lawn, sitting askew in his chair with one pepper-and-salt trouser'd leg cocked over the other as he flipped a hand slightly toward Phillip in greeting before his gaze returned to regard tolerantly the movements of the magician in a frock-coat of ancient pattern, with stand-up collar and cravat enclosing the strings of his neck; now taking up a black silk hat with concave sides and noticeably curly brim—the immemorial abode, spectacularly speaking, of generations of white rabbits, the latest tenant of which was, apparently, about to reveal its presence there.

Obviously to have made an entrance vulgarly, like something out of a Disney cartoon, blowing upon assorted instruments and wearing bizarre hats, would have irrupted the spirit of the party: although Captain Runnymeade, that mixture of the bohemian and the conventional, that *agent provocateur* of anything to dispel boredom and to stimulate entertainment, might not have found it unexpected. Indeed, his personality would have been partly the cause: for Phillip behaved in Captain Runnymeade's house in a manner, or character, quite different from his normal self. He became Runnymeade-Maddison. He was a little afraid of 'Boy': and often wondered what was the cause. Was it because he was forced to act a part, to be pretentious, because his true or real self was unacceptable to one whose whole mode of living and thinking had been formed in a mould that was now obsolescent? Even so, what was his real or true self? Often he felt that he was many kinds of a person, his personality a mixture or layer of innumerable impressions, like an old door of a carpenter's shop that is thick with many coats of paint from repeated brush-cleanings.

Out of the curved and curly silk hat upon the table topped with green baize was drawn a white rabbit. It squatted there, politely nibbling the lettuce, while awaiting the end of the show it probably knew by heart. Now the magician in the frock-coat had taken the hat with the curly brim, and holding it in the crook of his left arm, was pulling from it with his right hand flag after flag, each knotted loosely to its subsequent fellow, thus to fall in swathe on swathe of colour upon the table and thence to the level of the magician's elastic-sided boots, and to the bitter grasses of the lawn. Flag after flag cascaded down—France, Montenegro, Servia, Russia, Japan, Belgium, Roumania, Italy, the United States—all the flags of the Allies were there—but stay, where was the Union Jack?

The Magician paused, holding out his hat. Polite applause greeted the apparent end of the performance; but the audience was deceived, the climax was to come, for with a triumphant flourish the magician pulled out the Union Jack, then the Royal Standard, holding them high amidst a silence of unuttered cheers. Then he presented the Union Jack to Captain Runnymeade, who, having uncrossed his pepper-and-salt trousers, arose slowly to his feet, and with a smile on his ruddy face, held it up somewhat sheepishly for an appropriate moment of simulated appreciation before draping it over his chair-back with a gesture that seemed to Phillip to be saying, Thank God that's over.

Yes, the show was over: for the face of Rippingall, sans waxed moustachios, watching from behind the curtains of the sitting-room, was withdrawn; and hardly had Captain Runnymeade congratulated, and thereby dismissed, the magician, scarcely had he begun to move among his guests when from around the rear of the house appeared a file of white-capped-and-apron'd women led by Mrs. Rippingall and bearing between them the component parts of two trestle tables. Having fixed these, and laid thereon white damask tablecloths, they wheeled about, and filing back the way they had come, reappeared with a succession of trays bearing jugs of lemonade and ginger beer, plates of bread-and-butter, ice-cream, cakes of plum, ginger, fruit and macaroon, some iced and others heavy with almond paste set with walnuts and preserved cherries, together with bowls of various sliced and peeled fruits. Having put these down, they formed themselves into line as rehearsed by Rippingall, who then appeared, collar'd, cuff'd, and tail'd, to set in the centre of the table a silver-gilt engraved bowl holding a couple of gallons of cream, forthwith to be ladled on the plates of sliced and chopped apples, oranges, bananas, pears, apricots, peaches, grapes, plums, dates, and other fruits for the young mothers and their children.

Before this, while the conjuring had been going on, Phillip had glanced at the faces of the women, searching for beauty and light. Of the women he recognised only Felicity, but then, searching anew, he saw a face which quickened his spirit as no other face could. How calm and beautiful Melissa was, her fair hair under a Tyrolean straw hat, banded with little coloured flowers, set on the back of her head.

Captain Runnymeade was moving among the children and their mothers with an air of satisfaction in his face as he basked in soft looks. Had he once been a confident Edwardian, 'popular among the ladies'? What was 'Boy's' true self? Phillip imagined him as a small, lonely child who through the years had built up a façade of self-assertion to cover feelings of insufficiency and failure.

Stefania Rozwitz had told him that 'Boy' had had "a beautiful butterfly of a mother" whom he seldom saw. She had bolted from his father, after which her name was never mentioned. The boy had been left to a governess and later a tutor before going to one of the 'only three possible schools'. A gilded youth, with the right connexions—but always that sense of inadequacy. Freud had become significant only after the ruin of the former European plutocracy in the war. In 'Boy' the last of the Edwardian world was dying. He was a ghost still enfleshed.

"Ah, ha, Maddison. How's your god-dam' farm?"

Phillip presented the children. 'Boy' nodded to each, stroked Rosamund's head a moment, remarked, "Your father considers that leisure is a vice," and having seen that they had something to eat, led Phillip away into the house and poured him out a large glass of gin and lime-juice, while Phillip vainly protested, "Not so much please——"

"Then leave it."

The glass was topped up.

While they were there Stefania Rozwitz came in and said, "'Boy', you're a damned fool to drink that stuff if you want to make Felicity your mistress," and taking the glass from his hand, she went out of the room.

"The absence of manners in the world today is to be regretted," remarked Runnymeade, pouring himself some whisky which he promptly swallowed.

Phillip sipped his drink, waiting for a chance to get rid of it. He followed Runnymeade, who seemed to have forgotten him, into the garden, seeing past the open kitchen door the magician sitting at a table revealing shirtless bony shoulders and chest covered by a dickey tied on with tape. Starched cuffs were likewise secured to his wrists. There the old fellow was, enjoying himself with Guinness and platetful of York ham.

And there stood Rippingall, eyeing the bottle of Guinness, until the voice of Mrs. Rippingall said sternly, "Rippingall! Remember that Guinness is not good for you!"

Likewise this bloody gin, thought Philip, as he shot his glassful beside the threshold, by a rambler-rose root.

In the garden Billy and Rosamund and the other children were enjoying themselves. They had forgotten their disappointment at having missed the chance of seeing the rabbit slipped into the hat where obviously the flags had been hidden all the time. However, there was compensation, for the animal was now hopping about on the lawn, seeking not grass but bits of bread and butter and cake from small hands carefully guided by sleeves of grey uniforms. He saw Penelope, and went to her.

She told him that the magician was quite a figure in the district: in fact Mr. Gotobed Thurtle, said Penelope, was an Institution by himself. He was said to be any age between seventy five and ninety. Mr. Gotobed Thurtle, who liked to be called Professor, had shown off his tricks to children who were now grandparents. Years before the Great War, indeed before the South African War, the Professor was said to have been a professional mourning mute at funerals in Yarwich, wearing the same frock-coat, but with a band of crêpe six inches deep around his top hat.

Penelope smiled brightly. She was a social girl again, infected by uneasiness at the sight of so many starched nannies, symbol of all that from which she had run away. She said with extra gaiety, "What do you think of Felicity's new job? Didn't you know? She's secretary to Captain Runnymeade. To help him write his memoirs, or something like that. She tells me she's rented a cottage in Staithe, and her mother is coming to live with her and Edward." She added, "Brother Laurence, I understand, is returning to the Congo." She looked at him. "Do you always tand like that at parties, when you are nervous?"

"Am I nervous?"

"You are always nervous, but sometimes more so than at others."

Phillip was standing on his right leg, the foot at right-angles to that of the left leg, while the weight of his head was supported on the palm of his right hand, the elbow of which was held by the other hand: an angular figure, square shouldered, looking as though he had been drawn by a T-square, with something of the heron about him.

"Aren't you going to talk to Melissa?"

"I'm not sure she wants to see me."

"So that's why you're twisting yourself into a geometrical pattern."

"Or go back into my crystal pattern." To change the subject he said, "What do you think of 'Boy' Runnymeade? I can never feel quite certain about him."

"He's our host," she said promptly. "Did you see the Painted Ladies as you came along? There were clouds of them on the hedge. Some got in my radiator."

"Yes, I saw them. My father would have been excited—butterflies were his passion when a young man."

He thought that he had neglected his father: he had seen him only twice since his mother's death nearly three years before.

Polite goodbyes were being said, with varied phrases of gratitude, to Stefania Rozwitz standing beside Captain Runnymeade at the postern gate. As Phillip said goodbye, Runnymeade said, "You are expected for dinner tonight, 'Farm Boy'. We'll meet at the Frigate Inn for a drink at seven o'clock. Riversmill, the horse painter, is coming, and others."

Outside in the lane Melissa was talking to the children. He met the glance of her eyes lifted to his, and impulsively took her hand, and feeling its clasp knew that nothing had come between them. And it seemed on the way home that the Silver Eagle had never run so well, that the children had never looked so free, so gay, so light-hearted.

"Runnymeade has asked me back to dinner at the Frigate Inn, Lucy. Riversmill the painter is coming, and also George Burper the *Punch* artist, and his wife. Melissa will be there, too."

"I am so glad. You go and enjoy yourself. You deserve some relaxation after all you've done."

"What about you? I never seem to think of you, do I?"

"You are doing so now," replied Lucy. "I shall be perfectly happy here with the children."

"You once said they were all your life, d'you remember?"

Lucy's cheeks coloured, and she smiled an unsteady smile at Phillip. "I'm here, if ever you want me. If you are happy, that is all that matters to me."

"Illusion rules us all, but not you, Lucy. So while I rush back again, you remain content with the children."

"Oh, you're all right," she said, with a half laugh. "Now go you back, my man, and enjoy yourself."

"I *am* a bit of a cad, aren't I? Be honest, now."

"*I* don't think so," she replied cheerfully. "I don't want you to hurt yourself, that's all. But you won't do that with Melissa. Give her my love, I'm very fond of her, you know." She added, "Have you seen the paper today? Apparently tonight there's to be, all along this coast, a trial black-out."

He picked up the *Crusader*. Motorists were asked not to use their headlights after 10 p.m. It was not a precautionary measure, but only a routine practice for Anti-aircraft Command.

"Wind up. Well, I'll be off. Don't wait up for me. Goodnight, everyone."

"Goodnight," they cried, and Lucy said, "Don't let Captain Runnymeade ply you with too much 'hospitality'."

Back once more along the winding coast road, passing fields of sugar-beet and barley, all with fallen or broken gates; through the back road of the decayed little town with its silted-up port; round bends between marshes and a walled park from which strayed, every hundred yards or so, a wild pheasant: the demesne wall of a park built in another century by one who had called himself Giant Despair, not because he had taken on work beyond his strength, but because it was beyond his hope when he had found himself with a wastrel son and heir who cared nothing for that work. Through the drab and faded villages, round lanes of overgrown hedges, by a water-mill rising tall above a narrow bridge whereunder flowed a stream fast and deep. This was a place to stop by, and leaning over, to peer for trout in the eddies of the tail-race. He looked down into the water out of habit from past days when the mind had been free to find interest and refreshment in running water: then on his way.

Arriving at the Frigate Inn, he left the motorcar in the yard, and went to the place marked *Gentlemen*; and leaving there, thought to enter by the back way to the parlour wherein Captain Runnymeade usually met his guests, a room reserved for his sole use. The door to that room was not properly closed, and peering through the space he saw the side-whiskered face of George Burper, whom he had met once before, his gentle wife beside him; and there too was Riversmill the painter, neat of figure, small of face and head, Riversmill whose mordant wit and tremendous enthusiasm always gave Phillip a feeling of wildness.

Talking to Riversmill was another figure out of the 18th century, a stout figure in riding boots of black leather that ended half-way up the massive calves of legs in tight breeches of white moleskin giving him the appearance of a postillion. The red-faced figure wore a dark hacking-jacket of West of England cloth with high lapels, over which foamed a large white cravat.

And Melissa. Her poise of head and grace of movement calmed the wildness, as though all dross and fatigue were lifted from himself. She wore slacks of dark blue material, the trousers tapering from her thighs down to her ankles, with a suggestion of peg-top. Without a hat, and wearing a pale blue jumper, she was more beautiful than before.

"They're expecting you," said a voice behind him. In the passage stood a buxom smiling woman. "It's the Captain's birthday, you are just in time to drink his health."

"Who is the sporting chap in riding kit?" he asked. He thought she must be the cook, or someone of that station, when she replied, "Surely you know? Why, that's Mr. Valentine Sharkey! You *must* have heard of him? You haven't? Oh, you're new in this district. Well then, that's Mr. Valentine Sharkey of Sharkey's Riding Academy. I thought that everyone had heard of Mr. Sharkey's Riding Academy. Why, he and his father and grandfather, and *his* father, too, have taught children here to ride for the last hundred and fifty years."

"He sounds quite a local worthy. By the way, will my car be in the way where it is?"

"Of course it won't be. Besides, no motor of a friend of the Captain's could ever possibly be in the way."

He went down the passage and got a boisterous greeting from Riversmill. "Here he is!"

"Ah, 'Farm Boy'," said Captain Runnymeade, remaining seated in his armchair, on one arm of which sat Melissa. "Just in time to give us your opinion on a matter of some importance to our good friend Mr. Valentine Sharkey here. Mr. Sharkey is a very famous man. This is Mr. Maddison, Mr. Sharkey."

Phillip said how d'you do to Riversmill, his wife, and Stefania, leaving Melissa to the last.

Captain Runnymeade went on, "Mr. Valentine Sharkey is the fourth of his dynasty, all of them, judging by their daguerreotypes and photographs on the wall over there——" he jerked a thumb at an oblong frame with four figures in riding clothes and exactly alike—"all with hearts of oak like Mr. Valentine Sharkey the Fifth standing in the flesh before us."

"That's right," said the horsey figure, looking extremely solemn.

"Fill your glass, Mr. Sharkey!" 'Boy' Runnymeade leaned over Melissa. "I'll ring for Mabel. Ah, Mabel, just in time. Bring the same again, Mabel, will you, please? Mabel is my best friend, aren't you, Mabel?" Without heeding Mabel's reply, he turned to Phillip saying, "You're a man of ink, 'Farm Boy', so apply your vast knowledge of Fleet Street publicity to Mr. Sharkey's problem. It is a very serious problem, isn't it, Mr. Sharkey?"

"It is indeed, Capting."

"Stated simply, it is this. Should Mr. Sharkey change the name of his riding school, for over a century known as"—the voice pronounced the words slowly—"'Sharkey's Riding Academy, Livery and Bait'—into 'The Staithe Guest House and Riding School'—or should he not?"

"That's it, in a nut-shell," announced Mr. Sharkey.

"It is a very important matter, Maddison, for Mr. Sharkey does not want his forebears up there to turn in their graves, do you, Mr. Sharkey?"

"Too true, Capting."

Phillip, discomposed by Runnymeade's drawly, semi-patronising manner, and conscious of both Melissa and Stefania looking at him, said, "Why not have both? The Guest House on the board by the gate and the old style by the stables."

"Bravo," cried Riversmill. "Keep to tradition, and you can't go wrong! It's the same with all this formless rubbish spreading through the world in the name of Art. Look at Epstein, the sculptor. Look at——"

"Don't start off again on that line," said his wife, shortly.

"And don't you start off on me," replied Riversmill.

Runnymeade, waving a hand, said, "Tell us about your pal Birkin, 'Farm Boy'. I understand he's now saying, 'No war for Warsaw'."

Stefania Rozwitz, sitting on a straight-back chair the wrong way round, so that Runnymeade was behind her, cried out in a deep voice, "Don't be a damned fool, 'Boy'."

Phillip saw Runnymeade patting Melissa's knee. Was Stefania jealous, he wondered. He decided that she didn't care. Hairs were growing on her chin.

Soon afterwards Mabel came in with a magnum of champagne. She was followed by her sister, a woman thin and retiringly modest as Mabel was stout and jolly.

"It's the Captain's birthday," she said. "I want you all to drink his health with my sister and I."

"Mabel," said Runnymeade, "How can you expect me to take advantage of your great hospitality. However, as your very old friend, I intend to take advantage of it."

He remained seated when they drank his health, and in reply, proposed "Mabel and Maude, my oldest friends," sipping the wine but not drinking any. Phillip remembered what an old soak in the A.S.G. had once told him in 1916, *never mix malt and vine.*

"I haven't forgot you, Captain," said Mabel, bringing him an exceptionally tall tumbler of cut-glass holding half a pint of amber liquid. "I've got your special birthday drink." To Phillip, she explained with pride, "The Captain has it once a year. It's a real tumbler, very old. See, the bottom is round, so that it can't be stood up."

Runnymeade took the tumbler and drank the contents right off.

"Now Captain," said Mabel, "that is the last you will take tonight. Promise me?"

"Well, ladies and gentlemen," said Mr. Sharkey, picking up his curly-brimmed bowler, "I must be off. Thank you, Capting, for a most enjoyable evening."

"Au revoir," said Runnymeade, lifting a hand like a signal as he stared glowingly before him.

Four men and four women walking down the lane from the inn to the cottage on the edge of the marsh. A low sun casting long shadows before them on the yellow dust of the road. The wonder of evening, the close of a perfect summer day. Desmond and he walking side by side long ago, the last summer of the old world. Slanting evening sun upon the Hillies. Boys and girls sauntering through the green twilight of evening. Great box kites being hauled in. From afar a gentle singing in harmony, *We were sailing along, on Moonlight Bay.*

Keep it going boys, your race is nearly run——

'Boy' Runnymeade was happy. He was a host to artists, he was living in the timeless present, he spoke seldom, his face had a pink flush, his eyes glistened.

The dining-room was studded with sunset shells gathered upon the sea-shore and set in pattern on the wall above the sideboard where gold plate was displayed.

"A simple little dinner," he said, "Sit down anywhere," as they followed Stefania's wishes where they should sit.

Rippingall moved with genial aloofness, serving food and wine. He looked happy; he was devoted to 'the Captain'. He had cooked the sea-trout, caught in a longshore net in the gravel scours off the little harbour mouth. Grouse from Blubberhouses in Yorkshire. Dark red flesh, the essence of heather-tips, dark red wine, essence of limestone, sun, and tawny terraced soil above the Garonne. Bilberry tart, yellow crusty cream from Jersey cow. Mushrooms on toast. Fortune apples which must be eaten while a dry champagne is sipped, for champagne should never be drunk with anything but fruit.

'Boy' had eaten only cold bacon, drunk only whisky and soda. Edwardian splendour in fact and spirit.

How far I have travelled since my moon-calf days of the spring and summer of 1914, in that dark little office in Wine Vaults Lane.

By the time the port was on the table the guests were of a homogeneous happiness. Black-coated, yellow-waistcoat'd, cravat'd George Burper speaking across the table in his mild voice, sharing a gentleness of sensibility with his wife. Painter Riversmill on his feet reciting two of his ballads. When the cheering was over, George Burper saying, "You must print your ballads, Fred, before they're lost. They are very fine indeed."

"How you do it, beats me," cried Runnymeade. He waved an arm.

"Painters usually make good writers, 'Horse Boy'," said Phillip. "They have the gift of sight, which is also the basis of good literary style."

'Boy' Runnymeade, with a heavy smile, became *agent-provocateur*. "Tell us what is the position with the art-dealers and modern art, you Horse Painter. Let's have something from the horse's mouth."

Up rose Riversmill like a fighting Suffolk cock-partridge, churr-wocking against the oriental beaky fowls of art-dealers who bought and stored the pictures of rootless daubers who had neither sense of colour, skill in drawing, idea or form, until by agreement the racket operated, the critics were bought, and a sale arranged by which one painting was bid for by the ring and sold for a high price. Then the dealers unloaded and cashed-in.

To this outburst Runnymeade, playing his part, cried "Damn it all, Fred, critics and dealers must live, like anybody else," and so drew from the partridge cock what he wanted: an explosion of head, wings, body, and tail in the face of the imagined oriental vulture.

"By God, you damned ignoramusses can laugh! You think it's funny that these swine are ruining our English culture. That these rootless parasites who worship only the Golden Calf, control British painting. To hell with them all!"

Riversmill's hair shook with his roared-out rage. His wife pulled him down on his chair by his coat-tails.

"You're making a dam' fool of yourself, and you know it!"

"Not so much a fool as you've made of me since I married you!" yelled Riversmill, bobbing up to get on with his tirade.

"I told you to shut up," said his wife, pulling him down again.

Yet again on his feet, arms mixed-up railway signals, the painter let fly. All the four-letter Anglo-Saxon words flew into the air. Those around the table rolled about, helpless with laughter. The painter's arms became erratic windmills. His hair stood up and fell down as his head jerked about in abandoned rage. Then with arms upheld he finally bawled, "I hope Hitler bombs the bloody lot of them! Before the blasted swine destroys our culture based on the Greek ideal of the beauty of the human mind and form!"

"Don't take any notice of him," said Mrs. Riversmill. "When he's drunk he never knows what he's saying."

"You've never known a word of what I was saying," cried Riversmill.

"This is a party," chortled 'Boy' Runnymeade, tipping his glass. "By God, this is a party. 'Farm Boy', tell us about your friend Mr. Schicklgruber. It is true that his father had Jewish blood, so that the family name was changed to Witler, or Squitler or something?"

"Leave 'Farm Boy' alone, 'Boy'," growled Stefania, "and shut up."

"Shut up yourself!" yelled Riversmill, glaring at his wife.

"I didn't speak, you idiot!"

"Idiot yourself!"

"If I hadn't looked after your money for you, you'd have thrown it all away by now, and would be lying in the gutter, you ranting fool."

"Oh ho ho, ho ho!" cried 'Boy' Runnymeade, as he drew up his sagging torso and wiped his eyes, gasping with the effects of much laughter.

Phillip had not laughed so much for years. Only Melissa had not laughed as the others had laughed: she had smiled, a self-possessed sprite now in pale blue summery frock. She was watching Phillip. She had never before seen him laugh like that. She wanted to dance, to throw her arms round him, to hide her face against his chest, and rest, rest, rest.

Rippingall came in with the coffee. "Brother Laurence is waiting, sir."

"Ask him to come in."

The friar came in and apologised for Felicity's absence. "Her child has a temperature, Captain Runnymeade."

"Have a drink, Brother Laurence. Help yourself. We're having a discussion about certain matters. Now, 'Farm Boy', give us your views of the European crisis. Do I understand you to claim that Usury is the cause of the deteriorating international situation?"

Phillip said to himself that he was not going to be drawn.

"Come on, Phillip, speak up, man!" cried Riversmill.

"Come on, 'Farm Boy', give us a run for our money."

Phillip was sitting beside Stefania Rozwitz. She put her hand protectively over his. "The fox is a gentleman," she said. "The fox doesn't want to hurt the feelings of those who would hunt him."

Phillip said, "Winston Churchill wrote in his autobiography some years ago that the English power, based on world trade in English bottoms, or ships, for four hundred years has maintained that power by a policy of Divide and Rule in Europe."

"Well, what's wrong with that?" said Runnymeade. "Anyway, who is Churchill? Nobody thinks anything of him today. He finished himself over the Dardanelles in nineteen fifteen. Come on 'Farm Boy', tell us what Birkin says!"

"There's a man for you!" cried Riversmill.

"Birkin says, 'If there is another war between England and Germany, it will be money's war, and nothing to do with the English people'."

"Money's war?" growled Stefania. "What about my country-men? I am a Pole, do you not know that?"

"My remark was not intended personally."

"Why not?" said Runnymeade. "Let's have the gloves off. No holds barred."

Stefania gave 'Boy' a contemptuous look before saying to Phillip, "Why Money's war, 'Farm Boy?' Money is only a unit of energy, like a volt of electricity, or horse-power for an engine. You may as well say, 'It will be a volt's war', because electricity comes into it, to help drive one of your friend Hitler's tanks, or, 'It is horse-power's war', because somebody gets his rations in a lorry. Think straight, 'Farm Boy'."

"Well, you must agree that wars arise from a need for food, work, raw materials."

"And from damned gangsters who want what others have got," said Runnymeade.

"Europe has been divided too long. International money would lose its power to keep Britain on the dole if markets were stabilised by an Empire customs union. One more European war will wreck, as Riversmill has said, Western culture based on the Greek ideal. Greece was wrecked by rivalries between the city states, and the barbarians poured in."

"The modern barbarians are Hitler and his bandits," said Stefania.

"The modern barbarians are the dupes of Karl Marx," retorted Riversmill.

"Shut up," said Mrs. Riversmill.

"You shut up yourself."

Phillip turned to Stefania and said, "I respect you, not only as an artist; but surely, you, as a Polish patriot, do not want 'Only Russian spoken here' in your country."

"You would prefer 'Only German spoken here' in your country, 'Farm Boy'?"

"Of course not. English spoken here. I do not want to see another generation of British youths in their graves, head to head, boots to boots. I do not want to see German or Polish dead or French dead, while Oriental Commissars wait, like jackals, to grow fat on the killings."

"The hyaena comes before the jackal, 'Farm Boy'. For hyaena, read Hitler."

Runnymeade, half-gloating as he looked with semi-distaste at his voided mistress, said, "Tell us what Birkin says, Maddison."

"He says that Money is mainly in the control of those who have no national territory, whose virile qualities will always, until they do have their own territory, be subverted. I do not know about this myself, except to say that all money should be controlled by the Government. You will forgive me if this offends, but I am trying to answer 'Horse Boy's' question."

"What you lack is a sense of humour," said Runnymeade.

"I have no sense of humour about war. I lost some of mine in the first battle of Ypres, and again at Loos, and another little chunk of it on the Somme, and more at Passchendaele, and finally, in April nineteen-eighteen I found myself with no more humour whatsoever. At least, no *Punch*, or British upper-middle class humour. I except George Burper's drawings, of course. They are not patronising, but human."

"Go on lad, go on," said Riversmill, while Runnymeade filled his glass.

"If I speak of myself, it is because I can know only myself, who found the love of his life among the soldiers of a regiment. I was fortunate to be in a good crowd, where I was shown great friendship, or, as I know now, love."

"Now you are your true self, 'Farm Boy'," said Stefania Rozwitz. "I know what truth is, let me remind you. I—Rozwitz—who danced with Vaslov Nijinsky in 'Le Spectre de la Rose'." She put her hand on his. Phillip shook it before kissing it and returning it to her lap.

"One moment," said Runnymeade. "Do you mean to tell us that you found this feeling of brotherly love for the Germans?"

"I found it first in the Christmas truce of nineteen-fourteen, then in my regiment, where the *camaraderie* helped us all to carry on."

"Were you afraid?"

"Of course. But I was not alone any more."

"Then why don't you look forward to another war, to find more brotherly love for the Nazis?"

"I'd like to say one thing more, before the silence of personal opinion which may descend at the beginning of September."

"Why September?"

"The corn harvest will be in. And how wise and foreseeing is Birkin, whom I have the *honour* to know—a soldier of nineteen-fourteen like myself—how wise is he about the Jews. For years he has declared that they must be given territory within the British Empire, where they can settle and find their soul again as a nation rooted in its own soil. This soil must not be Palestine, because that would upset the Arabs, whose territory lies south of

Russia, with outlets to the Mediterranean. Who holds the Mediterranean holds the world, says Birkin. No! The Jews can be settled in the British Empire somewhere, and so fulfil the age-long vision of their prophets."

"Birkin's a great man," cried Riversmill. "I heard him speak in the Corn Hall at Fenton. He's a man alone, he won't work with other people, that's his trouble."

"Well, I don't know," said Runnymeade. "I heard him, too, and thought it a lot of hot air. I knew his father, and he was a waster. And I say, A plague on all your politics. Drink up."

"Birkin told me recently that every thug and crook in England had been through his party. Of course it's easy to see now where he went wrong, and others with him left over from the battlefields. If he had remained in Parliament, he would have had a platform where his speeches would at least be reported. Now, as you know, practically no paper prints them."

"It's the advertisers who control newspapers," said Riversmill.

"It's because Birkin strutted about in lion-tamer's boots and copied Mussolini, who is a clown," said Stefania. "But the Hyaena isn't—he's Anti-Christ, he's the devil, he's the modern Lucifer."

"Lucifer is the light-bringer," said Phillip.

"May I speak?" said Brother Laurence, quietly. "God had two sons. The elder, Lucifer, was arrogant, and wanted to usurp his Father's place. The other son was compassionate, all-embracing. Lucifer wanted a better world immediately. God said, 'You do not know my difficulties, the forces against me, my son. Your brother Kristos, has compassion for all life. He is love. And love will prevail when deep, dreadful night has absorbed all your light, my son.'"

"Did you hear that?" said Stefania. "After hearing that, never again talk to me of Hitler as a light-bringer, 'Farm Boy'! A false light, a false dawn, 'Farm Boy'—like those Northern Lights you told me about last winter, all electric storms. Very attractive, but no good as a steady constructive power. Your derided Money at least builds dynamos and power stations where electricity is harnessed, and not allowed to flash and terrorise and burn."

"Very interesting," said George Burper. "Very interesting indeed. I've never heard more interesting talk anywhere."

"We must agree to differ, 'Farm Boy'," said Stefania; and before she could cover his hand with her own, Phillip took hers and shook it in a friendly fashion. The defensive feelings due to her proximity went from him, and he felt compact once more.

"Well," said Runnymeade, "let's all drink to the damnation of Schicklgruber and his gang."

"To a Greater Britain!" cried Phillip.

As they left the table Melissa said, "Who's for a swim, 'on such a night as this'."

"I am," said Phillip.

In the dark days that lay ahead he was to remember that last peace-time party at Captain Runnymeade's—George Burper and his wife so quiet and happy, truly joined together by God, and Riversmill and his wife, and Brother Laurence saying, "Do not turn your talent into salt, Phillip. Your inborn love of the Kristos is your greatest protection—as it is mine—and you cannot rid yourself of it if you would."

There was the warm, moonless night outside, so still that it seemed natural to be walking in silence on the causeway across the marsh to the sandhills and the sloping shore beyond. At first he had been a little uneasy, for he had no bathing suit, and Melissa carried hers, with a towel; but the night was dark, the stars dim and small, and she seemed no more than a wraith as she moved unspeaking over the short turf of the golf-course beside him, and through a valley of loose sand to the shore, where the darkness seemed to be thick. Whither had the wraith disappeared? He did not know, he had lost her until her voice spoke quietly beside him and even the wet sands beneath the feet were unseen as they went towards the soft crashing waves; and entering, he saw that his feet were silvery, and wading farther in, that he had silver-green streaks for legs; and lying in warm water, in criss-cross movement with the short breaking waves of the North Sea, his hands were fins glimmering with silver.

He had no body, no feelings, he was a shadow, a water-sprite, the spirit had found its true home.

The tide was scouring along the shore to the east, and lying in two to three feet of water he was carried eastwards in the current, his face sometimes awash in a short cross-rush of breakers. The waves when rising were streaked electrically, they crashed in silver stabs and slashes on his body. Was that a seal with gleaming head rising near, was that a fish in the turmoil of waves? The silver streaks were Melissa. She was beside him in the wavelet rush, they were two glimmering water-things, drifting, drifting in the marvellous phosphoric sea of summer's midnight.

Never had he seen such a liquescence of light. The naked body of the nymph beside him was of a rare greenish pallidity, a thing entirely apart from ordinary life as the wash of waves bore them along, caressingly in greenish-silver water which had no undertow, no power to hold or to misdirect those pale watery forms which moved with the tumbling tide aslant the shoaling shore. Sometimes she glimmered among leaping sea-trout, a dim seal-like shape blurring into invisibility and revealed by a hand, a lock of hair, a shoulder laved in silver.

And the marvel was that this beauty of light was only of the warm sweep of water; it belonged only to the sea; this was baptismal beauty of the waters of night; for when he rose to his feet, all was dark. And once again the water sprite was an invisible presence beside him.

But night, yielding to all motion and bearing effortlessly the spirit over the shore to the sandhills a mile and more from where they had left the sea, had its wonders, too. There was no self, no thought, no problem, no feeling: only a calm everlastingness of the elements which, of their immense generosity, had created life. Desire, hope, striving, all were solved: the spirit was paramount, beyond even the beauty of words. For no word had been spoken between the time of coming on the shore, and leaving it an hour, or was it two hours, later. So it was, he thought, before he was born; so it would be, after he was dead.

He took her hand outside the garden gate of Marsh Cottage, whispering, "I won't come in. I expect they have gone to bed," for the upper windows were lit up. "Good night, Melissa."

"Good night, Phillip."

Covering the hand that he still held with his other hand he drew her nearer, kissed her cold cheek before touching her lips with his, then he was walking away in the soft dust of the lane, drawn by the thin wire of pain.

He could not face another heart-ache, which was all that falling in love had ever meant to him. Except with Lucy, whom he had never truly loved, or so it now seemed.

He wondered if Runnymeade, in alcoholic impotence, was in love with Melissa, a mental mistress of the hopeless spirit.

O Melissa, Melissa! Perfect sensibility; wordless understanding. Dare he still hope that his loneliness, his melancholy, his lost-rib-ache, would be salved by union with one of the generation following his own, a generation of sun, not like his own, of half-sun? Had he found his Isolde, Lily incarnate, Barley come again?

Looking back from rising ground, he saw that the sitting-room window was now alight. After hesitation he returned down the lane, giving himself the excuse that he must thank his host.

Re-entering the garden he had to pass the window. There was a gap between the curtains. He looked in, to see who was still up. He saw Melissa sitting in a chair. Runnymeade was kneeling before her. He was holding her two feet in his hands to kiss them. All this he saw in a brief glance before he turned away and walked over the lawn, keeping his back to the lighted window.

He drove along the serpentining coast road through the warm air of the summer night, jacket flung in tonneau, tyres whimpering on corners, headlights revealing the flint wall of the great park and then the cottages of the back road of the town, and home past fields of barley and sugar beet.

Watchers of the Observer Corps, Air Raid Precaution volunteers, regular members of the Police Force, Special Constables, and others reported by telephone that an open car, approximately one hour after midnight, was being driven at speed, with headlights full on, between two points on the coast—references and other particulars being given. An abbreviated report in due course reached M.I.5 in London.

Chapter 18

ROSEATE TERN

The barley was not yet rotten-ripe. Thistle-seeds were floating, set free by King Harrys, the twittering gold-finches of the East Anglian legend of the Field of the Cloth of Gold.

To Phillip delay was relief. Harvest time was crisis time: war when the harvest was in? He was troubled by doubts about the man whom for years he had thought to be the only true pacifist in Europe.

He carried in his pocket a copy of a speech made by Hitler to the Reichstag on May 21st, 1935. Reaching the creek where his dinghy was moored, he sat down and re-read the peroration.

> We believe that if the peoples of the world can agree to destroy all their gas, inflammatory, and explosive bombs this would be a more useful undertaking than using them to destroy one another.
>
> In saying this I am not speaking any more as the representative of a defenceless state which would have no responsibilities but only advantages as a result of such a procedure. I do not intend to take part here in discussions such as have recently been started in various places as to the value of other armies or one's own army and the cowardice of foreign soldiers and the supreme bravery of one's own.
>
> We all know how many millions of fearless opponents, contemptuous of death, faced us, alas, in the Great War. But history has certainly often shown us Germans that we understand less the art of living reasonably than that of dying nobly. I know that if ever this nation should be attacked the German soldier will do more than his duty, remembering from the experiences of one and a half decades what is the fate of a conquered people. This conviction is for all of us a serious responsibility, and at the same time a noble duty. I cannot better conclude my speech of today to you, my fellow fighters and trustees of the nation, than by repeating our confession of faith in peace. The nature of our new constitution makes it possible for us in Germany to put a stop to the machinations of the war agitators. May the other

> nations too be able to give bold expression to their real inner longing for peace.
>
> Whoever lights the torch of war in Europe can wish for nothing but chaos. We, however, live in the firm conviction that in our time will be fulfilled, not the decline but the renaissance of the West. That Germany may make an imperishable contribution to this great work is our proud hope and our unshakeable belief.

To escape—to be free—to be young again—to live, to love for ever. Sea-lavender, the misty blue of Melissa's eyes. The sea drew him, with memory of the phosphoric night. Why had he not come more often to this water which gleamed with sky as it moved up the channels of the marsh?

He set mast and rudder, put the anchor in the bows atop the coiled rope, and with leg-o'-mutton sail gently shaking glided down the creek, centre-board drawn up because the lapsing water was barely a foot deep. Lying back with tiller under arm, clad only in khaki shorts, dreaming of hair pale like the fine-ground sands of his destination. The bow touched, and leaping out he pulled the boat beyond the wavelets curling silently upon that windless shore. A whiteness of terns with scarlet mouths screamed and flapped a few inches away from his face as he walked among their young almost ready to fly.

There were Arctic terns, the colour of chalk and soot; and one roseate tern, a lone hen which had mated with an Arctic bird. From the watcher of the Yarwich Naturalists Society he had learned that the President, an aged man of eighty-two years living in the town, had ordered that the chick be killed when half-grown. It must not be killed when small, the parents might lay again, and so manage to bring off another hybrid, unwanted by the Society.

Phillip had written an article about that, ending with an ironical supplication to the President of the Society, which neither owned nor leased the sandhills of the Point and certainly did not own the wild birds of the air, to spare this solitary chick which was not responsible for its parents' sin.

The article, printed by *The Daily Crusader*, had made him locally unpopular. Who is this fellow from nowhere to lay down the law to us, the President had asked at a meeting convened to see what could be done about such unwelcome publicity. The paid watcher had made it known in the local inn that if the man who wrote the article came on the Point again he would pitch him back into the sea.

The fledgling was not in the same place. He sat down to watch for a tern's breast with a pale pink tinge. He focused his Zeiss monocular. There she was, sprat in bill, dropping behind a dune with its fringe of marram grass. Walking there he saw the print of feet smaller than his own. Topping the dune he saw Melissa.

She was pale. He sat beside her. She said, "I've hidden it. That's it over there. It can almost fly."

Cries of redshank and greenshank, curlew and stint, sandpiper and dotterel filled the morning air. And the larks. The steel of the sky was being drilled by a hundred drillings, bright minute steel dust sprinkling down.

"It takes after the hen," she said.

"Poor little Shicklgruber. He took after his mother, too."

The tide went out. The river-water in the channel was now shallow. They walked along the sea-wall in the direction of the harbour, which was silted. No ships ever called at the quay, which was of rubble and clay raised behind trunks of oak trees driven in as piles, with hand-sawn planks spiked to the posts. Beyond stood a malting of red brick and pantiles. It was empty and silent, with other warehouses. The walls were of flint and flaked brick rose-red in the intense clear light of the sky. The port was the home of small yachts. There had been a race that morning; the sharpies had just made their moorings against the ebb. Now the harbour was a prospect of mud, sand and reeds.

"Are you staying on at Marsh Cottage?"

"My last day tomorrow."

"I shall miss you, Melissa."

"I saw your face at the window. 'Boy' was warming my feet, after you'd gone. He's a kind man."

"I should have warmed all of you, Melissa."

"Darling Phillip——"

Hand in hand they walked back to the dinghy. The sands of the Point shelved, the ternery was afloat in mirage above the line of the sea. As they came near the end of the sea-wall a fresh breeze sparkled incoming waves. The tide had set north. It carried the dinghy at seven knots, soon leaving behind the drift of terns. The Great Barrier Sand lay to starboard. Upon this mound timbers of wrecked sailing ships stood up. Above one tatter of seaweed sat a cormorant.

Beyond the Great Barrier Sand the waves were smoothed stretches of foam.

"You're brown all over, Phil. Why does a woman have to 'observe the so-called decencies'?"

"Hold your arms over your head."

He pulled off her jersey, she wore nothing under it. She was chaste, she was beautiful. She took the tiller while he uncoiled the mackerel line and dropped overboard weight and spinner. Soon a fish was tugging.

Dropping the tackle over the thwart he took another fish. He stopped fishing when six were threaded on a string, enough for the family. Then he thought of Luke and Matt and the two other men who worked on the farm. Mackerel were cheap, a penny each, he told her, sometimes two a penny, from the monger who came round in his horse and trap.

"But a gift of fresh fish is always acceptable, better than boughten fish."

"*Boughten*, that's a good old English word."

She was beginning to feel small. Why did he avoid looking at her? Oh, why had she said what she had about the so-called decencies? But if he had been a little shocked, then why had he taken off her jersey? She felt cold.

"You look cold, Melissa. No wonder, with me, I'm no good."

"You are too good, I sometimes think."

"Why do I allow myself to be constricted, to be driven by this incessant idea to tidy up and to renew all the let-go things on the farm? People in the village are untidily happy, apart from their chronic anxiety about being out-of-work. They get by somehow, they've got cockle beds, and butts to spear in the creeks. Good fat fish they are, too. They get a bit of fowling in winter. And their gardens for vegetables."

"Yes, and they've got the night-cart, with its smoky red lantern, *clop clop* up the street in the darkness, tired horse, weary man—I thought he looked something like you, a good, little-boy face under his grey head—slopping contents of privy pails and creosote. All this poison spread, with ashes and broken glass and tins and other rubbish, on the glebe field, together with the blood and guts of the local slaughter house. Flies, rats and stink. Now do you see I'm with you, Phillip Maddison?"

"You're a bloody fine girl, Melissa." He felt his blood beginning to thrill.

Scylla slipped and wallowed past a seal that stared with opaque eyes. The sands of the Point were now remote. Inland the heat-misted Great Bustard Wood quivered above the line of the sheep-walk bordering the marshes—the woods that would be Billy's one day, and Billy's son after him—and perhaps more land until it was a sizeable holding of five or six hundred acres—and a house built among the beeches and pines above the chalk quarry. And forsake poor Lucy?

She drew the jersey over her head, she seemed to know his thoughts. Then he saw they were coming near to Marsh Cottage. He poled the boat up a creek. Got on the turf with the anchor.

"Do you want to see 'Boy', Phillip?"

"Not particularly."

"Let's go back then!"

They returned down the creek, and came to a strand of shingle, and lay on their backs among pink crab legs, the white and blue and grey of shells, amidst feathers and corks and dry seaweed under the bright stare of the sun.

This was what he had dreamed before he came to the East Coast. Here he was at last on the marshes with Melissa, among water-filled crevasses in the salt turf, the piping of birds, remote flicker of terns dropping to rise with sprats into the pale-blue sky above hundreds of acres of sea-lavender covering innumerable islets and peninsulas made by the wandering sea, which lay in the wider creeks wherein brown ribs of ancient wrecks rested.

They were alone with the sun. The breeze had left the earth. He sat up. The marshes were vacant. Far away, half-lost in mirage, a few lone figures on distant mud-beds bending over as they scraped for the 'blues', the dark-winged shells of fat cockles. He lay down again.

He dreamed of the time when Billy, helped by Peter, would be old enough to take over management of the farm, of the pedigree dairy herd and the modern equipment he would build up: and he would be free to come every day and wander in the beautiful desolation of this strange archipelago of the tides, to wander at will to the salt water, and sail out to Point of Terns. *Scylla* slipping and slapping against the tide. And when the sun was risen hot, to sail inshore and sit by the marram grasses, beside the shells and corks and bleached crab-legs in the sand; lie on his back, sun on face, thinking of what he would write in the books that had lain twenty years in his mind, and always on his spirit. Wavelets grating gently on shingle, farm in order, harmony dwelling there, all British men working their best at their jobs, flag of St. George floating over Merrie England again.

"Sir Henry Royce once said, 'Whatever is rightly done, however humble, is noble.' By myself, I dream of the past, or the future. With you, I live in the present."

At home there was a letter from Hurst. It was on writing paper with embossed address and armorial crest.

> Dear Phillip,
>
> For God's sake come to town and give us your help. Your name means such a lot to my generation. Cannot commonsense and the hopes of the common man prevail? Is 1914–18, despite the terrible lesson the world is supposed to have realised in the 'twenties, to be in vain? A line in one of your books haunts me: I think you quoted it from one of the minor poets killed in the war. *Speak for us, brother, the snows of death are on our brows.* Please come and help us. There is a meeting in a room in the Strand on Wednesday next. Could you come up for it, and speak? I hate to bother you, with the harvest imminent, and knowing you must be pretty weary with all the work to be done, but if you can't manage to come, perhaps I could come down and see you? I could sleep in the hay barn, among the pigeons . . .

"I'll have to go to London, to prevent Hurst coming here again," he told Lucy. "Or down to Kent, where he is working for Major Bohun-Borsholder and incidentally using his employer's personal writing-paper. I don't want to go," he repeated. "At the same time, this is a crisis in history. I often wish I had kept a diary all through the last war, instead of in spots. I've been keeping one for two years now, but most of the entries, except those dealing with farm details of crops, are what a critic of Conrad's letters to Edward Cornelian, published about nine years ago, called 'cries of pain'. Hard facts are best, they last longest. Though not the 'hard facts' of that columnist in *The Daily Crusader*, Tom Gamm, who is a Communist and loathes Birkin. I saw what he wrote about Birkin last week at Runnymeade's. All observed details, *clawing the air, the bull-roarer, the contorted face*, et cetera, but nothing about the ideas behind the words.

"It reminded me of what H. M. Tomlinson wrote about Kipling after the war, or during the war. It was to the effect that if Kipling had been the only recorder of the crucifixion 'we would have had a picture of the smells, the crowds, the physical scene, the three uplifted figures, that would have been immortal for its fidelity to common experience; but we would have known no more about the central figure than that he was a cool and courageous rebel'. It's a beautiful bit of writing, but might also with equal truth be turned around to prove that Tomlinson knew no more about Kipling than he declared Kipling knew about Jesus. The fact is, Kipling hated the war. He saw it as the old men's subconscious hatred of the young, their own fear of impotence with young women. Is this boring you?"

"No, but I must see that the stove in the wash-house is lit. Mrs. Valiant is coming to wash today."

"I must go to London first thing tomorrow morning. The barley won't be rotten-ripe for a few days."

It was a fast run over empty roads. He left the village at half past four, and had to go slowly at first, owing to the number of turtle doves picking up grit on the lesser road to Wordingham, but once through that town and on the better roads beyond it he kept his foot down and was passing up the broad and empty Whitechapel road at half past six—an average speed of fifty-four miles an hour.

Hurst came round after breakfast to his club. They sat on the grass of St. James's Park.

"London can be very pleasant," said Phillip, turning over to lie on his back. "These elms are fine creatures, lifting their arms to the sky. Byron must have known them, and Keats, and Shelley. W. H. Hudson, too. I saw a green woodpecker here in nineteen-twenty, during my first year in Fleet Street."

"How can you talk about that when the world is on the brink of a war that will end in the bolshevisation of Europe?"

"Did I ever tell you that my cousin Willie met Hitler at Beyreuth in nineteen-twenty-three, after the abortive *putsch*? My cousin said Hitler was the most sensitive and eager creature he had ever met, or was likely to meet. He was all idealism and hope and naked sensibility. And he had almost a mystic admiration for England. Willie, as an ex-service man, was invited by Frau Cosima Wagner to sit in her box during a performance of *Parsifal*. Hitler sat at the back, concealed from the audience. He was on the run. The music moved Hitler so much that the tears were running down his cheeks."

"I'd have given ten years of my life to have seen Hitler. He is *everything*. Birkin is a clod compared to Hitler."

"Now look here, Hurst! I'll be glad if you'll kindly keep such remarks to yourself, or to your pickpocket pals. Birkin is *my* generation, he is English of the English. I think it is a great pity that he resigned office from the Labour party. But then all history is a great pity. He belonged to the war generation, and we survivors all resolved to *do something*, to *be* something different when it was all over on the Western Front, that great livid wound that lay across Europe suppurating during more than fifteen hundred nights and days—torrents of steel and prairie fires of flame, the roar of creation if you like. Birkin should have remained in Parliament—that was his platform—but what's the use of talking about should-haves, or might-haves? Birkin remains the *only* man of prominence in England with the new spirit. He limped away from the battlefield determined that never again would it happen. Perhaps such a spirit can only be acceptable to a new generation after another war. When he is dead. And I hope I'll be dead, too."

"I still say you are the better man."

"I couldn't lead a party. I can't even lead my men on the farm. I used to think I could inspire a new way—through my books—but I've outgrown that conceit."

"Talk like that tonight, Phil! Let yourself go."

"I've got nothing to let go, Hurst—except my life. And who wants that?"

"England does."

"I'm afraid I am now only Hardy's 'man harrowing clods'."

Hurst briefed Phillip about the meeting as they finished their tea at a shop in the Strand.

"The meeting has been called by a man who was one of the 'Iron Ring' around Birkin. He says that Birkin is the weakest man in England."

"Every man is the weakest man in England at times. If you don't mind, I'd rather not hear any more of your reflections on Birkin."

"Very well. You'll see all kinds of people. There's Lord Eggesford, for a start. He's an authority on soil conservancy, and wrote a very fine book, according to Major Bohun-Borsholder."

"I've read it."

"Then there's the Admiral who commanded the Mediterranean Fleet in the last war. He's Anglo-German Link. Then there's the ex-M.P. who seized the mace in the House of Commons some years ago. I think you know the Duke of Gaultshire? He's promised to come. There are also heads of all sorts of societies, and associations, including an M.P. who fought with the Coldstream during the first battle of Ypres in nineteen-fourteen and was badly wounded. You'll meet a lot of men who were once with Birkin, but left him. The idea is to try and form a Committee to include all who see the danger of war, and want to try and form some sort of front to stop it. If you feel at the meeting that you can say anything, I do promise that it will be listened to eagerly. We desperately need a rallying point."

"I'm a smoking flax."

"For God's sake don't run yourself down so!"

They walked through ambient sunshine to the meeting. It was to be held in an upper room in a building off the Strand.

There sat and stood about fifty people, both men and women. They looked to be a little odd, all different, all of differing minds and animations. The Chairman briefly stated why the meeting had been called.

"We hope to try and find a formula of united resistance against the threat of decadent democracy's last resort to save itself by going to war. As Chairman I suggest that we listen to those who wish to speak. I must ask speakers to be as brief as possible, for time is short. Afterwards we hope to form a Committee, as a prelude to united action."

He sat down.

Speaker after speaker followed. From them came suggestions; qualifications to suggestions; diversions of the qualifications of proposals; counter-proposals, counter-suggestions. Phillip thought that a surrealistic painter might have had an idea for a picture of circular stones grinding faces like axes, while each arm turned its own grindstone heedless of all other abrasive circular motions.

Nothing was agreed upon, nothing decided when the meeting broke up.

Hurst, who had somehow become acquainted with various famous people, introduced Phillip to some of them. He said, "I am a member of Birkin's Party."

No comment was made by the polite faces; but the Duke of Gaultshire, whom Phillip already knew, invited him down to Husborne to see his collection of rare and uncommon pheasants in his park, saying that he had read his books with interest and instruction, and they might talk things over quietly together.

"I was a patient at the hospital, Duke, in nineteen-eighteen."

"So I am told," said the Duke, with nervous courtesy. "I do hope you will be able to stay. But of course your corn harvest is imminent. Pray propose yourself at any time."

What a gentle creature he was. A sad family, father against son, son in the wilderness. So it was throughout all classes of human society.

"His social credit programme isn't any good," said Hurst. "Come and see some of the fellows who believe in direct action."

A discussion was taking place on the wooden steps leading down to the lavatory. Talk ended when he and Hurst arrived. Phillip had an idea that he was being assessed.

"Tell us what you think," said Hurst.

"I believe in Birkin's potential. He is a true leader, if given the chance."

"He's had the chance. He can't work with anyone," said Hurst. "Everyone here knows it. They have all tried to do so, and he's failed us."

The Chairman, who had white hair and a young and hopeful face, squeezed past the group. "Still talking about Birkin?" he said. "Well, he's the weakest man in Britain."

He passed on down, and Phillip was regarded by six or seven composed faces.

"For years that chap was one of the Iron Ring around the Bleeder," said Hurst, "and he knows what he is talking about."

"All men talk about themselves. And so, perhaps, you won't mind not using that expression again," said Phillip, looking Hurst in the eye. "Derision does not become you or me or anyone else. Our words are boomerangs. As we judge others, so we judge ourselves."

"May I introduce you to William Frolich?"

Against the newel post at the bottom of the stairs stood a short man with a round face scarred by a razor slash down his right cheek, listening, half indifferent, to what was being said, but listening without discourtesy or egotism. Phillip recognised Birkin's ex-director of propaganda. Was this the man who, having rejected Birkin as the greatest patriot in Britain, the destined Leader to bring to full glory of service the Empire, now spoke contemptuously of Birkin as 'the bleeder'. What had happened? Phillip sensed in him a calm, easy force, a simplicity of nature, a singleness of mind. Hurst introduced him.

"Is Birkin the weakest man in Britain?" he asked, avoiding the razor scar.

"In no sense of the word is Birkin a weak man," replied the other, in a quiet, slightly nasal voice. "But he is not Britain's man of destiny, as the Führer is Europe's man of destiny."

"How can a man of destiny be known before he has 'achieved what was once only imagined'?"

"First, he knows himself to be that man. After agonised meditation, his life becomes clear. When others encounter him, they find themselves becoming clear. Those who are truly clear become his disciples, and endure to the death."

The scarred man hung by his elbow to the newel post at the bottom of the stairs and slowly swung round upon it as he smiled a little, as though to himself. A line of A. E. Housman came, without relevancy, into Phillip's head—*He wears the turning globe.*

The white-headed man who had been chairman at the meeting returned up the stairs. Seeing him close, Phillip saw that his umber eyes had a hurt look in them, as though he had passed through much mental confusion.

"He used to be a dipsomaniac," said Hurst, half contemptuously. "Birkin sent him to Germany to be cured. So he never forgave Birkin."

"He lost his fanaticism, perhaps? I suppose all eccentric ideas arise from a psychological basis, or condition." And how often do we use scapegoats by which to escape from our own inner chaos. Hitler and the Jews; himself and Lucy.

Now he must return for the corn harvest, a half-and-half man: a failure, as once his father said of himself. Poor father. Not one of his children ever thought of him as Daddy.

Poor Daddy.

Billy came home for the holidays from his school under Cranborne Chase, whither the sale of the Old Manor had helped to put him. He was eager to help with the harvest. On his first afternoon he went with Matt, who with a scythe cut round the field, 'opening of it up for the binder'—and helped to gather up the stalks into sheaves. Next morning he helped to put on the steel wheels of the tractor, and to fit the extension to the towing plate. The binder was drawn out of the barn by hand, lest the iron spuds of the tractor dig into and scrape the asphalt floor. It was the same old binder that had been used by the previous farmer. Phillip had bought it for £8 at the auction. Now it had been reconditioned, and he hoped it would change some of its habits, which were, literally, eccentric.

The binder being fastened to the towing plate, the slow procession went up to the Steep wheat. The steward drove the tractor, while Phillip's son sat on the high iron seat of the old horse-binder, stick in hand to bang the sheet-iron chain-cover should the thing become temperamental. The last of the old discoloured 1914 paint on the sheet-iron cover had long ago been thwacked off; for that binder in previous harvests had been liable to do the oddest things. Having cut a certain amount of corn, it would suddenly refuse to bind the stalks into sheaves, but throw them out loose instead. After a rest, and apparent adjustment by pokes of Luke's Shut-knife or Screw-hammer (the steward's two infallible tools), the binder would, on restarting and as though in repentance, drop off a series of sheaves tied together like sausages. BANG! THUMP! WALLOP! on the sheet-iron cover of the main driving chain. Another stop for adjustment. Onwards once more, a hundred yards or so of perfect tying, then BANG! again. This time the string was in a tangle: the sheaves looked as though a metallic spider had been at work. At each stoppage the steward with patience spoke to the machine, uttering soft and patient words of encouragement—a sort of incantation—"Yar'll see, we shan't be in no muddle." After this, for a period anyway, the reaper-and-binder behaved perfectly.

"I wonder what price we'll get for our barley this year, Luke."

"You won't lose like last season," replied Luke. "Not if the war come."

"Last season the price fell a hundred per cent, Luke, because of that cheap foreign barley flooding the market, Luke."

"You told me it was done to stop Hitler getting it."

"It was bought in the City of London, and led to the virtual closing of the corn exchanges in Poland, Roumania, Czechoslovakia and Hungary. All this caused a crisis in Berlin, since it upset the barter plans of a nation possessing only two million pounds gold reserve. And as you know, Luke, many farmers in this district went bust, and the banks foreclosing on mortgages couldn't get rid of the farms at any price."

"Come a war, you'll get a good price for your barley," said Luke.

"So you see, it's the same problem this year for Hitler, almost a problem of starvation, and then civil war. So he may have to go East."

"I don't know about that," said Luke. "But if war come, you'll be all right."

"Luke, we must cultivate the stubbles as soon as possible before the rains come. Cultivation will cut the thistles underground."

Luke looked unhappy. "No one else about here does that," he demurred. "It's a waste o' money in my opinion. If 'twas mine, I'd keep the money in my pocket."

"But stubble cultivation is a usual practice elsewhere. The cultivator tines penetrate into, and cut through, the top three inches of soil, and all the thistle roots. Then you cross the work again, leaving behind a loose tilth which dries out in the sun and kills the exposed thistle roots. You saw it on the Steep. When the rain falls, all the weed-seeds in the soil chit, the field becomes green with charlock, dock, fat-hen, and crab-grass. Then you plough. Thus you turn the growing weeds under and rot them. They help to put humus into the soil, they are destroyed."

"If 'twas mine I wouldn't do that," Luke repeated. He rolled a fag. "I never seen it done," he said, lighting the ragged fringe of British Oak shag.

"Because the 'art and mystery' of arable farming roundabout here is decadent."

"Well, I don't know about that," Luke said. "But the moles on the meadow do want trapping, and Horatio Bugg pays four-pence a skin, unless they're damaged by fighting. Father can catch them, if you buy the traps."

Interval for tea. All the wheat was cut (by permission of Messrs. Albion Binder, Shut-Knife, Screw-Hammer & Co.). After tea they were going to set up the heavy sheaves.

"Blast," said Matt, admiringly, "these sheaves are corny. Yar'll git twelve coombe an acre, yar'll see I'm right."

Matt went down to milk the cow for the house, feed his calves, and visit the sheep on the meadows with the bullocks. Then he would return and give them a hand. As he went to the sharp descent by the walnut tree at the edge of the wood he passed Phillip. "Come a war, guv'nor, and barleys will be making——"

"There mustn't be a war, Matt."

Matt looked at Phillip with his dark, Brythonic eyes.

"Yar'll see, guv'nor, barleys will be making three pun a coombe next y'ar. They did in the last war, ah, did'n'm tho'?"

He turned and walked away, like an offended prophet, for Phillip had repeated, "There mustn't be a war, Matt."

They carted for the first time by the New Cut. The lorry, driven by Brother Laurence (who had come for the harvest) came down with sheaves thrown into its body, the sides up.

On the way up again it passed the tractor with green trailer, driven by Billy. Meanwhile a tumbril, with lades, was being loaded; the second tumbril waiting. Thus men in the stackyard and in the field were kept going all the time. They didn't like the idea, since they were on wages, it was not a 'taken' harvest for a fixed sum. This wasn't practicable, since amateurs were involved.

When the three fields had been carried—a small corn harvest that year—when the last sheaf was pitched on top of the last load, Matt threw his cap into the air. That was on 28th August, 1939. Phillip never saw such an old rite happen again. He thought that perhaps it would never happen again anywhere in Europe.

Chapter 19

PRELUDE TO A WAR

Phillip backed the Silver Eagle from its bay in the hovel, filled up with petrol from the underground tank in the tractor shed, and with bag packed, set off for London with Brother Laurence.

Before leaving he posted two letters: one to Sir Hereward Birkin; the second to Lucy, enclosing his *Last Will and Testament*.

The day was fine, with much holiday traffic on the roads, most of it little black saloon cars, so that the superior speed of the sports-car was of little advantage until he got to the long road leading through the Brecklands to Heathmarket and the south.

Even when Brother Laurence was not reading his office, he never spoke unless Phillip spoke first: which was seldom.

The wind on his face, the exhilaration of moving at seventy miles an hour through familiar rows of twisted pines and sometimes tall poplars lining the road, the sense of personal freedom—leaving the farm behind, corn safe in stack—made Phillip optimistic, and he felt there could not be war, despite the power to decide having been given, virtually, to the Polish Government, so that any local brawl at a frontier inn followed by shooting might be the start of it. The real cause of the guarantee to Poland, he thought, was entirely unknown to the British public. What newspaper would print an account of the cosmopolitan financial interests in the Polish mines, whose workers were paid about fourteen shillings a week? Polish coal was bought, and sold in Britain at a price far below that of British coal; hence the years of dereliction in South Wales. Money was paramount; the Welshmen might rot so long as British *rentiers* could draw a good rate of interest on their Polish investments.

Back to farming 'interests'. The great Metropolitan Assurance Company—which twenty years before had owned his farm, then part of the estate on a foreclosed mortgage from the noble family which had possessed it for centuries—now had nine million pounds invested in Polish utilities—electric light, trams, in Warsaw. Few realised what the Money System was; the minds of ordinary people were entirely occupied with their own affairs. No one set of people or class was entirely to blame for the deteriorated world condition, certainly not the Jews—they had merely taken advantage of it until it was, for some of their racial purists, the return of the Golden Calf. Everyone must be allowed to see all these factors plain, if the new world of so many diversified hopes was to be made real and actual. Had not Hitler himself declared, in a speech, that of two opposing sides in a quarrel, both sides could be right?

If only Hitler could be persuaded to extend that theme, with the understanding that he had shown in private, according to Piers Tofield, in the Kaiserhof hotel in Berlin, so that each opposing section in the European division might be able to say, That is our case put for us. But Hitler had done that again and again, towards Britain: and every gesture had been countered.

What a luciferic phenomenon was that man. His self-will: a gem-hard flame of oxyacetylene cutting through steel underwater. His gaze, his double-handclasp on greeting, the instant appreciation of himself in that hotel at Nürnberg: as though he had been given oxygen, so that his mind had felt clear and direct: master of himself, without strain, without aspiration.

And yet, behind all the self-built will, was—fear?

Whoever lights the torch of war in Europe can hope for nothing but chaos . . .

That came from the better, truer side of the *man* behind the phenomenon of the clenched will-power, that amalgam of so many agonised contemplations upon a nation when it was in disintegration and dying. Behind the tensioned spring there was great sensibility, a dream of art and craftsmanship to replace mere counterfeit for greater profit. That was the side which, hearing that Chamberlain had offered to fly to see him a year before, had instantly offered to fly to England to save an older man possible air-sickness and exhaustion. Magnanimity, hope, generosity floated in that sensibility: a sensibility that easily became writhen when confronted by—professional chicanery.

What *was* the truth? People who knew said that Hitler had changed since 1935, more so since 1938. Was he, the ragged-voiced man, inextricably confronted by the implacable opposition of Money, being forced on to march . . . through *fear*? Money's economic blockage—'the strangulation'—had been on some time. *Germany must export or die; and Germany SHALL NOT DIE,* the blue-green flame had screamed at the last Rally. Seven million out-of-works had been put back to work on armaments: the vacant middle of Europe had been filled: the jigs were changed, the factories turned over to consumer goods, to . . . whither could they be exported? No one would, or dare, trade with such a system. Barter—or Batter.

Batter of guns, shatter of flying muscles . . .

How *could* that dilemma be resolved? Hitler, please do not march. Do not deny your *true* self. God, why am I not a 'Spectre' West, V.C., D.S.O., M.C. and bar, one eye gone, one hand off, and nine wound stripes? I would have prestige, I could hang myself up as a scarecrow, a scarewar.

I must think. If I could see Hitler, as the common soldier of nineteen-fourteen who fought the common soldier of his Linz battalion at Ypres, might I not be able to give him, the German common soldier, that amity he so desired from England—to beg him to halt his troops, and so save the two white giants of Europe, as Birkin has said, from bleeding to death, while Oriental Bolshevism waits on, to bring Asia to the chalk cliffs of Normandy?

It was said that Hitler now had only those about him who were afraid of hurting his feelings—afraid of precipitating one of those appalling moments of frustration and fear which came upon himself at times, as they came upon all sensitive men. Without reassurance, how could a man believe in his inspiration, that evanescent vision, indefinitely?

Hitler had said he believed in miracles; he had indeed achieved their equivalent. Would he then dismiss the offer of the common soldier's mite?

And yet—would he immediately be swept aside as a nonentity if he managed to get to the Templehof airfield? Hitler had made many gestures; and every one had been snubbed. The only Englishman of the first magnitude who had treated him as an equal and been treated as an equal had been Lloyd George. But then Lloyd George had been assailed on all sides for writing, in the *News Chronicle,* several thousand words of the highest praise and appreciation of Hitler. That had just about put paid to the

Liberal Party. Lloyd George had retracted; but he had known the truth. Lloyd George, an opportunist—a bit of a twister, but still a great man. He said one thing, he did another.

Hitler said one thing, and *did* another, it was knowledgeably said. Was he the only human being who did so? To how many men would that apply if they looked into their own souls with steady eyes? They would have to blink in the light of the inner truth. It was so much easier to blame the other fellow, to find a scapegoat, than to admit one's own weakness.

And yet, if minds were out of tune, only disharmony could result. Once again the words of gentle, innocent, unknowing Lucy passed through Phillip's mind. She had told him, laughingly, of what Ernest had said to her on his return to Dorset. *If I lived to be a hundred years old, I would never see eye to eye with Phillip*. And as he thought of that final judgment of himself and his ways by one whom he had only tried to help, a sense of frustration came over him, and with the need to hold himself against the thoughts that made him mutter to himself, as he felt strength being drawn from him.

"Just a little slower, d'you mind, Phillip?"

"Of course, mon père."

He drove steadily at fifty miles an hour, and lifted his goggles to feel air rushing past his eyes as they went between the grassy gallops before Heathmarket. By the Belvoir Arms they stopped and looked about the placid sunlit scene. Father Laurence left Phillip alone: he knew what the other man's thoughts were.

Here Phillip had been stationed as a junior subaltern in nineteen-fifteen. He tried to recall the details of the outbreak of that faraway war. In London there was much excitement and cheering. There was, in the man in the street, an unspoken but implied feeling of the Royal Navy's complete superiority over the Germans. Was there also a sense of impending tragedy? He could not recall any doubts, other than those in himself.

Was it the same war-psychosis in Europe now as in August nineteen-fourteen? Those cheering masses in London, Paris, Vienna, and Berlin—the masses which, like himself, had no glimmering or comprehension of the other fellow's point of view —were no more. Piers Tofield, who knew Germany well and who spoke the language fluently, had written that it *was* there, among the German storm-troopers: as well as a blazing determination to resist Hitler among the young Poles of the Corridor. Poles would always march to rescue Poles, Germans to succour Germans. And atrocity stories—mob-rousers—had already begun on both sides.

He was glad that Brother Laurence was with him, as they went into an inn with a gilt ham hanging over its green door. Inside were several York hams and barrels of ale. He sat down with a plate of sandwiches, and a pint of Burton, and tried to recall how the town looked when for a month or two he had been stationed there before going out to the battle of Loos. Twenty-four years ago, almost to the day! Strings of horses being exercised by thin small lads of all ages; Royal Naval Air Service men with Rolls-Royce tenders fitted with pom-pom gun or searchlight, dashing about the countryside at night supposedly following Zeppelins, and sometimes stopping to fire. The R.N.A.S. mess-room was in the Belvoir Arms. Beyond the open door one could hear a Decca trench-gramophone playing *They'd Never Believe Me* from the Gaiety musical comedy *Tonight's the Night.* 'Baldersby of Baldersby Towers, Baldersby, Berkshire' the senior subaltern, over whose head in the bar he had emptied a jug of water after Baldersby had poured a whisky-and-soda over his own, and then squirted a syphon at him.

Those splendid days would never come again, or their like, he told Brother Laurence as they went out, Phillip feeling rather proud of the Silver Eagle's lines until a small boy standing by said to another small boy, "Cor, there's a funny old-fashioned car, ain't it?" On the other side of the street a newsboy, running with a bundle of London mid-day papers under his arm, was crying, "Poles mobilise! Latest crisis!"

They reached the area left ugly by the maulings of London: speculative hire-purchase housing 'estates'—all trees cut down —tens of thousands of cubic yards of coke-breeze blocks and pink heaps of fletton bricks piled up. Life is big business, fornication, and death. Civilisation is chromium fittings, radio, love with pessary, rubber girdles, perms, B.B.C. gentility and the sterilising of truth, cubic international-type concrete architecture. Civilisation is white sepulchral bread, gin, and homosexual jokes in the Shaftesbury Avenue theatres. Civilisation is world-citizenship and freedom from tradition, based on rootless eternal wandering in the mind that had nothing to lose and everything to gain including the whole world. Hoardings, brittle houses, flashiness posing as beauty, mongrel living and cosmopolitan modernism, no planning, all higgledy-piggledy—thus the spiritual-material approaches to London, the great wen, Cobbett called it. Was the wen about to burst and pus to run throughout the body politic for the second time in his life?

At last the wearisome journey through dirty congested, narrow streets was over. Saying goodbye to Father Laurence—"I'll meet you at the Barbarian Club at half-past six"—Phillip drove over London Bridge, on the way to see his father. Richard, after returning from his world cruise, had declared that he was a new man. He spent his time in the garden, and flying his box kites on the Hill. He was cutting the lawn when Phillip arrived.

"I can't stay long, Father."

"Well, sit down awhile, old man. How is the farm going?"

"Oh, literally uphill work. I've just finished the corn harvest."

"Keep your corn in rick, take my advice. Prices will go up if there's a war."

"Father, if anything happens to me, will you keep an eye on Lucy and the children?"

"Why, are you thinking of going back into the army?"

"I might go abroad, Father."

"I don't follow you."

"Anyway, you will keep an eye on Lucy if——"

"Of course I'll do my best, my dear Phillip."

From Hillside Road he went to the flat in Charlotte Road where his sister Doris was living. He drank a cup of tea hastily, after being reassured that she was all right: she was teaching again, as well as receiving a small income from the money left to her by their mother.

Returning to the Barbarian Club he left the sports-car under the plane-tree and walked up the stone steps. It was quiet and cool inside. Nearly all the members were away on holiday. The porter was not in the lodge, so he put down his bag and walked up the stairs to the reading-room, with its wide windows overlooking the Park. No life here: only an occasional form on sofa or in arm-chair, eyes closed. There was three-quarters of an hour before Brother Laurence was due, so he went downstairs again and out into St. James's Park.

It was hot and quiet; the European harvest was in. A new era of life was beginning: he must be its historian. The detached part of him wanted to empty itself of preconceived opinions in order to get the feeling of the people. He walked to the lake, and watched the wildfowl. People sat quietly on the green seats, or strolled past, scarcely speaking. They seemed to be half-resigned to what might come, unable to alter or deflect in the least way the thing they all felt they should dread. Then along the asphalt path came two young men and a young woman. All three had an air of purpose, as they gave out hand-bills. *No war for Warsaw. Remember the War Dead of 1914–18. Have they died in vain?* and *Who the heck cares for Beck?*—with particulars of Birkin speaking that night near Trafalgar Square.

He wondered how the crowd would respond to Birkin that night, whether violently or with acclaim: Birkin who had given up all that he had (and he had great possessions) to the poor. What chances had he? If the idiom of history was anything to go by, Birkin's chances were small. He recalled the writings of his own grandfather Maddison, who had asked himself when the prophet would arise to lead the people back to the sun: poor, tipsy old grandfather, he had weakened and fallen down before he himself had been born.

After supper with Brother Laurence at the long table where sat comedians and authors, flute-players and surgeons, script-writers and gossip columnists, actors and scientists, they walked down Piccadilly with a club acquaintance through the strolling, seeming-careless crowds. Phillip felt that the people were not indifferent: but now behind the eyes of every man and woman was an evaded question, an avoided dread. What was to be, would be; meanwhile the sky is clear and bright, food and drink are pleasant things taken amidst laughter and the talk of friends, this new film is good, let us get in before the last house begins. Men still moving in the crowds with handbills: bold type on cheap paper barely glanced at before being dropped on the pavement, to be forgotten: to fall on stony ground, now trodden by the young men and their girls, the ghosts of tomorrow,

> 'whose world is but the trembling of a flare
> and heaven but as the highway for a shell'.

Down past the square of plane trees and gaudy lights of the cinema palaces the crowd waits, while under the wall of a tall brick building stands a black van with loudspeakers and platform on its roof, draped with the Union Jack; and beside and before it the displayed banner lines *Britons Fight for Britain Only*, and

People's Peace and Greater Britain upheld by men who have come here after their day's work inspired by Birkin's vision of a fairer country.

And then a roar of cheering and (strangely, Phillip feels) no booing, no opposition, no counter-demonstration, as the tall figure in the grey double-breasted suit climbs to the platform and stands gravely still, with set face, and then lifts his arm in salute and acknowledgment of the greeting. It takes some minutes for their devotion to release itself, and the words to come from the tense figure now crouching as though to attack an invisible giant, the Minotaur about to devour another generation of European youth.

Holding the stalk of the microphone with one hand the crouching figure cries—"Tonight the British people are here—to tell Parliament, to tell the old Parties, and their financial masters—the truth: that if any foreign power attacks Britain, every member of our Party will fight in defence of Britain—but just as straightly we tell them this—we will not permit a million British youths to die in their moneylenders' quarrel!"

A roar goes up from the faithful; a forest of salutes; cheers. Holding up his hand, Birkin continues—

Wandering away from his two companions, both soldiers of 1914–18, on the outskirts of the crowd kept by the police maintaining the traffic-flows from enlarging beyond the space allotted for the reception of free speech, Phillip again sought to find what the casual sightseers were thinking. They were not hostile to Birkin. Were they, with the exception of the followers massed under the high wall of the brick building, indifferent? Or were they those who accepted things as they were, as they were coming in the future, with no question—people who did not believe in miracles? Who felt the events of the world too much for them, who since early consciousness had been frustrated in nearly all, if not all, of the secret inner hopes and tenderness of the interior heart? Was their attitude that of people who could not help themselves? Were they, each one, crouching within the little ego, void of the still small voice, the glimmer of each soul dulled-out under the bushel of circumstance—the circumstance of one business against another business, of each for himself, of unemployment, poor housing conditions, malnutrition, the wheat berry permanently stripped of its goodness, people fed on the destroying white bread of ordinary life, with its eternal wars and mutilation, its diseases and frustrations, until the final peace of death?

Among these seemingly aimless ones there was no excitement, no resentment, no enthusiasm: there was passivity: and save from the figure now raving on the raised platform, there were no words. The gesture had been made; the gesture was suspended in time. At least this man had given hope and a vision of nobility to a few thousand men and women, said Phillip, returning to Brother Laurence and the gunner officer who had come with them from the Barbarian Club.

"I agree entirely about the Jews and their hidden power—*I* come from South Africa where I have been campaigning against the Jews' stranglehold for some years—but I object equally strongly to Hitler and his ways," said the old gunner, who had been decorated in 1917.

Birkin was crying,

"Let us put our own house in order before we interfere with others outside the great estate of the British Empire. Let us develop that estate, let us devote our lives in service to all within the Empire. We shall build a civilisation which will far surpass anything Germany or Italy or any other nation can build, for we hold one-fifth of the world in trust, while Germany has not one square metre of land beyond her boundaries. And if Germany has done so much with so little, how much more can we Britons build, with the resources of Empire? I beg you to believe in the possibility of this before it is too late, before Germans and Englishmen, the white giants of Europe who should be brothers, bring one another, and Europe, to the dust."

"Well, goodbye, and good luck," said the old gunner officer, as he went back to the club.

At least those who followed Birkin felt a light shining within themselves, thought Phillip, seeing the happy faces and hearing shouts of confidence as they marched in procession through the streets, believing that they were heralds of a great destiny, pioneers of a Greater Britain.

In this richer part of London, on that late August night, he heard amused laughter among the bystanders, saw sceptical tolerance on the faces of those looking from the windows of various buildings in which were clubs, for it was a warm night and many of the windows were open to the summer air of London. Phillip, walking alone on the pavement, accompanied the procession. He passed an old woman selling flowers, an old cockney in shawl, bonnet, and old-fashioned skirts who cried out to Birkin in a shrill voice, "Gawd bless you, Sir, you've always tried to save our boys!"

On through the lighted streets and lines of cars to the Embankment of the Thames. There Phillip turned back to his club and went up to the bar. While waiting to be served with a pint of beer he heard someone saying, "Same old speech. What rubbish he talks."

Yes, the same old speech; the same stony pathway; must the heart always die before resurrection. Leaving his drink untasted, he walked out of the club.

Omnibuses and motor-coaches moving to their assembly places. Evacuation of London children. Hitler would not start the bombing. Hitler wanted to go East only. Wandering down to the Embankment again he came upon Brother Laurence and told him what he had made up his mind to do.

"Of what use is it to fly to the moon, Phillip, if a man cannot bridge the abyss which divides him from himself."

"The world is too far gone for theosophy, mon père."

"You may never come back, Phillip."

"My life is nothing to me."

"Are you prepared to sacrifice the love, which is their security, of your little children?"

"They will be happier without me, mon père."

"You must not believe that, Phillip. But do not despair—hold on—the secret of a man's success lies in the mystical element which is in all of us. Bless you, my son."

I am a ghost among men, he thought, as he wandered through the warm summer night, I am in my right mind at last.

On a seat along the Embankment by Cheyne Walk he wrote *Apologia pro vita mea* upon a sheet of paper; and waited for words to come.

> The massed misery of existence in one battlefield after another, of life sapped by sleeplessness and exposure beyond the lost horizon of life is known by the enduring soldier of the infantry; and even then, only an exceptional integrity can resolve its Truth, maintain its inner clarity among normal human beings who do not think, who do not care to think, beyond the immediacy of their self-ful living. And what is the small and obscure life of one such man, its happiness or even its continuation, against such a threatening misery of un-understanding? Is there no formula, no idiom of understanding? Men talk of mysteries such as the mind of Shakespeare, or of Goethe, which are not mysteries to me.
>
> They were plain and simple men, as I see them; for I know the processes of elimination by which they came to their clarity, and so

built their worlds of deed and word. There is no mystery in a flower or a bird; there is infinite care and infinite work—the same things—and the essence of all things is the Holy Ghost, or the Spirit of Life. All things are made by work. To the true artist, the self-cleared man or woman, comes the Holy Ghost, to which he trusts himself, and can do no wrong. By study and by thought, by meditation and by observation, by knowing himself or by striving to know himself, in trust of the Holy Ghost or the spirit of life, a man comes to see plain, to see with truth; and thus he knows other men, the rare great workers called men of genius and the slower craftsmen and simple men who would live their lives in the sun, and ask no more than that they might work for their bread, and for a continuation of their useful work. Is all knowledge to be turned against itself, is all the self-hate of a repressive financial civilisation to destroy a generation, perhaps two generations, of European youth; and even what is called Europe? Is Russia waiting for the two giants of Europe to bleed themselves white, and then to step over the prostrate bodies and bolshevise the earth, as Birkin has said, has written, has shouted for years?

He tore up the letter and stuffed the pieces into his pocket. He walked up and down under the plane trees whose leaves were rustling with the congealed vapours of the night and the lights of the river. A lost moth was beating its wings against the glass, the lamp casting its pattern of shadows upon the seat.

What will it avail my life, or what is left of that life if after twenty years of striving for that plain-seeing called truth I turn away from my knowledge and hide myself in the little fearful ego, a farmer not thinking beyond his family on a farm? Have I no wider responsibility? In the growing fear and apprehension coming over the world, is it better to remain silent, or is it better to risk losing all by speaking out, however ineffectually? I do not want fame, or my name to be known among men; I know the vanity of such illusions; but the poor man working in the fields, the man in the thin coat in the dole-queue, the artisan soon to be taken from his home to wear a uniform and carry a rifle and bayonet, or to be told to fly through the air and sooner or later to be broken by iron or charred by fire, who else is there to speak for him? Have I not when trusting myself to the Holy Ghost, the gift of clarity? Will not this immediately be recognised if I go, my unafraid self, in the name and spirit of the *camaraderie,* with all the hopes of the dead and the living of the Western Front on Christmas Day, 1914?

Might not such a gesture, for once in history, be taken at its just and truthful value, and with the aid of that modern miracle, the radio, and served by the hope of all men of good-will, so promulgate the beginning of the new world, the *brave* new world?

Speak for us, brother; the snows of death are on our brows.

When the sun arose upon the Thames east of the bridge he walked to a coffee house in Covent Garden. As the day grew, and movement of men and vehicles impinged upon his eyes and ears, he felt an extreme coldness growing upon him, and when just after noon he went before the man in whose ability and realistic vision he believed, he could not speak more than a few words. With his invariable courtesy Birkin rose to greet him, but the calm and aloof strength of Birkin's usual self was withdrawn, as though for the moment his life, too, was suspended. He held Phillip's letter half-crumpled in his hand, as though it had been pushed hastily into a pocket.

"I have been thinking about your letter," he said.

Phillip waited. He knew the answer. Birkin looked before him a moment before saying, "I am afraid it is too late to try to see Hitler. The curtain is down."

As he prepared to leave, Phillip said, "What will you do?"

Birkin shifted his weight from the leg ruined in the war, and with eyes averted he said, "They might shoot me, as Jaurès was shot in Paris in August nineteen fourteen, for opposing the war."

Phillip waited another few moments.

"I shall keep on, Maddison, while I can, to give a platform for peace, should our people want it."

Phillip paused with his hand on the door-knob.

"I cannot see my country sink, without trying to do something to save it."

"I understand, sir."

Outside in the street the newsbills read:

NAZIS SEIZE DANZIG CUSTOMS

Chapter 20

FLITTER-MOUSE

On the Saturday morning as Phillip was leaving his club the hall porter, who was sorting letters, said casually, "Well, it's begun. They've bombed Warsaw this morning. Will you be wanting your bedroom tonight? I could do with it. Members are returning to Town."

"No, thank you. Who told you?"

"Mr. Olson just came in and told me. I'll cross your name off No. 10 then. Going home to the farm?"

"Yes, I'm a farmer this war. How queer."

"Yes, it's a queer business altogether," the porter replied grimly. He was an old soldier from Belfast, with a wound from the Schwaben Redoubt at Thiepval on July the First, 1916, still unhealed. "Bloody queer, if you ask my opinion," he iterated, and as his grim stare was maintained upon him, Phillip began to wonder if Irish Jack thought he might be responsible.

"I heard where you'd been last night," he said in a lowered voice, "and I reckon Ould England could do with a few more blokes like him." Then in a harsh Belfast brogue as another member came in, "I hear the Nationals of Golders Green and St. John's Wood have bought up all the bully beef in London, and all I can say to that is, they can have their bully beef. Well, goodbye, sir, and good luck to ye. I'll post any letters on to you. You're lucky to be a farmer. Well, you got in at the right time. Wish I had your head. Goodbye, and don't forget a turkey for me at Christmas."

It was a dull journey home. All the way he passed omnibuses and coaches, filled with children with labels on their jackets. Nobody where he stopped for food or drink or petrol spoke of the war. England seemed quiet, as at something that was passing away; the old way of life, the old world.

"Oh," said Lucy, as Phillip walked into the parlour, "so you've come back." She seemed disappointed. He sat down in a chair. "I didn't expect you," she went on. "So I'm afraid you'll find the place rather untidy."

"I am sorry to haunt your mind so greatly with my horrible tensions of tidiness and efficiency."

"If I had known——" she said. "Oh well, I expect you'll want some tea. But, if only I'd known, I could have got everything ready for you. Rosamund said she would polish the table, but the little boys wanted to go bathing on the marshes, so she took them, it's been so hot today. I'll get you some tea."

"Didn't you get my letter?"

"Oh, did you write to me? I didn't see any letter. Here's your post."

"What could have happened to it? Are my letters being censored already?"

He lay dejectedly in his leather armchair before turning to the heap of letters. Looking at the unopened envelopes, he saw that his letter to Lucy was among them. He was relieved; and put it in his pocket.

Lucy went into the kitchen. He heard her filling a kettle. The electric motor with its automatic switch throbbed with the pump, and water from the well splashed into the tank above.

Through the open door he saw the swallows, which had a late brood. One dived twittering from a purlin supporting the rafters. It returned almost at once, and flew into the parlour, and fluttered delicately from corner to corner, hesitating by the beam which crossed the ceiling, where hung a pipistrelle bat, a small model of a Sopwith Camel, and another of a Bristol Fighter. Then the bird fled silently through the doorway into the air outside.

The family was as used to the swallows, as the birds were used to them. The children loved them; as they loved the pipistrelle bats which sometimes at night came in the open windows and flitted to and fro across the room, to and fro erratically. One flitter-mouse had apparently decided that it liked the place because it lived by day on the beam. It flew off at twilight, and when it returned it did so by making an Immelmann turn, to cling with its feet and then to hang, with folded wings, beside the model of the Sopwith Camel, and watch with its jetty glinting eyes. It was tame.

Now the bat had a baby at her breast. Once Phillip had given her a drop or two of sherry on a match-stick; for bats like sherry. After taking several drops the bat flopped about on the floor ticking with emotion. But with a nursing mother one had to be careful; alcoholic milk might cause her child to lose its grip on her fur, then it would fall off.

"Oh yes," said Lucy, coming into the room, "before I forget. Captain Runnymeade called here while you were away, with Melissa and that Polish dancer, Stefania Rozwitz. They stayed to tea and got on very well with the children. The children remembered Stefania at the magician's party."

"Did Melissa say anything?"

"Only that she had to go back to London the next day. Oh yes, she asked me to tell you that the hybrid roseate tern had flown. Well, that's about all that's happened since you went away. Oh, how silly of me, I nearly forgot. Captain Runnymeade rang up this afternoon, and asked me to tell you he will be at the Frigate Inn tonight, and would you dine with him. I told him you were away, and I didn't know when you were returning. He asked me to give you a message. He said, 'Tell him that this war will mean the last of the country houses'."

While she was getting tea he burned the letter to Lucy. Then, sitting on the floor he hid his head on his arms resting upon the form, and said, "I've been thinking that we ought to make a hiding place under the Bustard Wood, tunnelling into the chalk half-way up the steep slope from the meadows. It ought to be on the pattern of the German dug-outs in the downlands of the Siegfried Stellung. After all, the harbour here is the only deep-water anchorage at all tides on this coast. The children and you will be reasonably safe there during any bombardment."

He noticed that Lucy was stitching some black cloth. "What's that for?"

"The black-out curtains. It's on the wireless, and also in the papers."

"Half-way up the Bustard Wood will ensure good drainage. The entrances must be concealed, and the tunnel go deep into the hill. At night we can make a fire in the stove removed from the granary, and cook. The smoke can go up a shaft to the ground above, and up a pipe into a hollow tree there, where it will stray away."

He saw himself stealing down at night to fetch water from the spring which flowed along a dyke in the meadow below. Rabbits abounded in the wood; he would shoot them with his yew-wood bow. Barley could be stored in one of the galvanised bins he had bought, and ground for griddle cake with pestle and mortar.

When bombs fell, and perhaps rockets, and the invasion passed on, they would come out. If the rest of the countryside were laid waste they would have a chance to survive for a week or two.

Lucy made the tea and put a cup near him on the floor.

"Yes, the children will love the idea of living in a cave. Oh, I forgot—my memory nowadays is like a sieve—Mr. Riversmill the painter came over this morning, and was painting the church across the river when Billy came down from scuffling the stubbles on the Bustard, and saw that he had taken one of the millboards out of your trouser press, and had painted the view on it. Mr. Riversmill turned round and shouted at him to go away. Billy said, 'You've got my father's trouser-press board, he wants that.' 'Who cares?' said Riversmill. 'This painting is more important than your father's damned trousers.' Billy told him you wouldn't be able to get the picture of the church off, because paint hardened on cloth. 'It's my picture, you damned boy,' shouted Riversmill. 'And it's my father's trouser-press' said Billy. He was quite upset. Anyway, I told him it didn't matter, we could easily get some more board."

"Good for Billy."

"I suppose in London everyone was very much occupied with getting their children away?"

"Yes, there were lots of them obediently holding hands in queues."

"Did you see anyone in particular?"

He lifted the cup slantingly so that it spilled a little before he put it down without seeming to know what he was doing. "I saw Birkin. He was rather subdued."

"He did try so hard, poor dear."

The bat dropped from the beam to his shoulder. He did not move, but sat there with head on arms.

"There," said Lucy, "someone wants you, you see."

The bat shuffled to seek the warmth at the back of the bent head, and settled against his neck.

"Did you like Birkin when you met him at Lady Breckland's?"

"Oh yes. He was so courteous to everyone, wasn't he?"

Journalised: Devon 1935–Norfolk 1941
Drafted: Devon 1952–56
Recast and rewritten: Devon-Sussex-London 1964–5

4882198R00229

Printed in Germany
by Amazon Distribution
GmbH, Leipzig